W9-ANU-168
09/2020

DISCARD

THE
BLACK
SONG

THE BLACK SONG

A RAVEN'S BLADE NOVEL

ANTHONY RYAN

ACE

NEW YORK

ACE
Published by Berkley
An imprint of Penguin Random House LLC
penguinrandomhouse.com

Copyright © 2020 by Anthony Ryan
Penguin Random House supports copyright. Copyright fuels creativity, encourages diverse voices, promotes free speech, and creates a vibrant culture. Thank you for buying an authorized edition of this book and for complying with copyright laws by not reproducing, scanning, or distributing any part of it in any form without permission. You are supporting writers and allowing Penguin Random House to continue to publish books for every reader.

ACE is a registered trademark and the A colophon is a trademark of
Penguin Random House LLC.

Library of Congress Cataloging-in-Publication Data
Names: Ryan, Anthony, author.
Title: The black song: a Raven's Blade novel / Anthony Ryan.
Description: First Edition. | New York: ACE, 2020. | Series: A Raven's Blade novel; 2
Identifiers: LCCN 2019056305 (print) | LCCN 2019056306 (ebook) |
ISBN 9780451492548 (hardcover) | ISBN 9780451492562 (ebook)
Subjects: GSAFD: Fantasy fiction.
Classification: LCC PR6118.Y3523 B54 2020 (print) | LCC PR6118.Y3523 (ebook) |
DDC 823/.92—dc23
LC record available at https://lccn.loc.gov/2019056305
LC ebook record available at https://lccn.loc.gov/2019056306

Printed in the United States of America
1   3   5   7   9   10   8   6   4   2

Cover art by Cliff Nielsen
Cover design by Judith Lagerman
Book design by Tiffany Estreicher
Maps by Anthony Ryan

Dedicated to the memory of the late Lloyd Alexander,
author of the Chronicles of Prydain, the truly wonderful series
that started me on a lifelong adventure as both a reader and a writer of fantasy

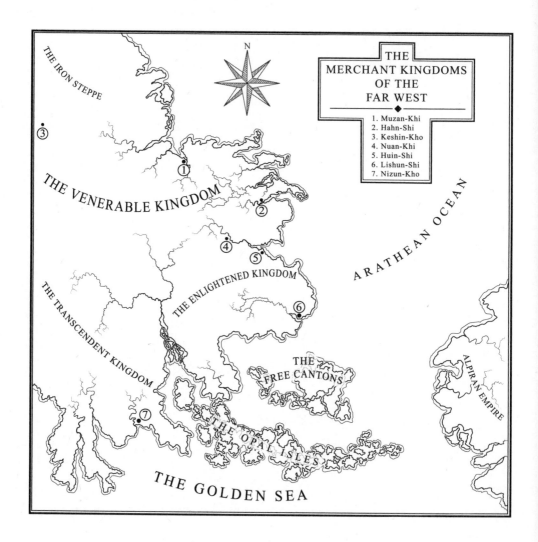

THE
MERCHANT KINGDOMS
OF THE
FAR WEST
◆
1. Muzan-Khi
2. Hahn-Shi
3. Keshin-Kho
4. Nuan-Khi
5. Huin-Shi
6. Lishun-Shi
7. Nizun-Kho

THE IRON STEPPE

THE VENERABLE KINGDOM

THE TRANSCENDENT KINGDOM

THE ENLIGHTENED KINGDOM

ARATHEAN OCEAN

ALPIRAN EMPIRE

THE FREE CANTONS

THE OPAL ISLES

THE GOLDEN SEA

THE
FREE CANTONS AND
THE OPAL ISLANDS
◆

1. Lishun-Shi
2. Askira
3. Nakira
4. Tokira Peninsula
5. Margentis
6. Ruined Temple

THE ENLIGHTENED KINGDOM

THE FREE CANTONS

THE OPAL ISLES

ARATHEAN OCEAN

THE GOLDEN SEA

N

THE
BLACK
SONG

PART I

Even the greatest lie
Can be undone
By the sharpest blade.

—SEORDAH POEM, AUTHOR UNKNOWN

Obvar's Account

Luralyn once asked me, "What does it feel like to die?"

Sensing the desire for comfort that lay behind this question, I said, "Like falling. It's as if the world shrinks to a single point of light far above whilst you descend into an eternal abyss. Then . . . it's gone and there is nothing."

But this somewhat poetic response was, I must confess, a lie. I can, of course, speak only for myself, and others may have enjoyed a death little more troubling than a gentle drift into endless slumber. But my death held no such comforts.

I knew the wound was mortal the instant I felt Al Sorna's blade scrape across my spine to erupt from my back. The pain was everything you might imagine it to be. But I knew pain. For I was Obvar Nagerik, anointed champion to the Darkblade himself and second only to him in renown amongst the Stahlhast. Many were my battles, and it is no boast to say I could not and in truth still cannot recount the exact number of lives I had taken. Such a life breeds wounds, also too many to count, although some live larger in the memory than others. The arrow at the Battle of the Three Rivers that pierced my arm all the way to the bone. The slashing sword that laid my collarbone bare the day we slaughtered the first great host the Merchant King sent against us. But none hurt so much as this, nor dealt such a grievous blow to my pride. All these years later I remain uncertain as to which hurt more, the pain of being skewered from chest to back, or the certain knowledge that I was about to die at the hands of this condemned interloper, this Thief of Names. For his words had angered me, and in those days few who stirred my anger survived my response.

He is not a god. You are not part of a divine mission. All the slaughter you have done is worthless. You are a killer in service to a liar . . . *His words. Infuriating, hateful words. Made worse by the truth they held, the truth revealed by the song of the Jade Princess, although I had known it in my heart for far longer.*

I believe it was anger that kept me clinging to life then, even as the blood bubbled up into my throat, starving my lungs of air. Even as the pain wracked me from head to toe and my bowels began to loosen, leaving me no illusions that once-mighty Obvar would soon be rendered just another shit-stained corpse littering the indifferent face of the Iron Steppe. Even then my grip on the sabre never faltered and my arms retained enough strength to drag the blade clear of Al Sorna's flesh. He remained upright as I took a wavering step back, gabbling something at him. The mingled rage and pain ensured that whatever I said in that moment made no purchase on my memory, but I prefer to think it was something suitably defiant, perhaps even noble. I could tell he was dying from the whitening pallor of his skin as he stared at me, face set in rigid, unflinching expectation. No fear, I recall thinking as I raised the sabre to finish him. There was some satisfaction in that, at least. Despite a well-won reputation for cruelty, I had in fact never enjoyed killing men who begged.

The stallion's ironshod hoof slammed into my thigh first, snapping the bone as easily as dry kindling, sending me sprawling. There was no time to roll clear, had I possessed the strength to do so, for the beast's blows fell like an iron rain, crushing bone and sundering flesh. I had imagined the pain of Al Sorna's killing thrust would be the worst I might endure. I was wrong. There was no sensation of falling, no shrinking point of light to send me off to blessed oblivion, just the terror and agony of a man pounded to death by an enraged horse until, finally, there was an overwhelming sensation of being wrenched. It brought a new form of pain, deeper, more fundamental, a pain that seared its way into my very being rather than merely my body. Somehow I understood that the very essence of my soul was being stretched and torn like meat scraped from a carcass.

Soon the sensation gave way to a sickening, lacerating disorientation. Contrary to the lie I would tell Luralyn, I did not fall when I died, I tumbled. Images and emotions assailed me in a swarm that allowed no room for coherent thought. Although the agonies of my physical self had vanished, in many ways this was worse, for it brought the deepest of fears, a panicked, desperate realisation that what lay beyond life was naught but eternal confusion. However, the panic abated as the flurry of images gradually coalesced into discernable memory. Here was I staring up through a child's eyes into my mother's cold, angry glare. You eat more than the fucking horses, *she muttered, shoving me away as I reached for the oatcakes she had baked.* Other wombs are blessed by the Divine Blood, but I get a walking stomach. *She threw a skillet at me, hounding me from the tent.* Go take food from the other brats if you're so hungry! Don't come back until nightfall.

The memory fragmented, shifting into confusion before once again settling into something familiar. Luralyn's face the day I fought Kehlbrand. I knew this one well, having revisited it so often, or at least I thought I knew it. In my conscious remembrance it was always the fight that dominated, the feel of fist on flesh, the iron taste of my own blood as Kehlbrand delivered the most complete beating I ever took. But this time it was different, for Luralyn's face, bunched in impotent fury, tears streaming from her eyes, was all I saw and Kehlbrand's blows merely a distraction. Her face changed then, taking on the fullness of womanhood and stirring a much-resented but persistent mingling of lust and longing.

What a disgusting animal you are, Obvar.

Her expression was scornful now, half-lit by the fading sun and the dim glow of the myriad fires from the camp that surrounded the Great Tor. I recall thinking how pleasing the shifting colours were on the smooth curves of her face. There was wine on my tongue, Cumbraelin wine, although in those days I had no notion of its origin nor did I care. Beyond her I could see the tall figure of her brother standing over the corpse on the altar. Tehlvar was denuded in death, as is typical, his long, muscular form a pale, limp thing stained by the drying blood that had gushed from the knife wound in his chest. The day the Great Priest asked Tehlvar the second question, *I realised, watching Luralyn take a grudging sip from the wineskin my younger self handed to her.* When it all began.

I felt it all again as the memory unfolded. Another lurch of anger and lust at Luralyn's now-customary rejection, honed to a greater pitch when Kehlbrand summoned her to his side and dismissed me. Whatever would be said here was not for my ears. Why would it be? What sage counsel could I offer? I was to become the Darkblade's champion, but never his advisor. The passage of years has allowed a keener appreciation for the true course leading to a point in history where the name Kehlbrand Reyerik is fast slipping into the realm of dark legend. I had imagined it to commence with the moment of my death, but I know now it had begun here as a hulking brute stomped away into the darkening camp intent on venting his frustrations through all manner of foul deeds. In his heart the brute knew himself to be no more than a valued dog, mighty and vicious to be sure, but still, just a dog.

Is this what death is? I wondered as the memory shifted again, the Great Tor and the camp whipped into swirling mist. Endlessly reliving the hurts suffered in life. If so, could I truly claim not to have deserved it?

When the vision coalesced again it seemed to confirm my suspicions, for this was another moment I would have preferred to forget. I stood alongside Kehlbrand in the chamber beneath the Sepulchre of the Unseen. The bodies of the priests we had slaughtered here were well rotted now, desiccated flesh crumbling away from dry bone in this arid and ancient cavern. The taint of death, however, still lingered in the air.

I recalled how he had surprised me by insisting on a return to the Great Tor after the fall of Leshun-Kho. Such a great victory should have brought a night of revels, with all the indulgence that entailed. The hunger my mother had scolded me for had never faded as I grew, and had been joined by other appetites as manhood dawned. But the Darkblade allowed no revelry. When the slaughter was done and Luralyn had made her pick of the captives, he put the city in the hands of a trusted Skeltir with ten thousand warriors to ward against a counterstroke from the south.

"You intend to move on Keshin-Kho?" I had asked, keen anticipation mingling with apprehension in my breast. Although ever eager for battle, the great fortress city was a formidable target, even with our ever-swelling ranks.

"No, old friend," he told me. "We're going home. It's time to prepare."

"For what?"

I saw his eyes narrow a fraction as he glanced at his sister. Luralyn's aspect had been somewhat grim since the city's fall, due I assumed to her squeamishness, which had always struck me as worryingly un-Hast-like. Kehlbrand, however, had never displayed anything but absolute trust in his sister, at least before now. "I'm not entirely sure yet," he said, climbing into the saddle, "but it will require something of you, a service it pains me to ask of you."

"You are the Mestra-Skeltir," I reminded him. Even then I refrained from using his other name, his godly name, something he saw fit to ignore. "Ask for anything, and I'll give it."

He settled a steady but otherwise expressionless gaze on me. When he spoke his voice had a faint note of regret, something I rarely heard him express. "A promise I'll hold you to, saddle brother," he said.

And so we rode home with the Stahlhast horde at our back. The Tuhla were sent east and west to visit what mischief they could on the border garrisons, but the Stahlhast went north, back to the Great Tor where Kehlbrand bade me follow him to the Sepulchre and what lay beneath.

"Touch it."

The stone's surface was flat and black save for the veins of gold that ran through it, veins that seemed to pulse in the light of Kehlbrand's torch. I recalled Luralyn's terror of this thing the night we killed the priests and found I couldn't fault her for it.

"Someone is coming," Kehlbrand added. "An enemy I know you cannot defeat."

I lifted my eyes from the stone, fixing a broad smile on my lips to mask the uncertainty provoked by being in such close proximity to the most feared object in Stahlhast lore, an object so sacred the Laws Eternal decreed death for any who looked upon it unless chosen by the priests. But the priests were dead and the Laws Eternal now just a rarely spoken vestige of the time before Kehlbrand's rise. What use had the Stahlhast for laws when we had the word of the Darkblade, the word of a god?

"There is no man I cannot defeat," I said.

"Oh, but there is, be sure of that. He stole my name, and soon enough he'll come to steal everything we have built." He reached across the stone to grasp my forearm. "Touch it." His gaze was fierce now, implacable in its command and resolve. It was the face he wore when he became more than the Mestra-Skeltir, the face of the Darkblade. "Touch it and mighty Obvar will become mightier still."

It is a hard thing to refuse a god's command, despite my many poorly suppressed doubts as to the truth of his divinity. Before this moment I had often entertained the notion that his mantle of the Darkblade was just another stratagem, a means of winning over those we had once enslaved and those we would soon conquer. If so, it had certainly proven a successful ploy. But, looking into *his eyes now, I understood for the first time that Kehlbrand Reyerik had not been playing the role of a god. In his own mind, at least, he was the Darkblade, and in that instant, I too believed. I have come to understand, all these years later, that it is these small moments of weakness that damn us, the brief instances when reason and doubt are overthrown by blind faith and love.*

My fingers opened, splaying out as Kehlbrand gave a grim smile of satisfaction and slammed my palm onto the surface of the stone.

It was like touching flame, but the pain was far worse than a mere scalding. It seared its way through the flesh of my hand, through my arm and into the core of my body. White fire exploded in my eyes, accompanied by a roar that deafened my ears to my own scream. The fire faded as quickly as it arrived, and for the briefest second I found myself confronted by a pair of eyes. Black pupils set within yellow orbs flecked with green and surrounded by a pattern of striped fur that was as complex as it was symmetrical. Tiger, *my agonised mind realised as the eyes stared into my soul. I heard no words, saw nothing beyond those eyes, but I felt the intent of their owner more keenly than any wound suffered before or since:* Hunger. Deep, ravenous, unquenchable hunger.

The eyes blinked and vanished, heralding a grey mist and sudden absence of all sensation. When the mist cleared I found myself on my back, staring up into Kehlbrand's concerned face. "It was different," he said, voice soft and contemplative, speaking more to himself than me. "Why was it different?"

"Different?" I asked, groaning and taking his hand as he helped haul me to my feet.

"I have bestowed gifts on many before you, brother. There was confusion, but no pain." He searched my features with intense and uncomfortable scrutiny, brow furrowed with an uncharacteristic consternation. "Do you feel it? Do you know what it is?"

"Feel it?" Kehlbrand let out a thin sigh of frustration at my baffled expression, causing me to add, "It hurt."

"And nothing else? You feel nothing else?"

I stood back, drawing in a ragged breath, uncaring of the tainted air of this place. In truth, I felt only the ache of a recently vanished pain. My arms felt as strong as ever, but no stronger. Similarly my vision, now cleared of the grey mist, was sharp but I perceived nothing beyond the solidity of this chamber. "I am . . . myself, brother."

"No." He shook his head, brow still creased and his voice coloured by a faint note of anger. "Your tune is different." He angled his head, voice dropping to a whisper. "I'm not sure I like it."

He blinked and I found myself unable to suppress a small shudder, for in that moment his eyes so resembled those of the tiger I suffered a spasm of remembered pain. When he spoke again the furrow of his brow had smoothed and his tone was one of casual reflection. "Oh well, I'm sure it'll make itself known soon enough."

"Luralyn might know . . ." I began only to be swiftly silenced.

"No," he said, voice flat with command. "In fact, Obvar, I would prefer it if, henceforth, you avoided my sister's company completely. She finds you try-ing at the best of times, and frankly, your attentions have always been unwar-ranted, even unseemly. She is, after all, the Darkblade's closest and most cherished kin. She is not for you."

It was then that I felt it, through the sting of the slight that told me I was unworthy of his sister's heart, through the anger provoked by his flippant tone, the tone of a master to a slave. Through it all I heard and felt something more. It was as if the words were spoken by two separate mouths at once, one pos-sessed of Kehlbrand's blithely insulting inflection, the other far more sibilant, like the hiss of a wretched, deceitful cur. The words were identical but the tone left no doubt that every one was a lie, every syllable dripping with falsehood. It told me that, although it was true that Luralyn had always delighted in shunning my advances, this was not why he wished me to avoid her. He fears what she will tell me, and what I might tell her.

My gaze slid back to the stone, an otherwise unremarkable black plinth save for its golden veins, pulsing with even greater life now. This is its gift, I understood. Lies.

"Oh, don't be angry," Kehlbrand told me, smiling as he came forward to clap a hand to my shoulder. "In your heart, you knew it would always be this way." His grip tightened into one of sympathetic reassurance. "There'll be wives aplenty when we take the southlands. I hear the Merchant King Lian Sha has an entire wing of his palace filled with the most comely concubines."

Just a dog, the leering cur's tone informed me. To be thrown scraps from the Darkblade's table.

A warrior's instinct is a valuable thing, similar in many ways to that of the coward, for it is at its keenest in moments of extreme danger. I knew as Kehlbrand laughed and shook my shoulder with brotherly affection that he would kill me in a heartbeat should my next words be anything but those expected of his most faithful hound.

"As the Darkblade commands," I said, lowering my head.

Memories came swiftly after that, tumbling into one another like ragged sheets caught by a whirlwind. The great victory over the Merchant King's host, their lines breaking apart under the assault of Luralyn's Gifted family, the ecstasy of slaughter that followed. The return to the Great Tor and the arrival of the Jade Princess in company with the healer and the Thief of Names, the one Kehlbrand had expected for so long. I was long used to ascertaining the danger posed by potential enemies and found this one disconcertingly enigmatic. Tall and strong to be sure, but not so much as I. Possessed of a keen mind and shrewd cunning also, but I did not feel myself to be in any way awed by his acumen, nor, in truth, did I fear him. Perhaps this is what doomed me, for if I had, I might have actually beaten him.

The song of the Jade Princess came next, the truth it held as horribly inescapable as before. Although the stone's gift gave me the ability to hear lies, making me somewhat rich in trinkets when I employed it at the gambling tent, it did nothing to reveal the extent of the lies I told myself. I had consoled my wounded pride at Kehlbrand's slights by making much of the respect he had shown me since. The Stahlhast do not reckon wealth the way the southlanders do. Although we value gold and sundry treasures, true wealth lies in renown, and by now my legend was outshone only by that of the Darkblade and his divinely blessed sister. It became a shield against my doubts, a comforting fur to wrap myself in whenever the leering cur's voice returned to taunt me. But, against the song of the Jade Princess, there could be no shield.

It is all a lie. I could see it now as her song slipped effortlessly past my defences, invading my soul, the tune both beautiful and terrible. All his acclaim, all his gifts, the pretence of brotherhood going all the way back to boyhood. Lies. The song forced me to regard him with new eyes, forced me to see the artifice in every expression, the calculation that lay behind every word. Amongst it all I discerned only two truths: his love for Luralyn and his belief in his own godhood. A lying god but, in his own mind, also a living one.

The memory came to an abrupt halt the moment Kehlbrand struck down the Jade Princess, sparing me the spectacle of my duel with Al Sorna. I felt myself to be fixed somehow, ensnared. For what seemed an age I saw nothing, *heard nothing and felt nothing beyond the sense of confinement. I fancied I could hear the raging thump of my heart, but soon came to understand that it was merely the memory of a pulse, for I no longer possessed a heart, nor a body to house one. Despite my reputation, fear had not been any more absent from my life than from that of any other man who repeatedly faced death. But I had always possessed the ability to master it, control it, channel it into rage that would blossom when the battle became joined. Yet here there was no battle; there was only the knowledge of being trapped, like a fly cursed to endless squirming in the spider's web. Fear quickly became terror, the kind of terror that swallows a man whole and sets him screaming, but I had no mouth with which to scream.*

The roar came then, brief but angry, and rich in impatience. I discerned no words in it, but somehow intuited its command immediately: QUIET!

My vision returned as I felt myself twisted in the web, a faint grunt of curiosity thrumming my being. Two eyes resolved out of the gloom, eyes I had seen before, narrowed in scrutiny. It will eat me! *The thought bubbled to the surface of my mind from the raging torrent of fear. I could feel its hunger, as depthless as before. But the tiger apparently saw little sustenance in my soul, for its jaws remained closed. The relief this birthed in me vanished quickly, however, for its eyes loomed closer, cold and unblinking. It roared again, louder and longer this time, and once again the command was clear:* I WILL RETURN YOU! AND YOU WILL FEED ME!

Its will enveloped me like a giant fist encircling a gnat, squeezing hard. Then came the feeling of being wrenched once more, torn free of the web and cast away, a mote of dust tumbling through a formless void, falling and falling until something caught me once again, another web, but this one crafted from pain. It flooded me, coalescing into fiery orbs that lengthened and stretched, becoming limbs. More pain followed quickly, flaring bright into a heart that began to labour even as newly forged ribs closed around it. Tendrils of agony became veins, and a curtain of fire fell upon the naked muscles of a new body, a different body, forming itself into skin. The pain abated as the body solidified around my soul, but didn't diminish completely, lingering in my gut like a hot, angry flame.

I cried out in both joy and distress, rejoicing at the knowledge that I now possessed a voice with which to shout. Also, I had skin to feel the hard stone beneath my body and the caress of chilled air. But any joy soon evaporated at

*the realisation that the pain in my belly was building, spreading with a feroc-
ity I knew would soon kill me.*

"The antidote!" a curt, familiar voice instructed. "Hurry!"

*The sting of something acrid on my tongue, choking me into convulsions
as it made its way down my throat. Another, brief burst of agony deep within
then it was gone, quenched by whatever foulness I had swallowed.*

*"Open your eyes," the same voice said, and I felt the grip of strong fingers
on my jaw. Tears streamed in thick torrents as I blinked, gasping at the harsh-
ness of the light from a flaming torch held close to my face. He loomed over me,
eyes staring into mine, hard and demanding in their inquisition.*

*"Do you have a message for me?" he asked, speaking the language of the
southlands then blinking in surprise when I answered in the Stahlhast tongue,
the words harsh and seemingly ill fitting in the mouth that formed them.*

"Kehlbrand . . ." I croaked. "Brother?"

*His hand slipped from my face as he rose to his full height, the harsh scru-
tiny on his face twisting into a smile of welcome. Whatever the nature of my
recent travails, the stone's gift had somehow contrived to remain entangled in
my soul, for I heard the lie he spoke as clear as a tolling bell. "Welcome back,
Obvar." It returned my dog to me, the leering cur translated.* Perhaps, finally,
he'll prove himself useful.

◆ ◆ ◆

*The great fortress city of Keshin-Kho lay under an ashen grey miasma that
seemed immune to the stiff northerly wind sweeping off the Iron Steppe. The
streets were void of inhabitants save for wandering bands of Stahlhast, Tuhla
and Redeemed, all busy in search of loot. Some corpses lay here and there but
most had been cleared away in the two days since the city's fall. I could, however, discern the ferocity of the battle from the many blackened ruins still adding smoke to the lingering shroud above.*

*"Thirty thousand or more," Kehlbrand told me, gauging the track of my
thoughts with typical ease. "That's what it cost me to take it, Obvar. It was
quite the spectacle, I must say. I've already set several scholars to work on the
account. Another chapter to the Darkblade's epic, once suitably edited, of
course."*

*He clapped a hand on my back, guiding me along the battlement. He had
led me to the innermost and highest wall in the city, all the while relating a
commentary of his achievements since my death whilst my still-confused mind*

struggled to grasp hold of the pertinent details. I had missed a great deal, the taking of Keshin-Kho being the principal omission. It had been the object of Stahlhast ambitions for generations, and even in the throes of my disorientation, the shame of having played no part in the city's fall rankled more than I liked.

"Have no fear, old friend," he told me. "There'll be a feast of renown to reap when we move south. Though, sadly, it will be your new name that garners the plaudits."

I looked up at him, suddenly beset by the strangeness of it all. Kehlbrand was a tall man, but I had always been taller and found I disliked this new disparity in stature.

"Don't fret over it too much," Kehlbrand assured me with a smile that held an aggravating level of amusement. "As I understand it, this is but your first shell. Perhaps the next will be more to your liking."

"Where . . ." I began, trailing off as another wave of disorientation swept through me. Images I had never seen flicked through my head along with emotions I had never felt. A shell, I reminded myself. This is just a shell, stolen from a man driven by poison to the point of death.

"I had to force him to touch the stone first," Kehlbrand had told me in those first moments after waking, as I reeled about the room in utter confusion. "Otherwise you wouldn't have found purchase on this body. Apparently he gained an uncanny ability to calculate numbers. A trifling gift to be sure, but I'm sure we'll find a use for it."

I gritted my teeth, forcing away the rush of alien memory to concentrate on my question. "Where is Luralyn?"

Kehlbrand came to an abrupt halt, all humour fading from his features. The hand on my back suddenly bunched into a fist before he withdrew it with a small sigh. "Gone, old friend. She chose the traitor's path."

"Luralyn . . . betrayed you?" The absence of any lie in his voice was palpable, as was his grief. I found myself staggering again and might have stumbled had he not reached out to steady me.

"All will be made clear. For now"—he inclined his head towards the inner streets of the city's uppermost tier—"I need you to perform the role we spoke of."

We halted at the edge of the battlement, looking down on the broad expanse of barracks, temple and courtyard below. A large body of men was *arrayed in the centre of the courtyard, all sitting with heads bowed under the watchful glare of a large contingent of Stahlhast with sabres drawn. A hundred or more archers also patrolled the overlooking wall, ready to unleash a hail of arrows should it prove necessary. The prisoners numbered perhaps six thousand by my reckoning, all that remained of a garrison tens of thousands strong.*

"Before we could surround it, the general emptied the city of all save soldiers," Kehlbrand said with a note of grudging respect. "Clever bastard. I assume he thought he was sparing his subjects our barbarous attentions. Instead he denied them the Darkblade's love and left me only with this lot." He flicked a hand at the prisoners. "Cowards too craven to die fighting. I was hoping for more, but it's a start. Come," he said, moving towards the stairwell, "time to meet your army, General."

The prisoners started to stir as we approached across the courtyard, the grim listlessness of defeated men expectant of death giving way to alarm at the sight of the Darkblade himself. A murmur of disquiet passed through their muddled ranks, but they remained seated due to fear of the Stahlhast. However, their unease turned to outright confusion as my features came fully into view. Some let out shouts of alarm whilst others, veterans presumably, sprang to their feet to stand at rigid attention.

"Stay your blades!" Kehlbrand called out as the Stahlhast made ready to hack down those who had risen. "Good soldiers should show due respect to their general."

Clearly taking this as some form of signal, the entire contingent of prisoners got quickly to their feet, former sergeants and corporals hissing out orders that had them shuffling into a semblance of order. Although they stood to attention, their faces were all locked on mine, some unable to conceal a frown of suspicion, others staring in desperate hope that my presence might mean deliverance. Scanning the faces, I felt a strange rush of recognition, picking out several and finding their names coming easily to mind. I know these men. I *closed my eyes, shaking my head to clear the rush of confusion.* No. He knew these men.

"Have you no words for your soldiers?" Kehlbrand asked, voice soft but insistent.

I straightened, clearing my throat. I had only a rudimentary knowledge of Chu-Shin and expected the words that emerged from my mouth to be halting, accented by the comparatively soft vowels of the Steppe. Instead they flowed with unhesitant fluency, and no one in my audience displayed the slightest doubt that they were being addressed by the man who had worn this face.

"You know me," I told them. "You and I fought together in loyalty and trust. You served under my banner with courage and fortitude through the worst of days, and I am honoured by your service. This day I ask once again for your trust. It is time you learned the truth, the shameful facts of our betrayal. We fought to save this city and spilled our blood for days, watched our brothers die at our side, all on the promise of salvation from the Merchant King. But no salvation ever came. I know now that it was never coming. The Merchant King sent no reinforcements. We were abandoned here to die so that he might continue to sit in his palace and enjoy his riches. It has always been this way; the wealth of the Merchant Realms has ever been purchased by the blood of their soldiers."

Most continued to stare in confused fascination, whilst I saw several frown in either anger or disgust. Was their leader now a turncoat?

"Know that my words are true, for the Darkblade speaks only truth." I extended a stiff arm to Kehlbrand, who now wore a perfectly composed expression of regretful anger, the image of a man grieved to hear of his friend's suffering. "He has spoken unto me, and I have heard the truth of his words and the greatness of his mercy. He offers us life, he offers us freedom from the shackles of the Merchant King. No longer will we be slaves to an old man's greed, no longer will our wives and children know only servitude. The Venerable Kingdom is naught but a diseased monster in need of killing. I, Sho Tsai, once your general, once a fool who spent his days bowing before an undeserving miser, pledge my sword to the Darkblade's service." I swept my arm towards them, fingers spread in urgent invitation. "Join me. Together we will sweep away the corruption and filth of the Merchant Kings. Join me!"

An angry murmur rippled through the ranks, men exchanging glances of despairing bewilderment. Sho Tsai, commander of the Red Scouts and defender of Keshin-Kho, the most faithful servant ever known to the court of the Merchant King Lian Sha, now called for treason. The murmur grew into muttering, the words "mad" and "treachery" audible amongst the babble. The orderly ranks lost cohesion as muttering blossomed into shouts and many took on the crouch of those about to engage in combat, heedless of the danger. It was clear to me that these men were about to die under a hail of arrows and *slashing sabres, that all they had heard in the words of their general were the lies of a traitor.*

Then Kehlbrand stepped forward.

The prisoners fell to immediate silence as he spread his arms out wide, the parade of angry faces becoming the blank masks of an enraptured audience. I felt something as he walked into their ranks and they parted before him, a pulse of power only I amongst this company could feel. I had long known Kehlbrand gained a powerful gift upon touching the stone, but now I understood he had gained more than one. He spoke as he moved amongst them, face and voice possessed of a soft but commanding sincerity. "Heed your general's words," he told them, clasping hands as he made his way through the crowd. "Hear the truth he speaks." But I could see it was not the words that captured them, it was him; his mere presence sent hard-faced veterans and callow youth alike to their knees, eyes moist with adoration. But not all—some failed to kneel, a few dozen amongst the many, retreating from his progress in obvious repugnance. From the practiced swiftness with which the Stahlhast guards moved in to drag these unseduced souls away, to the utter indifference of their kneeling comrades, I discerned this to be a scene that had played out before. This was how he had recruited his army of Redeemed. This was how the Darkblade assured his ascendancy over all other gods.

"You will be the seed of a new host," he told his new adherents, arms outstretched to receive their obeisance, every head bowed now, some reaching out to him with tremulous hands. "Under the leadership of the hero Sho Tsai you will free first the Venerable Kingdom, then the world entire so that all may know the love of the Darkblade."

◆　◆　◆

I found over two dozen freshly slaughtered prisoners in the temple, along with a multitude of bandaged corpses who had evidently died the night of the city's fall. The general's memory, still mostly a jumble of gratingly unfamiliar sensation and image, allowed a dim remembrance that this structure had been given over to the care of the wounded during the siege. The Darkblade, it appeared, had little use for those not whole in body. The scene stirred a fresh image in the mind of this shell, brighter and clearer than the others. A woman, dark of hair and pale of skin, resembling many a Stahlhast in fact, a face also known to my living mind. The healer, I realised. The one the southlanders called the Grace of Heaven. She travelled with the Thief of Names. Sherin, her name was Sherin.

I recalled how she had tended to the scratches on my back the night Kehl-brand took Al Sorna to the Sepulchre. My indulgence in the revels had been enthusiastic that night, causing me to seek out those of similar enthusiasm. Carnal instinct led me to a pair of sisters from the Wohten Skeld who took as much delight in causing pain as in receiving pleasure. Despite the welcome distraction they provided, my mood remained sour. The arrival of the Thief of Names, after so many months of waiting, led me to brooding on Kehlbrand's lies and the grim realisation that his most pertinent statement on the matter had been spoken before I possessed my gift. Someone is coming . . . An enemy I know you cannot defeat.

Another lie, *I consoled myself.* Just a taunt to stir my pride.

"Uhhh!" I had gasped as the healer's ointment stung the scratches on my back, causing me to hiss, "Have a care, you foreign bitch!" Glancing over my shoulder at her I saw only the weary forbearance of one who had no doubt heard many such curses. "I'm going to kill your man tomorrow," I told her in my halting Chu-Shin. "You know that?"

Her eyes flicked to mine, the gaze steady and irksome in its lack of fear. "He is not my man," she said, and I heard no lie on her lips when she added, "but, for your sake, I implore you, don't fight him. He'll kill you."

A shrill cry banished the recollection and brought me back to the temple, a woman's cry.

"Found her under a pile of coals in a basement," a Stahlhast said, dragging a woman across the tiles by the hair. She was tall and about the same age as the general's shell, and even under the coating of coal dust I detected a certain handsomeness to her features. A half-dozen other Stahlhast closed in as the warrior released the woman, leaving her gasping on the floor.

"Servant of Heaven," one of the Stahlhast grunted, a hatchet-faced woman with the scars of a veteran who prodded at the tall woman's besmirched robe with the tip of her sabre. "The Darkblade will want her to answer the question."

"What's the point?" another asked in a weary tone. "They always say no." He crouched to rub away a portion of the dust on the woman's face. "Not too ugly, for a southlander. We could sell her to the Tuhla. They like unspoiled meat."

I was impressed to see the woman's features harden into a defiant glare, teeth gritted as she began to recite a prayer litany through clenched teeth. I had seen this before in Leshun-Kho when we killed the monks. All would be asked to surrender their faith in Heaven for subservience to the Darkblade and their only answer would be a stream of prayers. The words were spoken in an archaic version of Chu-Shin far beyond the understanding of her tormentors, but the shell I wore had little difficulty discerning the meaning. "The mercy of Heaven is eternal. The judgement of Heaven is eternal . . ."

"Another babbler," the veteran sighed, rolling her eyes. "Why do they always babble?" She jerked her head at the crouching warrior. "Slit her throat and spare my ears."

The woman's litany continued unabated as the warrior drew a dagger from his belt, her furious gaze locked on his, refusing to look away until he grabbed a fistful of her hair, jerking the head back to bare the throat for a killing slash. As he did so her gaze found me and instantly widened into startled recognition.

"Servant of the Temple!" she gasped, sending a rush of memory into the forefront of my mind. The High Temple . . . The Temple of Spears . . . It was too much to comprehend all at once, an accumulation of experience going back decades. A wiry man with long dark hair and judgemental countenance imparting a lesson, the words were too garbled to make out, but I saw that he held a plain wooden staff stained with blood. The iron sting on my tongue told me the blood belonged to this shell. In placid moments, the tutor said, thoughts may flow like a gentle stream through verdant fields. In the midst of combat, however . . . The staff whirled in his hands and a hard pain exploded in my guts. Thought is a luxury, and action must surrender to well-honed instinct. To be plain. Another blow from the staff cracking against my shins. Stop allowing yourself to be so fucking distracted . . .

There followed a tumult of military servitude and battle interspersed with fleeting glimpses of an unfolding life. I felt Sho Tsai's blossoming of affection for a woman, severe in both face and word but that only made him love her more. A pair of squabbling children played in a modest but well-appointed garden. This vision darkened almost instantly into a disordered mess, overgrown with weeds, the house beyond unlit and empty but for the three corpses it held, claimed, I understood, by one of the plagues that periodically swept the Merchant Realms. Then more battle, bandits and sundry scum felled by his blade as he led a troop of red-armoured men from one corner of the Venerable Kingdom to the other. The tumult calmed as the memory once again settled on the judgemental tutor, standing beside another *figure that blurred and shifted as I tried to focus on it. I sensed a glimmer of something in this figure, an occluded gem of knowledge of great significance. It darkened and receded as I reached for it, the shell I wore taking on a cold, uncomfortable shiver. For the briefest second I knew myself to be looking at the world through two sets of eyes, sharing a mind with a second awareness, something that railed against me like a prisoner at the bars of his cell.*

You're still in here, I realised as the awareness diminished and retreated into the morass of memory, taking the gem of knowledge with it. What are you hiding from me?

I blinked, seeing the woman's bright, pleading eyes still locked on mine as the edge of the warrior's dagger pressed into her skin. "Stop!" *I snapped, bringing the Stahlhast's blade to a halt. They all stared at me as I moved closer, waving a dismissive hand.* "Get you gone. I have business with this one."

The crouching warrior let out a half snarl as he rose, face tense and brows dark with the frustration of the born killer denied a victim. "You don't command me, southland fucker!" *he said, fingers twitching on the dagger's handle.*

"You were at the Three Rivers," *I said, angling my head in recognition. I saw his fury falter slightly at the sound of his own language, spoken with a fluency that should have been beyond a southlander's tongue. The fury, however, returned in full measure as I smiled and added,* "You ran from Obvar's blade. He could smell the shit leaking from your craven arse."

The veteran woman reached out a restraining hand, but it was too late, the warrior's lunge was automatic and impressive in its speed, the dagger blurring as it jabbed at my unarmored chest. I had intended to bat the thrust aside and beat him unconscious, but my shell had a different notion. Moving of their own volition, my hands ensnared his wrist, twisting and breaking it like a twig before forcing the weapon to a vertical angle and stabbing it upwards. The dagger pierced the warrior under the chin, the long, triangular blade penetrating all the way to the brain. In combat, action must surrender to well-honed instinct, *I thought, grunting in satisfaction.* This shell might not be mighty of stature, but it definitely had its uses.

I tore the dagger free, letting the corpse fall and whirling to face the other Stahlhast who had all retreated a step, hunching with sabres half-drawn.

"You fight me," *I said, levelling the bloodied blade at the Stahlhast woman's scarred face,* "and you fight the Darkblade. Is that what you want?"

Her jaws bunched as she glared in response, but good sense soon overcame rage and she looked away. "She still has to die," she muttered, gesturing for the others to gather up the body of their unwise comrade. "He decrees it."

I waited for their footsteps to fade before crouching at the tall woman's side. Her bright, beseeching gaze had darkened into suspicion now, and she shuffled back from me. "Brother?" she said, dust-covered brows creasing as she searched my face.

Her name came to me then, plucked free of the mess of memory. As it did so I felt a faint trill of anger deep in the recess of my mind where the soul of this stolen shell still lingered. "Mother Wehn," I said, holding out my hand. "Let me help you."

Her eyes flicked to my hand then back to my face, suspicion becoming certainty. "I have known Sho Tsai for two decades," she said in a low, angry murmur. "You wear his face, you have his voice, but you do not have his soul. I know my brother."

A rueful smile played over my lips as I lowered my hand. "No, I do not have his soul. But I do have his memories." She drew back as I inched closer, impressing me with her defiance despite the fear that set her trembling. "The Temple of Spears," I said. "My old . . . teacher. Once gave me something. What was it?"

She took a breath and closed her eyes, the lips moving in a whisper as she resumed her prayer litany. The words were different now, but spoken with even more intense certainty. "The true servant of Heaven knows no fear. The true servant of Heaven knows no pain . . ."

A crosscut to the soles of the feet, *I thought, grabbing hold of her ankle.* Always a good place to start.

Her litany continued even as I pressed the edge of the blade to the bare flesh of her foot, the words continuing to flow, absent of the barest whimper. I found myself holding the dagger in place for some time, baffled by the fact that my hands refused to make the cut. Is this you? I asked Sho Tsai, wondering if he had somehow infected me with his southland scruples. Mercy is weakness, *I reminded myself.* Compassion is cowardice. Wisdom is falsehood. *The priests' teachings—for me they had always been true to the heart of the Stahlhast despite the Darkblade's injunctions against speaking them aloud. But now, I found them empty, incapable of forcing my hands into motion. I simply had no desire to cause this woman pain.* Death brings changes, even in mighty Obvar.

"Just tell me," I said, releasing my hold. "Please."

Her litany stopped and she opened her eyes. Fear had begun to master her now, the tears streaming from her eyes to carve rivulets through the dirt on her cheeks, her body shuddering in terror, but still she shook her head. Perhaps it was the tears that did it, finding some echo of this woman in Sho Tsai's mind and stirring sufficient emotion to lead me to the required memory.

"You were there," I realised as the images resolved into clarity. Mother Wehn stood close by wearing a broad smile on younger features as she regarded the youth at the tutor's side, a youth this shell had known and loved for all the years that followed.

Guide him, teach him, *the tutor said.* Above all, protect him.

◆ ◆ ◆

"No sign at all?"

A shiny tendril of sweat trickled down the neck of the Redeemed as he bobbed his lowered head in response to Kehlbrand's question. "None since we found the collapsed tunnel, Darkblade."

"And the canal?"

"Only the bodies, Darkblade."

I watched Kehlbrand turn his expressionless face back to the tubular contraption on the tripod, pressing his eye to the narrow end. "The bodies," he murmured, "but not the horse." He swivelled the device back and forth, scanning the landscape below. I had climbed the many steps to the top of this tower to find him in conference with this sweating man, a borderlands native judging by his clothing, which was hardy but lacked any martial accoutrements. He was a few years my junior, or rather Sho Tsai's junior, and had the lean but sturdy look of a man who spent his days in the wilds.

"I," the Redeemed began, swallowing before speaking on in strained tones, "I divined that the foreigners became separated, Darkblade. Those I tracked to the Tomb Road; the others are still on the canal."

"He is not on the canal," Kehlbrand said, turning back from the viewing glass. "Hence the absence of the horse." He stared at the Redeemed for the space of a few heartbeats, which I knew must have felt much longer, before his gaze slid to me.

"General," he said. "Give greetings to Master Lah Vo, most famed huntsman of the Northern Prefecture."

I exchanged a shallow bow with the Redeemed who seemed no keener to meet my gaze than he was Kehlbrand's.

"It is said Lah Vo can smell a dagger-tooth from five miles upwind and as a boy felled a bear with but a slingshot," Kehlbrand went on. "And yet he can't catch the smallest scent of my sister or the Thief of Names."

"Send me," I said. "I've an account to settle with him, as you know."

"You have an army to train." Kehlbrand moved to Lah Vo, provoking a shudder as he clapped him on the back and guided him to the stairwell. "Worry not, my friend. The Thief of Names is cunning and so is my sister. Rest and restore yourself. I'll have fresh quarry for you soon enough."

He returned to the viewing glass as the huntsman's relieved steps echoed into silence. "That Ostra bitch was supposed to finish him," I heard him mutter. "The tune was clear. Now I hear nothing."

"I suspect you'll see him again soon enough," I offered. "Al Sorna struck me as a man unlikely to let a grudge fester for long."

Kehlbrand gave a soft laugh. "Is that regard I hear in your voice, old friend?"

"A man should know his enemy."

"Keen for a second try, eh? Well, I regret to disappoint you. Babukir's penance is almost done, and I have to find some use for him, after all." He moved back from the viewing glass, fixing me with a questioning look. "I sense you have something to tell me. What can it be?"

"I remembered something, something the general knew. A name of some importance."

Kehlbrand gave an amused grin and came closer, I assumed so he could look down on me once again. "And what could that be?"

Still just a dog to him, I thought. Faithfully bringing prey back to its master. Even so, a dog of vicious temper can bite an overly trusting hand. But first, trust has to be won. "The name," I said, "of the lost heir to the throne of the Emerald Empire."

CHAPTER ONE

He felt Ahm Lin die as he drank. A faint, almost imperceptible exhalation and a final shudder, then his friend was gone.

Vaelin forced away the surge of despair to suck in the last few pulses of blood streaming from the mason's wound. The thick metallic stream flooded his mouth and caught in his throat, making him gag. Heedless of his disgust, he forced the thick torrent down. Vaelin felt the gift blossom as soon as the first few drops entered his gut, spreading through his being with lightning speed, and bringing with it a song, a song that had more in common with a scream.

The music was deafening, painfully so, filling his mind with an overlapping cascade of notes that somehow retained a tune of sorts despite their ugly discordance, a tune that held both certainty and meaning: *Death comes from all sides. IT COMES NOW!*

He sprang away from Ahm Lin's corpse, crouching low and ducking under the whistling slash of a sabre as its wielder, a hulking Stahlhast in full armour, came surging out of the long grass that covered the canal bank. The warrior cursed and tried again, both hands on the hilt as he thrust towards Vaelin's chest. The song continued to scream as Vaelin found his gaze captured by the Stahlhast's blunt, heavily creased features. The tune told the tale of a man steeped in blood and happiest in moments of violence. A man who had fought, killed, raped and looted his way across the Iron Steppe and the borderlands. A man who hungered for more when the horde swept into the heart of the Venerable Kingdom. A man who had also neglected to repair the small plate of armour that covered the space above his left hip, hacked away during the final assault on Keshin-Kho. All this the song screamed into Vaelin's mind in the space of a heartbeat.

He twisted as the Stahlhast closed, allowing the sabre to pass within an inch of his chest, then stabbed his sword point into the gap in the Stahlhast's armour. The blade sank deep, slicing through vein, tendon and cartilage to sever all connections between leg and hip. The warrior shouted in shock and fury as he collapsed, glaring up at Vaelin, lips forming a last defiant obscenity. Vaelin withdrew his blade and hacked down, the warrior's final word swallowed by the gush of blood that erupted from his mouth.

The song's shriek snapped Vaelin's gaze to a fresh threat, two more Stahlhast thrashing through the tall grass barely yards away. He hacked again at the dying warrior's neck, delivering two fast blows then taking hold of the man's helmet as his head came free of his shoulders. The first Stahlhast to clear the grass took the thrown head full in the face and reeled back on his heels, stunned and blinded by the impact and explosion of gore. He managed to scrape the red mess from his eye in time for it to receive the tip of Vaelin's sword, the blade skewering his brain before he had time to register the fact of his own death.

Vaelin kicked the twitching corpse aside, pulling the sword free in time to parry the slash delivered by the second Stahlhast. He stepped close before the warrior had the chance to retreat, delivering a swift headbutt to his unguarded nose then snatching a dagger from the man's belt before whirling and driving it into the unarmoured rear of his thigh.

More pealing cries from the song sent Vaelin sprawling into the grass as a criss-cross hail of arrows snapped the air. The unfortunate Stahlhast, still upright and staggering as he tried to pull the dagger from his leg, took a trio of shafts in the chest, evidently loosed from close range judging by the ease with which the steel arrowheads punched through mail and plate. As Vaelin crawled away, his belly scraping the earth, he heard the warrior's choking death rattle. Shouts echoed through the fog-shrouded bank interspersed by the occasional snap and whistle of a loosed arrow, but none came close.

It's different, Vaelin thought as he crawled, wincing as the song's grating tune continued. Its pitch rose and fell continually, sibilant as a snake's hiss one second then screeching like a distressed hawk the next. With every peak he felt his vision darken and his pulse quicken, accompanied by a rarely felt but familiar hunger. He had first felt it in the Martishe Forest many years ago, when his friend lay dying and Vaelin sprinted in pursuit of the archer who had felled him. It was bloodlust, a need to kill born of this song. *A different song*, he knew with growing certainty. *Not my song.* Not the song he had left in the Beyond after bleeding himself to the point of death at Alltor. Not the song he had ached for ever since.

He came to a halt as the new song's tune rose again, although the tune was not quite so discordant and the sensation it brought held no tinge of hunger. Still there was a sour note to it, a grudging thrum of welcome.

The horse's hoof came down a few inches from his head, stamping in impatience. Vaelin looked up and grimaced as Derka's snort showered hot vapour onto his face. The stallion angled his head to regard Vaelin with a single, insistent eye, shaking his neck to allow the reins to fall free.

"Yes," Vaelin grunted, reaching for the reins, "it's good to see you again too."

A fresh chorus of shouts erupted as he vaulted into the saddle, swiftly followed by another volley of arrows. They met only air as Derka bore him away, spurring unbidden into a gallop to be swallowed by the fog. The song let out another shrill cry of warning an instant before a mounted Stahlhast came thundering out of the mist directly ahead, a tall woman whirling a double-bladed axe above her head. Vaelin took a firmer hold of the reins, intending to guide Derka to the rider's left, but the stallion had a notion of his own. Earth and shredded grass fountained as he came to a halt, rearing with a whinny as the charging horse closed. The hard crack of shattered bone sounded as Derka brought a hoof down on the opposing horse's head, sending it and its rider into an untidy tumble.

Vaelin started to spur Derka forward but stopped as the song surged again, the tune not as loud this time but somehow even more painful. The notes were harsh and insistent, seeming to dig deep inside him to conjure images of the siege, all the soldiers he had commanded now dying at the hands of the Darkblade's horde, and Ahm Lin's bleached, pleading face at the end. *Please . . . my gift to you . . .*

His vision blurred as the song rose to a deafening, near-agonising pitch, turning the world into a reddish grey haze. He was aware of his hand on the reins, of the sword's handle turning against his palm and the flex of his arm, but had no control over any of it. He couldn't say how long it took for the song's tune to fade and his vision to clear—it might have been just a few seconds or an hour—but when it did he found himself staring down at the Stahlhast woman, now slumped against the flank of her slain horse. Her features were a curious mirror of Ahm Lin's at the end, whitened by blood loss and imminent death. She looked up at Vaelin and blinked once before turning to regard the jet of blood pulsing from the stump of her severed arm, watching her life drain away in rapt fascination rather than horror.

Dragging his gaze away, Vaelin slid his sword into the sheath on his back and spurred Derka into a gallop, disappearing into the fog once more. Shouts and bowstrings continued to echo through the haze but faded soon enough. Slowing Derka to a walk, Vaelin cast around for a landmark, some indication of where he might be. The fog had thinned to a low-lying mist unveiling the sun and revealing a plain of tall grass that rose into undulating hills to the south. The dim conical bulk of Keshin-Kho dominated the skyline to the north and he could see the unerringly straight line of the canal a few hundred paces to the west. The only appreciable cover consisted of a dense patch of woodland off to the east and, knowing pursuit would not be long in coming, he turned Derka towards it and set off at a steady canter.

As he rode, the sight of the dying Stahlhast woman's face lingered. He had taken many lives but always, he preferred to think, out of necessity. With the Stahlhast dismounted he could have ridden on. Killing her was unnecessary, and yet he had done it. A sharp snarl came from the song then, the tone one of harsh rebuke that carried a new thought: *An enemy is deserving only of death.*

He found his hands tightening on the reins, bringing Derka to a halt. Glancing over his shoulder Vaelin peered into the misted grass, hearing the faint but growing shouts of his pursuers. *They killed Ahm Lin,* he thought as the song's tune grew more melodious, becoming almost seductive in the promise it held. *They killed Sho Tsai and so many others, all in service to a false god. And I have a blood-song once again. Would it be so hard to kill them all? Would it not, in fact, be an insult to Ahm Lin's memory if I didn't? He gave me a gift, after all.*

Derka gave a loud, irritated nicker, breaking through Vaelin's burgeoning hunger and provoking another snarl from the song. Vaelin clenched his teeth and determinedly turned his gaze east once more, kicking the stallion into motion. *No*, he decided as the hungry tune persisted, setting a continual ache in his head as he refused to answer its call. *This is not a blood-song. Blood is the stuff of life. This is a song of death. A black-song.*

◆ ◆ ◆

By the time they reached the trees the song had diminished into a sullen murmur and the ache in his head subsided to a dull throb. He brought Derka to a halt a few yards in, dismounting and crouching with his eyes closed to gauge the sounds and smells of the forest. *Earth damp from recent rain*, he concluded, fingers probing the ground. *Bird calls muted . . . Woodsmoke, drifting from the south.* There were people in these woods.

The forest was dense and the branches low, obliging him to lead Derka through the trees, maintaining an eastward course to avoid whatever lay south. He intended to reach the far end of these woods before striking out to find the canal, an easy task and following it south would inevitably lead him back to Nortah, Ellese and the others. He hoped they had had the good sense not to come looking for him and consoled himself with the knowledge that, for all his faults, Nortah was no fool and not easily swayed by sentiment, especially when sober. *He'll lead them on*, he decided. *All I need do is find them.*

His progress, however, stalled when the song, the black-song, rose in sudden insistent volume once more. The tune remained harsh and grating but the tone lacked the vengeful hunger from before, possessing instead a note that combined warning with necessity. It also prodded him south towards the persistent scent of woodsmoke. *Something there*, he thought, finding the song too compelling to ignore. *Something that must be dealt with.*

He led Derka through a quarter mile of thick forest until he spied wispy tendrils drifting through the treetops ahead. *At least three fires*, Vaelin surmised, eyeing the smoke then wincing as a scream sounded through the trees. This time it didn't come from within, but was the unmistakable product of a human throat and shot through with the plaintive terror unique to torture. It continued for several seconds before abruptly choking off, the subsequent silence filled by a faint ripple of laughter. *Something that must be dealt with*, he repeated to himself, the scream and the laughter having dispelled any doubts about the song's course.

Derka gave a truculent snort and tossed his head in annoyance when Vaelin began to fasten his reins to the fallen branch of a yew. *I sang to him,* the Jade Princess had said during the trek across the Iron Steppe. *Just a small tune to bind you together.* "Wait here," Vaelin whispered, letting the reins fall and smoothing a hand over the stallion's snout before crouching and slipping into the concealment offered by a stretch of ferns.

The laughter grew louder and more discordant as he crept forward, making out several voices speaking a language he didn't know. Pausing to listen, he detected some resemblance to both the Stahlhast tongue and the form of Chu-Shin spoken in the borderlands, but the phrasing and accents rendered the words unintelligible. Lowering himself to the earth he began to crawl, moving with steady, practised slowness, his hands sweeping the ground free of twigs or fallen branches that might betray his presence. He stopped as a familiar hissing sound reached his ears, his eyes picking out a rising patch of steam beyond the trunk of an ash tree. A slow sideways creep revealed the sight of a man in leather armour, face set in bored distraction as he pissed into the undergrowth.

Tuhla, Vaelin concluded, recognising the man's garb. His eyes flicked left and right, finding no others whilst the laughter and conversation continued in the distance. *Never a good plan to piss alone in a time of war.* Vaelin watched the man finish his task and turn away, looking down to fasten his britches as he walked off. Vaelin rose to a crouch, moving swiftly, the sound of his footfalls causing the Tuhla to pause and turn, but too late to ward off the arms that encircled his chest and throat. Vaelin kicked the Tuhla's legs away and jerked his head up and to the right as they fell, Vaelin taking satisfaction from the double crack that told of a snapped neck. He clamped a hand over the man's mouth to stifle his death cries, pinching the nose to prevent a last intake of breath, maintaining his grip until his twitches stilled.

Rolling the corpse off him, Vaelin checked it for anything useful. The Tuhla wore a scimitar on his belt along with a flask of some foul-smelling concoction with the sting of strong liquor. He also had a bone-handle hunting knife of good steel tucked into his boot. Vaelin took the knife and moved on, once again adopting his slow, steady crawl, keeping to the densest undergrowth. He found two more Tuhla twenty paces on, both markedly less careless than their recently despatched comrade. One held a strongbow with an arrow nocked to the string whilst the other gripped a drawn scimitar. Both were scanning the surrounding trees with the predatory awareness of men well versed in detecting fresh danger.

"Ulska!" the archer said in a restrained shout, presumably calling out to a man who had taken too long over a piss. Vaelin flattened himself to the soft ground as they came closer. He was partially concealed by the broad trunk of an aged oak and a covering of ferns, but this would prove scant protection when they drew closer. Vaelin palmed one of his own throwing knives in his left hand and adjusted his grip on the stolen Tuhla weapon, waiting until the two warriors closed the distance to five paces.

He drew back his arms and threw as he rose from cover, both knives arcing towards the targets with a precision he had thought lost to his youth. The left-hand throw was marginally the less accurate of the two, the steel dart striking at the join of the Tuhla's neck and shoulder, but still managing to find a vein of sufficient import to send the warrior to the ground with blood gurgling from his mouth in a dark torrent. By contrast, the archer somehow remained standing despite taking the bone-handle knife full in the throat. He even tried to draw his bow as Vaelin made an unhurried approach, though the Tuhla's spasming limbs soon shook the weapon from his grasp. Vaelin stooped to retrieve the bow before pulling the knife free and relieving the Tuhla of his quiver when he finally collapsed and choked out his last strangled breath.

Vaelin put an arrow to the string as he moved on, the black-song growing into an ugly murmur. It was coloured by a sensation he hadn't felt for many years, the hum of recognition that meant only one thing: *Another Gifted is near.* A fresh upsurge of laughter led him to the rest of the Tuhla, a dozen standing in a loose circle around a small group of kneeling men. The kneelers were all bare chested, but a pile of discarded armoured jerkins nearby marked them as captured soldiers of the Merchant King. Also, Vaelin saw as he crept closer, men he knew.

Cho-ka knelt at the forefront of the group, flanked on either side by the prone corpses of two fellow members of the Green Vipers. His sweat-beaded features bunched in mingled hatred and frustration as he stared up with admirable defiance at the portly man standing over him.

"Where is he?" the portly man asked in Chu-Shin. Unlike the Tuhla, he was unarmoured and carried no weapons, and was garbed in clothing typical of the borderlands. As the man angled his head and leaned closer to Cho-ka, Vaelin felt a blossoming of power along with a rush of recognition. *The Darkblade's tent*, he remembered. *The day he killed the Jade Princess.* It had been this one who had frozen Vaelin in place when he tried to avenge her murder.

"Tell me," the portly man went on, playing a hand over Cho-ka's furious visage. "We know you helped him escape the city. So why isn't he with you now? Did you kill him? Steal from him?"

Cho-ka gave no answer beyond a sneering curl of his lips, which provoked a soft, regretful sigh from the portly man. "You have already witnessed the price paid by those who shun the Darkblade's love," he said, gesturing to the bodies on either side of the kneeling smuggler. Vaelin was unable to see the nature of their injuries but the ground beneath them was dark with blood and the stench was familiar to anyone who had witnessed a disembowelment. "Why suffer such a fate for a foreigner?" the portly man enquired. "A vile and treacherous foreigner at that." He leaned closer, voice softening into an insistent plea. "Spare yourself and these others. Redeem yourself in the eyes of the only true living god. Tell me, where is the Thief of Names?"

Cho-ka's sneer turned into a snarl, although his teeth remained clenched and his body rigid. Vaelin saw that his arms were unbound but remained tight against his flanks. "Such a closed soul," the portly man said, shaking his head in meagre despair. "I think you should set it free from your cage of flesh." He shifted his gaze slightly, focusing on Cho-ka's bare torso. Vaelin felt another swelling of power and the smuggler shuddered, his arms coming up in a spasmodic jerk, hands forming into trembling claws. "Although," the portly man added, "the soul of one such as you will be hard to find. Dig deep."

Cho-ka's hands slapped against the flat muscles of his belly, his entire body shuddering in fruitless resistance as the fingers began to gouge at his skin. The black-song started to shriek again when Vaelin saw the first trickle of blood on the smuggler's skin, the music full of an all-encompassing rage. *There are too many*, a small, still-rational part of his mind protested as he raised the bow, the string scraping over his cheek as he drew it to the full. The song's only answer was a small, vicious trill of amusement before his fingers loosed the arrow.

Vaelin saw the shaft skewer the portly man through the chest and felt his gift dwindle and die. Before the red-grey mist descended once again to obscure the world, he was aware of casting the bow aside and drawing his sword, charging forward and throwing the bone-handle knife so that it sank into the ground near Cho-ka. Everything went away when the first Tuhla raised a sabre to parry his thrust, the last clear image Vaelin caught being the man's bisected features as the star-silver blade cleaved him from forehead to chin.

◆　◆　◆

"Shouldn't we stop him? They won't get any more dead."

"Feel at liberty to try."

The voices were little more than dimly heard murmurs beyond the red mist, but held sufficient meaning to snare the vestige of reason not drowned by the black-song's clamour. Vaelin felt a rush of sensation as the song subsided into the headache he was beginning to understand as its resting state. His body shuddered with recent exertion, muscles throbbing and chest heaving as sweat coursed down his back. Even so, he felt no sense of exhaustion, although his sword arm ached as he lowered it, squinting at the blood covering the blade from tip to hilt. A man lay at his feet, or rather what was left of him. His jaw had been hacked away along with a good portion of his upper lip, teeth gleaming white amongst the red mess. Shifting his gaze, Vaelin saw another body lying facedown a few feet away, the leather armour on his back rent and cut away along with the flesh beneath, all the way down to his spine.

"Lord?"

Vaelin jerked towards the voice, sword rising in instinctive reflex. Cho-ka stepped back from him, lowering the scimitar he held, his free hand open in placation. "We need to be gone from here," the smuggler said.

"We?" another voice asked. It belonged to a stocky man Vaelin remembered from the ranks of the Skulls. He had been a good soldier, resolute in the face of the Darkblade's repeated onslaughts. Now, however, he eyed his former commander with a mixture of suspicion and deep trepidation. Another surviving Viper stood at his back, his face displaying much the same sentiment.

"Shut your yap, Kiyen!" Cho-ka snapped. "An unsettled debt is a curse. Or don't you value your hide?" The words had a sense of authority to them, as if the smuggler were reciting a solemn rule not to be broken.

The stocky man's face hardened at the rebuke as he flicked a hand at their surroundings. "You really want him travelling with us?" he asked.

Looking around, Vaelin counted six more bodies, most in a similar state of mutilation to the one at his feet. "Did I . . . ?" he began, trailing off as the pain in his head made him wince.

"We did for two ourselves," Cho-ka told him, patting the bone-handle knife tucked into his belt. "A bunch ran off after they saw . . ." He inclined his head at the bodies with a grimace. "This. Can't say I blame them."

"They'll be back with more," Vaelin said, shaking his head to clear the last traces of red mist from his vision. "If the Darkblade doesn't execute them for cowardice."

"Lucky they left us these, then." Cho-ka started towards a rope line where a number of horses were tethered. "Any preference, lord?"

A stamp of hooves drew Vaelin's gaze to the sight of Derka emerging from the trees nearby. "That won't be necessary."

"This isn't smart, Cho," Kiyen, the stocky man, said as Cho-ka and Vaelin mounted up. He shot a cautious glance in Vaelin's direction before moving close to his fellow Viper, voice lowered. "Even if he wasn't mad as a starved dagger-tooth, the Darkblade's lot will be scouring every inch of this country for him."

"A debt is a debt," Cho-ka stated flatly, jerking his head at the pile of discarded armour and weapons. "Get your gear and mount up or piss off. But if you do, you'll never again call yourself a Green Viper." He fixed Kiyen with a cold stare. "And you know the rules when it comes to outcasts."

The stocky outlaw bit down on a retort, shifting his gaze to Vaelin. "I'll travel with you, foreigner, because he wills it. But no more lordly shit. I took my last orders from you back there." He stabbed a finger in the direction of Keshin-Kho. "I'm done fighting the Merchant King's war, understand?"

Vaelin saw little point in answering and turned to Cho-ka, thoughts of his friends rising to the forefront of his mind. He knew Nortah would have the good sense to try to stop the others interrupting their flight from Keshin-Kho to look for him, but had severe doubts Ellese would be inclined to listen. His niece's frantic calls after he plunged into the water had echoed very loud in the fog. "We need to get back on the canal," he told the outlaw. "My friends . . ."

"No boats for miles." The smuggler shook his head. "Besides, we'd be far too easy to find. We'll make for Daiszhen-Khi. It's where the Great Northern Canal joins the others. It's likely swamped with boats trying to get through the locks. Best chance you have of catching up to the other foreigners."

"It's open ground all the way there once we clear these trees," Kiyen said, climbing into the saddle with a sullen glower.

Vaelin saw Cho-ka hesitate before replying, his voice tight with forced surety. "Not if we take the Tomb Road."

The other two Green Vipers exchanged wary glances. "That place holds a curse worse than any unsettled debt," the taller of the two pointed out. Unlike Kiyen, this one hadn't made much impression on Vaelin's memory during the siege, other than an apparently incurable tendency to march out of step.

"My word stands," Cho-ka stated, meeting the eye of each man. "Travel with us and settle your debt or make your own way, knowing what it means down the road."

He kicked his mount into motion, setting off at a steady trot with Vaelin following. Behind him, he could hear a muted but fierce discussion amongst the two Vipers as they failed to follow. He concluded they had decided to risk the ire of their outlaw fraternity after all, then detected the sound of inexpert riders guiding horses through dense country. The song, however, saw no reason for comfort in their decision, voicing a sharp note of discordant but easily discerned meaning.

"They're planning to kill us," Vaelin told Cho-ka. "Me out of fear. You out of necessity. With you gone, there'll be no one to tell the Vipers of their treachery." He gritted his teeth as the song's volume rose, causing him to continue in a hungry rasp. "We should finish them now."

"I know their schemes, lord." The outlaw's tone was one of distracted preoccupation rather than concern. He rode with much more expertise than his companions, guiding the long-legged Steppe-born mount around fallen trunks and hazardous tree roots with practiced ease. "My brothers are not hard men to read."

"Then why not allow them to leave?"

"Four swords will be better than two if we run into trouble." Cho-ka steered his mount between two trees and into more open ground. The forest had thinned now and Vaelin could see the rolling grassland to the east. The smuggler's voice grew softer as he spoke on, his tone one of grim resolve although the black-song translated it as a deep sense of guilt. "And I've travelled the Tomb Road before. It cannot be walked alone."

Chapter Two

They spurred to a gallop upon clearing the trees, Cho-ka striking out on a south-easterly course. Vaelin scanned the long stretches of swaying grass for any sign of more Tuhla or Stahlhast, although the black-song had now subsided into the customary ache that told of no impending danger. *Why is it different?* he asked himself continually. *Ahm Lin was a good man. How can his song be black?*

He searched his memory for every scrap of knowledge concerning the Dark he had accumulated over the years, finding it a surprisingly useless mélange of lore, legend and anecdote. All the time spent poring over books in his ever-growing library in North Tower seemed pointless now. He knew the Seventh Order had an archive dating back centuries that would surely have provided some clues to his current malaise, but he had been scrupulous in shunning them since the end of the Liberation War. The schemes and secrets of the Order of the Dark had always aroused his disdain, and Caenis's lies still felt like a betrayal, despite the manner of his death and the part he played in bringing down the Ally. *There were many things you never told him,* he reminded himself. *Who betrayed who?*

Cho-ka slowed his mount to a halt as the sky reddened, Vaelin reining in alongside to see his brows furrowed and eyes bright with unabashed fear as he stared at the dimming horizon. As far as Vaelin could see, the only feature breaking the otherwise unbroken line was a low, flat-topped rise a few miles distant. He would have taken it for a hill but for the odd regularity of its dimensions. "The site of an old fortress?" he asked Cho-ka.

"The Emperor's Mound, they call it," the outlaw replied, lowering his gaze. Vaelin assumed it to be an effort to conceal his fear. If so, the tremble of the man's hands and the whiteness of his knuckles as he gripped his reins told the tale well enough. "The entrance to the Tomb Road," he added with a cough.

"Is it guarded?" Vaelin asked, receiving a harsh, short-lived laugh in response.

"Not even the Merchant Kings have enough wealth to pay a man to guard it. In any case, only the mad or the desperate ever come here."

Vaelin glanced over his shoulder at Kiyen and the other Viper bringing their mounts to an untidy halt. The song murmured louder as Vaelin took note of the way they avoided his gaze. *The mad or the desperate*, he thought. *Fortunate, then, that we are both.*

"What threat lies in this place?" he said, turning back to Cho-ka.

The outlaw didn't reply immediately, continuing to regard the distant mound with his overly bright eyes, hands now tight on the pommel of his saddle. Vaelin was well accustomed to such a demeanour, having seen it at the dawn of many a battle, the posture of a man summoning his courage. "I once heard that your people worship the dead," Cho-ka said finally. "Is that true?"

"Not exactly. It's . . . complicated and would take quite some time to explain."

"So you do not commune with them? They do not speak to you?"

I have spoken with the dead. They reached to me from the Beyond and saved us all. He left the answer unsaid, knowing it would do little to alleviate the man's fears. "Mere superstition," he said instead.

Cho-ka voiced another laugh, even harsher and shorter than before. "What awaits us on the Tomb Road is not superstition." Vaelin detected a shift in his voice, the words becoming more precise and spoken with the inflection of a man who had received some education, if not refinement. "It is not the vague conjuration of a fearful mind. It is real. What you hear and see in there is as real as everything else." Cho-ka's gaze grew intent as it shifted to Vaelin. "To survive, you must accept that."

"Cho!"

Vaelin and Cho-ka wheeled their mounts around at Kiyen's shout. Assuming the two Vipers had chosen this moment to attempt their betrayal rather than risk whatever lurked in the Tomb Road, Vaelin's hand flashed to his sword. However, the stocky outlaw's attention was fixed on the northern horizon. Despite the gathering gloom, Vaelin could make out the roiling silhouette of a large group of riders, accompanied by the sound of dozens of horses at full gallop.

"Tuhla or Stahlhast?" the taller Viper asked, peering into the gloom.

"What does it matter?" Cho-ka said, jabbing his heels into his horse's flanks to spur it forward. "Ride!"

Vaelin soon gained an appreciation for the impressive scale of the Emperor's Mound as Derka brought him closer. The feature's grass-covered slopes rose to a height of at least a hundred feet and extended towards east and west for over a mile. In the fast-gathering gloom, however, he could see no sign of an entrance.

"This way," Cho-ka called out. Vaelin guided Derka in pursuit as the outlaw led them towards the eastern slope. Rounding a corner brought the realisation that the mound was in fact a pyramid, the thickness of the grass that clothed it and the irregularity of its surface speaking of something constructed centuries ago. Cho-ka reined in at the base of the slope and dismounted to slap a hand against his horse's rump, sending it into a gallop.

"Horses can't walk the Tomb Road," he told Vaelin, starting up the slope with a rapid stride. "Best set him loose, lord."

Vaelin quelled his reluctance and climbed down from the saddle, drawing a confused huff from Derka who evidently sensed his intention. "You'll find me again," Vaelin told him with a sigh, unfastening the ties on his bridle and taking the bit from him mouth. "Or I'll find you." He smoothed a hand over the stallion's neck before stepping back, looking intently into his eyes. Derka snorted and stamped a hoof to the earth before wheeling about and galloping away into the dark.

"Lord!" Cho-ka called to him from above as the thunder of fast-approaching hooves grew ever louder. Vaelin scaled the slope at a run, flanked by the dismounted Vipers. He found Cho-ka standing before what appeared to be a miniature temple of some kind. It was partially ruined and degraded by the elements, the pillars that supported its triangular roof cracked and weathered so much that the script inscribed into the stone had long been rendered illegible. It lacked any doors and Vaelin peered into its darkened opening, gaining an impression of unfathomable depths. Cho-ka spent a few seconds rummaging through the rubble at the base of a pillar before grunting in satisfaction.

"Still here," he said, hefting aside a chunk of masonry to reveal an iron-shafted torch. He tore rags from his shirt to cram into the torch's basket, soaking them in oil from a small flask on his belt before striking a flint. Moving to the opening, he paused, Vaelin watching the light from the torch glisten on his sweat-beaded brow as he swallowed. "Keep your eyes on the flame," he said, voice hoarse. "And it's best not to speak unless you must."

He straightened and stepped into the opening, Vaelin waiting to regard Kiyen and the other two outlaws with a pointed stare until they followed Cho-ka into the gloom. Vaelin allowed a decent gap before proceeding into the entrance a few paces, then called for them to wait as an obvious problem rose in his mind.

"We can't tarry, lord," Cho-ka insisted.

"What's to stop them following?" Vaelin asked, inclining his head at the unbarred opening.

"Good sense," Kiyen muttered.

"This place is greatly feared," Cho-ka said. "With ample reason."

"By your people," Vaelin pointed out. "The Tuhla and Stahlhast may not share the same fears. Or may fear the Darkblade's wrath more than anything that lurks below."

He turned and pressed his shoulder to the nearest pillar, feeling it give a little under the pressure. "Help me," he told them. Cho-ka muttered a curse and handed the torch to Kiyen before moving to join his strength to Vaelin's. The pillar's stones leaked ancient mortar and groaned in protest, a sound soon swallowed by the shouts of many voices from the base of the slope. "Hurry!" Vaelin grunted, renewing his efforts. The other Viper pressed in, adding his weight, and soon a loud crack sounded from the base of the pillar.

"Back!" Vaelin said, pushing them into the passage as the pillar toppled. The templelike entrance collapsed an instant later, birthing a dense cloud of dust that flooded the passage and sent them all coughing.

"Shit!" Kiyen exclaimed as the dust swallowed the torch's flame. The darkness that claimed them was near absolute save for faint glimmers of moonlight leaking through the remnants of the entrance.

"Give it here," Cho-ka said. A few moments of cursing and jostling followed by the sound of a striking flint and the torch burst into life once more, revealing a descending passageway and steps several times the width of the entrance. It reminded Vaelin of the entryway to a castle rather than a tomb, its dimensions being sufficient to allow the ingress of at least twenty men abreast.

"How many people are buried here?" he asked Cho-ka.

The outlaw descended the first step, extending his torch into the gloom, his reply echoing long despite the softness of his voice. "Just one."

The clatter and scrape of shifting stone drew Vaelin's gaze back to the rubble-crowded entrance, hearing the muted murmur of voices. "Stahlhast," he said, recognising the language if not the words. "They're digging through."

"Then let's not linger," Cho-ka said, starting down the steps.

By Vaelin's reckoning the passage descended well over a hundred feet into the earth before coming to an end. The space it led to was truly huge judging by the length of the echo raised by their footfalls, but Cho-ka's torch illuminated only a few paces in either direction, leaving Vaelin with the sense of being lost in a sea of darkness. Looking down, he saw that the floor consisted of perfectly flat tiles of finely worked granite, their smoothness and lack of cracks indicating they had barely been touched since being set down.

"What in Heaven's arse is that?" the tallest Viper asked in a tremulous whisper, peering into the gloom as the light caught the edge of something several yards away. It was hard to make out with such meagre illumination but Vaelin gained the impression of a stunted horselike shape before Cho-ka's voice snapped his gaze back to the torch.

"Eyes on the flame, remember! And don't talk again. You don't want them to hear you."

Vaelin stopped himself asking the obvious question and followed as the outlaw led them on, keeping to the rear of the group. His distrust of this pair hadn't abated and he was unwilling to show them his back. However, their treacherous intentions seemed to have been overcome by fear, at least for now. Whilst he kept the bobbing flame of the torch firmly in the centre of his gaze, he caught flickers of movement from the Vipers as their eyes strayed repeatedly into the surrounding gloom. Their breath came in short, shallow gasps and Vaelin could smell their sweat. Despite their terror, he heard no particular alarm from the black-song. The steady ache in his head had changed a little but held no note of warning. If anything, the impression it gave was one of recognition rather than danger. *The Dark knows the Dark,* he thought. *That's what lives in this place.*

Cho-ka set a fast pace, moving in a steady half run as their boots sent a cacophony booming through the cavernous space. Vaelin caught glimpses of tall, rectangular pillars at the edge of his vision, along with numerous vertical shapes too poorly lit by the torch to make out. The impulse to take a long, inquisitive look was strong, but he held to Cho-ka's injunction, reasoning the smuggler knew this place and he did not.

"Gotta have a rest," Kiyen gasped after close to an hour at the run, stumbling and nearly falling before Vaelin reached out to steady him.

"Just a few minutes," Cho-ka said, coming to a reluctant halt. "Keep your eyes down and tongues still."

They huddled in a circle with the torch at the centre, the outlaws all shivering in various states of distress whilst Vaelin felt only the song's ache of recognition and the strain of moderate exertion. The tallest Viper shot him a glare that mingled suspicion with puzzlement, muttering, "He can't hear them."

"Hear what?" Vaelin enquired.

"Tongues still!" Cho-ka snapped.

"He can't hear the voices," the Viper insisted in a quavering hiss, his gaze sweeping across the other outlaws. "Why can't he hear them?"

"Shut it, Johkin," Cho-ka told him, his voice kept low but hard with dire promise. Vaelin saw how his shoulders were hunched and understood him to be resisting the urge to turn away from the torch flame.

Johkin took a shuddering breath and crossed his arms tight, head lowered and eyes closed. Vaelin cocked his head, straining to hear some whisper from the dark, but there was nothing beyond the grating breath of these terrified men. The song sounded a new note then, still offering no warning but full of amused contempt. *They shiver like children spooked by ghostly tales, but there is no threat here. Not to me, at least.*

Letting out a weary, derisive snort, Vaelin got to his feet, turning about to take in what little he could see in the flickering light. Ignoring Cho-ka's urgent, garbled warning he focused on the massive, angular bulk of a pillar rising from the tiles a dozen paces away. Moving towards it he reached out to run a hand over the many characters chiselled into its surface. He had some familiarity with Far Western script but this possessed only a vague resemblance and he could find no meaning in it. It was as he stepped around the pillar's sharp corner that the armoured warrior came looming out of the dark, teeth bared and spear held low for a thrust to the gut.

Vaelin stepped to the side, drawing his sword and crouching in readiness for a counterstroke, then paused. The warrior hadn't turned to face him. In fact he continued to stand completely immobile, spear aimed at the empty space before him. Peering closer, Vaelin made out a web of fine cracks in the man's skin, skin that caught the torchlight with an unnatural sheen.

Letting out a rueful laugh, Vaelin straightened, sheathing his sword and stepping closer to the statue. *Remarkable*, he thought, touching a finger to the warrior's stone shoulder. It was mostly free of dust and had been painted in a faint reddish pigment that cracked and flaked under the pressure of his fingertip. He wondered if some vestige of Ahm Lin's soul still lingered in his song to stir a heart-lurching admiration then. The skill with which the statue had been carved was astonishing. The spearman seemed to have been frozen in the act of readying his thrust, the pose of his limbs and the expression of his face a perfect and unglamourised depiction of a man in combat.

"Please, lord!"

Cho-ka stood a few feet away, eyes still lowered and speaking in a rasp of fear and poorly concealed anger. "You will doom us all!"

Vaelin ignored him and turned his gaze to the space beyond the stone warrior, finding the torch had revealed others. He could make out several dozen, but there were far more stretching away into the darkened recesses of this chamber, a vast stone army. He saw more spearmen, others with swords, kneeling crossbowmen. Pony-sized horses were frozen in the act of towing two-wheeled chariots. Each figure had been carved with the same remarkable skill, and Vaelin felt his amazement deepen when he saw that each was different. Every face, every pose was distinct from the one beside it. This was an army of individuals.

"What are they?" he asked Cho-ka.

"The Guardians of the Tomb," he whispered back. The outlaw winced then, features bunching as if pained by an ugly sound, but still Vaelin heard nothing. "They don't appreciate our presence."

Vaelin's gaze tracked across the frozen army, reckoning their number to be well over a thousand, and these were all he could see. "They speak to you? What do they say?"

"Things best left unsaid." Cho-ka winced again, hunching as if shrinking from a blow. When he spoke once more his voice had diminished to a faint murmur and Vaelin saw his eyes flick towards his fellow Vipers. "We will pay in blood for our trespass."

"The first emperor," Vaelin said. "He built this?"

"We have no time, lord." Cho-ka reached out a trembling hand. "Please."

The black-song's contemptuous tune changed then, flaring with an ugly note of warning. This time Vaelin did hear something, the tumult of many boots on stone echoing ever louder, soon accompanied by the sound of Stahl-hast voices. "Seems they've dug their way through," he observed.

"Move!" Cho-ka snarled at Kiyen and Johkin, kicking them to their feet. Both men were now white-faced with fear and barely seemed capable of responding. "Run or die," Cho-ka told them over his shoulder as he sprinted away. "Your choice."

Vaelin started off in pursuit of the bobbing torch, hearing the two out-laws follow after an instant of terrorised indecision. Johkin was babbling now, the words streaming from his mouth in a shrill torrent. Vaelin could discern scant meaning in the dissonant prate, which was soon swallowed by the cacophony of the oncoming Stahlhast. As they ran, Vaelin glanced left and right, picking out the dim shapes of the Guardians, realising that they were more easily discerned now, partially lit by a faint silver glow. The source soon became apparent as he returned his gaze to Cho-ka's torch, seeing a rapier-thin ray of moonlight descending from the cavernous roof of this chamber. It appeared to end at a point some thirty feet in the air, occluded by an angular construction of some kind. As they drew nearer, Vaelin saw the torch illuminate a series of steps and realised they were approaching a huge pyramidal platform.

Cho-ka started up the steps without pause, the three of them hurrying to follow suit. The stairs were steep, obliging them to scramble on hands and feet as they made their ascent, coming to a broad, flat summit after a fren-zied climb. Vaelin drew up short at the sight that confronted him, another statue, as finely carved as the others but twice as large. It was flanked on either side by a pair of stone sentries, shorter in height but both impressive in stature. Unlike the soldiers below, they wore no armour and stood bare chested, their finely honed muscles tensed in the act of hefting their weapons. One held an axe and the other a hammer and they both wore expressions of stern, implacable resolve.

However, it was the central figure that captured Vaelin's attention. It loomed above them, bathed in the thin stream of moonlight, a man of advanced years but also straight-backed and broad-shouldered vitality. The incredible talent that had carved this had managed to imbue his features with a sense that mingled peerless authority with great wisdom. He wore an ornate suit of armour bearing many similarities to that still worn by Far Western soldiery, but each tile had been inscribed with a single character in the same ancient script. In one hand the figure held a leaf-bladed sword, which he pointed out at the darkened army below, whilst in the other he bore a scroll. The skill of the mason that crafted this so long ago was once again evident in the way the unfurled scroll seemed to catch the wind.

"The first emperor, I assume?" he asked Cho-ka.

"Mah-Shin, founder of the Emerald Empire," the outlaw replied, keeping his gaze averted from the statue. He nodded to a large circular motif set into the stone beneath the first emperor's feet. "His bones lie beneath and he is not honoured by our visit."

A fresh tumult of shouts drew Vaelin's gaze to the dozens of torches bobbing in the gloom below. The Stahlhast were about to reach the steps. "Shouldn't we move on?"

"No point now." Cho-ka took a breath before raising his gaze to the face of Mah-Shin. "The first emperor will pass judgement." With that he sank to his knees and bowed his head to the stone surface of the platform, hissing at the others to do the same.

Seeing little reason not to comply, Vaelin duly knelt and bowed, as did Kiyen. Johkin, however, remained standing. His babbling had ceased now and he stood staring up at the commanding yet sagacious face of the long-dead emperor, eyes bright and unblinking. "Yes . . ." Vaelin heard him whisper. "My crimes are many . . . but this . . . defilement is the worst of them . . . I am forever beyond Heaven's reach . . ."

"Bow, you shithead!" Kiyen said, his own forehead pressed to the stone.

But Johkin was clearly beyond all reason. After a few heartbeats of gasping terror and baffling whispers he drew his sword and charged to the edge of the dais, starting down with heedless speed that soon set him stumbling. At the sound of his fall the black-song prodded Vaelin to his feet with another amused thrum. Moving to the top of the steps he watched Johkin tumble into the glow of the accumulated torches below. The Stahlhast were thronging the base now, Vaelin hearing the scrape of drawn sabres amongst the angry shouts. He detected true rage amongst the tumult. Evidently, they had seen what he had done to their comrades on the canal bank and hungered for a reckoning. However, amongst the anger he discerned something else. Not all the voices below were raised in vengeful fury; some were babbling, in much the same way as Johkin.

It was as the tumbling outlaw clattered to a halt at the base of the steps that the Stahlhast's clamour abated. Vaelin heard a few laughs of anticipation at being presented with so easy a victim, but others continued to babble, soon joined by more. He watched Johkin get unsteadily to his feet, expecting the Stahlhast to cut him down. Instead, no weapon was raised against him as he let out a strangled, terrorised cry and began a hobbling charge through their ranks. They either stepped aside or ignored him, Vaelin realising that all were now seized by the same maddening terror. Shrieks and entreaties echoed through the chamber and shadows swayed as the Stahlhast cast their torches aside and charged off into the surrounding gloom.

The shouts and screams rising from the chamber depths would have been taken for the din of battle but for the fact that there was no clang of clashing steel. Vaelin managed to track Johkin's course through the partially lit chaos, watching the Viper charge headlong at the statue of a spearman, his speed sufficient to impale himself on the levelled weapon. He bucked and screamed as his life drained away, still babbling out the mysterious diatribe against his own perfidy until finally sagging in death. Vaelin's gaze flicked from one patch of illumination to another, finding variations on the same scene in every one. A weeping Stahlhast woman knelt before a stone swordsman, craning her neck to carefully press her exposed throat to his blade. A powerfully built warrior kept up a forceful commentary as he methodically sawed his forearm along the length of a chariot's wheel spike.

The shrieks and screams continued for some time, the black-song trilling with enjoyment the whole while, apparently unmoved by his disgust. *More blood to balance the scale*, its music seemed to sing. *But not near enough.* It dwindled to the familiar ache when the last of the screams choked off and

Vaelin turned away from the carnage. Kiyen was still kneeling and knocking his forehead against the platform but Cho-ka had gotten to his feet. He busied himself by replenishing the oil on the torch, unwilling to meet Vaelin's eye.

"What did you mean?" Vaelin asked him. "When you said this place cannot be walked alone?"

Cho-ka's throat bunched as he swallowed, his eyes flicking towards the statue of Mah-Shin. "He passes judgement on all who come here. At least one is always taken. It is his due, payment for trespass."

"That's why you needed Johkin and him." Vaelin nudged Kiyen's kneeling form with his boot, provoking a high-pitched gasp. "To pay the price. How did you know he wouldn't take you, or me?"

"I didn't. But legend says he takes the least worthy. It seems he also saw little worth in the Stahlhast." Cho-ka aimed a kick at Kiyen's rump. "Get up! Time to go."

"I can still hear them," the kneeling outlaw protested in a wet mumble. "The voices . . ."

"So can I." Cho-ka kicked him again, less gently. "And we will until we leave this place. Now get up."

Slowly, Kiyen got to his feet, sniffling in fearful misery although Vaelin judged him not so terrorised as before. "Another mile and we'll reach the tunnel," Cho-ka said, starting towards the far edge of the platform.

"Tunnel?" Vaelin enquired.

"Dug by the forebears of the Green Vipers centuries ago when this place was still guarded. They imagined there were treasures worth looting in the tomb of the first emperor." He gave a humourless laugh. "They must have been greatly disappointed. But the tunnel's still there and it's the only way out."

"Wait," Vaelin said, causing Cho-ka to pause before taking the first downward step.

"Lord?"

"I've never met a ghost," Vaelin murmured, running his eyes over the first emperor's statue in careful scrutiny. "Not one who lingered in this world, at least. I doubt there are any here."

"The voices," Cho-ka pointed out. "Even if you can't hear them, you saw what they did."

"I've seen men do all manner of things when their reason is stripped from them." Vaelin circled the statue, peering closely at the stone, finding only ancient and finely worked marble. "It's the manner of stripping that intrigues me."

A choking gasp of horror came from Kiyen as Vaelin reached out to run a hand over Mah-Shin's robe, the stone smooth to the touch. He recalled the tale Reva had told him of the statues of the old gods in the Meldenean Isles, statues that could place words in the minds of the living. He had assumed them to be fashioned from the same material as the grey stones he had found in the Martishe Forest and the Fallen City, stones that held memories of the distant past. If so, this one clearly had been fashioned from something else.

It was a murmur from the black-song that drew his gaze down to the circular motif beneath the statue's feet. The symbols that had been carved into its surface were as beyond his knowledge as the other script in this place, but the way the stone glittered as it caught the moonlight stirred his recognition. *So that's it.*

Crouching, he extended a hand to the centre of the motif, feeling the black-song surge. Its tune was cautious but not overly alarmed. If anything, his overriding sense was one of keen, almost predatory curiosity that gave him pause. *This is not wise*, he thought as his hand continued to hover. *A cat will doom itself if it becomes too inquisitive.* The surface of the stone was grey like the others, but flecked with the same golden material he had seen in the black stone in the Sepulchre of the Unseen. *This holds more than mere memory.*

"We must go, lord," Cho-ka said, but Vaelin ignored him. The black-song became more insistent the longer he held his hand in place, the music coloured by an increasing hunger. *So, it lusts for knowledge as well as blood.* His hand began to shake as he resisted the song's compulsion, the ache in his head redoubling as if in punishment.

"It does not command me," he stated through a cage of clenched teeth, then gasped as a wave of agony flared in the base of his skull, spreading through his body and sending him into a spasm that forced his hand onto the chilled surface of the grey stone.

The voices began immediately.

CHAPTER THREE

iar, betrayer, deceiver . . .

Vaelin shuddered as the voices invaded his mind. It was a vast chorus spoken by multitudes, the words overlapping but each one impossibly comprehensible.

Murderer, warmonger, assassin . . .

The chorus ripped into his memory, dragging forth events and images he had no desire to see. Steam rising from the wounds of bodies cooling in the aftermath of battle on a cold morning. The face of the first man he ever killed in the Urlish Forest when still just a boy, the man's face slackened in death and speckled in blood. Frentis suffering under One Eye's knife. Dentos staring up at him as the desert sand turned red beneath him . . .

Coward . . .

Sherin's pale, unmoving features when he placed her in Ahm Lin's arms . . .

"Enough!" Spittle flew from Vaelin's lips as he unclenched his teeth to voice the shout. The black-song surged and the voices quelled, not completely but enough to return him to reason. Realising his eyes were closed tight he forced them open, finding himself still on the platform, but it was indistinct, rendered into a misty semblance of itself. Another swell of music from the black-song and the vagueness surrounding him began to coalesce, the platform becoming solid once more. It was brightly lit by four glowing braziers placed at each corner. The chamber echoed with the sound of metal on stone and the discordant drumbeat of many hammers at work. There was no sign of Cho-ka or Kiyen, and in place of the statue of Mah-Shin, there stood a man, identical to the stone figure in all but height and the fact that his arms were folded.

He regarded Vaelin over his shoulder, eyes cold and features hard with the anger of a man unused to disrespect. "Even foreigners are required to bow in the presence of the emperor," he said.

"You're not my emperor," Vaelin told him. "And I doubt you have any power in this memory."

The tall man, surely Emperor Mah-Shin himself, angled his face up-wards in a gesture of stern superiority before turning his back. Moving to stand alongside him, Vaelin surveyed the scene below, finding masons everywhere, working away at blocks of stone. A warrior stood alongside each block, posed with sword or spear in hand as the masons sought to mirror their forms with hammer and chisel. "The creation of your army of Guardians," Vaelin noted. "Was each one modelled on a different soldier?"

"Yes, and all were honoured recipients of my favour," Mah-Shin replied, eyes narrowed as he scanned Vaelin from head to toe. "Men of distinguished service and great courage. All willing to spill their blood to protect my leg-acy in this life and the next."

His words were immediately and graphically illustrated when one of the warriors, a charioteer wearing a bronze helm and blue lacquered armour, stepped down from his two-wheeled conveyance and knelt beside the statue that depicted him with uncanny precision. He spent several seconds in silent meditation, eyes closed and face lowered, before raising his head and speak-ing a single word. A nearby swordsman abruptly abandoned his own pose and moved to the rear of his kneeling comrade who once again bowed his head. Reversing the grip on his blade, the swordsman drove it down into the exposed neck of the charioteer.

"Their lives belong to me," Mah-Shin said. "And so when I pass into Heaven's embrace, they will protect me from the enemies I am sure to find there." The old man's eyes lingered on Vaelin's face as he watched the mason stoop to press his hand into the spreading pool of blood before smearing it onto the stone face of the charioteer's effigy. "Who are you?"

"A foreigner, as you said." Vaelin turned to face the emperor's stern vis-age. "One who finds your customs disgusting."

"I have sent emissaries to all corners of this world and their reports of your people tell of illiterate savages wallowing in superstition. Speak not to me of disgust. I have built an empire greater than any on the face of the world. An empire of learning, law and peace. And I built it with blood."

"And in blood it will crumble."

Mah-Shin's mostly impassive features twitched then, his eyes narrowing further. "You are not from my time," he said in a low mutter of realisation, gaze flicking momentarily to the stone circle set into the platform's surface. It had yet to receive the decoration from Vaelin's time and remained smooth apart from the flecks of gold that shone bright in the braziers' glow. "So much power these hold," the emperor murmured. "More than I ever imagined."

"You have others?"

Vaelin saw a familiar glimmer of calculation in the old man's expression, one he had seen on the face of two kings now. But never his queen's. Lyrna had always been far too skilled in concealing her thoughts for that.

"It seems I possess knowledge you require," Mah-Shin observed. "If you want it, I require knowledge from you, barbarian. You said my empire will crumble. How?"

"Why ask? It's already happened. You are just a memory captured in this stone. You cannot change it."

"Tell me!" Mah-Shin bared his teeth as he voiced the demand, and Vaelin saw that they were black and rotted, the breath that emerged from his mouth foul with sickness. *It's said he went mad in his later years*, Erlin had said during their voyage to the Far West. *Believing himself to be a living vessel of divine grace and therefore infallible.*

"Before you die," Vaelin replied, "you will decree that all your laws will forever remain unchanged. As the years pass your laws will become a cage. Emperors clung to ancient ways that no longer had meaning, tried to govern according to arcane custom. Discord grew amongst the people, the last emperor was cast down and the Emerald Empire was sundered into the Merchant Realms. Now they face annihilation by the Stahlhast."

"You lie." Mah-Shin's lips formed a faint sneer. "The Stahlhast are even more primitive than your kind."

"They grew in number and power, came to be led by a madman who believes himself a god. And they have a stone of their own. One that holds more than just memory."

Mah-Shin's sneer faded as he straightened, taking on a bearing of regal indifference that failed to mirror the uncertainty Vaelin saw in his eyes. "Did you invade my sacred tomb just to torment me?" he asked. "You have travelled a long way to indulge your cruelty."

"I came here for refuge. The Northern Prefecture has fallen and the Stahlhast will soon invade the heartland of the Merchant Realms. Are you content for that to happen?"

The old man blinked and turned away, moving to stand at the edge of the grey stone, staring into its glittering surface. "I touched this and captured this vestige of my soul here in the hope that my descendants would come to partake of my wisdom and guidance in years to come. None ever did. I spent decades meditating on the reason for this before enlightenment dawned. This stone took the worst of me and amplified it, found echoes of all my rage and fear in the souls of the soldiers who died here. No sane man would ever make pilgrimage to this tomb. For centuries my only visitors have been outlaws and fugitives, all driven beyond the edge of madness." Mah-Shin turned back to Vaelin, the calculation returning to his gaze. "Apart from you. Something protects you. Something in your blood, yes? A blessing of Heaven?"

Unwilling to give this calculating soul more knowledge than he had to, Vaelin confined his reply to a short nod.

"Is it a great power?" Mah-Shin's voice grew soft as he stepped closer, angling his head in catlike scrutiny. "Unfeasible strength, perhaps? The ability to conjure fire from the air?"

Vaelin returned his scrutiny in full, saying nothing.

"You shouldn't fear me, for we are like brothers, in blood if not culture." The emperor's lips formed a thin smile as he retreated, moving to the edge of the platform. "You see, from the age of thirteen I could hear the thoughts of others. My family was noble, but not rich, my father a soldier of middling rank and as unthinking as the horse he rode to war. My mother, however, was more than capable of thinking for both of us. My ability became our family's greatest secret, and our greatest asset. It began as small things, little tasks she would set me, making it a game of sorts. A servant with overly light fingers caught in the act and duly flogged. A debtor who pleaded poverty and was sent to the mines for it when his riches were laid bare. With every task she would praise me, and I cherished every word of it, for she was a woman for whom affection did not come naturally. In time, our game became more serious. My father's rivals for promotion had all manner of secrets. Some were exposed and eliminated whilst Mother persuaded others to stand aside and pay a regular stipend for our silence. I learned then that power does not derive from wealth; wealth and power derive from knowledge.

"Our machinations eventually made my father a general, a role for which he was palpably unsuited, but with me at his side to read the thoughts of enemy prisoners and duplicitous spies, his victories were many. Ever an unwise soul, he became enamoured of his own success, deluding himself that he was the architect of our rise, all the while increasing his clutch of concubines, much to Mother's annoyance. Eventually, she had me guide him into an ambush, and with his death, his armies became mine. Securing what was by then the Northern Kingdom was a relatively simple matter, as was conquering the southern realms, all accomplished in less than a decade. But the blessings of Heaven, as I presume you know, always exact a price.

"In my youth I could focus my ability on one mind at a time, shutting out the babble of others to seek out the knowledge I needed. But as I grew older it became harder to maintain such focus. Other thoughts would inevitably intrude, and they were all very ugly. My retainers, generals and servants showed me only the utmost honour and regard, but behind every respectful face lay a swirling, fetid pool of fear, envy and ambition. I was not loved, not even admired. I was feared and hated, even by my own mother. How she had hidden it from me for so long, I never knew, but when I looked beyond her mask of loving pride, I saw the same thing as in all the others." Mah-Shin let out a soft sigh. "I allowed her to drink poison in the end. I believe she deserved that much. The others were not so fortunate.

"After that I chose only the dullest attendants, men with minds incapable of schemes or intrigues, and communicated with my courtiers and generals via messenger. I chose wives, as was required. I fathered children, as was required, but I had no true family. I never met my daughters and saw my sons only once in every year and the meetings were always brief, for I feared what the blessing would reveal. But still, the thoughts intruded, somehow seeping through the walls of my palace to whisper of treason and rebellion. It never stopped; regardless of the purges and the public tortures, still the river of discontent would stream into my mind. I drank the strongest liquor. I took the most potent drugs. My body grew weak and my teeth black from the indulgence, but none of it stemmed the tide of hatred. It is one thing to be a tyrant, but another to know the nature of your own tyranny. Then, one day, a messenger from the Northern Prefecture brought word of a strange stone dug out of the mountains, a stone with remarkable properties."

Vaelin looked again at the grey stone and its gleaming flecks of gold, hearing in the black-song voice an inquisitive murmur, as if it had happened upon something of potential importance. "This place is not truly a tomb," he said. "You built it to contain this."

"The power it held could not be simply loosed upon the world. Even at my worst excesses, I knew that. The last decade of my reign was spent overseeing the construction of this chamber and the army that guards it. I came here as you see me now, sickened and fully aware that mere months of life remained to this body. I touched it and it took me, imprisoned me, made me bereft of knowledge as to the fate of my empire, save for now when it brings me a barbarian to speak of disaster."

"Disaster that can be averted." Vaelin nodded at the grey stone, the meaning of the song's tune becoming clearer. "You would have searched for others like this. It was not in your nature to forego the chance of finding more."

Mah-Shin inclined his head in surprised and grudging respect. "You see much, or your blessing tells you much."

"Did you find any?"

"I set my best scholars scouring every scrap of paper in every library, had my most able soldiers traverse vast tracts of desert, mountain and sea, guided by the meagre clues they found. All returned empty-handed. Had I known the Stahlhast possessed a stone, I would have depopulated the Iron Steppe to claim it. Now, it seems, I should have done so in any case."

The black-song let out a harsh note, its meaning clear. "You're lying," Vaelin said. "Your scholars found something."

Mah-Shin raised his eyebrows and unfolded his arms, two clawlike hands emerging from the sleeves of his satin robe. Each nail was formed of a steel barb set into the flesh of his fingers and they flickered as he flexed his hands. "I have no power here, as you said. But, I suspect, neither do you. What reason have I to assist you? My empire has already fallen, my line is extinct and the monarchs of these Merchant Realms you speak of share no blood with me."

The song's tune took on a familiar ugliness, stirring the hunger, although this time the music was shot through with impotent rage. *The old bastard's right.*

Vaelin closed his eyes, trying to calm the song's fury and wincing at the throbbing pain it birthed in his head. It only began to abate when he recalled something Mah-Shin had said, something that stirred an idea. "It imprisoned you," Vaelin said, opening his eyes. "That's how you regard yourself, a prisoner."

Mah-Shin flicked a steel nail and shrugged. "What of it?"

"What if I could free you?"

He made a brief attempt to hide it, but the emperor's face became a twitching mask of suspicion and near-desperate hope. "Don't toy with me, barbarian," he hissed.

"It's this that keeps you here." Vaelin tapped a boot to the grey stone. "And in the waking world it's within my power to destroy it." He moved closer to Mah-Shin, feeling a pulse of approval from the black-song. This manner of bargaining appeared to be to its liking. "Tell me what your scholars found," Vaelin said, voice soft and intent with promise. "And I'll send your soul to whatever awaits it in Heaven's embrace."

Mah-Shin let out a long, hungry breath. "What . . ." He faltered, his thin neck bulging as he swallowed. "What assurance do I have that you'll keep your word?"

"None. But you have my assurance that I'll happily leave you to your prison if you don't. Perhaps, in a few centuries, another with a blessing will turn up. But I wouldn't wager on it; we are a rare breed. Or"—he paused to offer the ancient emperor an empty smile—"the Stahlhast's living god might choose to visit once he hears about this place. I doubt you'll relish his company."

The creased, leathery mask continued to twitch, Mah-Shin's grey tongue sliding over the black stubs of his teeth. The depth of his madness shone in the brightness of his eyes and the drool sliding over his chin, much to the black-song's amusement. The tune became mocking, stirring a caustic realisation: *The rewards of power are always empty in the end.*

When he spoke, Mah-Shin's words came in a rapid, flowing torrent, as if he feared Vaelin might withdraw his offer at any second. "An ancient legend spoke of a mighty sorcerer who laid waste to the Opal Islands, long before the foundation of the first kingdoms. The legend had been set down in a language few had the knowledge or skill to understand, but one phrase was clear: 'From stone he drew his strength and with it did all manner of foul deeds, for he had stolen the wolf's favour.'"

"Wolf?" Vaelin asked, stepping closer. "What did it say of the wolf?"

"Only that and nothing more. It was a slight thing, a scrap of knowledge at best, but still I sent a fleet to comb through the Opal Islands from end to end. They found nothing but beast-infested jungle, except there was one ship that went missing during the expedition, thought lost to storms or pirates. Months later it was found adrift, the crew vanished and the decks stained dark with long-dried blood. A search of the captain's cabin yielded a log, but the last entry was incomplete and garbled, set down in haste and ended mid-sentence. However, the words 'grey stone' were legible. I sent more ships, of course, but the winter storms were fierce and many were lost. Those that returned found nothing save more jungle and animals of unfriendly disposition. By then the sickness was upon me and I had other concerns."

The Opal Islands, Vaelin thought, trying to recall what little he knew of them. *A haven for pirates, lacking law or civilisation. Not an inviting place to search, and so far away.*

"I have told you the truth," Mah-Shin said, the steel talons of his fingers reaching out to pluck at Vaelin's arm. They passed harmlessly through his flesh but left an icy chill.

"Why did you do that to yourself?" Vaelin enquired, looking closer at the steel barbs set into the tips of the emperor's fingers. The flesh that surrounded them was dark with the kind of corruption that Vaelin's experienced eye knew would soon require amputation.

"My enemies were many. A man is at a disadvantage if he must reach for a weapon." The fingers plucked again, desperate and beseeching, the chill they birthed causing Vaelin to retreat in disgust. "I told you the truth," Mah-Shin repeated. "Fulfil your promise to me!"

He was weeping now, tears streaming down the creased mask of his face as fresh drool flowed from his lips. Vaelin gave no answer, hearing the black-song rise in sadistic mirth, its music swelling to a roar that turned the platform to mist once more. Vaelin heard Mah-Shin's final wailing cry of despair, dwindling into a pitiful sob and then silence, before the scene faded completely into blackness.

◆　◆　◆

"Lord?"

Vaelin blinked and looked up into Cho-ka's eyes. The outlaw's fear seemed to have abated somewhat, though a sheen of sweat lingered on his forehead. Despite his lessened fear, something he saw in Vaelin's face troubled him enough to make him retreat a few steps. "Are you . . . well?"

Vaelin realised a smile had formed on his lips, a smile that felt disagreeably unfamiliar in the way it twisted the muscles of his face. Had he possessed a mirror he knew he would be looking upon the visage of a man enjoying a moment of cruel triumph. "Quite well," he said, forcing the smile from his lips and rising from his crouch. Kiyen stood as far from him as the platform allowed. Unlike Cho-ka, his face was pale and frozen in unalleviated fear, and Vaelin wondered how much reason remained to him.

"The voices stopped when you touched it," Cho-ka said, frowning and shaking his head. "Now they've returned, but they're quieter, somehow."

And will grow louder if the old man doesn't get his reward, Vaelin thought, glancing up at Mah-Shin's stern features. This statue, like so many others, was a lie. The man had never been wise, just possessed of a gift and the ruthlessness to wield it in pursuit of power, though it cost him his mind in the end. The black-song filled Vaelin with a grim, satisfying resolve then, coloured by the cruelty he now knew underlay all its music. *Leave the old monster to his prison. The Darkblade will delight in tormenting him.*

The music took on a discordant note of frustration as Vaelin moved to the hulking form of the statue on the emperor's left. The double-bladed axe it held was fashioned from steel rather than stone, its blade tarnished but lacking rust thanks to the dry air of the tomb. Vaelin was obliged to spend some time pounding at the guardian's stone thumb with the pommel of his sword before the axe came free.

"My sister once showed me how to destroy a stone," he said, hefting the weapon. "First you have to split it."

Moving to stand over the grey stone, he raised the axe above his head and brought it down on the centre of the intricately carved surface. Ancient symbols shattered and golden flecks came loose under the impact, the entire edifice rendered a chaotic mess as Vaelin delivered a dozen more blows with the axe. With every strike the black-song let out a harsh, truculent growl of protest. Tossing the axe aside, Vaelin went to the guardian on Mah-Shin's right and hacked at his hands until the hammer fell free.

"Then you pound it," he said, the weapon's brick-sized head grinding across the platform's surface as he dragged it towards the grey stone. It took several long minutes of pounding to accomplish the task. This grey stone wasn't as large as the others Vaelin had seen, extending into the platform to a depth of only two feet, but ensuring every shard of it was rendered to dust required hard and assiduous labour. When it was done, a pile of granular powder sat in the circular hole that had once housed the grey stone. The gold flecks remained, still glimmering in the moonlight.

"They've stopped again." Cho-ka sighed in relief, a puzzled smile coming to his lips. "Folk have lived in terror of this place for generations, and all it took to end it was an axe and a hammer."

Some measure of reason must have returned to Kiyen then, for the outlaw shuffled closer to the piled dust, tentative hand reaching out to claim one of the shining specks of gold.

"I wouldn't," Vaelin told him.

"Are they dangerous?" Cho-ka asked, stepping closer to peer at the tempting metal. "Looks much the same as other gold."

A sullen, grudging pulse of warning from the black-song was enough to convince Vaelin that this pile of detritus should be left untouched. "Take it if you want," he said, "but don't expect any good to come of it."

Cho-ka gave a reluctant nod and stepped back whilst Kiyen saw no reason to heed the warning, plunging both hands into the dust to gather all the gold he could find into a leather pouch.

"Hurry up, you greedy shit," Cho-ka snapped at his fellow Viper. "I'm keen to be gone from here, voices or no."

"Just one other thing," Vaelin said, turning back to Mah-Shin's statue and hefting the hammer once more.

He shattered the emperor's feet with two well-placed blows. The tall figure swayed and tottered for what seemed an unnatural interval, as if somehow resisting its fate. Finally, Vaelin delivered a hard kick to Mah-Shin's imperial posterior and the statue toppled forward to shatter on the steps below, the remains tumbling down into the gloomy depths to scatter across the floor of the tomb.

Chapter Four

T he sun had risen above the horizon by the time they emerged from the tunnel, Vaelin brushing an accumulation of loose earth and bugs from his hair as he straightened from the crouch he had been obliged to adopt for the past few hours. Judging by the patches of brickwork that lined its walls, the tunnel had once been a well-constructed passage, but age had taken its toll. They were forced to pause several times to clear away blockages, and soil leaked continually onto their heads. Once clear of its cramped confines Cho-ka took his sword and jabbed at the tunnel roof, collapsing it to seal the exit.

"Should slow them down, at least," he said, sheathing his sword. "Assuming they'll brave the tomb."

"They'll brave it," Vaelin assured him. "Their god will command it."

He shielded his eyes against the rising sun to survey the surrounding country, finding a pleasing landscape of low misted hills and shallow valleys, often thick with forest. *Good country*, he thought, grunting in satisfaction. *Many routes to take, none easy to track.* "How far to Daiszhen-Khi?" he asked Cho-ka.

"By foot, it would usually take four days." The outlaw brushed dirt from his hands, squinting towards the south-east. "But we'd be best advised to take the less obvious route. There are trails known only to the Green Vipers. It's hard going, but if we push we could make it in six days."

"And if we were on the canal?"

"A day or two."

They'll already have reached Daiszhen-Khi, Vaelin concluded, wondering if Nortah would allow the others to wait. Much as he wanted to rejoin them, he assumed his brother would have the sense to move on quickly. Even so, if they had passed through the town it was his best chance of following their path, unless he sought the black-song's assistance. The notion summoned a small murmur from the song, a dull, indifferent tune. Whereas he greatly wished to reunite with his companions, the song, it seemed, didn't much care.

"We need to get under cover before the sun's fully risen," Cho-ka said, starting off for the nearest patch of woodland at a fast walk. Vaelin paused to regard Kiyen, standing with shoulders hunched, bright eyes staring at Vaelin from a face that shone pale under the dirt. The outlaw clutched his bag of gold in both hands, fingers continually kneading the leather in the manner of a child with a comforter. He started when Vaelin wordlessly jerked his head in Cho-ka's direction. Although the black-song sounded no threat, the man's suspicion and possibly unhinged mind still made Vaelin wary. Sniffing and blinking moist eyes, Kiyen shuffled past him before following in Cho-ka's wake, the stiffness of his bearing making it plain that he was resisting the urge to look over his shoulder.

Upon reaching the trees, Cho-ka led them through dense woodland then along a series of deep gullies for several miles, allowing only brief halts for rest. Whilst the outlaw moved with the unhesitant stride of one completely familiar with their surroundings, Vaelin found the forest was an unknowable maze of impassable bamboo groves, junipers and the occasional yew, all carpeted in ferns and rich in low-hanging branches and foot-entangling tree roots. It made for plentiful hiding places should they need them, but also ensured a frustratingly slow pace. As the day wore on Vaelin felt his stomach begin to growl. They had replenished their water from streams but had no food at all, something that would need to be remedied if they were to spend days in these woods.

"Worry not, lord," Cho-ka told him when Vaelin raised the question of stopping to hunt. "The Green Vipers will provide."

He had them press on until the forest grew dark with the onset of evening, eventually calling a halt in the shadow of a wide-trunked yew standing atop a mound composed mainly of its own roots. The mass of roots dipped on the tree's west-facing flank, creating a shallow depression. Climbing into the dip, Cho-ka crouched to work loose what at first appeared to be a wall of intertwined roots, but revealed itself as a door after several hard shoves.

"The Vipers learned long ago," he said, crawling inside, "a smuggler can never have enough places to hide from the Dien-Ven."

Vaelin waited for Kiyen to make his way into the hole before following suit. Cho-ka spent a moment fixing the door in place, sealing them in the damp, musty darkness, before Vaelin heard the scrape of his flint and a small oil lamp flared into life. The glow revealed a den of surprisingly broad and deep dimensions. Whoever had constructed it had dug six feet into the earth before hollowing out a circular bowl easily wide enough to accommodate the three of them. A number of small barrels had been set into the earth in the centre of the bowl, and Cho-ka spent some time levering open the lid of one with his bone-handle knife.

"Looks like it's been a good while since anyone happened by," he grunted when the lid finally came loose. Reaching inside, he extracted a leather flask, which he tossed to Vaelin. Removing the stopper unleashed a pungent aroma similar to the rice wine typical to the Far West, but of much greater strength.

"Cured pork, if you want to risk it," Cho-ka added, nostrils flaring as he gave a muslin-wrapped bundle an experimental sniff.

"I'll take it," Kiyen said in a dull mutter, catching the bundle as Cho-ka tossed it over. Vaelin took the smallest sip of rice wine before grimacing and handing it to Kiyen, who showed no hesitation in downing several hard gulps. From the way the outlaw's eyes continually flicked over Vaelin's face in brief, fearful glares, he seemed like a man girding himself for some unwise action. The black-song, however, still sang a relatively placid tune.

The barrels yielded several flasks of water and a form of dense bread resembling hardtack, which proved edible once doused with sufficient liquid, but was hardly appetising. More welcome were the jars of dried dates Cho-ka extracted from the last barrel, which also yielded a brass scroll-tube.

"News from the brotherhood," he explained, chewing dates as he unfurled the paper it held. "Increased patrols around Daiszhen-Khi, soldiers as well as Dien-Ven. The boss of the Western Link had his throat cut, something to do with a woman, so personal rather than business." He gave a caustic laugh. "That one always did think more with his cock than his brain."

"Western Link?" Vaelin asked.

"It's a grouping within the brotherhood, like a company in an army. The Green Vipers are a chain, strong when united, and each part is a link in that chain." He read through the rest of the scroll reporting mostly trivia. "It's dated close to three months ago. Who knows what's happened since."

"The Darkblade came and took Keshin-Kho," Kiyen said, voice little more than a whisper. "And soon he'll take everything else. That's what happened."

Cho-ka settled an expressionless gaze on his fellow Viper of sufficient length to send him back into sullen silence. "Hand it over." Cho-ka gestured to the half-empty flask of rice wine clutched tight in Kiyen's hand. Upon snatching it from Kiyen's reluctantly outstretched hand Cho-ka poured the contents onto the earth. "Get some sleep," he told them, wrapping his stolen Tuhla cloak around him and settling onto his side.

"It's cold," Kiyen protested in a peevish groan.

"Light a fire in here and we suffocate in seconds." Cho-ka flicked the edge of his cloak over his head in dismissal.

Vaelin watched Kiyen's gaze flick towards him once more before the outlaw turned his back and huddled, arms folded tight about himself. It wasn't until Vaelin heard the soft grating breaths of men at slumber that he lay back and let sleep claim him, his fatigue sufficient to overcome the black-song's ache. It was smaller now but still lingered like the buzzing of a fly beyond reach of swatting.

◆ ◆ ◆

He dreamt of ripples spreading across placid water, the red and gold of an evening sky folding together before being scattered by a splash.

"I know my uncle." A voice he knew. Young, female, strident with insistence but also coloured by a poorly controlled quaver as it continued, the words spoken with firm deliberation. "He is not dead."

"I don't believe so either." Another voice, also female and familiar, but older and much more controlled, the tone reflective and carrying a weight of grief he found hard to hear. *She doesn't grieve for me.* "I've often thought that there isn't anything in this world, human or beast, capable of killing your uncle, except perhaps his own misjudgement."

The waters bobbed and settled as the ripples faded, revealing two figures. They were dark against the evening sky, features rendered vague by the twisting reflection, but he had little difficulty in recognising either. Ellese sat with her legs dangling over the lip of a barge's prow, shoulders hunched and stiff. Sherin stood behind her, arms folded. The fading light played on the smooth curve of her forehead as she raised it, and he caught a glimpse of the same unflappable compassion he knew so well, still shining clear despite her sorrow.

"Lord Nortah is right . . ." she began only for Ellese to cut her off.

"He's a craven drunkard is what he is." Ellese turned, casting yet more scorn over her shoulder. "All of them, cowards! Flee if you want! I choose to search for my uncle!"

Vaelin saw a stiffening of Sherin's form before she moved to sit at Ellese's side. "And how do you imagine you will find him? You know nothing of this land and can barely speak more than a few words of the language."

"I do!" Ellese shot back, shuffling a little and adding in a lower voice, "Enough to get by, anyway."

"The way you pronounce the word 'arrow' sounds more like the Chu-Shin for chicken gizzards. In any case, the region south of Keshin-Kho will be crawling with Stahlhast and Tuhla by now."

"I do not fear them . . ."

"Then your uncle hasn't taught you well, because you should." Sherin took a breath to cool the heat in her voice before speaking on. "You are still pledged to follow his lessons, are you not?"

Ellese's head sank lower before bobbing in the affirmative.

"And what do you imagine would be his lesson now?"

Ellese didn't answer immediately, instead shattering the reflection once more with a hard-thrown stone. When it settled she had raised her face to the sky, and Vaelin wondered again at her ability to remind him of her adoptive mother. Reva had always worn much the same expression when forced to confront hard reality.

"Mother told me he would be cruel," Ellese said. "When she'd finally had enough of my . . . transgressions, she had me pack just one chest of belongings and told me she was sending me to the Northern Reaches. 'The Tower Lord will not fail as I have,' she said. 'He will not spare you as I have. Whatever delight you may take in shaming me and the name you bear will be nothing to him.'" She paused, Vaelin hearing a soft laugh. "So I was escorted north and put on a ship, all the time expecting to fetch up in a frozen wasteland ruled by a monster. Instead, I found him."

Her shoulders hunched lower and Sherin smoothed a hand over them, Vaelin catching the faint choke of a sob. "He's not dead," Ellese whispered. "I know it . . ."

"As do I." Sherin sat beside her, pulling her into a soft embrace. "As do, I . . ."

Vaelin let out a gasp as the reflection shattered again, not by a stone this time but cut through by the kiss of something cold pressing against his throat. The vision unfolded then, falling away like severed halves of a curtain to reveal Kiyen's crimson features, flesh quivering and eyes bulging.

Vaelin's hand went to the sword at his side but Kiyen jerked back before he could draw it. The cold caress of the knife he held vanished from Vaelin's throat as it fell from hands that began to claw at the cord about his neck. "A debt is a debt!" Cho-ka hissed through clenched teeth as he jerked the garrote, heaving Kiyen away. Kiyen kicked and thrashed as Cho-ka forced him face-down onto the soil, pressing a knee into his fellow Viper's back and flexing his wrists to draw the garrote's cord ever tighter. Vaelin watched soil and blood blossom as a final explosion of breath came from Kiyen before subsiding into an ugly rattle. Cho-ka, clearly experienced in such matters, continued to hold the garrote taut until the last twitch faded from the corpse.

"Lost his mind back on the Tomb Road," he muttered, loosening the garrote and drawing Kiyen's head back to pluck it from the furrow it had carved into his flesh. "Should've knifed him in the tunnel."

No warning, Vaelin thought, finding that the black-song hadn't risen at all during the entire confrontation, maintaining the same steady if unpleasant murmur throughout. He wondered if it had become indifferent to his death, harbouring some kind of grudge over his refusal to leave Mah-Shin to his prison, but could fathom no reason why that should be. *Without me it ceases to exist. So why not warn me? Unless survival means nothing to it.*

It was as Cho-ka turned Kiyen's body over and began to search it that the black-song rose again, in faint trepidation rather than outright warning. It was much the same uneasy murmur it had voiced after he had destroyed the grey stone in Mah-Shin's tomb. *The gold*, he recalled as the pouch fell loose from Kiyen's belt. *It didn't like the gold.*

Rising, he shuffled closer to retrieve the pouch, hearing the black-song let out a growl of protest as he did so. *There is more than gold here.*

"Take this," he said, holding the pouch out to Cho-ka.

"My thanks, lord," the outlaw said, regarding the pouch with a dubious eye and making no move to take it. "But, I'm happy to forego some spoils . . ."

"Just take it." Vaelin grasped Cho-ka's wrist and placed the pouch in his hand. "Now," he said, shuffling back. "Lie to me."

The smuggler's gaze shifted from Vaelin to the pouch and back again, clearly wondering if Kiyen's hadn't been the only mind lost to the Tomb Road. "Lord?"

"Tell me something that isn't true. Something I wouldn't know."

"Such as?"

Vaelin swallowed an exasperated sigh. "Your father. What was his profession?"

Cho-ka's gaze darkened a little and he lowered it, shrugging. "He . . . was a Viper, like me. Had charge of the Canal Link south of Daiszhen-Khi."

The black-song's pitch didn't change, maintaining the same uneasy groan. Vaelin reached out to take the pouch from Cho-ka and placed it as far away as the hiding place would allow. "Tell me again," he said. "The exact same thing."

"My father was a Viper who had charge of the Canal Link south of Daiszhen-Khi."

This time the song flared with the harsh note of dishonesty, and judging by its volume, the lie Cho-ka had told was very far from the truth. Also, Vaelin realised as he listened closer, coloured by a deep well of shame.

"Your father was no outlaw," he said, closing his eyes to gauge more of the song's meaning. "He was a learned man. Well respected, widely read . . ."

"What," Cho-ka broke in, voice suddenly hard as flint, "is the point of this?"

Opening his eyes Vaelin found the outlaw's gaze dark with warning. Plainly, this was a subject he didn't wish to explore. "These," Vaelin said, moving to recover the pouch and loosening the ties to reveal the glittering contents, "are more valuable than we thought."

"In what way?"

"The Darkblade has . . . abilities. A blessing of Heaven that helps him track his enemies. With these, we might be able to evade him."

"A blessing that you appear to share, lord."

Vaelin met Cho-ka's steady gaze and gave a short nod. "Is that a problem?"

"Not if it gets us clear of the Darkblade's horde, but don't ask me to pretend joy at the prospect of travelling with one so cursed. Those who bow and scrape to Heaven's idols might delude themselves that such things are a blessing. The Vipers know better."

Vaelin gestured for Cho-ka to hand over his own pouch and tipped half the gold into it. "I'm not fully sure how it works. I'd guess his song will track me rather than you, since I've been in his company, but it's best to be safe."

"Yet another curse to bear, the first emperor's curse," Cho-ka said as Vaelin held out his pouch to him, the outlaw eyeing it with deep suspicion.

"The first emperor is gone," Vaelin told him, adding in a gentler tone when the outlaw continued to hesitate, "I doubt your father was prone to such superstition."

A flash of anger passed across Cho-ka's face before he snatched the pouch from Vaelin's grasp. "Still some hours till dawn," he said, turning away to huddle into his cloak once more. "We'll have to bury Kiyen come the morning. Can't leave him to stink up this place."

CHAPTER FIVE

T he town of Daiszhen-Khi put Vaelin in mind of a beached octopus
in the way it sprawled across the junctions of eight separate canals.
The densely packed houses followed the course of each canal, clinging to the banks to form blocky grey tendrils extending for a mile or more
in each direction. The town's unique geography made a protective wall
redundant and its defences were composed of a series of stout guard towers
positioned so they sat astride the locks of each canal terminus. The largest
tower bestrode the lock of the Great Northern Canal, possessing much the
same height and girth of North Tower but little of its architecture. The
curved walls and uneven brickwork typical to Realm fortifications were
largely unknown in the Far West, this tower being no exception with its
smooth sloped walls and hard angled buttresses supporting the battlements.

"We need to wait for nightfall," Cho-ka advised from their vantage point
atop a craggy mound a few miles north of the town. He squinted as he surveyed the mostly flat plain surrounding Daiszhen-Khi, pointing out the
distant specks of ranging horsemen. "The report wasn't wrong about the
patrols, unless you'd rather just walk up to the gates and introduce yourself,
lord. You are here as a servant of the Merchant King after all."

"I'm keen to avoid any further complications." Vaelin focused on the forbidding edifice of the tower. Whilst it was true he had been sent to the
Northern Prefecture at the Merchant King's behest and subsequently promoted to a senior command position at Keshin-Kho by a duly appointed

general, he felt no surety such eminence would avail him much here. Sho Tsai was almost certainly slain, and his final instruction to Tsai Lin had been clear: *Survive this place and return to the Temple of Spears. Follow their counsel, for I see the age of kings is done.*

The recollection stirred the black-song from its torpor, its tune one of growing certainty as his eyes roved the curious spectacle of Daiszhen-Khi. "They're not here," he told Cho-ka. "And this place will fall to the Stahlhast within days."

"Perhaps not, lord." The outlaw pointed to the main tower's iron gate, which had begun to rise. Soon a long column of cavalry emerged, two full regiments by Vaelin's reckoning. Behind them came an even larger contingent of infantry. They marched with the ragged step of the recently trained, and their columns lacked the straight-edged cohesion he would have expected from regular soldiery. Still, as ever more regiments trooped through the gate, it made for a force of impressive size.

"Forty thousand, I reckon," Cho-ka said as the rear guard of the army emerged from the tower and the host began to snake its way northward.

"Closer to fifty," Vaelin said. "It seems General Tsai's reinforcements have finally arrived."

"Fuck all good they'll do anyone now." The outlaw shook his head, lip curling in grim dismay. "Why march out? They must know Keshin-Kho has fallen."

"I imagine their commander has orders to either relieve the garrison or retake the city." He needed no sign from the black-song to know the fate of this army, but it provided one anyway, a lilting, mocking cadence that told of inevitable doom. Most if not all of these men would soon be dead. He knew he could seek out their general, provide a warning and sound advice to retreat to Daiszhen-Khi and evacuate its inhabitants. The army could then fight a series of delaying actions to hinder the Darkblade's southward march. He also knew such an attempt would be pointless. Sho Tsai might have listened to the word of a foreigner, not without reluctance, but he had been a man of unusual practicality. The mere fact that the commander of this force had chosen to follow orders of the worst folly meant he was no more than a functionary, an unquestioning servant of the Merchant King's will.

"There's nothing to be done here," he said. "Except the chance to witness another city's fall."

"Then where . . . ?"

"Do you know of a place called the Temple of Spears?"

Cho-ka squinted at him in amused puzzlement. "Of course. Who doesn't?" His amusement faded quickly when he saw the resolve on Vaelin's face. "That's where you want to go?"

"I do. Is it far?"

"Yes, it's far, but that's hardly the issue. The monks guard their temple well and they are not to be crossed. Only those who are invited may even approach its gates. It's not a place people just travel to on a whim, lord."

"This is no whim. My friends will be there. Guide me to the Temple of Spears and our debt is settled."

Cho-ka turned a sombre gaze towards the town once more. "The Canal Link has many brothers here."

"Then let's hope they've had the good sense to flee before now." Seeing the conflict play out on the outlaw's brow Vaelin added, "I won't raise a hand to stop you if you want to warn them, if you feel your debt to them outweighs your debt to me, that is."

He saw the outlaw bite down on a retort and felt a murmur of unease from the black-song. Apparently, Cho-ka's forbearance had limits, debt or no debt. "We'll keep to the hills," he said in a flat mutter, starting off towards a neighbouring rise. "Head west then hook south. Less likelihood of running into any patrols, and I know a trading post where they ask few questions."

◆ ◆ ◆

It took two days and a night of sleeping in the open before they reached the trading post. It consisted of a small huddle of shacks clustering around a bridge that spanned an otherwise featureless stretch of the western canal. The hour was still early when they approached, finding the hamlet wreathed in low-lying mist. Also, Vaelin noted, no smoke plumed from any of the chimneys.

"Wait," he said, sinking into a crouch and motioning for Cho-ka to do the same.

"Something wrong?"

Vaelin peered at the misted shacks, listening to the black-song voice a grim tune that told of death but no danger. "I doubt we'll find much to trade for here," he said, rising and starting forward.

The first body lay amidst a vegetable patch, a man of middling years, his threadbare dun-coloured tunic stained by dried blood that had streamed from the several stab wounds in his back. A glance inside the nearby hovel revealed a woman of much the same age, stripped naked and lying splayed on the dirt floor. From the shallowness of the many cuts that marred her flesh from groin to neck, Vaelin deduced it would have taken her quite some time to die.

They moved on, counting another dozen corpses, either cut down in the open whilst trying to flee or tormented to death in their own homes. The large shack that housed the trading post yielded another four bodies. Two men, one old, one young, plus a woman lying huddled in a corner with deep slashes to her arms. Further inspection revealed the infant she had been trying to shield, a girl, staring up at Vaelin with blank eyes in a near-perfect doll's face, unmarked by the blow that had shattered her skull.

"Lohn-va," he heard Cho-ka murmur and turned to find him crouched next to the body of the older man.

"You knew him?" Vaelin asked.

"All the Vipers of the Canal Link knew him. Best fence in the Northern Prefecture, and always a fair dealer." He jerked his head at the other corpses. "His daughter and son-in-law."

"And granddaughter." Vaelin's eyes tracked over the ransacked interior. The floor was carpeted with shards of broken jars and splinters of shattered barrels. The black-song's tune told of pillage driven by desperation, the work of men acting as much through fear as cruelty.

"Wouldn't've expected the Stahlhast to range so far so soon," Cho-ka commented, nudging at some wreckage with his boot.

A glimmer of something in the wall caught Vaelin's eye, confirming his suspicions when he took a closer look. "Not the Stahlhast, or the Tuhla," he said, plucking the object free of the wall and tossing it to Cho-ka.

"Crossbow bolt." He held the steel-headed projectile up to the light. "From the Merchant King's own armoury, if I'm any judge." Tossing the bolt away, he grimaced as he knelt to rifle through the dead trader's pockets. "Soldiers, then. Deserters, probably, and in a rush. I'd guess they didn't relish the prospect of facing the Stahlhast, and who can blame them?" His lips twisted in grim amusement as he extracted a handful of coins from the lining of the unfortunate Lohn-va's jacket. "Didn't even bother to do a proper search. If you're going to rob a man at least make a good job . . ." He fell abruptly silent as a loud snort sounded from outside, a horse's snort.

Muttering a curse, Cho-ka drew his sword and crouched next to the doorway. Vaelin, however, made no move to arm himself, exiting the shack to find Derka standing in the midst of the ruined hamlet. He had contrived to retain his saddle and bridle and stood tossing his head, hoof dragging at the ground in impatience.

"Tracked us all this way," Cho-ka said, sliding his sword back into its sheath. "Never seen a horse so fond of a rider. Think he'll have any objection to riding double, lord?"

"Yes." Vaelin's voice emerged in a dull sigh and the black-song flooded his being. The faces of the slaughtered villagers flicked through his head in a continual montage, the song's tune birthing an irresistible rage that banished all goals, save one.

"Lord?"

Vaelin barely heard Cho-ka and was only dimly aware of running to vault into Derka's saddle. The black-song rose to claim him entirely as the stallion reared before bearing him away at a gallop. The tracks left by those who had done slaughter in this place seemed to glow upon the earth as he rode away, rendered into bright red rubies by the song, now deafening in its hunger.

◆　◆　◆

When he recovered the ability to hear anything but the black-song, it was to the sound of a man begging.

"Pluh . . . pleeease . . ."

Vision remained beyond his reach, but Vaelin could feel the chill air of night on his skin. It was harsh enough to make him shiver, the bite of it worsened by the presence of something wet covering his face and hands.

"Pleeeeease . . ."

Blinking, Vaelin found himself looking at a pair of bloodied hands, his hands. He held them out to a fire, fingers spread to catch the warmth. He sat on the ground in a small forest clearing, the fire casting embers into a cloudless night sky, flames dancing and tree limbs creaking due to a stiff, chill wind. Vaelin saw a corpse lying on the other side of the fire, a man in unkempt armour typical to Merchant soldiery. A man lacking a face. His teeth glowed pale orange in the firelight as they grinned up at the starlit sky, the glistening flesh of revealed muscle telling of a death barely an hour old.

"Please . . ."

The voice, faint to the point of a croak now, drew Vaelin's gaze from the fire to the sight of a man tied to a tree. He was naked, arms drawn back at a sufficiently acute angle to break them before being secured around the trunk. From the tone of his frame Vaelin would have taken him for some kind of athlete, but reckoned him too slight for a fighter. An acrobat perhaps? However, the most salient aspect of the man's form was not the leanness of his body but the sight of the entrails partly spilled from the slit in his belly. Some of the glistening tubes had unravelled and dangled onto the ground, but it seemed to Vaelin that whoever had done this had paused in their work, leaving the victim to suffer.

He caught a flicker of movement beyond the bound man where three more naked forms were illuminated by the fire's glow, each also secured to a tree. The injuries inflicted on each varied. One had been blinded, Vaelin assumed before his rib cage had been hacked open and his heart pulled out. The one to his right lacked his legs below the knee, the stumps blackened and burnt, presumably to stem the bleeding and prolong his agonies. It was the third one that had caught his eye, for he was still twitching, some vestige of life slowly ebbing away despite the swords stabbed into each shoulder and the third protruding from his groin.

"Kuh—"

Vaelin's gaze snapped back to the disembowelled man, finding him straining against his bonds, blood-spattered features riven with pain, eyes wide and beseeching. "K-kill meee . . ." he hissed as blood flowed down his chin. "Please . . . kill . . . me . . ."

The black-song, which until now had receded into its customary ache, rose again, full of mocking enjoyment. *He raped a child back in the village,* Vaelin recalled, quelling a shudder as the memory of extracting this piece of information flashed through his mind. *Then he cut her throat. I gave him too merciful an end.*

There came the hard snap of a crossbow's string followed by the thwack of a bolt finding a body. It sank into the centre of the bound man's chest up to the fletching. He jerked, let out a final, rattling breath and sagged in death.

"You found them, then," Cho-ka said, emerging from the darkness with crossbow in hand. "Took it from the sentry you left in the woods," he explained, hefting the weapon before surveying the scene. His expression had been one of forced joviality but soon morphed into something that mixed fear with disgust as his gaze tracked from one mutilated deserter to another. "Not going to argue that punishment wasn't merited, lord. But this . . ."

The song's tune changed again, taking on an angry note as if it resented the outlaw's judgement. *I could just kill him too*, Vaelin mused as the song wound itself around his thoughts. *He's not so different from this scum. Finding the Temple of Spears can't be that difficult . . .*

"NO!" he hissed, reeling away and clenching both hands together to banish the urge to reach for his sword. The black-song began to roil, making him stumble about like a drunkard as he fought to quell its hungry cacophony and the ugly notions it birthed. *In fact, why travel to the temple at all? The Darkblade lies north and I have a great debt to settle with him. What I did to this lot will be a child's game in comparison . . .*

"Stop!" He was on his knees now, double fists pounding the earth and head bobbing, no doubt resembling the most abject supplicant to indifferent gods. He had always thought such people either foolish or deluded, but now understood the actions of a desperate soul. *You are not me*, he told the song. *This is not me.*

It subsided a little then, its tune taking on a mirthful note that also held the same grating tinge that came from having heard a lie.

"Lord?" Cho-ka crouched close by, wisely keeping out of arm's reach.

"How did you find me?" Vaelin asked him, his voice weighed by a mingling of despair and weariness.

"We're only a couple of miles from the village, and your horse leaves deep tracks. These shit-wits should have put a greater distance between themselves and their crime."

Vaelin glanced over at Derka nuzzling at a juniper by the clearing's edge. If what had occurred here disturbed him, it failed to show in his placid chewing.

"You should go," Vaelin told Cho-ka. "It is not safe for you to travel with me."

Cho-ka's gaze slid over the carnage of the camp as he frowned in contemplation. "This is not just madness, is it? Something drives you to this."

Sighing, Vaelin nodded and sat back on his haunches, face raised to the sky. On such a clear night the stars formed a majestic spectacle that felt like an affront. *What right do I have to look upon beauty?* "The blessing of Heaven I carry," he said, "is no blessing. I once possessed a similar gift, years ago. But it guided me, saved me more times than I can count, saved others too. I lost it and grieved that loss for a long time. When it was given back to me, I thought . . ." He shook his head and let out a soft, empty laugh. "I was a fool. The Dark always exacts a price, but I never knew it could be so high. I don't know why it's different. I don't know why it makes me do . . . what I did here. I do know that I may never be free of it, and so should not be in this world."

He got to his feet and strode towards Derka. "I ride north," he told Cho-ka, "where I will kill Kehlbrand Reyerik and put an end to this war."

"*That* would be madness." Cho-ka hurried to block his path, stirring a dangerous murmur from the black-song. "Thousands of his followers stand between you and him. I've no doubt you'll kill many, but you must know you'll never get within sight of him, not unless he wills it, and he'll only do that for the pleasure of prolonging your death."

"I cannot . . ." Vaelin faltered, hunching with the effort of quelling the song-born urge to cut the outlaw down. "I cannot be like this anymore!" he grated, spittle flying from clenching teeth as he made to step around Cho-ka. "I will welcome death."

"And your friends?" Cho-ka asked, barring his path once more. "The man you call brother, the girl you call niece. The hunter, the healer. Will they welcome it?"

"I'm as much a danger to them as the Darkblade is. Whilst this song keeps singing . . ."

"What if it doesn't?"

Vaelin had begun to edge around him again but stopped at the sincere insistence in Cho-ka's voice. "What?"

"It wasn't just Lohn-va's coins they missed." The outlaw reached into his jacket and extracted a large leather wallet, opening it to reveal a dark, sticky substance.

"Redflower paste," Vaelin said, slipping back into Realm Tongue.

"A mix of white-petalled poppy juice and purple lotus seeds. Lohn-va's finest. He was famous for it. Called it Jade Fox." Cho-ka held up a long-stemmed wooden pipe. "Never knew a man to keep hold of a single bad thought after a bowl or two of this, lord."

Vaelin gave a tired shake of his head. "How will I travel all the way to the temple if I'm drugged?"

"I've guided men in far worse straits than you for greater distances. Besides"—Cho-ka forced a grin that didn't alter the deep trepidation in his eyes—"what choice do you have?"

Chapter Six

He was contemplating the similarity of a particular cloud formation to a herd of great elk when Cho-ka gently shook him back to
a semblance of consciousness.

"I saw elk in the sky," Vaelin told him, a serene smile on his lips. "I wonder where they were going . . ." He trailed to silence, brow furrowing in
bemusement at the sight of the horse Cho-ka rode. It was a fine mare almost
the same height as Derka, and black save for a blaze of white on her forehead.
"Where did you get a horse?"

"I stole her a week ago, lord." Cho-ka's tone was that of a man bored with
repeating the same story. "From those dim-witted cavalrymen, remember?"

"Cavalry." Vaelin gave a vague nod then stiffened as a dark thought
occurred. "Did we kill them?"

"No, lord."

"Good. That's good." Blinking, Vaelin took in his surroundings. They
had paused amidst a series of rolling, grass-covered hills. In the distance,
sunlight slanted through clouds to illuminate a range of mountains. "The
canal's gone," he observed.

"Left it behind ten days hence." Cho-ka's bored tone belied the caution in
his gaze as he leaned closer to inspect Vaelin's features. "Do you . . . hear
anything, lord?"

"No." Vaelin wasn't exactly sure why this was a good thing, but the
absence of any sound save the huffs and snorts of their mounts was very

comforting. "No, I don't." His head lolled as a wave of weariness swept over him, shot through with a strange kind of craving. His tongue was dry but it wasn't thirst, exactly, or hunger. This was something deeper, something that soon banished his fatigue and brought a tremble to his hands.

"I think it's time we made camp," Cho-ka said, his eyes slipping from Vaelin's face to his hands, shuddering as they clutched Derka's reins. The outlaw, glancing up at the increasingly dark sky, let out a soft curse as a low rumble of thunder sounded from above. "Looks like rain, lord. Lucky I know a place nearby with a roof, of sorts."

He led Vaelin through a series of shallow valleys, eventually coming to a copse of trees nestled between two steep slopes. The rain began as a thin drizzle but soon blossomed into a deluge. Despite the cover offered by the trees, the chill and the damp were sufficient to cut through Vaelin's lingering confusion. The vague memories of the last two weeks sprang into sudden clarity, the miles of tracking the southern canal at a distance, hiding from ranging patrols and avoiding the ever-growing number of beggared people fleeing the Darkblade's onslaught. There had been ugliness aplenty along the way. Deserters, looters and outlaws dangled from gallows and tree branches, victims of the Merchant King's summary justice. Clutches of bereaved, dis-possessed people, mostly old and lacking the fortitude or will to continue the southward trek, sat down to await their fate. It was these that pained him more than the sight of the hanged men, the utter defeat and despair on their faces reaching through his drug-induced fug to stir hungry whispers from the black-song. The land grew emptier once they veered away from the canal and began to traverse pastoral lands where farmers laboured in their fields, apparently ignorant of any danger from the north.

"It was a tin mine once," Cho-ka said, breaking into his thoughts. Vaelin shivered and watched the outlaw heave away a covering of fallen branches to reveal a small opening in the hillside. "Dug and worked for years, all without a single fee paid to the Dien-Ven. The Green Vipers have always been more than mere smugglers and robbers. The last scrap of tin was mined out years ago but it still makes for a useful refuge."

He was talking faster than usual, casting furtive glances at Vaelin as he worked to clear the mine entrance. As the traces of Jade Fox began to fade from Vaelin's veins, the black-song would inevitably rise to full volume, and Cho-ka had learned to fear its music. Several nights ago he had barely finished lighting the pipe before Vaelin's hand began to reach for his sword. The song, apparently, found the outlaw's company increasingly irksome.

"In you get, lord," he said, forcing a smile and ushering Vaelin into the narrow shaft. He was obliged to stoop to gain entry, proceeding into the gloom for a dozen feet or more before stopping at an impassable wall of tumbled stone. Cho-ka followed him inside and dragged the branches into place before using his knife to saw off some wood for a fire. Peeling away the bark, he arranged the sticks into a small bundle before striking his flint. "There's a fissure in the rock," he explained, leaning down to blow air onto the glowing embers. "Carries the smoke away."

Vaelin sat and watched him build the fire, his arms crossed tight about his chest in an unsuccessful attempt to keep his hands from shaking. The song was rising fast now, its tune sending all manner of unwelcome notions through his mind. *Kill this one and ride north, the Darkblade's waiting. No, torture him first to extract the location of other hiding places . . .*

"Hurry," he told Cho-ka, words clipped by his clenched jaw.

"Nearly done." The outlaw used his fingers to scrape a thimble-sized measure of Jade Fox into the bowl of the long wooden pipe before taking a stick from the fire and touching the glowing tip to the drug. The sweet, musty odour filled the shaft as Cho-ka placed the pipe in Vaelin's eagerly outstretched hands. As usual, the first inhalation brought a moment of clarity, a brief instant of rational thought in which the black-song fell silent before the fog descended. "Do we have enough?" he asked, smoke blossoming from his mouth and nostrils. "To get us there?"

"If it's carefully rationed, I think so."

Vaelin watched Cho-ka evade his gaze as he added more sticks to the fire. "For an outlaw, you lie poorly."

Cho-ka gave a slight shrug and went about preparing their meal. Vaelin had eaten sparsely throughout the journey; Jade Fox did little for the appetite and he could feel his growing weakness whenever its effects faded. At Cho-ka's coaxing he forced down a few mouthfuls of salted pork, apparently something else stolen from the dim-witted cavalrymen, before the effects of the drug began in earnest. The black-song's angry muttering dwindled to silence as his vision dimmed and a pleasurable warmth flooded his body, the cold and the wet becoming little more than vague irritants.

"How far . . . ?" he heard himself ask, his voice sounding dull and distant.

He slumped against the wall of the shaft and would have surely collapsed if Cho-ka hadn't settled him onto his back. "How far . . . to the Temple of Spears?"

"Just five or six more days, lord," Cho-ka assured him.

"You said that five days ago . . . I think." Vaelin's vision grew darker as the warmth spread to his limbs, sending tendrils of confusion into his thoughts. "I wonder," he murmured, "why do you stay with me?"

He watched Cho-ka's shadowy form retreat to huddle close to the fire, muttering, "A debt is a debt."

"No, that's not it." Vaelin's head lolled and he winced with the effort of raising it. "You've broken deals before, shirked debts before. Every outlaw does. But, you choose to stay with me. Why?"

Cho-ka's shadow raised its hands to the fire, saying nothing.

"Is it your father?" Vaelin persisted, voice slurring now. "Is there something about me that reminds you of him?"

A small laugh as the shadow's head turned to regard him. "Be assured, lord, you in no way remind me of my father." He turned his gaze back to the fire, his silhouette becoming almost formless as the Jade Fox dragged Vaelin closer to oblivion. When Cho-ka spoke again, his voice was soft, reflective, the voice of a man speaking to himself rather than a drug-addled companion who most likely wouldn't remember a word come the morning. "My father was an engineer, a man of great learning and accomplishment. He built bridges for the Merchant King all over the Venerable Kingdom. He oversaw the construction of roads through mountains that had previously defied all attempts to traverse them. He built towers taller than any before to house the king's long-eyes. Many were his rewards and great his esteem, but never was he truly raised high, never was he allowed into the Merchant King's presence, for he was lowborn, the product of the Hahn-Shi slums. Everything he knew, he taught himself. But, my father was not a prideful man, and however much my mother railed at the slights and injustices heaped upon him, he would only ever smile and press a kiss to her cheek before taking himself off to his study wherein resided his true passion. You see, lord, much as he loved his bridges, roads and towers, my father loved his books more. More even than he loved his family.

"Wherever he travelled he would seek them out, spending considerable sums, much to my mother's annoyance, to purchase obscure tracts from ages hence. In fact, the more obscure the better. He would pore over these scrolls and parchments for days on end. As a boy I once asked him, 'What do you look for, Father?' He smiled and said, 'Anything they care to show me.' An innocent pastime, you might think. The harmless indulgence of a man with money to spare, but books, as any king well knows, are far from harmless.

"It was one of the supposedly lost commentaries of Esteemed Kuan-Shi that spelt his doom . . . our doom. The man he bought it from was an agent of the Dushan-Ven, the Merchant King's guardians of knowledge. It was a trap, you see. The commentaries have long been suppressed due to Kuan-Shi's uncomfortable musings on the corrupting nature of power and the vacuity of greed. Consequently, any copies are extremely rare and sought out only by those with the most curious minds, and a curious mind is a dangerous thing in a land where change is abhorred. I was twelve years old when they came for him, watching from beneath the floorboards where my mother had hidden me. You might have imagined, lord, that his many services to the Merchant King would have offered some measure of protection, limited his punishment to a loss of property and status, perhaps just a stern warning."

Cho-ka's voice took on a bitter edge, his shadow flickering as he tossed another stick on the fire. "They flogged him, dragged him out to the garden and dumped his beaten body onto the pyre they'd made of his books. Then they burned them together. I'm tempted to think he might have appreciated that. They killed my mother too, for the family is always judged to be as guilty as the father. They slit her throat as she knelt wailing before the fire, then they came for me, but even then I was a difficult bastard to catch."

He shifted, adjusting his cloak and settling onto his back. When he spoke again his voice was just a murmur, hard for Vaelin to catch as the Jade Fox's grip began to strip away all senses. "Two years grubbing and fighting for scraps on the streets of Muzan-Khi made me vicious and feared, and the Green Vipers have always had an eye for talent. So, now you know why I had no intention of dying to defend the Merchant King's city. I'd happily watch him perish along with his entire arse-licking court. But they won't die alone when the Darkblade's horde reaches Muzan-Khi. Why do I stay with you? Outlaw or no, I do honour my debts, but you're right, that's not all of it. This kingdom is about to fall, and I've a sense I might live through it if I stay at your side . . ."

His voice dwindled to a distant echo as the Jade Fox dragged Vaelin into a darkness so absolute he wondered if he might never see light again.

◆ ◆ ◆

The next few days would always be little more than a blurred collection of mostly meaningless memories. As Vaelin's tolerance for the drug increased, Cho-ka began to alter his dosage. A half bowl smoked at first light ensured mornings were spent lolling in Derka's saddle with little awareness of the country they passed through. Come noon, Cho-ka would have him smoke a full bowl, which was usually sufficient to see them safely to the next campsite. With their supply of Jade Fox diminishing rapidly, the nighttime dose was the smallest, Cho-ka relying on Vaelin's exhaustion to see him into slumber without too much danger of arousing the black-song. It proved a successful stratagem but also meant Vaelin's sleep was no longer free of dreams, as the song seemed to take great delight in rummaging his memory for tormenting images. His nights became a fitful and feverish trial of old battles and the loss of those he had loved. Often he would wake with a name on his lips, sometimes Caenis, most often Dahrena, leading to several minutes of shivering distress as Cho-ka hurried to light the pipe.

He guessed it was six days after leaving the mineshaft that he became aware of a commotion, the sound of raised voices and the grunts of men in combat cutting through the fog. Blinking, Vaelin looked around at a broad rocky slope, much of it concealed by a drifting mist that told him they had finally reached the mountains. The sounds seemed to be coming from the left, although he could make out only a vague dance of shadows. More through ingrained instinct than intention, he reached over his shoulder to draw his sword, despite the warning from a dim corner of his mind that he would be of little use in his current state. He had half drawn the blade when the noise abruptly subsided, Vaelin recognising the faint gurgle of a man choking on his own blood.

"Pair of shitheaded farmers trying their hand at banditry," Cho-ka said, sliding his sword into its sheath as he emerged from the mist. "A man should have the sense to stick to what he's good at."

"Bandits?" Vaelin asked in a slow mumble, hand still gripping his sword.

"Called themselves wardens of the mountain." Cho-ka climbed onto the back of his mare, kicking her into a walk. "Wanted to charge a toll for safe passage. I gave them a chance to run, lord, but starving men are never lacking in courage."

I might've disarmed them, Vaelin thought as a breeze shifted the mist to reveal two slumped, lifeless figures in threadbare clothes. *Sent them on their way with a beating.* Apparently, this notion was sufficiently amusing to the black-song for it to overcome his shield of drugged numbness. It flared, hot and loud in his breast, the music full of cruel mockery, allowing no doubt that, whatever merciful instincts he might imagine himself to possess, the song was stronger.

He reeled as the song's pitch rose to deafen him, and Derka let out a loud whinny when he slipped from the saddle. He lay on the rocky ground, clutching himself tight until the song finally began to abate and he opened his eyes to find Cho-ka regarding him with a deeply furrowed brow.

"I'll fix the pipe," he said, rising to unfasten one of his saddlebags. "But this is the last of it, lord."

"Leave it." Vaelin groaned and got to his knees, finding himself too weak to stand without the outlaw's assistance. "It doesn't work anymore." The tremble in his hands made it a difficult task, but after some fumbling he managed to unbuckle his sword. "Take it," he said, pressing it into Cho-ka's grip. He also handed over his hunting knife and the five throwing knives concealed about his person. "You may have to kill me," he told the outlaw. "If so, don't hesitate."

"It's another night and a day to the temple," Cho-ka said. "How . . . ?"

"You have a rope, don't you?"

◆　◆　◆

Riding with both hands tightly bound and a thick coil of rope encircling his arms and chest proved too arduous a task after the first couple of miles, obliging him to dismount and walk. Cho-ka kept hold of the rope that bound him, meaning they must have appeared as captor and prisoner to any observer. Derka needed no tether, trotting along in their wake with occasional forays into the surrounding slopes to nibble at the sparse gorse sprouting amongst the rocks. All the time the black-song grew ever louder as the last of the Jade Fox seeped away with the copious sweat flowing from Vaelin's pores. He knew his body had developed a hunger for the drug, that his addiction was now a match for Nortah's thirst for drink. Flashes of fever vied with bone-deep chills to inflict the most pain upon him, making every step a test as he fought against the urge to sink to the ground and beg Cho-ka for all that remained of the drug. Perversely, he found that he welcomed the waves of pain and sweat; the greater his discomfort, the less loud the song.

"Never climbed so high in my life, lord," Cho-ka said as the slopes they traversed grew steeper. He had maintained a constant commentary since Vaelin insisted on being bound. It consisted mostly of tales from his criminal career interspersed with observations of the absurdity of life in the Merchant Realms. Vaelin assumed the outlaw was trying to distract him from his pains, or attempting to assuage his own fear, which became more evident in the wavering temper of his voice the higher they climbed.

"Once scaled a mountain in the north to raid a tomb dug into the side of a cliff," Cho-ka went on. "Even that was a midget compared to this. It was a fine tomb, to be sure. Marvellous columns and statues carved from bare rock, so long ago no one was even sure whose body lay within. We thought there'd be jewels, or at least gold. All we found was a coffin full of dust and some very strange pictures painted on the walls. One of my brothers fell and broke his neck on the way down. I've tended to avoid mountains ever since . . ."

Cho-ka's voice dwindled away and he reined his mare to an abrupt halt, causing Vaelin to stumble and fall to his knees. Looking up he saw the outlaw staring fixedly ahead, and Vaelin made out a tall figure through the drifting vapour that lingered continually on the slopes. The figure stood surveying them in silence for some time, Cho-ka's horse fidgeting all the while as she sensed her rider's agitation.

"We come seeking refuge in the most revered temple in all the Merchant Realms!" Cho-ka burst out finally, casting a hand towards Vaelin's kneeling form. "This is a great warrior from across the sea, a renowned foe of those who come to ravage our lands . . ." His voice lessened in volume as the tall figure started down the slope, resolving into a man of impressive stature clad in an unadorned black robe. He bore a plain wooden staff and his hair was long, trailing in the stiff mountain breeze as he drew nearer. Vaelin thought him perhaps the largest person he had as yet encountered in the Far West, standing even taller than Obvar, the Darkblade's hulking and thankfully deceased champion.

"He is in need of Heaven's mercy," Cho-ka continued after a cough, his next words emerging in a strained whisper when the tall man paused to regard him. "His name . . ."

"We know his name," the tall man cut in. His voice was surprisingly soft, his gaze more curious than fierce as he scanned Cho-ka from head to toe. Vaelin also found the man's features to possess an unexpected youthfulness, putting his age at somewhere shy of thirty. "He is expected," the tall man added, his eyes coming to rest on Cho-ka's face. "You are not. Who are you?"

"Corporal Cho-ka." The outlaw pressed his fist to his chest in a semblance of a military salute. "Late of the Skulls Regiment of the Merchant King's Host . . ."

"That is not who you are." The tall man turned away, moving to stand over Vaelin. His features remained mostly passive as he took in the sight of the sweat-covered, hollow-eyed man kneeling before him, but Vaelin detected a small flicker of something in his expression. He might have taken it for pity if a caustic note from the black-song hadn't confirmed it as disappointment. It disappeared quickly, however, and the tall man forced a smile before lowering his head in a bow of grave respect. "Welcome, brother."

He straightened and turned about, starting up the slope at a purposeful stride. "Bring him," he told Cho-ka over his shoulder. "Follow my path and do not stray."

He is not alone, Vaelin concluded, struggling to his feet and following as Cho-ka urged his mare into motion. He saw nothing but drifting clouds and rock to either side, but the song was clear. The tall man was not the only one who had come to greet them. From the song's tune he judged there to be at least another dozen men dotted about their path, each one armed with a bow. *They welcome me, but fear me.* He let out a humourless laugh, seeing the tall man stiffen a little at the sound, although he didn't turn. *And well they should.*

The wall came into view after another hour's climb, a forty-foot-high barrier stretching between the flanks of two peaks for a distance of over three hundred paces. It was of sturdy and ancient construction, buttressed with thick stone at regular intervals and featuring several raised towers where the vague shapes of sentries watched their approach. Vaelin gained an impression of a larger construction beyond the wall, dark angles and hard edges in the thick mist, which concealed its true shape.

The tall man led them to a gateway in the centre of the wall, its huge doors of iron-banded oak standing open. A dozen or so men waited in the courtyard beyond as they passed inside, all dressed in the same black robe as the tall man and with hair of similar length, but none matching his stature. The structure Vaelin had glimpsed from outside now stood revealed as a tower rising at least a hundred feet, its summit obscured by the pale, swirling sky. It consisted of five storeys, each delineated by a slanting roof, the gutters dripping a continual and presumably unending rain of accumulated moisture onto the wide expanse of flagstones surrounding its base.

"The Temple of Spears," he said in a groan as a wave of nausea swept through him, sending him to his knees once more. Glancing around at the onlooking men he grunted in slight amusement. "And yet I see no spears."

"Weapons are like thoughts," the tall man replied. "Best kept hidden until needed."

Vaelin glanced over his shoulder at the grinding whine of heavy metal, seeing the great doors of the gate come together with a thunderous rumble before the black-robed men hurried to heave a tree-sized bar in place to seal it closed.

"Dismount," the tall man told Cho-ka. One of the other men came to take the reins of his mare as he complied, whilst another took charge of Derka, displaying impressive reflexes as he dodged a sweep of the stallion's head before leading him away. "You are required to disarm," the tall man added. After relieving the outlaw of his weapons, the tall man took the bone-handle knife and moved to crouch at Vaelin's back.

"That is not a good idea," Vaelin warned, feeling the tug of the blade against his bonds.

"Worry not, brother." The tall man gave a grunt as he cut through the final knot and the rope fell away. "You can do no harm here."

The black-song flared as Vaelin shrugged off the rope and got to his feet; however, the violent impulses he expected failed to materialise. For the first time its voice seemed uncertain, even confused, sounding discordant notes when Vaelin's eyes tracked over the ascending majesty of the Temple of Spears. *There's something here it doesn't like*, he decided. *Or doesn't understand.*

"My brothers will provide you food and a place to rest," the tall man told Cho-ka before starting towards the base of the temple and gesturing for Vaelin to follow. "Come, brother. Our abbot awaits you."

"Abbot?" Vaelin asked, pausing to watch Cho-ka be led away by a pair of monks. The outlaw initially shrugged off the hands they placed on his shoulders but calmed himself at a warning glare from Vaelin. Weapons or no, these men all displayed the same leanness and fluency of movement possessed by well-practised warriors the world over.

"The head of our temple," the tall man explained, halting with a pointedly expectant glance until Vaelin consented to follow. "He is very keen to make your acquaintance."

"I came here in search of my companions," Vaelin said. "One of whom I believe is known to you, a Dai-Lo named Tsai Lin . . ."

"Yes, he is known to us. His recent visit was very welcome, if all too brief."

"You mean, they already left?"

"Indeed. Tsai Lin's business elsewhere was pressing."

Vaelin came to a halt beneath the shadow of the first-storey roof, the tall man pausing in the wide entrance, frowning in puzzlement. "Brother?"

"I'm not your brother. I don't even know your name, and if my friends have left there is no reason for me to be here."

"My name is Zhuan-Kai and I believe there is every reason for you to be here. What resides within you poses a great danger to all who might happen across your path."

What resides within you . . . Vaelin felt it then, the murmur of recognition from the black-song. "You possess a blessing of Heaven," he said, angling his head to study Zhuan-Kai more closely. The monk said nothing, though Vaelin noted how his fingers flexed on his staff. "Is it powerful enough to keep me here against my wishes?"

Seeing Zhuan-Kai's eyes flick from left to right, he turned, finding six monks barring his path to the gate. The fact that he hadn't heard their approach was impressive, although the black-song's failure to sound a warning was more concerning.

"Please, brother," Zhuan-Kai said, stepping aside and gesturing to the temple's gloomy interior. "Be assured the temple is a refuge, not a prison."

The song coiled within him like an angry snake then, its tune one of petulant consternation he assumed stemmed from finding itself confronted by something more powerful. *Something I can't fight, or kill.* He found a grim satisfaction in this, banishing his caution sufficiently to allow him to step into the cool interior of the temple. It was a wide space, swept by a wayward breeze that made embers bloom from the blazing iron braziers in each of its corners. A smaller fire guttered in a brick-lined pit in its centre, casting a long flickering shadow from the small figure seated before it.

"I shall leave you to make your own introduction," Zhuan-Kai said with another bow before turning to go.

Seeing little reason to loiter, Vaelin approached the fire, standing on the opposite side of the seated man. He wore the same plain black robe as the other monks, his hair swept back from his forehead in a long cascade of silver and black. Examining his lean and deeply lined features, Vaelin guessed him somewhere over fifty, but the weight of experience evident in the gaze he turned on Vaelin told of a far older soul. Although his eyes were dark instead of grey, Vaelin saw a distinct similarity to Master Sollis. The sword master who had guided him so ungently through those many years at the House of the Sixth Order had a gaze possessed of the same kind of implacable resolve. Although a Servant of Heaven, Vaelin knew instinctively this man had little to offer in the way of mysticism or musings on the spiritual. This man was a warrior, but like his brethren, he carried no weapon.

"You're in my home," he said as the silence became prolonged. His voice had a gravelly quality that added to the impression of age, though it lacked any note of frailty. "In these lands it is the visitor who first offers greetings."

"I'm told you know who I am," Vaelin replied. "So why bother?"

A slight narrowing of the dark eyes and a small twitch to the lips, either in anger or amusement. "Rude bastard, aren't you?" the old man grunted. "Is it that *thing* inside you that makes you so?"

The black-song coiled again in response to the barb, but still failed to stir Vaelin to violence. Its tune was now so uneven as to be tremulous, conveying a distinct and surprising impression of fear even though, unlike Zhuan-Kai, he could sense no gift in the abbot.

"Vaelin Al Sorna," he said, sketching a bow.

The old man raised an eyebrow in apparent expectation when Vaelin fell silent once more. "I thought you had a rather long list of titles. Battle Lord of something or other, Tower Lord of somewhere or other. Why not state them?"

"I doubt you would be impressed if I did."

The abbot grunted again, returning his gaze to the fire. "Rude but not stupid, at least. Sit." He jerked his head at a nearby stool. It sat barely six inches above the flagstones and proved so narrow as to provide scant comfort when Vaelin perched himself atop it.

"Every day," the abbot said, "I spend two hours sitting in silent contemplation of this fire. Do you know why?"

"To think, I assume," Vaelin replied. "Enjoy a moment's respite from your responsibilities."

"No. I do it because my brothers and sisters expect it. Because all the abbots before me did it. Every day I sit here bored shitless and stare into this fire. This temple is a place that binds us in rituals, some worthwhile, many pointless. It is the worthwhile ones I wish to share with you, Vaelin Al Sorna, Tower Lord of somewhere or other."

"I didn't come here for rituals . . ."

"Then why did you come? To find your friends? Did you delude yourself they might harbour some form of remedy for the poison you carry? I assure you, they did not. Even the Healing Grace of Heaven possesses no concoction that can quiet it." The abbot blinked and shifted his gaze once more, meeting Vaelin's eye. "But this temple does."

"You know what it is?" Vaelin leaned forward, searching the abbot's face. "You know why it's . . . different?"

The old man gave a small shake of his head. "No, but the temple will." Seeing the bafflement on Vaelin's brow he raised a hand to gesture at their surroundings. "What do you see? Stone, mortar, tile. Some of it very old, some the result of recent repair. But make no mistake, the Temple of Spears is a living thing. It does not belong to my order; we belong to it. And for reasons it has chosen not to make clear, it wishes to help you."

"How?"

"In the same manner it helped me all those years ago when I fetched up at the walls, as wretched and unworthy a soul as you could imagine. At any given time there are perhaps five hundred brothers and sisters within these walls, all called to the temple by means they do not truly understand. Some will spend all their lives here, others merely years, bending every effort towards achieving but one goal." The abbot pointed at a doorway in the far wall, the firelight playing on a staircase within. "Ascend the temple, all the way to the top."

"I was told novitiates were required to spend days scrubbing courtyards before being allowed to study here."

"Something we make the youngsters do when they turn up, a small and amusing tradition. But we do not choose who ascends the temple; it does."

"Is it so simple? I climb to the top and I can leave?"

"No, of course it's not that fucking simple." The abbot laughed in disgust. "There are five tiers to the temple. Upon reaching each tier you will be tested. Pass the test and you ascend. Fail and you repeat it until you pass."

"What manner of tests?"

"They change with every soul who takes them according to whatever the temple decides it needs to teach you. My first tier involved four brothers doing their best to beat me unconscious with clubs. I was only permitted to ascend when I avoided every blow." He grimaced in painful remembrance. "It took a long time."

"I assume Tsai Lin told you what is happening beyond these walls. You would have me waste time playing games whilst your lands crumble around you?"

"I said much the same thing to the abbot when I first came here. There was a war going on then too, some dynastic dispute or other. He was a man of more poetic inclination than I. 'Time,' he told me, 'is both precious and worthless. It is eternal and fleeting. Like clay, you may make of it what you will, if your hands possess the skill to do so.'" He smiled then sobered at the sight of Vaelin's glowering visage. "Suffice to say," the abbot told him, "you will not leave here until you have ascended to the top tier of this building. You will be fed, you will be watered and sheltered, but you will not be permitted beyond these walls until you have fulfilled the temple's plan for you."

"Then I'd best do that." Vaelin bit down on a groan as he rose from the uncomfortable stool and started towards the doorway.

"You should wait a few days," the abbot called after him. "Recover strength . . ."

Vaelin ignored him and the upsurge of warning from the black-song as he entered the shadowed stairwell and began to ascend.

CHAPTER SEVEN

The song faded to a dull throb as he entered the first tier, finding a broad space with a polished wooden floor lacking any features beyond the shuttered windows, the pillars supporting the roof and another doorway presumably leading to the next tier. Vaelin spent a few moments wandering the space in search of some clue as to the task he was required to perform and, finding nothing, started towards the doorway. As he did so the drum of feet sounded to his rear and he turned to see four monks enter the tier at the run. There was no preamble or formality, all four simply charged towards him, their long hair tied back from faces hard with the tension of men intent on violence.

At least they don't have clubs, Vaelin thought, ducking under a punch. He blocked another fist with his forearm and drove a kick into the chest of its owner, sending him onto his back. Old lessons sprang to mind as he back-pedalled, including Master Intris's mantra during those bruising days on the practice field: *When faced with multiple opponents, make them into one. Always seek to deny them the advantage of numbers . . .*

Vaelin sidestepped a kick and darted towards the nearest pillar, spoiling the attack of another monk whose fist collided painfully with the hard wood edge. Vaelin delivered a kick to his leg and slammed an elbow into his face as he collapsed to one knee. Fists and feet whistled within inches of him as he ducked and rolled away, sprinting for the next pillar. Jumping, he gripped it and swung his body around, intending to plant both boots in the face of the pursuing monk. Instead the man performed a roll of his own, sliding under the attack before springing to his feet and whirling a kick into the back of Vaelin's head. He staggered, blinking away red and white flashes and managing to dodge a flurry of punches, replying with several of his own and feeling the satisfying thud of fist on flesh, before one of the monks managed to deliver a two-punch combination to his exposed ribs. Doubling over, Vaelin covered his head with his forearms and charged, bulling aside a pair of monks as he tried to gain space. The others, however, opted not to allow him the luxury, and a series of roundhouse kicks to the back and legs sent him to the floor. After that everything became a confused morass of pain and frustrated attempts to rise until his vision dimmed and he felt himself slide towards unconsciousness.

The monks left off as his body sagged, Vaelin rolling onto his back, gasping air into strained lungs, bruised flesh stinging. Eventually, his vision cleared to reveal the abbot's face, lean muscle and lines formed into a caustic frown. "I did tell you to wait," he said.

"No time . . ." Vaelin grated, shifting to plant a hand on the floor and push himself upright. His arm gave way before he managed a few inches and he found himself kissing the smooth wood of the floor, the iron sting of his blood mingling with the scent of polish.

"You are suffering the effects of addiction," he heard the abbot say. "In fact, your attempt to pass this tier could be considered an insult to this temple." His voice faded as Vaelin heard the sound of his retreating footsteps. "Take this silly bastard to Kish-an. He's not permitted within the temple again until pronounced fit . . ."

◆　◆　◆

Kish-an was a portly monk of middling years with a penchant for obvious observations. "You have many scars," he said, dabbing a cloth loaded with some form of salve onto the most livid of Vaelin's bruises. "You must either have killed many men or be a very poor fighter."

He met Vaelin's glare with an unrepentant grin and dabbed the salve onto a cut on his upper arm, provoking a hiss as the substance stung its way into the wound. "Doesn't look like you need any stitching done." Kish-an dropped the cloth into a bowl and ran a hand along the long row of bottles and jars crowding his shelf. The monks, it transpired, did not live within the towering temple itself. Kish-an's healing house consisted of a small brick dwelling in the centre of the cluster of ancient buildings. This collection of archaic architecture nestled between the tower and the unscalable edifice of the tallest of the three-peaked mountain upon which the temple complex had been constructed.

"Let's see," the healer mused. "Ah." His finger came to rest on a small yellow glass bottle. "Pipe-smoker's ruin. The oldest remedies are usually the best." He unstoppered the bottle and poured a few small droplets into a clay cup before adding a measure of water.

"I don't want any more drugs," Vaelin said when Kish-an offered him the cup.

"Your body thinks otherwise. Whatever you might want, you're an addict now, my foreign friend. The concoction you were dosed with is the most potent form of poppy milk I've encountered, the kind that seeps into the very fibre of a man. It'll always be there, lurking away in a small corner of your mind, ready to grow back into a hungry monster when opportunity arises. Drink this and you'll have a much better chance of keeping it at bay. Don't and I'll be forced to tell the abbot you cannot attempt the temple again."

Vaelin sat up and swung his legs off the couch, reaching for the cup then hesitating. "There is . . . something within me," he began, unsure of how to explain the danger posed by the black-song. "Something the drug keeps contained . . ."

"I know," Kish-an cut in with a tight smile. "I can feel it. But so can the temple, and it will allow no evil within its walls." He proffered the cup again. "Drink, brother."

Recalling the song's coiling discomfort from before, Vaelin quelled his fears and took the cup, downing the contents in a single gulp. The taste was bitter and faintly floral, but not particularly unpleasant, making an easy progress from his throat to his gut. "What will it do?" he asked, wiping his mouth.

"Piss, shit, vomit and sweat. Not necessarily in that order and sometimes all at once." Kish-an stood back as Vaelin doubled over, gasping at the sudden lurching nausea bursting in the pit of his belly. "If you would, brothers." Clenching his gut to keep from soiling himself, Vaelin was only dimly aware of a pair of monks draping his arms over their shoulders to carry him from the room. "Take him to the basement cell, the one with the drain," Kish-an called after them. "And make sure you strip him first."

◆ ◆ ◆

The grinding creak of the cell door woke him from a dream in which he had been trying to strangle his father. It was, in fact, one of the milder spectacles his mind had subjected him to over the course of what felt like weeks suffering in the dark. The cell stank of his own effluent, only partly denuded by the bucketfuls of water they drenched his naked form with at regular intervals. Although his ability to gauge the passage of time had waned amidst the waves of pain, vomiting and tormenting delusions, he had counted five separate drenchings, which could mean he had been here for an impossibly brief five days.

Light flooded his eyes as they swung towards the open door, causing him to shrink back against the wall, shielding his face. The stride of purposeful feet upon stone then his hands were batted aside. "Look at me." Strong fingers gripped his face, shaking it until he blinked and opened his eyes. Light blinded him and sent tears coursing down his cheeks until the glare faded to reveal Kish-an's face, the glow of a lantern playing on brows drawn in appraisal.

"Well?" a voice enquired as the healer's inspection continued, Vaelin recognising the abbot's impatient tones.

"He's not screaming, that's a good sign." Kish-an stared into Vaelin's eyes for a second before grunting and releasing his grip. "Pupils are normal. He's as clear of it as he's ever going to get, but he'll be weak as a kitten for a while."

"Then clean him up and feed him." The echo of retreating footsteps overlapped with others as two monks appeared out of the gloom.

"You're in luck, my foreign friend," Kish-an huffed as he and the monks dragged Vaelin to his feet. "Sister Lehun is making her famous onion soup today."

◆ ◆ ◆

Sister Lehun's long features regarded Vaelin with cold suspicion as she ladled soup into his bowl. She was a tall woman, only an inch or so shorter than he was, with a stature to match and apparently no intention of acknowledging his muttered thanks before he took his soup to a nearby table. Upon Vaelin being carried from the cell, Kish-an ordered he be taken first to the healing room where he was given a more thorough examination and a hefty draught of something that mixed water with a lemon-tinged concoction. It tasted foul but Vaelin's parched throat had him gulping it down without hesitation, finding it to be sufficiently invigorating to return a small measure of strength to his limbs. After that, Kish-an took him to a small garden where he was provided a bucket of clean, hot water and a scrubbing brush. The brush slipped from Vaelin's grip several times and he inevitably fell when trying to retrieve it. Kish-an looked on with his arms folded, offering no assistance as Vaelin climbed slowly back to his feet to resume scrubbing. Once Vaelin was cleansed of his own filth, Kish-an tossed him a black robe and a pair of shoes.

"My weapons?" Vaelin asked, receiving only a laugh in response before the healer led him to the meal hall and Sister Lehun's soup. Kish-an inclined his head and departed, leaving Vaelin alone in a large chamber where other monks and nuns sat in groups of four or more, all conspicuously avoiding looking in his direction. Silence reigned as he took a seat, making him wonder if they were forbidden to speak, but the slow murmur of resumed conversation led him to the conclusion that he was in fact the cause of this less-than-convivial atmosphere.

"Wouldn't take it too personally, lord. Seems the temple doesn't summon the friendliest of sorts."

Vaelin looked up to find Cho-ka regarding him with a mix of concern and relief as he settled onto the bench opposite. Like Vaelin, he wore a black robe. He also sported a livid bruise on his jaw and a cut above his eye.

"Did they do that?" Vaelin asked.

"The first tier is hard," Cho-ka replied with a shrug.

"You attempted the temple?"

"The abbot said I had to, or I could just piss off back to whatever dung heap I crawled out of. He's got a colourful turn of phrase for a Servant of Heaven." Cho-ka tapped his spoon to Vaelin's bowl. "Please eat, lord. You, uh, look like you could do with it."

At another time he would have judged Sister Lehun's soup as overcooked and underseasoned but found himself wolfing it down as if it were the finest meal ever produced by the queen's kitchens. "Why did you stay?" he asked Cho-ka, scraping the last dregs of onion from the bowl. "Our debt is more than settled. If anything, I'm now obligated to you."

"Beatings aside, this is probably the safest place in the Venerable Kingdom just now. Besides, I'm curious as to what the third tier has to offer."

"You completed the first two tiers?"

"That I did." Cho-ka gave a rueful chuckle. "Wasn't easy."

"What waits on the second?"

A guarded look crept into the outlaw's gaze as he swallowed some soup. "Not supposed to say," he said, shifting uncomfortably under the weight of Vaelin's lingering stare. His eyes flicked to his right, settling on a slim figure at a table close to the door, a nun, sitting alone unlike the other Servants of the Temple. Her hair concealed her face like a veil, but Vaelin felt a faint sense of familiarity upon glimpsing her profile as she leaned forward to put her spoon to her lips. Her features possessed a youthful near-perfection he felt he had seen before but, thanks presumably to his still somewhat befuddled state, couldn't place where.

"Who's she?" Vaelin asked Cho-ka, seeing the outlaw quickly shift his gaze back to his soup.

"The second tier," he said, voice low and clearly reluctant to elaborate. "Suffice to say, it's not a test of combat."

◆ ◆ ◆

Kish-an took another four days to pronounce him fit to attempt the first tier once again. Vaelin spent the first day wandering the temple grounds searching for a potential avenue of escape. Much as he detested the black-song, he had entertained some hope it might provide a clue as to how to safely remove himself from this place. Nortah and the others slipped further away with every hour spent here. Added to that was the certain knowledge that Kehlbrand Reyerik would now be leading his horde across the northern border, facing scant opposition in the process. The song, however, provided no help, rarely rising in pitch above the same dull ache, except when his gaze strayed to the top of the temple, and even then its distress remained muted.

His wandering did uncover a grated sluice in the eastern portion of the wall through which the denizens of the temple would cast their used water and food scraps. Every morning and early evening the detritus tumbled down a steep narrow channel to form an ugly cascade as it slipped over the edge of a sheer drop a few dozen feet below. The bars of the grate would normally have prevented any egress, but with his denuded frame Vaelin suspected he might be able to squeeze through.

"You'll die, brother," a cheerful voice informed him on the morning of the next day as Vaelin stood watching refuse being cast into the drain. He turned to find Zhuan-Kai regarding him with an apologetic grimace as he rested his chin on a hand placed atop his staff. "No handholds, you see?"

the big monk elaborated. "Just a channel worn smooth over countless years. I'd guess it would take you some time to hit the bottom."

"So," Vaelin said, "if I tried it now you wouldn't raise a hand to stop me?"

Zhuan-Kai laughed, stepping back to heft his staff, twirling it briefly with the effortless skill of one who knew his chosen weapon with absolute familiarity. "I didn't say that." He planted the butt of his staff on the ground and gestured to the group of nuns and monks assembling in the shadow of the temple. "I'm about to teach them the best way to disarm an opponent armed with a spear. You are welcome to join us."

Vaelin ignored him, pausing to cast a final glance at the drain before stalking off towards the meal hall where he hoped to elicit an extra helping from Sister Lehun. Despite her continuing refusal to speak a single word to him, she was at least usually willing to provide all the food he wished, presumably at the abbot's order.

With little else to do, he spent his time watching the temple's servants undergo their daily routine, finding to his surprise that this was not exclusively an order of warriors. Whilst many spent much of each day sparring or partaking of the tutelage in combat offered by their senior brothers and sisters, others were fully occupied in various crafts. It became Vaelin's habit to watch them work. Some displayed an initial irritation at finding themselves with an audience, but as he had observed during his years in the Northern Reaches, skilled people were often proud of their abilities and took joy from showing them off.

Dei-yun, a blacksmith of limited height but thick muscles, grew tired of Vaelin watching him hammer steel into blades and soon enlisted his help with working the bellows and grindstone. The smith's skill was undeniable but his work was entirely functional and lacking ornamentation. Racks of swords and spears lined his workshop, alongside barrels piled high with arrowheads. From the gleam of the freshly polished metal, Vaelin deduced the weapons to be of recent manufacture.

"You must have many hundreds of these in your armoury," he ventured, nodding to the weapons as he worked the grindstone's treadle. "If this is all you do."

"Six months' labour," Dei-yun muttered, squinting amidst a shower of sparks, his fingers moving the blade over the stone with expert precision. He was taciturn but at least willing to speak, if briefly. "Before that nails and brackets and such, for the gates and windows."

"Just six months?" Vaelin pursed his lips in contemplation. "Why the change?"

The blacksmith's gaze flicked up at him, but only for a second. "The temple called and I answered. Do you want to work or pester me with questions, foreigner?"

The stoop-backed weaver was equally busy and no more forthcoming. He wouldn't allow Vaelin near his loom but did enlist his help in folding and piling the many cloaks he had crafted. They were all black and hooded, the dense wool waxed to ward off the rain. The cobbler was no less busy, and Vaelin noted that Sister Lehun, when not preparing the daily meals, spent a good deal of her time curing and salting pork before sealing it in earthenware jars. He expected her to shoo him away when she noticed his attention but instead handed him a cleaver and set him to chopping ribs from a pig carcass.

The only artisan to shun his company was the nun he had seen sitting alone in the meal hall. Her workshop was the most secluded of them all; in fact it was more a cave than a house, having been hewn in ages past into the side of the mountain. Peering through the open door he saw her slender form bent over a table, the brush in her hand tracing ink across a broad sheet of paper. Other sheets hung from the ceiling, immediately capturing his attention with the clarity and precision of the images portrayed. It was very different from the art of the Realm, the figures rendered in clean lines of ink rather than oils, lacking the attention to light and shadow and delight in perspective so beloved by his sister. However, he had little doubt Alornis would have found a great deal to admire here; the people depicted on every sheet possessed an undeniable vitality and realness despite being formed from only a few lines. Each picture was also decorated in Far Western script, the characters flowing around the subject in smooth, natural curves. He had no difficulty in recognising a portrait of Zhuan-Kai, smiling as he raised his staff amidst a mass of characters that swirled around him like flocking birds. The abbot was also easy to discern, kneeling before his fire, the flames forming script as they rose into the air. However, it was the next image that caused him to take an involuntary step across the threshold. *Sherin.* Her face had been captured in profile, the few lines that described it somehow conveying a deep well of grief. The Far Western script surrounded her in a spiral, resembling cherry blossom petals caught by the wind.

His fascinated gaze was interrupted by the scrape of a stool, his view shifting to see the nun rising to her feet. Her features were still obscured by a cascade of silken black hair as she approached the door, head lowered and eyes fixed on his intruding foot. When Vaelin withdrew with a bow and apology, she gave no reply, instead softly closing the door. He heard the double click of a lock followed shortly after by the dim sound of her stool scraping back into place.

CHAPTER EIGHT

The monk's mouth emitted a crunching rattle of broken teeth as Vaelin's fist collided with his jaw. The young man spun into the nearest pillar, spattering the wall beyond with a spray of white-flecked crimson before he slid slowly to the floor. Vaelin dragged air into his lungs and unclenched his fists, flexing the fingers and arching his back in an effort to banish the ache of a well-placed kick. The other three monks lay around him, one stunned and groaning, the other two unconscious. The fight had been too long, leaving him with several additional bruises. Still, the effects of Jade Fox and his time in the cell had abated sufficiently to allow at least a partial return of his old strength and skills. His four opponents were all some years his junior and well-practised in the various forms of unarmed combat taught in the Far West. If anything, he thought them too practised, their fighting style almost like a dance that eschewed the inelegant but useful expediency of brute force. It gave rise to the notion that the abbot hadn't yet sent his best or most experienced Servants to contest Vaelin's ascent of the temple.

He turned towards the doorway at the sound of feet on the stairwell, crouching in readiness as eight monks emerged into the tier. Instead of attacking, however, they ignored Vaelin and paired off to carry away their fallen brothers. Within seconds he was alone again, standing in contemplation of the stairwell to the second tier. *It's not a test of combat*, Cho-ka had said, Vaelin feeling a twinge of unease as he recalled the grimness of the outlaw's tone.

Ascending the stairwell brought him into another mostly bare space. The only furnishings were two low stools and a table positioned in the centre of the polished floor. Assuming there would be little point in simply making his way to the next tier, Vaelin chose the furthest stool and sat down to wait. The sound of light footsteps on the stairs was not long in coming, and he was unsurprised to see the slender nun emerge from the stairwell. She carried a rolled-up sheet of paper and a satchel as she moved to take the stool opposite. The polite "Good morning" he offered received no response as she unfurled the paper on the table and weighed down its edges with two pots she extracted from her satchel. She went on to set out two stoppered bottles that she used to fill the pot on the right with water and the one on the left with black ink. That done, she produced a long-stemmed brush and spent a long interval staring at the blank sheet of paper before her.

As the silence grew, Vaelin began to voice an enquiry about her purpose here, biting down on the words when he noticed the tip of her brush was shaking. The shallowness of the woman's breath and small heaves of her shoulders told of a deep, barely controlled fear. *Is it me?* he wondered. *Am I so terrifying?* For some reason, he doubted it. If what Cho-ka told him was correct, this woman must have performed this task many times, and a small intuitive murmur from the black-song told him she had been scared every time, but perhaps not so scared as she was today. Also, the note of recognition it held was clear if muted; this woman was Gifted.

Finally, she drew in a deep breath and raised her face to his. He was once again struck by its strange perfection, but this time the reason for the sense of familiarity it stirred became clear: *the Jade Princess.* This woman was far from her twin, but there were definite echoes of the ancient but youthful princess in the soft curve of cheek and chin. The eyes, however, were markedly different. The princess had always displayed the knowing, if somewhat impish, air of a very old soul who may well have been incapable of fear. At this moment, this woman exuded mostly fragility, the fear in her eyes he recognised as the kind that came not from ignorance, but knowledge.

"Tell me who you are," she said in a tight, controlled tone.

"My name is . . ."

"Tell me who you are." Her voice took on an edge as she repeated the instruction, a hard insistence shining in her otherwise fearful eyes.

So, names have no meaning in this test, he decided. After a moment's consideration he replied, "A man in search of his friends."

The nun frowned, gaze narrowing as she shook her head. "Tell me who you are."

Vaelin sighed and looked away from her, sorely tempted to get up and leave. He would wait for darkness and ascend the mountain to the far side, climb down come the morning and go in search of Nortah and the others. But that would mean once again traversing the outside world with the black-song, its terrible music unconstrained by whatever power the temple possessed. The abbot had promised a cure and there was but one way to get it.

"I am," he began, meeting the nun's gaze, "a man with a great sickness within him. A great danger . . ."

He trailed off as she lowered her eyes to the paper, dipped her brush into the ink and began to paint. The brush flowed rapidly across the sheet, forming lines that initially seemed to intersect in an abstract, meaningless concordance, but soon took on a disturbingly familiar clarity. Also, with every stroke of the brush he felt a strange tugging pain in his head, barely perceptible at first but soon growing strong enough to make him wince at each mark left on the paper. He found himself grunting in discomfort as she joined the two lines that completed the wolf, the tugging becoming more of a harsh slashing when she dipped her brush in water and began to shade the wolf's fur. It was as he remembered it from the encounter in the Urlish Forest all those years ago. The same eyes, the same fangs revealed in a snarl when it dealt an ugly death to the assassins who had been sent to kill him. Except now it wasn't killing assassins but seemed to be engaged in a struggle with an invisible enemy, an enemy soon revealed when the nun returned her brush to the ink and began to outline a larger and yet more ferocious shape.

Vaelin was shuddering continually now, white flashes obscuring his vision and blood trickling from his nose. The urge to stop her was strong, to banish the now-unending pain, but he fought it down. *Her brush is merely a conduit,* he realised. *The means by which she interprets the thoughts she pulls from my mind.* But, as the second shape took form on the paper, it seemed she could drag forth thoughts he didn't know he possessed.

The tiger's snarl was more feral than the wolf it fought, drool flying from teeth bared by gaping jaw. Its entire form bespoke a vast, savage hunger, save for its eyes, which shone with hate for its opponent. The two beasts coiled together on the paper, locked in a spiral of combat that seemed to swirl before his eyes, causing him to blink until it once again became a static image. He saw that the nun's brush had stopped and she sat with her head bowed. Vaelin heard a soft sob then saw a teardrop land on the paper, blurring the tiger's head in a manner that somehow failed to rob it of meaning. If anything, the mingling of ink and salt water formed it into something even more ferocious. The sheer hungry malice of it was as transfixing as it was disturbing, Vaelin's pulse quickening as he continued to stare into its hating gaze.

"I . . . hoped." His gaze snapped to the nun, finding she had risen to her feet and backed away from the table. Her long hair only partially veiled her face and he could see the tears streaming from her eyes. Even so, her voice remained steady as she spoke on, "I hoped that you would never come here, even though I always knew you would."

She took a long shuddering breath and turned away, her voice little more than a whisper as she made her way to the stairwell. "You may ascend to the next tier."

◆ ◆ ◆

The third tier was a marked contrast to the others in being far from featureless. Whilst its floor remained bare the walls were lined with racks of weapons. Swords, spears, axes, maces all gleaming in the light of the torches set into the pillars. Vaelin was quick to recognise most of the weapons as Deiyun's work, the precision and uniformity of design mirroring the product of the forge. Some were clearly older and possessed a less functional appearance, the blades of several spears and swords bearing inscriptions in archaic script that echoed those in Mah-Shin's tomb. The temple, it appeared, dated back to the founding of the Emerald Empire, if not before.

"Which are you?"

Vaelin turned to see Zhuan-Kai entering the tier, staff in hand and visage cheerful as always. His other hand held the nun's picture Vaelin had been happy to leave in the tier below. "The tiger or the wolf?" the monk asked, holding up the image.

"Neither, I suspect," Vaelin replied.

"Ah." Zhuan-Kai frowned as he strode towards the far end of the floor, carefully rolling the sheet into a scroll. "It's true the meaning of Sister Mi-Hahn's work is not always easily discerned, to anyone but her. My own was less . . . violent in nature, but it still took me many years of pondering to arrive at a meaning."

"What was it?"

The monk placed the furled paper on a windowsill before strolling to Vaelin's side. "A tree."

"Just that?"

"Just that." Zhuan-Kai inclined his head at the row of engraved swords in the rack. "Beautiful, aren't they? The product of an age when artistry was more valued than it is today. An age before greed became the law, you might say. They're well cared for," he added, moving away to stand at the far end of the floor. "Still as sharp as the day they were forged. So any will serve very well, if that is your choice."

"Choice?" Vaelin asked.

"Indeed." The monk hefted his staff and adopted a fighting stance, nodding at the weapons. "Choose."

"We are supposed to fight, I presume?"

Zhuan-Kai's smile broadened into a laugh. "We are."

Vaelin's gaze settled on the plain wooden staff in the monk's grip before slipping back to the row of swords. "I've no desire to kill you," he said.

The monk's laugh grew louder. "You won't."

Vaelin's gaze lingered on the swords for a second, feeling the black-song coil in response, still muted but possessed of a deeper note of malice than before. Gritting his teeth, Vaelin turned away from the swords and moved to the neighbouring rack of spears. He chose one of the plain, recently forged weapons. It was typical of Far Western design: a five-foot shaft topped by a footlong curved blade. Reversing it, Vaelin placed the blade's hilt between the base of the rack and the floor. Stamping down with his boot he broke the shaft, leaving him with a staff of his own, albeit with one end formed of a splintered stump.

"That wasn't necessary," Zhuan-Kai said as Vaelin took his place before him. "But," he added with a shallow bow, "your consideration does you credit, brother. And please know, I'm sorry."

Distracting an opponent with a statement begging a question was a trick Vaelin knew well, so the monk's first and impressively swift attack was easily avoided. He ducked under the jabbing staff then swayed clear of the sweep that followed, replying with an overhead strike aimed at the monk's shoulder, hard enough to break a bone or two but far from lethal. The shaft of the spear rebounded from Zhuan-Kai's staff with a clack of colliding hardwood, and Vaelin caught the monk's appreciative grin before he launched into a series of countermoves. His staff whirled and blurred as he advanced, Vaelin fending off blow after blow, all delivered with a speed that prevented a response. He repeatedly dodged to either side in an effort to gain space enough for a riposte, but Zhuan-Kai was quick to employ his advantage in height and bulk to block any such attempt. The blurring whirl of his staff was increasingly hard to follow, at times the weapon becoming near invisible due to the speed with which its owner wielded it. Retreating step by increasingly irksome step, Vaelin knew he would soon find himself forced into a corner where defeat would come quickly.

Wincing in anticipation but seeing little alternative, instead of blocking the next blow he raised his left arm and allowed the staff to thud into his side, turning at the last moment to deflect a portion of the force. Even so, the impact was almost enough to send him to his knees as the shock thrummed through his body. Vaelin clenched his jaw against the pain, bringing his arm down to trap the monk's staff whilst swinging his own at his head, intending to deliver a stunning blow to the temple. Zhuan-Kai's plate-sized hand came up in a flash, catching the broken spear before it could land, but leaving his midriff open in the process. Vaelin put all the strength he could into the kick, driving his foot into the centre of the larger man's chest. The kick was a tribute to his training and years of experience, precisely placed with sufficient energy to leave any opponent gasping and retching on the ground.

Zhuan-Kai grunted as the kick landed, retreated a single step then lashed out with a kick of his own that sent Vaelin reeling into the rack of maces behind. Hard metal scraped him as he fell amidst a shower of displaced weaponry. He paused for the fraction of a second it took to partially fill his lungs then rolled clear of the descending staff. It thudded repeatedly onto the wooden floor, chasing him as he scrambled free. Zhuan-Kai loomed above him, impossibly fast despite his size, face set in determined concentration rather than anger as the staff jabbed again and again. Vaelin's broken spear was gone, jarred from his grip when the monk landed his kick, but as he scurried back his palm landed on the steel shaft of a mace. A small ugly pulse from the black-song was enough to make him grasp it, his prior moderation forgotten in the instant it took him to swing the mace. He aimed for the monk's knee, a shattering blow that might well never heal, but the staff blurred into its path before it could land. Vaelin expected the monk's weapon to dissolve into a cloud of splinters but instead it coiled, wood creaking as it stretched and curled, enveloping the spiked metal club.

The black-song voiced its note of recognition as Vaelin's gaze snapped from the mace, now trapped in an overlapping lattice of wood, to Zhuan-Kai's face. His smile was back, though it was impressed rather than mocking, the monk's eyebrows raised in admiration.

"Remarkable," he said. "I don't normally need to use my blessing until at least the fourth attempt."

With that he pulled on his staff, heaving the mace away to embed its spiked head in a pillar. Whirling, he thrust one end of the staff into Vaelin's midriff, just below the sternum.

"I can see this is going to be very interesting, brother," Vaelin heard him say, retreating voice and footsteps dulled by the pain that made him gag and double over on the floor. "Until tomorrow, then."

◆ ◆ ◆

"You could've warned me," Vaelin admonished Cho-ka over supper in the meal hall. Sister Lehun's offering tonight consisted of an aromatic stew of chicken and dumplings seasoned with thyme and some form of spice that brought a pleasant tingle to the tongue. The lingering ache below Vaelin's chest, however, left him with only a marginal appetite.

"About what?" the outlaw enquired, cheek bulging as he chewed on a dumpling.

"The third tier. What he can do with that staff."

Cho-ka shrugged, blank faced. "Brother Zhuan, you mean? It's not him I face on the third tier, it's that weaselly-faced little fucker." He jerked his head at the table nearest the door where the senior brothers and sisters tended to congregate. Vaelin's gaze picked out a diminutive brother of middling years with a slightly pointed chin exchanging a muted conversation with the abbot. "Still hasn't bothered to tell me his name. I choose a weapon, we fight." Cho-ka's features, discoloured by yet another bruise, darkened as he turned back to his meal. "He wins. Five times now."

"What weapon does he choose?" Vaelin asked, drawing a sour glare from the outlaw.

"That's the worst of it," he replied in a sullen mutter. "Short-arsed bastard needs only his bare hands to beat me."

Vaelin did his best to finish his meal, knowing he would need his strength for the next day as he pondered various unlikely stratagems for defeating a man with the power to bend wood to his will. The black-song was more quiescent than ever since his defeat, offering no clues and leaving him to idle speculation as his gaze wandered the hall, inevitably coming to rest on the solitary form of Sister Mi-Hahn. *Do they shun her?* he wondered, watching her economical, precise movements as she ate. *Or is it she who shuns them?*

"Where are you going?" Cho-ka asked as Vaelin got to his feet, bowl in hand, and started towards the sister's table.

"In search of more enlightening conversation."

Her spoon froze an inch short of her mouth at the bench's scrape and he saw her eyes widen behind the black veil of hair. "Good evening, sister," he said, sitting down.

Sauce dripped from her spoon as she continued to stare at him, Vaelin becoming aware of the hush that had descended over the hall. "Mi-Hahn, is it not?" he went on. "You already know my name, so formal introductions would appear to be redundant."

She lowered her spoon back to her bowl, head dipping further and eyes averted.

"I've seen many with the blessing of Heaven," Vaelin went on, continuing to eat. "But none quite like yours. My sister is an artist, you see. I believe she would find your work fascinating."

He caught a small glimmer behind the veil as her eyes darted towards him before flicking away once more.

"She works in oils, mostly," Vaelin continued. "Charcoal too, and has been known to try her hand at sculpture . . ."

He fell silent at the loud thud of Zhuan-Kai's staff on the flagstones. The large monk stood at the table's edge, his smile for once completely absent from a very serious face. "Our sister," he told Vaelin in an unambiguous tone rich in warning, "prefers to eat alone."

As his gaze tracked from Zhuan-Kai to the still unspeaking nun, Vaelin recalled the care the monk had shown for her picture of the wolf and the tiger. "As I'm sure she's quite capable of telling me herself," he replied, eyebrows raised as he partook of another spoonful of stew.

Zhuan-Kai's shoulders tensed, fists bunching on his staff as he started forward, stopping at a small, barely audible utterance from Mi-Hahn. "Oils?"

She had raised her head a little, her hair parted sufficiently to reveal the centre of her finely made face.

"Yes," Vaelin said, "pigment mixed with oil and applied to canvas. Such things are not known here?"

Her head moved in a fractional shake before her eyes flicked to Zhuan-Kai. Vaelin felt something pass between them in the brief meeting of gazes, an unspoken understanding that had nothing to do with their gifts. The monk's features softened a little, although the hard stare he afforded Vaelin before turning and stalking back to his own table promised tomorrow's trial would be a difficult one.

"You know how to do this?" Mi-Hahn asked. "Mix pigment and oils?"

"I've watched my sister do it many times." Vaelin smiled. "I'd be happy to show you."

She thought for a moment then lowered her gaze once more, the hair falling back into place. "Tomorrow," she said. With that she rose and made an unhurried exit from the hall, leaving her meal mostly untouched.

CHAPTER NINE

"Y ou should sit."

Vaelin gave a strained smile and shook his head, continuing to grind the mix of chalk and dried juniper berries in the mortar and pestle. Mi-Hahn's smooth brow showed a small crease as it formed a dubious frown. He had arrived at her dwelling with a badly grazed forehead and a bruise on his cheek more livid than any collected by Cho-ka over the recent days.

"Sit," she said, pointedly dragging a chair into place. He took it without further demur, trying unsuccessfully to conceal a groan at his protesting ribs. He didn't think any were cracked but couldn't be completely sure.

"Brother Zhuan is always kind," Mi-Hahn told him. "Until you make him angry."

"I noticed."

The morning's attempt had been brief, if painfully instructive in the nature of Zhuan-Kai's gift. Vaelin had chosen an axe this time, reasoning that any wood, even if commanded by the Dark, could be chopped in two by a sufficiently keen edge. The monk had nimbly dodged his first swing and whirled, the staff stretching and coiling like a whip that wrapped itself around Vaelin's torso and began, slowly, to squeeze. When the axe had fallen from Vaelin's blood-starved hand, Zhuan-Kai jerked the staff, launching him face-first into the nearest pillar. The monk then departed the tier without a word.

"My sister preferred ochre to chalk," he told Mi-Hahn, tapping the pestle against the mortar to loosen the powder from it. His scouring of the artisans' workshops had yielded only the bare minimum of ingredients required. The chalk came from Dei-yun's forge and everything else from the kitchen. "And linseed oil, but that seems to be the one ingredient missing from Sister Lehun's larder."

He reached for one of the eggs he had purloined and cracked it, draining the white away to leave the yolk before adding it to the mixture along with a few drops from the bottle of rice vinegar. He used a spoon to stir the concoction before emptying it out on the slate he had brought. "This takes some time," he said, using a small, flat knife to work the dark red glop into a paste. He had seen Alornis spend hours at this task and worried that the nun might soon lose interest through sheer boredom, but she continued to observe the whole process with keen fascination. Her hair was tied back today, affording him the first clear view of her face, her similarity to the Jade Princess now so pronounced he found it hard not to stare.

"It would normally require much longer on the slab," he said, setting the knife aside. "But this should suffice for a demonstration."

He paused to wash his hands then took hold of the canvas frame the weaver had been kind enough to fashion for him. It was coarser than he would have liked and retained a brownish tinge, but Mi-Hahn didn't seem to mind. Taking up one of her brushes, she lost no time in dabbing it to the crimson smear on the slate and applying it to the canvas. Vaelin saw her lips form a small but perfect bow at the result, her hand returning the brush to the paint as if in automatic reflex.

"You can grind pure white chalk or charcoal to create different shades . . ." Vaelin began but trailed off when it became clear she wasn't listening. He continued to hold the canvas as she worked, the brush blurring at times, her features taking on an intense concentration he had seen on his sister's face many times. He half expected her gift to manifest itself but felt no tug at his mind. Whatever she was creating came only from within.

The brush finally stopped after near half an hour's feverish work, Mi-Hahn stepping back with head tilted in appraisal. Vaelin propped the canvas on a table and joined her silent review. Somehow, despite working with only one shade, she had managed to fashion a portrait of remarkable accuracy, the shadows crafted only through applying varying pressure to the brush. The man it depicted was somewhat grim of aspect, his eyes dark and his features half-veiled in shadow. The image conveyed a sense of barely contained threat, of violence suppressed but always present. This was a man people would do well to avoid, a man with a fresh bruise on his cheek and a scrape on his forehead.

"My nose isn't that big," he said, glimpsing another small curve to Mi-Hahn's lips before she turned away.

"She said you weren't a vain man," she replied, washing her brush clean in a bowl of water. "Despite the legends that surround you."

Vaelin's gaze went to the portrait of Sherin hanging from one of the ropes criss-crossing the ceiling. "The Grace of Heaven spoke of me?"

"She spoke of many things. She was there when the Jade Princess fell. I wanted to know the manner of her death."

"I too was there. Her passing was . . . a great regret to me. I had cause to resent her, the scheming she had done to bring me to these lands. But I could see no malice in her."

"Malice." She set the brush aside and reached for a cloth to dry her hands. "No, she was never burdened with that."

"You knew her?"

"I did, although we never met. Distance was no barrier to her, as I assume you know."

"She reached out to you with her mind?"

"In my dreams. I was just a child the first time, barely able to discern the difference between dreams and the waking world. But it was through her guidance, and with some assistance along the way, that I eventually came to the temple. They had been waiting for me." She met his gaze, the first time she had done so since their meeting in the temple, all trace of timidity gone. When she spoke again, her voice lacking any hesitancy, he understood her previous manner to be an act, a role she had been playing for a long time. "As they have waited for others, like you."

"You share her blood," he said. "You are kin to the Jade Princess."

A sad, reflective smile played on her lips as she nodded. "A long time ago, so long there is no word for the number of years, she came to love a man. He was no great man. Neither a warrior nor a scholar nor a king, but he had a great heart and he loved her as she loved him. She married him, stayed with him and in time bore a daughter, the moment she said was the greatest joy and the greatest sadness of her long, long life. For she knew this was a child she couldn't keep. So one night she left, leaving no word behind, knowing her kindly husband's heart would break but at least he would have a daughter to salve it. In time the child grew and bore children of her own, who in turn did the same. And so as her grandchildren became great-grandchildren and her blood spread throughout these lands, the Jade Princess kept careful watch on her progeny, knowing one day there would be one born who would allow her to forsake her mantle. That is how she found me, through the blood that binds us."

"Forsake her mantle? You're supposed to take her place?"

"For now I'm supposed to be here, painting pictures at the temple's behest. Although, with your arrival I sense that is about to change."

"That's why you hoped I would never come here."

"I've grown comfortable behind these walls. Here, apart from my occasional visits to the second tier, I am left in peace to paint as I wish amongst people who respect my privacy. The world outside was never so kind to me. I have no great desire to see it again."

"The world outside will be at your door soon enough, whether you wish to see it again or not. When the Darkblade learns of your existence, and he will, he'll come for you. He'll try to claim you as he tried to claim her."

She raised an eyebrow, shoulders moving in a small shrug. "The tiger sends his creature, as she promised me he would. Now the wolf has sent his. Another promise she made me. We'll see who triumphs in due course."

He began to voice another question but she forestalled him by moving back to the slate, smoothing a finger through the paint. "I thank you for your gift, brother. It was unexpected. Rest assured I shall make extensive use of it."

There was a finality to her tone that left him in little doubt that this conversation was at an end, so it was a surprise when she spoke again, halting him at the door. "Didn't it occur to you," she said, moving to place a small earthenware jar in his hands, "that even the hardest wood can become ash when it meets flame?"

She stepped back, one hand on the open door and head once again lowered as he stepped outside, the door slowly closing in his face.

◆ ◆ ◆

Zhuan-Kai proved to be only marginally less angry than the day before, maintaining an expressionless silence as Vaelin entered, ignoring the racks of weapons as he traversed the tier to stand before the hulking monk.

"You're supposed to choose," he said, inclining his head at rows of weapons.

"I already have," Vaelin replied, jabbing a punch at Zhuan-Kai's face. He avoided it easily, stepping back and raising his staff, which instantly began to stretch into its whiplike form. As he raised it, Vaelin palmed the small jar Mi-Hahn had given him from a black silk pouch at the small of his back. Launching himself forward he brought the jar down with smashing force onto the elongated wood of the shaft, covering the centre span in a slick of glistening oil. He then turned and rolled, feeling the whoosh and snap of air as the monk lashed the staff at him. Coming to his feet, Vaelin sprinted for the nearest pillar and snatched one of the torches from its stanchion, spinning to hurl it at Zhuan-Kai now charging in pursuit. Moving with a speed that Vaelin would have thought beyond a man of his size, the monk twisted, whirling the staff clear of the torch as it blazed by. Despite his efforts, a trailing ember must have caught the lamp oil smeared on the staff, for it ignited as Zhuan-Kai swung it at Vaelin's legs.

He leapt over the uncoiling snake of fire, rolling to his feet in a crouch to see the monk casting the staff aside. It stiffened the moment it left his hand, clattering to the floor, just a blackened stick wreathed in smoke and ash. With a shout of rage Zhuan-Kai turned to the nearest rack and took hold of one of the antique swords, charging towards Vaelin with blade levelled and murderous intent marring his broad features. Vaelin leapt towards the nearest rack, drawing one of the unadorned modern blades and spinning with the sword at a vertical angle, the ring of steel on steel filling the tier as he turned Zhuan-Kai's blade.

Shouting again, the monk began to assail Vaelin with a series of thrusts and slashes, all dodged or parried without undue difficulty. The man was evidently skilled with a blade but lacked the finesse and economy of force he had displayed with his staff. He was also angry, which was never a sound tactic when dealing with a skilled opponent.

Vaelin let him come on for an extended interval, fending off his repeated assaults without a riposte, allowing the monk to tire himself whilst stoking his rage. Several times he didn't bother to parry the man's thrusts, simply stepping aside or ducking with his sword held behind his back. It all combined to provoke Zhuan-Kai into an enraged overhead strike aimed at cleaving Vaelin's skull in two. Vaelin stepped close with his sword upended, allowing the opposing blade to slide over his own as it made passage to the floor, the steel tip biting deep. Vaelin kicked Zhuan-Kai's wrist, the toe of his boot precisely placed to find the nerve behind the thumb joint. The monk's hand spasmed and lost its grip. He cursed and reached again for the sword's handle but froze as Vaelin's sword point pressed into the flesh below his chin.

"You need a broader education," he said.

The monk's blocky features turned a fierce shade of crimson, nostrils flaring and muscles quivering. A loud crack snapped Vaelin's gaze to the floor, seeing the boards surrounding their feet suddenly warped. Splinters rose as the boards twisted and stretched, separating into a dozen or more coiling timber snakes that began to wrap themselves around Vaelin's legs.

"Don't!" Vaelin commanded, the tip of his sword drawing blood as he pressed it deeper into Zhuan-Kai's flesh. The monk bared his teeth, eyes now livid with unreasoning defiance, the wooden snakes tightening on Vaelin's legs.

"Enough!"

The pressure abruptly slackened at the sound of the abbot's voice, then disappeared completely as Zhuan-Kai closed his eyes, taking a deep breath. The reddened fury dominating his features faded when Vaelin lowered his sword and they stepped away from each other. The monk lowered his head, Vaelin catching a glimmer of shame before he closed his eyes.

"Your students will be gathering for their midday lesson, brother," the abbot said, inclining his head at the door. "Best piss off and see to it, eh?"

Zhuan-Kai nodded and bowed to both of them, each gesture deeper and more respectful than Vaelin had seen from any Servant of the Temple so far. The abbot watched him leave before turning a caustic eye on Vaelin. "He's worked for years to master his rage," he said. "I'd prefer if you didn't taunt him."

"The true master must always be tested," Vaelin replied. "Or he is a master of nothing."

"I see the philosophers of your lands are just as fucking pretentious as ours." The abbot flicked a finger at the sword in Vaelin's hand. "Put that back and come with me."

Vaelin expected to be led from the temple, possibly to receive a profanity-laden diatribe on his latest failure, so he was surprised when the abbot guided him to the stairwell to the next tier.

"This means I passed, I take it?" he asked as they ascended.

"Combat is always a puzzle," the old man replied. "The key to victory is different for every battle. In order to complete the third tier I had to defeat a brother who could make his skin like stone. After a year of having the snot beaten out of me, I spent one rainy morning in miserable contemplation of the mountain. My gaze became preoccupied with the way the many centuries' worth of rain had carved such deep channels into so vast an edifice. Water, you see, can undo stone, especially if you boil it first." He paused at the doorway to the fourth tier, eyes narrowed in suspicion as he glanced over his shoulder. "Strange that you managed to reckon a solution to your own puzzle in only a few days, though."

"Fire undoes wood," Vaelin said with a bland smile. "Merely the application of logic."

The abbot grunted and moved on, leading him into a space lacking any resemblance to the one below. At first glance it looked like a greatly enlarged version of Sister Mi-Hahn's dwelling. An uncountable number of pictures hung from a network of ropes, creating a veritable maze of art. Those closest to the door were clearly Mi-Hahn's work; a pair of portraits depicting Sister Lehun and an aged monk Vaelin didn't recognise but guessed from the wisdom and authority rendered by the nun's brush that he must be the former abbot.

"Does this test consist of getting to the other side without damaging anything?" Vaelin asked, casting a doubtful eye over the fragile and densely arranged contents of the tier.

"Don't be such a shithead." The abbot proceeded inside without further pause, shouldering his way carefully through the gently shifting sheets and gesturing for Vaelin to follow. "What do you see?" he asked.

"The work of many talented hands," Vaelin replied, his gaze slipping from one image to another. The deeper they went, the less recognisable the faces until soon he saw nothing but strangers. It was also clear that Mi-Hahn was not the author of every work. Some were old, the paper foxed with age and the edges ragged, and the images they held, whilst accomplished, lacked her facility for capturing expression. Nor did all the art here consist of paper and ink. He edged his way past tapestries and carved wooden panels, eventually finding himself nearly tripping over a cluster of waist-high statues.

"What else?" the abbot enquired with a note of impatience.

"Servants of the Temple, going back many years."

"Quite so. Sister Mi-Hahn's role is an ancient one, although I'd say she is its most expert exponent. There is no scripture in this temple. No archive of ancient scrolls to pore over. We call this the Forest of Memory. This is our history, though it may fall to ruin and dust as the ages pass. The temple remembers, and preserves what is most important."

Upon reaching the centre of the tier the abbot came to a halt. The forest was not so dense here, creating a clearing of sorts. A number of pictures had been arranged in a circle, all portraits of varying age. "Welcome to your test, brother," the abbot said, raising his hands to gesture at the pictures before folding his arms. His face remained impassive as Vaelin's puzzled gaze tracked over the portraits.

"You . . . want me to paint something?" he ventured, drawing a disgusted sigh from the abbot.

"Of course I fucking don't. Look"—he nodded to the nearest portrait—"see, learn, reason. The temple has no need for those who can't think. Insight is the test here."

Vaelin went to the picture he had indicated. The image was clearly not Mi-Hahn's work, but was still highly accomplished. It depicted a thin-faced man somewhat shy of his fiftieth year. His expression was pinched, almost sour, conveying a sense of judgemental disappointment. However, Vaelin found the man's clothing more interesting than his face. Unlike most of the pictures, this one featured vibrant colours, none more so than the shade of green that dominated the thin-faced man's elaborate robe. It flowed around him in complex folds, an emerald cascade shot through with veins of gold and silver. *Emerald . . .* Vaelin's gaze returned to the subject's face. Was there a regal air to the narrow scowl of disappointment? A sense of ingrained superiority perhaps, worn by a man enveloped in a completely impractical emerald robe?

"An emperor?" he asked the abbot.

"Yes." The old man's voice held a note of respect, albeit grudging. "Hai-Shin, the last to ever sit the throne of the Emerald Empire."

"He came here?"

"Once, many years ago. No retinue, no guards, just turned up at the gate. Seems he had a dream and needed help divining its meaning."

"He came alone? I heard he was so pampered he never even walked on his own two feet."

"That's a widely believed pile of pig shit. It was long before my time, but when I first came here there was an ancient sister who remembered his visit. She said he walked well enough, and yes, despite the doggerel heaped upon his story since, he knew how to read. Although, the sister did think him something of a dullard. But, to be fair, it would've taken a political and military genius to prevent the empire's fall, and he was neither."

"And this dream of his?"

"Some lurid vision of impending disaster, most likely the fruit of the poppy pipe. It's often easy to mistake the effects of a drug for a missive from Heaven. Or maybe the temple really did send him a dream, it's impossible to know. In any event, he came here in search of guidance. Someone painted his portrait whilst the abbot told him something suitably cryptic. Apparently satisfied, he duly took his divine self off to oversee the series of disasters that led to the dissolution of the empire and the rise of the Merchant Realms. He was dead a few years later, poisoned by an overly ambitious cousin, so they say."

"If his visit here failed to save the empire, why is this significant?"

The abbot's only reply was an empty smile as he angled his head, arms still folded. Sighing, Vaelin turned his attention to the neighbouring picture, blinking in surprise as the face of the youth it depicted sounded a loud note of recognition. His face lacked the weathered lines of a veteran soldier, but the frown of concentration that had been captured as he raised a sword to an unseen enemy was unmistakable.

"Sho Tsai," Vaelin said. He knew from their visit to the High Temple that the general had studied here in his youth, but seeing him was still jarring, stirring images of Sherin's grief and accusation after the last wall fell in Keshin-Kho. *Did you see him die . . . ?*

"Perhaps our finest student," the abbot said. "You fought together, did you not?"

"Yes." *And we lost.* "He was a great warrior and a fine general, deserving of a better king."

"On that, at least, we can agree. I told him not to go but he didn't listen, as is the way with young men. Shitheads, the lot of them. But, in his case, I always knew the temple wouldn't be his home forever. From the moment he arrived at the gates, a half-starved orphan, I knew the time would come when his hunger for the world beyond these walls would take him from us."

"Did he complete the tests?"

The abbot shook his head, face growing sombre. "He stood where you are now, looking at his own array of images drawn from the temple's memory. It's my belief that he gained the insight it wanted for him, but instead of compelling him to climb to the final tier, it confirmed his desire to leave." The abbot's gaze slid to his right where another picture hung from the ropes, the smallest so far. "But at least his regard for the temple was enough to compel him to return when requested, although it took some urging from the Jade Princess."

Moving to the small picture, Vaelin saw it to be a charcoal sketch of only a few lines depicting an infant. The child was barely a month old by his reckoning, eyes open wide and cheeks bulging as its tiny lips curved in a smile. Another charcoal rendering was positioned just beyond, this one larger, depicting a boy of about ten holding a staff in a defensive stance. Vaelin felt another note of recognition as his eyes lingered on the boy's face, but it wasn't until he turned to the next image that realisation dawned. "Tsai Lin," he said. The youth was only a few years older than the boy with the staff, but his features were fast adopting the angular handsomeness that would come in manhood. "His father sent him here to be trained," Vaelin mused, noting the sword in Tsai Lin's hand.

"Look," the abbot said, the impatience returning to his voice. "See, learn, reason."

Vaelin spent some time looking at each picture in turn, finding little beyond what he had already discerned. The abbot clearly expected him to arrive at some kind of deduction, but all he saw were the faces of two men he knew and one he didn't. *Faces* . . . It was the first true note he had heard from the black-song since coming here, a note of singular importance that compelled him to look closer at each face. As he did so, he felt something else, another song rising to answer his own. It was far deeper than the black-song and carried a sense of vast age. The black-song shrank from it, becoming a small, tremulous whisper as the ancient song continued to sing.

The abbot and the Forest of Memory went away, banished by this new, implacable voice. Vaelin found himself staggering under the weight of it, the sensation of power entangled with boundless knowledge. Images swirled in his mind, a bare mountaintop beneath a red, smoke-blackened sky. A blizzard of ash blinded him for a second, and when it cleared, the mountaintop returned, this time with a five-tiered tower rising from its summit. The sky was mostly blue now, save for a circular cloud formation that swirled and coiled with unnatural energy. It was shot through with myriad colours, some dark, others bright. Light and dark hues coalesced as it continued to swirl, its energy becoming furious, the merging colours forming two distinct shapes. At first they were vague, shifting like smoke, but soon took on a more definite form.

The tiger and the wolf, Vaelin thought as the two shapes fought in the sky. They lashed at each other in a frenzied dance, one momentarily gaining an advantage over the other but never for long. The dance continued as the combatants descended, their contest swirling around the tower, which began to glow as if imbued by the energy of their battle. The glow built until the tower became a vertical bolt of shimmering white whereupon it burst. The tiger and the wolf were shredded by the explosion, blasted apart and scattered in an instant to leave the tower intact.

The voice and the images disappeared in an instant, Vaelin blinking and finding himself in the Forest of Memory once more. He was surprised to discover that he was still on his feet, his head ringing with the echo of the ancient song. "What was that?" he demanded of the abbot.

The old man wore a frown that spoke of mingled puzzlement and, more disconcertingly, envy. "Showed you something, did it?" he asked, and Vaelin understood he had no notion of what had just transpired. "What was it?"

"I don't know," Vaelin replied honestly. Shaking his head to clear the fading vestiges of the vision and the song, he looked again at the portraits. They seemed clearer now, more vital somehow, as if the ancient voice had allowed him to see them with new eyes and new understanding. For the first time it struck Vaelin that, whilst they shared a basic similarity, the resemblance between Sho Tsai and his son was not close. Vaelin might have assumed that Tsai Lin favoured his mother, but his fresh insight prodded him to look again at the long-dead emperor. *The eyes*, Vaelin thought, gaze flicking from Hai-Shin to the youth with the sword. *They have the same eyes.*

Moments from the journey to the Iron Steppe began to tumble through his mind, moments he now understood to be of great significance. *Third egg, that's what the other Scouts called him. Their captain had a third child when two is the norm in the Venerable Kingdom.* The Jade Princess back on the Steppe the night after they had caught up with her and Sherin, the appraisal in the ancient but youthful gaze as she regarded the apprentice officer. *He is a credit to you*, she told Sho Tsai. *The Servants of the Temple chose well.*

"Tsai Lin is not Sho Tsai's son," he said to the abbot. "Is he?"

The abbot replied with only a raised eyebrow, saying nothing as Vaelin looked at the pictures again. "The same eyes," he mused aloud, nodding first to the portrait of the youthful Tsai Lin then to the emperor. "The same blood. Tsai Lin carries the blood of the last ruler of the Emerald Empire."

This time the abbot raised both eyebrows, grunting in satisfaction. "And so insight finally arrives. Hai-Shin had no less than eight wives and over thirty children. Those who came to fight over the spoils of his fallen empire were scrupulous in hunting them down, all save one, an infant girl with a nursemaid of deep Heavenly convictions. She took the child to a nearby temple but the monks there knew she would never be safe in their care and so had her smuggled here. She grew, she married a suitable man summoned by the temple for the task. They had a son. In time he grew and married and fathered a son of his own, and so it went as the Merchant Kingdoms blossomed in their greed and sowed the seeds of their own destruction. We raised the emperor's heirs until the time came to allow one out into the world, one we knew could rebuild what was about to fall."

"You knew this was going to happen," Vaelin realised. "You knew the Stahlhast were coming."

"It has long been the role of the Temple of Spears to safeguard these lands and their people from dangers both internal and external. For centuries uncounted the temple has gathered unto itself those with skills and blessings deserving of the knowledge we impart. Those who will not abuse the power to kill, but employ it for the good of all. Amongst these chosen souls there have been a precious few with the power to glimpse the shifting shadows of the future. Added to that we had the dreams conveyed to Sister Mi-Hahn by the Jade Princess. Yes, we knew the Stahlhast would come."

"You didn't warn them, the Merchant Kings. You told them nothing, did you?"

"For something to be rebuilt, it must first be destroyed. The Merchant Realms are corrupt, rotten from head to foot. They were always destined to fall. If not to the Stahlhast then to their own venality. The Darkblade's horde will be the tide that washes them clean, and Tsai Lin will be the seed that grows a new empire in their place."

"Does he know?"

"The truth of his blood was told to him when he followed Sho Tsai's final command and returned here. But what a man hears is not always what he believes, or wishes to believe. Tsai Lin's lessons here produced hard answers. His regard for our order is stained with bitterness, probably even more so since the death of Sho Tsai, something that was not foreseen. He only came here because it was his father's last order, and he proved deaf to what I had to tell him. He will not heed my words, but he will heed yours. He will know them as truth, as if he heard it from his own father."

"And then what? Do you have any notion of what the Darkblade has built in the north? It's not some cleansing tide, it's a mass of believers in thrall to a living god, and it grows with every conquest. How many will die because of the decades you spent in secret scheming?" The abbot's face remained impassive as Vaelin advanced, looming over him. The anger he felt had nothing to do with the black-song; this came from an older place. "Do you imagine yourselves to be unique in the world? You are not. I have met your kind before. I was raised by your kind. Wallowing in secrets, deluding yourself about your own wisdom, your own grand foresight that will only bring death and ruin to what you intend to save."

"Were your people not saved?" the abbot enquired, staring up at Vaelin with uncowed eyes.

"Yes, they saved themselves and died by the thousands doing it. Your people will die by the millions." He turned and started towards the stairwell to the lower tiers, pushing his way through the mass of paper without care for any damage he might cause. "I'm done playing games in this temple of liars, and I advise that you tell your brothers to raise no hand against me."

"And what will you do when you leave?" the abbot called after him. "What will the poison inside you make you do?"

Vaelin came to a halt, jaw clenching and pulse pounding as he fought his rage. "You promised a cure," he grated, refusing to turn around. "I've seen no sign of it."

"You haven't ascended to the final tier." Paper rustled as the abbot came to his side. "Face and overcome what awaits you there, and the temple's promise will be fulfilled."

Vaelin's hands itched as he stood there, eyes still closed. If he opened them to regard the abbot's unafraid, knowing face, he feared what he might do. "Then let's get it over with," he said, turning around.

"Not yet." Paper rustled afresh as the abbot made his way to the exit. "The hour grows late and an old man needs his dinner. Wait a few days; all should be ready then."

CHAPTER TEN

He found a once again freshly bruised but triumphant Cho-ka in the meal hall, happily chomping his way through a roasted pig's trotter in between recounting the details of his victory in the third tier. "Turns out choosing a weapon was the point," he said. "Or rather, not choosing one. The little fucker was an expert in fending off men armed with a blade, not so expert when it came to a no-holds-barred brawl. So I just walked in and started swinging punches." He bit down on the trotter and winced a little, drawing back to rub at his jaw. "Still knew plenty of tricks though, but so did I. Not many can beat a Green Viper when it comes to a lawless scrap."

He wiped his mouth with his sleeve and leaned closer, voice lowered. "What's waiting for me in the next tier? Come on, lord," he added in response to Vaelin's frown. "I told you."

"I think it'll be different for you," Vaelin replied. "But, most likely the abbot will show you some pictures and you'll try to make sense of them. If he likes your answer, you get to ascend."

"That's all?" Cho-ka laughed and returned his attention to the half-gnawed trotter. "Sounds like a piece of piss."

◆ ◆ ◆

The next few days were spent in impatient stalking of the temple whilst being mostly ignored by its inhabitants. Vaelin's visits to the artisans' work-shops were brief and quickly abandoned when he found their skills failed to reignite his interest. Mi-Hahn was something of an exception. She had taken to leaving her dwelling on a daily basis, drawing surprised glances from her brothers and sisters as she set forth laden with newly mounted canvases and jars brimming with freshly mixed paint. Catching sight of her struggling to climb the steps to the top of the wall, Vaelin relieved her of the canvases and followed her to the battlement. He sat and watched her paint the partially misted landscape below for the next hour, his fascination in her abilities overcoming his otherwise sour mood of pensive expectation.

"Does your sister paint mountains?" Mi-Hahn asked, adding a few flecks of bluish grey to the summit of a ridgeline. She remained a largely silent companion, although he noted she became more talkative when the brothers stationed on the wall wandered out of earshot.

"She paints all manner of things," Vaelin replied. "But people were always her preferred subject." The words brought to mind the last portrait he had seen Alornis paint, three years ago just before she announced her intention to return to Varinshold. He had known it was coming but still the ache of separation lingered even now. She had fought tears that day, keeping her back to him as she stepped away from the painting, words forced and choked when she asked what he thought. He had thought of replying with various witticisms as he surveyed the man gazing at him from the painting, *He was never so sober* chief amongst them. But they would have been lies, attempts to deflect the emotions she had stirred in him. *Alucius was a great man*, he had said instead. *Though many didn't know it, even him. Now, everyone will.*

She had turned and pressed herself against him, slender shoulders moving in his arms as she wept. *I can't stay here*, she told him through her tears. *You know that, don't you? I've been hiding in the Reaches for too long, and so have you. I wallow in paint whilst you distract yourself endlessly hunting outlaws. We both need to face the world once more.*

The scrape of charcoal on paper brought him back to the present where he found Mi-Hahn had temporarily abandoned her painting for a sketch. Her face showed the same deep concentration he had seen on the second tier, and as her charcoal stick moved, blurring at times as her strokes grew more urgent, he felt the familiar tug at his mind. It wasn't as painful as before, in fact it wasn't truly painful at all, instead provoking an upsurge of sorrow that only grew when her charcoal halted and she came closer to show him her sketch.

"You miss her greatly," she said. "Perhaps this will make you miss her less."

His sister's face blurred as he blinked tears. The image was perfect, capturing the moment he had said goodbye to her at the harbour. Her expression mingled trepidation with hope, and not a little sadness. *I'll write*, she said. *Every week*. And she had.

"Thank you," he told Mi-Hahn in a hoarse rasp, and consigned the sketch to the folds of his robe.

"I see only what my Blessing allows," she said. "Mostly the past, very rarely the future, so I do not know what awaits you. But I feel certain you will see your sister's face again."

Vaelin found his gaze drawn to the temple, his eyes tracking over its angled roofs to the uppermost tier. "That," he said, "worries me more than anything else."

◆ ◆ ◆

It was the next day when the abbot called him to the final tier. As Vaelin made his way through the Forest of Memory, he paused at the sight of a picture in the clearing where the abbot had shown him the set of portraits. They were gone now, replaced with a single image. It was unmistakably Mi-Hahn's work, an ink rendering of what appeared to be a bonfire. The smoke and flame were depicted with her typical economy of line but clarity of meaning, as was the charred and slumped shape of a kneeling man amidst the flames. Like the portraits in the sister's dwelling, the central image was surrounded by Far Western script. The characters were arranged in a cloud that merged with the smoke arising from the flames. Before moving on, Vaelin noted a small but deliberate rip in the picture's lower edge, the paper creased and rumpled as if someone had tried to tear it apart.

He was unsurprised to find the abbot waiting in the fifth tier, but puzzled to see that he wasn't alone. The top tier of the Temple of Spears was about twenty feet square and open to the elements on all sides. Cho-ka knelt in the centre of the floor with his head bowed whilst the abbot stood with his back turned, his long hair whipping in the stiff, icy wind sweeping in from the surrounding mountains.

"Much to my disappointment," the abbot said, not turning as he gestured at Cho-ka's kneeling form, "the temple has seen fit to allow this lawless cur the chance to be confirmed as a Brother of the Spear."

Cho-ka gave no reaction, though when Vaelin came to stand at his side, he noted the clenched rigidity of the outlaw's body. His eyes were firmly closed and nostrils flared as he drew rapid breaths. *His father*, Vaelin thought, recalling the image of the burning man from the tier below. *Burned for his books.* "What did you do to him?" he asked the abbot, not bothering to keep the anger from his voice.

"What the temple required." The abbot's voice was no less angry, lacking any note of guilt or regret. "This is what the temple does. You needed to know your purpose in these lands. He needed to know the consequences of failing to fulfil his."

The abbot turned, unfolding his arms to reveal a small glass bottle in his hand. Holding it up to the light Vaelin saw it to contain a clear, viscous liquid. "The cure you were promised," he said. "Brother Kish-an possesses a blessing that gives him remarkable insight into the effects of various compounds when properly mixed. One drop of this a day and the monster inside you will be tamed. It won't kill it, but it will make it your servant. And, unlike the drug this dog nearly killed you with, you will suffer no ill effects from drinking it." He fell silent, eyes narrowed in appraisal as he watched Vaelin fight the urge to rush forward and snatch the bottle from his hand. "The temple's gift to you," the abbot went on, "once you complete the final test."

With the abbot's free hand he reached behind his back, drawing forth a plain, straight-bladed dagger. A ring of well-honed steel sounded as the abbot tossed the dagger onto the flat slate tiles between Vaelin and Cho-ka. "Fight," he instructed.

Vaelin's gaze snapped from the dagger to Cho-ka, still kneeling with his eyes closed.

"What is this?" Vaelin demanded of the abbot.

"Two begin the journey, only one can finish it." The abbot nodded at the dagger. "Fight. When one body is cast from the top of this temple the victor will be confirmed."

Rituals, Vaelin recalled. *This temple is a place that binds us in ritual.* He let out a disgusted laugh and shook his head. "I care nothing for your temple or its ancient superstitions." He stepped forward, gesturing to the bottle in the abbot's hand. "Give that to me."

The abbot exhibited no fear as Vaelin approached, merely blinking. "I couldn't give the smallest shit for what you care about," he said. "And neither could the temple." His placidity faded as he stepped closer, lips forming a snarl. "Fight."

"No." Vaelin began to reach for the bottle, aware that his anger was compelling him to an unwise action but finding it irresistible. He understood Tsai Lin's resentment of this place now, his disregard for the abbot's words. In some ways Vaelin thought the Temple of Spears worse than the Sixth Order, for at least they had changed, slowly and in the face of catastrophe it was true, but still they had changed. Those who secluded themselves on this mountaintop continued to cling to ancient custom, inflicting suffering and even death on their adherents whilst a mass slaughter raged beyond their walls.

"Just give it to me, old man," he hissed as his hand closed on the bottle. "Or I *will* take it, and the temple will have its corpse, but it won't be either of us."

From behind came the scrape of steel on slate, Vaelin whirling in time to block the thrust Cho-ka aimed at his heart. His hands closed on the outlaw's wrists, clamping tight as Vaelin stared into Cho-ka's desperate visage. "What are you doing?"

"What I have to." Cho-ka lashed out with a kick, Vaelin turning to avoid most of the force, but the impact on his hip was enough to jar the wrist from his grasp. He ducked under the outlaw's second thrust then backed away from repeated slashes as Cho-ka chased him to the edge of the tier.

"Stop this!" Vaelin shouted, sidestepping another thrust and driving his shoulder into Cho-ka's flank, sending him into a pillar. Grunting, Cho-ka renewed his attack, reversing his grip on the dagger and crouching to duck under Vaelin's blocking arms to stab at his midriff. Vaelin managed to dodge the dagger's point but the blade sliced through his robes to score his skin, birthing a stinging pain. His reaction was born of decades of experience, the reflex of one tuned to survival through more fights than he could easily remember. Sinking to one knee, he looped his arm under Cho-ka's knife hand, trapping it whilst driving a blow into the outlaw's temple. As Cho-ka's gaze lost focus, Vaelin jerked him closer, twisting his arm at the precise angle to loosen the grip on the dagger, sending it clattering to the tiles. Vaelin drew his fist back for another blow but Cho-ka, ever the seasoned scrapper, was quick to recover his wits, pulling away to allow the fist to graze his head before replying with a punch of his own.

Vaelin grunted as the fist drove into his ribs, suffering another blow before bringing his knee up into Cho-ka's midriff. The outlaw doubled over with the force of it, but retained sufficient strength to respond by snapping his head up, the crown connecting painfully with Vaelin's chin. They reeled about the tier in an ugly dance of punch and counterpunch, Vaelin repeatedly failing to bring Cho-ka down with kicks to his legs. For his part, the outlaw employed every trick he had learned over the course of an extensive criminal career to break Vaelin's grip on his wrist. Vaelin jerked his head clear of attempts to gouge at his eyes or press a thumb into his jugular. When Cho-ka resorted to biting his other arm, he decided it was time to end this dance.

Allowing another blow to land on his jaw, he feigned a moment of confusion, loosening his grip just enough for Cho-ka to draw back, clearly intending to tear free and dive for the dagger, which lay only a few paces away. Vaelin sank low, lashing out with his foot to trip the outlaw, sending him flat onto his face. Pinning him to the floor with his greater bulk, Vaelin clamped an arm around his neck and dragged him to his feet.

"Why?" he demanded, grunting with the effort of manoeuvring the outlaw to the edge of the tier. "What did he promise you?"

Cho-ka's reply was a backward jerk of his head, and Vaelin tasted blood as the man's skull impacted on his lips. His grip remained strong, however, and within seconds the outlaw's toes were tapping on the edge of the floor. The ground below seemed very far away and the wind threatened to propel them both into the void.

"Tell me!" Vaelin demanded, tightening his hold. "Why save my life only to try and take it?"

"My father . . ." The words emerged in a strangled whisper, but the depth of sorrow and guilt they held was enough for Vaelin to stop short of casting Cho-ka from the tier. "Now . . . he will not be . . . ashamed . . ."

The sketch of the man burning in the fire. The book collector beneath the cloud of words like smoke, carried up to Heaven's embrace. "You think he sees you," Vaelin said. "You think he looks down from Heaven and sees what you are?"

"I know it. I've always known it. But the sister's picture . . . made it real. You need to leave this temple and find the heir to the Emerald Empire, and I need to die to make it happen."

"You put too much stock in this liar's word." Vaelin released his grip, stepping back as Cho-ka fell to his knees.

"I felt it," Cho-ka insisted in a breathless rasp, jabbing a finger to his head. "In here. This is what must happen, lord."

Vaelin looked at the abbot, still standing with the bottle in his grasp, face as expressionless as before. The temptation to wrest the cure from him had gone now, as had Vaelin's anger. *I'll kill but I won't murder.* A promise he had made to himself so many years ago. A promise he had kept, regardless of the cost.

"Here," he said, kicking the fallen dagger. It skittered to a halt before Cho-ka's kneeling form. He stared at it for a heartbeat before his eyes snapped up to meet Vaelin's. "Do it," Vaelin told him, spreading his arms. "If the temple demands blood, it can have mine."

Doubt warred with resolve on Cho-ka's face as he reached for the dagger with a shaking hand, slowly climbing to his feet. "He said it had to be me . . ."

"A pox on what that old bastard said!" Vaelin stared into Cho-ka's fear-bright eyes. "He lies. They all do, these servants of things unseen. Long ago I learned that prophecy is always built on shifting sands and destiny an illusion used to banish fear of the chaos that is life. I trust what I know. I've seen what waits on the other side of death so I know it's always better to cling to life. But," he sighed, shoulders sagging in resignation, "I also know that I have made myself a monster, and this world should be spared its violence." He straightened and slapped a hand to his chest. "Come, brother. Finish it."

Cho-ka looked at the knife in his hand then at the abbot, apparently finding no answer in either. Gritting his teeth, he lowered the weapon, letting it clatter to the floor once more. "It has to be one of us," he murmured and stepped towards the edge of the tier. Vaelin lunged for him, catching hold of his forearm as he leapt. Vaelin wrapped his free arm around a pillar as Cho-ka's weight threatened to drag them both over the side.

"Are you mad?" he shouted, staring down into Cho-ka's suddenly bleached features. His resolve had abruptly vanished, replaced by unalloyed terror as he darted a look at the ground below.

"I . . . think so, lord," he replied with a weak smile. "Or I was." He glanced again at the drop below his dangling feet and let out a fearful yelp. "That's quite a distance."

Grunting, Vaelin hauled the outlaw up until he could grasp the tier's edge and drag himself the rest of the way. Vaelin sank down next to him and they spent a few moments panting in relieved exhaustion, the breaths eventually giving way to laughter. Their humour, however, faded when the abbot's shadow fell across them, a hard frown of disappointment on his brow.

"It seems," he sighed, tossing the small bottle into Vaelin's grasp, "the temple has use for both of you."

"But," Cho-ka said, squinting in bemusement, "we both failed."

"Willingness to kill and willingness to die. That is what the temple requires." He turned about and started for the stairwell. "Eat and rest well tonight. Tomorrow, we leave."

PART II

From the moment we are born we are but vessels of destiny.
The storms of life wear away the outer shell of our being to reveal the
truth of who we have always been and where we have always been going.

—INTRODUCTION TO "COLLECTED MUSINGS" BY THE MOST
ESTEEMED KUAN-SHI, PHILOSOPHER AND POET, EMERALD EMPIRE,
C. LATE FIRST CENTURY OF THE DIVINE DYNASTY

Obvar's Account

"Why don't you kill me?"

I ignored her question, it being so often repeated as to have lost any real meaning. It had become something of a ritual between us, the words spoken either on waking or when I returned to my tent after a day in the Darkblade's service. Come nightfall, Mother Wehn would ask the same question. Lately, the fear had faded from her voice almost entirely, replaced by a dull lassitude that did little to endear her to me. I found I much preferred the defiant woman I had met in the temple in Keshin-Kho.

I sighed as I sank onto the campstool, an ornate furnishing looted from the tent of the fool general who had tried to oppose us north of Daiszhen-Khi. The man had survived the disaster he had ordained for his troops, more through luck than any martial skill, but Kehlbrand hadn't felt him worthy of recruitment into the ranks of the Redeemed. The general's ineptitude aroused my contempt to the degree that I had expressed no pleas for mercy when the fellow was forced to his knees beneath the tulwar. However, I did find some measure of admiration for his refusal to beg.

"Are you hurt?" Mother Wehn asked me, seeing how I grimaced as I divested myself of the hauberk's red-lacquered armour. I saw some concern in her gaze as she rose from the mats where she spent most days attempting to meditate. I assume it stemmed more from fear at losing her sole protector than any genuine regard.

"Street fighting is dog's work," I muttered, tossing the hauberk aside. But then, *I added inwardly*, I am but a dog.

"You're bleeding." *She crouched to inspect the red stain on my shirt, the product of a wound to the right side of my back I didn't recall receiving. The final struggle amidst the streets of Daiszhen-Khi had been a fierce and confusing frenzy, the resistance of the townsfolk stirring a surprised pride from the former owner of this body. Although the town's defenses were in a poor state of repair, the winding, close-packed streets and numerous obstructing waterways created a maze perfect for ambush and barricade. With most of the soldiers slain on the field days before, the burden of opposing the horde had fallen on the civilian population. The duly appointed governor had apparently found a conveniently pressing matter in the south some weeks ago, leaving command in the hands of his deputy. When eventually captured, he was revealed as a former bookkeeper with no prior experience of soldiering. Nonetheless, his inventive contrivances, coupled with the sacrificial will of his compatriots, managed to embroil the horde in three bloody days of costly combat. Upon capture the deputy governor had also proven to be one of those souls with an ingrained immunity to the lure of the Darkblade's love. Not without regret, Kehlbrand ordered his head taken and impaled along with the few hundred others now arrayed alongside the canal.*

"Must've been that skinny bastard with the carving knife," I muttered, raising an arm to allow her to inspect the wound. *The fellow had launched himself from a second-storey window as my company passed beneath, latching onto my back and stabbing away with wanton abandon until one of the Redeemed cut him down.*

"It requires stitches." *Mother Wehn moved to retrieve the canvas bundle that held her various surgical instruments and healing curatives. This had become another ritual between us; her tending to my so-far-minor wounds after every slaughter. Like any ritual it required an exchange of words.*

"How many died?" *she asked, ignoring my aggressive grunt as she used rice spirit to swab the blood from the wound.* "How many were taken?"

"Four thousand, six hundred and ninety-two dead," I replied, *teeth gritted as she squeezed the lips of the wound to insert the needle.* "Eight hundred and thirty-eight captives." *Such numerical precision was another part of the ritual, the product of the blessing obtained by Sho Tsai when Kehlbrand forced his hand to the stone. I could now provide a full and accurate count of any grouping with a single glance, whilst also calculating the circumference of a circle or area of a square with no effort at all.*

"So few captives?" she asked.

"Most of the women and children were taken away over the last few days. Packed into barges and gone south as far as they can get." I closed my eyes against the pain as the needle did its work. *"It seems these people gave their lives to secure the escape of their loved ones."*

"Admirable." She tugged the thread tight and bit through it before dousing the wound with another splash of spirit. "Wouldn't you say?"

There was a deeper question in her eyes as she drew back, a sense of searching for something beyond the bitter, fatigued mask of the man before her. "He's not coming back," I told her. Although, there's part of him that can hear you well enough. *This I left unsaid. It was better if she thought all remnants of Sho Tsai gone for good. Better for me, at least.*

She lowered her gaze, eyes closed as a sigh of pure sorrow escaped her lips, the question following soon after. "Why don't you kill me?"

I had only one answer for her, the same answer I had given every day since the horde began its southward march. "I don't know."

◆ ◆ ◆

Kehlbrand had Daiszhen-Khi burned to the ground the next day, a spectacle watched by a dozen captives who had been spared despite proving themselves immune to his godly wiles. They were set free soon after, each given a horse and provisions and told to go wherever they wished. Of course, they all galloped south as soon as their tethers were cut, carrying forth the fate of any town or city that chose to contest the Darkblade's advance. The tale must have spread far and fast, for the next three towns we encountered were all but empty save for a few elderly souls too infirm to join the growing exodus of beggared wretches fleeing the barbarian horde.

"How many?" Kehlbrand asked, gesturing to the dusty haze in the distance beneath which a disordered mob of humanity trudged another weary mile. He had led a scouting party ahead of the horde for several miles, twenty of his most trusted saddle brothers. They were all men I had known for over a decade, warriors I had fought alongside, even saved a few. I can't claim a particular fondness for any of them, but they had still been my brothers in the Hast who had once shown me the respect I was due. Now they ignored me, shunning every glance as if it might carry some manner of curse. They knew

who lived behind this face, and yet still saw only a southlander. It made me want to kill them very badly, and if not for Kehlbrand's presence I surely would have.

"Fifty-nine thousand, seven hundred and twenty-nine," I said. "That I can see."

Kehlbrand laughed, displaying his usual delight in my numerical gift. A few days before, he had several bundles of arrows scattered onto the floor of his tent and had me count them, setting a trio of captives to work checking the answer. When the three of them disagreed on the number, he had them stand and watch as he counted each arrow himself, a process requiring a two-hour interval after which he arrived at the answer I had given him. "It's a pity," he had said, shaking his head in regret, "that your inability to accept the Darkblade's love also seems to have addled your wits." With that, he had them handed over to the Tuhla for one of their amusements, typically involving wagering their spoils on the outcome of a contest between a captive and a pack of starved dogs.

"Why do they flee so?" Kehlbrand wondered now, watching the dusty progression. "Do they not know I have come to save them?"

Recently, when he adopted a rhetorical tone it had become increasingly difficult to distinguish between humour and sincerity. As a consequence, I found it wise not to offer a response at such times, opting instead to placidly await whatever insight or pronouncement that was sure to follow. This was a lesson one of my former saddle brothers had evidently failed to learn.

"Does something amuse you, Timurik?" Kehlbrand asked, casting a sideways glance at the veteran warrior on his left, freezing the smirk on his face. Next to me, Timurik was probably the most feared fighter amongst the Darkblade's saddle brothers, an experienced war-band leader who had won considerable renown at the Three Rivers and countless lesser battles. Now he strove not to quail like a child beneath the glare of his father's wrath.

"Darkblade?" was his only answer, delivered after a prolonged pause and several darted glances at his brothers, none whom felt obliged to meet his eye.

"Does the plight of these unfortunates make you laugh?" Kehlbrand asked, voice soft and sincere with genuine curiosity. He nudged his horse closer to Timurik, staring into his scarred, lean features with implacable insistence. "Do you think it right and proper for so many to be denied the deliverance I have come to offer?"

I should have enjoyed this moment, seeing the humbling of one who had *shunned me; instead I felt only a dull pity. Timurik was a snide bastard who gloried in slaughter and was always first to lay claim to the loot. But he also never lacked in courage and hadn't faltered at my side. Now, he was likely to meet his end for a mistimed smirk.*

"No," Timurik coughed, moulding his face into as neutral a mask as he could. "No, Darkblade, I do not."

"That is good." Kehlbrand sat back in the saddle, turning once again to the distant host. "I would know why they shun me so. Bring me"—he paused for an instant of contemplation—"a dozen, so that they may enlighten me. Just you, Timurik," he added as the warrior turned to summon more riders to his side. "Just you."

Timurik's features tensed for a second, in either fear or a final spasm of defiance. I couldn't tell which and the expression was soon gone in any case. "Darkblade," he said with a formal nod before kicking his horse into a gallop and speeding away towards the fleeing mob.

"If threats don't work," Kehlbrand called after him, "you could always tell them a joke!"

Watching the rider and horse merge into the dark mass of trudging humanity, Kehlbrand's brow creased into a thoughtful frown. "This new emperor, Obvar," he said. "This Tsai Lin of apparently lowly rank but royal blood, how would he treat these fleeing unfortunates, do you think?"

"With the weakness of compassion," I replied, shrugging.

"That is a Stahlhast answer, old friend. I require a father's answer."

I felt the small angry ball of Sho Tsai's remnant stir within me, coiling tighter in stern refusal to offer any insight. However, I was able to discern a few tendrils of emotion amongst the fury and contempt.

"He will do what he can to aid them," I said, "but possesses enough of a soldier's heart to know that retreat is his best option, for now. He will continue south and try to gather strength before opposing us."

"With the aid of the Temple of Spears, no doubt." Kehlbrand gave a rueful sigh. "I was warned they would be a complication. It's why I was forced to show our hand at Keshin-Kho when the Merchant King sent the Red Scouts in search of the Jade Princess. An attempt to extinguish the man whose face you wear. I knew he was an agent of the temple, but not the true nature of his agency. It seems I aimed an arrow at the wrong target. Still, I find that the unexpected always brings opportunity."

He fell to silence and had us wait for the hour it took to conclude that *Timurik was not going to return with his dozen captives. "In the morning," he told me as we began the journey back to the encampment, "take your Redeemed and force march them south-east of these misguided souls. I'll have the Hast and the Tuhla drive them towards you. Spare about half, if you can. It would be more, but I can't very well let the death of one of my most trusted saddle brothers go unpunished, can I?"*

◆ ◆ ◆

I never discovered where Kehlbrand found Uhlkar and concluded at my first sight of him that I never wanted to know. The many scars that marked his frame, still stick thin and frail despite recent provision of copious food and the care of the best healers, bespoke a life filled with suffering and privation. He had appeared amongst the Darkblade's growing cluster of Divinely Blooded children after the burning of Diaszhen-Khi and even those little horrors gave him a wide berth. Although the boy's scars were ugly, his face was the most off-putting aspect of his appearance, so denuded of flesh it was effectively just a skull with a thin covering of bleached skin and two overlarge eyes staring out from pitlike sockets. For one raised amongst the Stahlhast where strength and fortitude were the highest virtues, such a sickly and seemingly pathetic soul aroused considerable disgust. However, my remade self no longer allowed refuge in basic emotions, and I knew that my repugnance was merely a mask for a shameful measure of fear. Simply put, this emaciated, wasted boy with his skull face terrified me.

"He plays, you say?" Kehlbrand asked, smiling fondly at the boy as he crouched in front of him.

"Yes." Uhlkar spoke in a faint, reedy voice that reminded me of the tuneless product of a poorly carved flute. Unlike the other blessed brats, he never addressed Kehlbrand by any reverently inflected title, or even with particular respect. His answers were prompt and toneless, but often cryptic. Kehlbrand, however, never seemed to mind the boy's lack of adoration and confused utterances, regarding him with the fond aspect I remembered from our youth when he occasionally took a liking to the runtier curs roving our camp.

"And what does he play?" he asked the boy, brows raised in sincere curiosity.

"War, with ships. He thinks they're real sometimes. Other times he knows they're not and this makes him sad and angry, but never for very long."

"Good. Well done, Uhlkar." Kehlbrand held up a sugared nut, which the

boy swiftly snatched and crammed into his mouth. "And the bad man? The man I told you to look for?"

"Not here." Uhlkar shrugged, the threadlike muscles of his bleached face working as he chewed on the nut. "So he's not there either. Needs to be here so he can be there. Don't see him otherwise."

"And the nice lady? The one who looks like me."

"Was here and there, talking to him about something." I felt an ignominious lurch in my chest as Uhlkar's gaze swung towards me. His eyes were free of any emotion, but I couldn't help but imbue his words with a sense of accusation. "Don't know what," he went on, blinking as he refocused his overlarge eyes on Kehlbrand. "It was far away and they were old. But she's not here now too, like the bad man, so not there either."

"Not here, like the bad man," Kehlbrand repeated softly, face darkening. "So, he's found her again." He rose, patting Uhlkar on the head and handing him another treat. "Good boy. Go and play now."

After the boy departed the tent, Kehlbrand sank onto his mats, reaching for a finely engraved crystal goblet filled with wine of excellent quality. Conquest had made the horde rich in loot as well as recruits. I was the only other soul present in Kehlbrand's voluminous tent. The further we marched the less the Darkblade had need of counsel. There were no longer any gatherings of Skeltir, Tuhla chieftains or Redeemed commanders. Nor any effort to seek advice from knowledgeable servants. After all, why would a god require the insight of others?

"What do you imagine you were discussing with my sister?" Kehlbrand asked.

"Discussing, Darkblade?"

"Don't play the fool, Obvar. It's tiresome. He has glimpses of the future, you know this. In one of those visions he saw you and Luralyn talking. What could it have been about?"

"We always had little to say to each other in the past. I find it hard to credit we would have much to say in the future. The boy is plainly wrong in the head, in any case. If I didn't sense the Divine Blood in him I'd call his visions the riddles of a deranged mind."

"Deranged he is, and riddles they are, but useful nonetheless."

"Useful, Darkblade?"

"He said you were old, you and Luralyn. It speaks well of my victory if you have both survived into old age, don't you think? Also, my sister's eventual salvation and return to her brother's embrace. As I was promised . . ." His words faded as his gaze slipped to the dark shape behind a silk curtain at the far end of the tent. He had explained its presence amongst the horde by pointing to the need for more Divinely Blooded servants, but I suspected it stemmed from a primal desire not to be separated from the source of his power. His features remained impassive as he contemplated the indistinct silhouette before slowly turning back to me, voice dull and preoccupied.

"Before that can happen we have many other kingdoms to conquer, once we're done with this one. What do your scouts tell you of the Merchant King's preparations?"

It had been four weeks since the destruction of Daiszhen-Khi, time enough for the Darkblade's host to advance over a hundred miles into the heart of the Venerable Kingdom. Opposition had been scattered, but often fierce when encountered. Isolated garrison towns barred their gates and refused offers of mercy, suffering dire consequences when the Redeemed boiled over their walls in numbers too great to contest. The host had grown by a fifth over the course of the preceding month, swelling the ranks of Redeemed, often with recruits lacking any training or martial ability. My efforts to school them were frustrated by the need to keep marching, meaning I commanded a mob of fanatics rather than a true army. It raised severe doubts as to their performance should we face disciplined opposition.

"Still south of the westward canal," I said. "But growing in number. Mostly half-trained conscripts by all accounts, but some mercenary Sehtaku hired from the Free Cantons too. And we shouldn't forget that the Merchant King also retains a good number of regulars; they didn't all perish at Keshin-Kho."

"Two questions, old friend," he said, sipping wine with an air of distracted calculation, putting me in mind of a man forced to contemplate trivia instead of more interesting matters. "What would Obvar do? And, what would General Sho Tsai do?" His gaze narrowed above the raised goblet when I didn't answer immediately. "He is still in there, isn't he? Some part of him at least."

His gift, I reminded myself. The song only he can hear. It tells him much. "A small part," I admitted.

"And what does he tell you?"

In fact, the remnant of Sho Tsai's consciousness rarely consented to communicate anything to me beyond the occasional swell of disgust or rage, *although he sometimes leached a small current of concern when in Mother Wehn's company. "Manoeuvre," I said, trusting more to intuition than any wisdom from the man who once owned this body. "Send the Tuhla to harry their flanks and supply lines. Despatch large contingents east and west to compel the Merchant King to split his forces then strike at each in turn, wear them down through a series of skirmishes and smaller battles. Eventually, they'll have to hide in their fortresses, and the road to Muzan-Khi will lie open."*

"Eventually," Kehlbrand repeated in a sigh. "Not a word I'm fond of, old friend. And Obvar, what is his counsel?"

"March for Muzan-Khi with all our strength, gathering more Redeemed along the way. Lian Sha will have to oppose us with every soldier in his army."

"Thereby bringing about a great and terrible battle for the capital of the Venerable Kingdom, eh? The entire matter settled in one glorious, blood-soaked day. That's the Obvar I remember." He drained his goblet and rose, laughing as he put a hand on my neck, grip fierce with brotherly affection. "Good to have you back. I had begun to wonder if that nun had drained your spirit as well as your balls."

He smiled, feeling me tense under his grip. I'd told him nothing of Mother Wehn's continued survival, striving to keep her from my thoughts at every meeting. Of course, it had all been fruitless.

"You puzzle me, old friend," he said. "All the beauty we have gathered in this march, all the willing young flesh who would like nothing more than to please the Darkblade's most favoured general, and yet you spend your nights with a southland nun. One who," he added in a more serious tone, "has yet to answer the question I put to all her kind."

"She will," I said, my voice filled with a conviction I didn't feel. "If you wish it."

"I don't like it when you lie to me. A man shouldn't lie to his god." All trace of humour had disappeared now, leaving only the intent face of a man I hadn't known until my reawakening. Or was this always his true face? *I wondered as my mind scrambled to form a reply that might spare Mother Wehn's life.* All through the years we shared, was he just waiting for the chance to throw away his mask?

In any event, he spared me the effort and terror that would come from speaking another lie, squeezing my neck once more before stepping away. "Keep her, brother," he said. "If that's your wish. A small indulgence for the architect of my coming victory. Spread the word to every Skeltir and chieftain, tomorrow we strike camp and march for Muzan-Khi, the Darkblade being keen his new subjects do not suffer the horrors of a prolonged war. You'll get your bloody day, Obvar; just be sure to win it for me."

◆ ◆ ◆

"So, I am to be spared by virtue of your false god's whim."

We lay in darkness, together but apart, as had become our custom. She on the comfortable bed I had procured for her from yet another mound of spoils, me on the leather and fur mats I had known from birth. Despite Kehlbrand's assumptions, I had never laid a hand on her, nor any other woman since waking in this body. Although lust still stirred within me, it was a small flickering itch, more an annoyance than a desire to be indulged.

"Not a whim," I said. My voice sounded tired even to my own ears, the day having been spent in preparation for the coming march, but sleep was elusive. So many thoughts crowded my head it felt as if it might burst from within. Such feelings had mostly been absent from my previous life, stirring nostalgia for simpler times and less sympathy for Mother Wehn than she deserved. Besides, I had never enjoyed any skill in voicing comforting lies. "You are his insurance against my failure," I told her. "I fail and you die. It seems my undying loyalty is no longer enough. He imagines us to be . . . lovers."

The resultant silence was briefer than I expected, a testament to her courage, although her voice possessed the thick quality of one forcing words through a barrier of fear. "Then fail. Orchestrate his defeat and cleanse this world of him."

"He can hear any lie, sense every deception. He will kill me, after he has taken a long time in killing you."

Another pause, longer than the first, her voice yet more strained as she pushed out further words. "Then kill me now. Remove his hold over you . . . Or the hold he imagines he has."

I shifted, turning to regard her vague, shadowy form on the bed. She lay on her back, rigid with expectation, then shuddered as I let out a faint, bitter laugh.

"It's so easy for you to think me a beast," I said. "A savage wearing the body of a civilised man. But I am not a beast and my people are not savages. There once was greatness in us, but it has been corrupted. Yes, we were fierce, cruel at times, but no more so than the greed-obsessed southlanders. There is no renown in slaughter for its own sake. No greatness in the death of children or *fleeing peasants. He is making us a scourge upon this world, and I will not have that."*

"You intend to kill your god?"

"He is not my god. His divinity is a lie worse than any of the priests' deceitful babbling. As for killing him, I labour to keep all such notions from my thoughts, for fear he might hear them. I'm not sure he can be killed, not by my hand at least. Something protects him, guides him. The stone..." I trailed off, mention of the stone always provoking painful remembrance of my demise and the being that had snared my tumbling soul. You will feed me...

"Brother?" A soft, tremulous whisper in the dark.

"Don't call me that," I said, turning away from her. "My name is Obvar; use it. And tomorrow you might as well start showing yourself outside this tent. Find something useful to do, tend the wounded. Anything but sit here and wallow in your fears. It irks me."

Silence descended and I finally began to feel the tug of sleep's embrace, broken by a whisper. "Mai." Her voice was faint but I could hear the gratitude in it.

"What?" I muttered back.

"My name, before I was called to the High Temple to serve the Jade Princess. Mai Wehn."

I pulled my furs over me, sleep momentarily postponed by the promise I sensed in her words. "Get some sleep, Mai Wehn," I said. "Tomorrow you and I will discuss the Jade Princess in greater detail, including everything you haven't yet told me."

◆　◆　◆

I learned later that Lian Sha had chosen to name his grand army the Heavenly Host, conscripting every monk and priest he could lay hands on to continually douse each step of their northern march with blessings. The Merchant King, or whichever unfortunate soul he had placed in command of his forces, had taken the offered bait with such enthusiastic determination I suspected there might be a ruse hidden somewhere in this mindless advance. If so, it never revealed itself. The Heavenly Host of the Venerable Kingdom marched north from the Eastern Prefecture and followed an unerring course towards the Darkblade's horde for the next two hundred miles. Initially numbering over two hundred thousand soldiers of variable quality, it incorporated numerous garrisons and impressed large numbers of peasants along the way. As a consequence, when the host reached its greatest strength, even my unnatural facility for calculation was unable to establish a full tally of its size.

"Somewhat over three hundred thousand, brother?" Kehlbrand enquired as we watched the Merchant King's regular cavalry crest the low ridgeline to the south. "I've come to expect better of you."

"Their conscripts are prone to desertion and their rations are poor," I replied. "So the full count changes by the day."

"Even so, it would appear we are in fact currently outnumbered. Is that not the case?" His question was accompanied by a raised eyebrow that told me his caustic tone was in jest, or rather, he wanted me to believe so.

"We are," I conceded. "By at least a hundred thousand untrained mud-grubbers who will most likely shit themselves all the way back to whatever hovel they were dragged out of."

"And our own mud-grubbers, General?" The same raised eyebrow, though his tone was marginally less caustic. At my request he had allowed a weeklong pause upon entering the verdant heartland of the Venerable Kingdom. I had used the time to instill as much discipline and martial skill into my mob of Redeemed fanatics as I could. Former sergeants and officers from the garrison of Keshin-Kho, plus a few others lured by the Darkblade's love during the march, were placed in charge of companies five hundred strong and told to use any means necessary to transform their charges into soldiers, or at least fight-ers. The results were mixed. Most still couldn't march in step, and I took per-verse heart upon finding the scant few who knew how to properly thrust a spear. Despite remaining mostly a mob, their failings as soldiers were partially negated by their keenness to fight and die for the Darkblade. The drudgery of endless marching and the hardships of camp life would wear on the hardiest souls. Even the Stahlhast were known to lose heart if the season's campaigning wore on too long. Not so the Redeemed. However many succumbed to dysen-tery or found their feet turned to blistered meat, their devotion never wavered. The Merchant King's Heavenly Host might shrink by the day, but the horde only grew.

My chosen battlefield comprised a range of low hills in the otherwise fea-tureless farming country two weeks march north-west of Muzan-Khi. The hills formed a shallow valley a mile long and lacked the annoying encumbrance of a river or marsh that might impede an advance from either side. The horde had taken up position on the crest of the northern slope in the early hours, awaiting the arrival of the Heavenly Host. In the event, the enemy proved to be tardy, their outriders not making an appearance until midday. It required another two hours' ponderous manoeuvring before their full order of battle had been arrayed to face us. Their commander showed some modicum of sense in placing the bulk of his regulars in the centre and on the right flank, whilst various mercenary contingents and a great mass of conscripts formed the left wing. This army with its forest of banners and densely ordered ranks made a fine spectacle that would once have stirred a swell of appreciation in the heart of mighty Obvar. This was to have been the greatest battle of my life, one every Stahlhast had been taught from the cradle to hunger for, and yet I felt no exultation.

"Pity, brother?" Kehlbrand asked, reading my emotions with customary ease.

"I was expecting more," I said, forcing a tone of grim amusement.

"You should rejoice, for this will be a tale they'll tell for generations. It has all been as you ordained; they present their full strength for destruction."

"Two-thirds, in fact," I replied, nodding to the left flank of the Merchant host. "Massing conscripts there invites our main advance. I suspect the other third of this army, probably the best troops, waits on the far side of the ridge, ready to block us once we have exhausted ourselves hacking our way through so many peasants. When they do, their right will swing around to encircle us. The Merchant King's general is not a complete fool after all."

"And your counterstrategy, General?"

"Send half the Redeemed towards his left, holding back the rest until they engage, then advance against his right to prevent the encirclement. The Tuhla and Stahlhast will skirt both flanks to fall upon their rear. In short, we create an encirclement of our own."

"Clever," Kehlbrand said, though his tone lacked enthusiasm. "No." He shook his head after a short pause for contemplation. "You have to understand that today is not merely a battle, brother. It is another chapter in the Darkblade's story, one of the most significant, for here he will doom the Venerable Kingdom and signal to the world entire that his day has come. A blundering general obligingly marching his army into your carefully constructed trap doesn't possess the right"—his brow creased as he fumbled for the right word, eventually choosing one from the southland tongue that had no equivalent amongst the Stahlhast—"drama."

Arranging his features into a mask of stern, ardent resolve, mixed with a faint glint of sorrow to his eyes that completed the image of a soul driven to heroic sacrifice, he spurred his mount forward. Today Kehlbrand wore newly crafted armour, still of mostly Stahlhast design but with a few changes chosen to incorporate the aesthetics of the Merchant Realms. It was a mix of steel burnished to a silver sheen and black enamel, every plate flawless and catching the noon sun so that he seemed to shimmer as he wheeled his fine stallion about. Apart from his small guard of saddle brothers, he had opted to position himself at the head of the Redeemed, every single one of whom fell to abject silence as the Darkblade raised his sword and began to speak.

Although I find much of what has been written about the Darkblade's conquests to be ill-informed nonsense or outright lies, I cannot in fact contradict the many chroniclers who claim that on the eve of what became known as the Battle of the Vale, his voice carried effortlessly to every ear in the horde. Perhaps, as some assert, it was a result of his divinity, or as I have long suspected, it had something to do with the cluster of mostly silent, hollow-eyed children that rarely strayed far from his side. Whatever the cause, when he spoke we all heard every word as clear as day.

"So it comes at last to this," he said, his voice as rich in truth as it was in fortitude. "Every step taken, every victory won and loss endured brings us here. We have suffered much, it is true. We have lost those we loved, brothers . . . and sisters." He faltered for a moment, straightening in the saddle and speaking on with a slight catch to his voice, a grateful god acknowledging the sacrifice of his supplicants. "And it pains me to ask for more. But we have come so close. The end of the Merchant King's tyranny is at hand, if we can but grasp it. He sends his whores against us." Kehlbrand's voice grew savage then, his arm lashing out at the army arrayed atop the ridge opposite. "Men mired in greed, as he is. Men who rejoice in cruelty, as he does. Men who would see this great march brought to ruin and all our hopes crushed, as he would. Will you let them?"

The answer roared from tens of thousands of throats at once as blades stabbed the air and the Redeemed at my back convulsed with mounting blood-lust. "NO!"

"Know this," Kehlbrand went on as the shout faded, tears now streaming from his eyes. "Know that whatever happens on this day, you have my love. Know that even though our foes outnumber us and hope may seem lost, you

have my love." He drew his sabre, raising it high as his stallion reared. "And know that your god will die for those he loves!"

Another roar erupted from the horde as Kehlbrand wheeled about and spurred his mount to a full gallop, charging straight towards the centre of the enemy's line. There was no holding the Redeemed, nor did I try. All I could do was urge my own horse into motion for fear of being crushed by the surging tide of humanity. It swept me into and across the valley as I fought to restrain my mount from outdistancing the mass of Redeemed. I could see Kehlbrand ahead, still pelting towards the Heavenly Host and apparently immune to the blizzard of crossbow bolts loosed by their skirmish line. I saw dozens of Redeemed fall in the first volley, soon joined by more as seemingly every archer, slinger and crossbowman in the Merchant army launched their missiles. To my left I saw a young woman who couldn't have yet seen her twentieth year continue to charge despite the crossbow bolt jutting from her shoulder and the blood streaming from a slingshot wound to her head. I winced and ducked low in the saddle as a bolt skittered off my armoured shoulder, then tugged hard on the reins to steady my horse as a Redeemed with a bolt to the throat staggered into our path to be trampled.

Ever more corpses littered the ground as repeated volleys struck home, birthing an unfamiliar sense of vulnerability in my supposedly calloused mind. I was no stranger to the threatening hiss of massed projectiles, but charging headlong into such a storm was not the Stahlhast way. Better to veer off and assail a foe with your own arrows, wearing them down before the final rush. But such tactical finesse was not present on this field of the mad and the faithful. As Redeemed fell in their hundreds around me, I spurred my mount to a faster pace, reasoning that the archers and slingers would continue to aim for the densest part of the onrushing mob rather than directly in front of it.

My thinking proved sound, providing a respite as my horse drew me clear of the deadly rain, but it was only a temporary reprieve from danger. Kehlbrand, now thirty paces ahead, cut his way through the opposing skirmish line with a few strokes of his sabre, a small knot of crossbowmen withering around him, before charging towards the massed ranks beyond. A few bolts were launched at me as I followed him through the gap he had created, but either through panicked aim or plain luck, none came closer than a few inches. Watching Kehlbrand close on the first rank of Merchant soldiery I underwent the curious experience, one might say privilege, of contemplating the certainty of my own death for the second time. Whereas my first such ordeal had been rich in fear, it had been far richer in grim acceptance, something I hadn't understood before now. Then, as Al Sorna's horse trampled me into the dust, despite it all, there had been a small corner of my mind that was actually grateful. I would be spared everything to come. I would not have to watch the man I called brother transform into a monstrous perversion of what it was to be Stahlhast. But even that solace had been taken from me and now, as I saw him barrel headlong into an entire army, his sabre whirling with unnatural speed, the only emotion filling my heart was one of purest terror. I knew now what waited beyond the veil of death and had no desire to feel its dreadful grasp once more.

So, as I followed in Kehlbrand's bloody wake, I fought. I hacked my sword into the upturned faces of spearmen and stabbed frantically at every glimmer of exposed flesh that caught my eye. By any logic of combat I should have been cut down within seconds, but, incredibly, Kehlbrand's charge had created a path through the Merchant ranks. His stallion's stride barely slowed as he rode through, his sabre a flickering blur that claimed limb and life from any soldier who tried to bar his way. It was as if he could sense each thrust of spear or sword before it happened, his sabre parrying every stroke and leaving the attacker dead or dying as his charge continued unabated. The passage he carved through the army would close partially once he passed by, obliging me to keep hacking my own path. Since I possessed no ability to sense an attack before it was launched, I had only years of hard-won experience to sustain me, enhanced by enough terror to banish the strain of such a furious assault. I was aided by the mingled awe and fear Kehlbrand birthed in these men, veteran regulars who stared at the Darkblade with the frozen panic expected of callow youth experiencing their first taste of battle. Not all were frozen, however. Many sergeants and officers proved immune to the fear and, denied the opportunity to cut down the Darkblade, tried desperately to visit their wrath on his apparently fanatical turncoat general.

"Traitor!" one stocky, blunt-faced sergeant roared as he swung his spear at my horse's legs. Fortunately, my own stallion, the product of many generations of Stahlhast stock, leapt the blade with instinctive ease. The sergeant reeled back as I slashed my sword across his face and sped on, blade rising and falling without pause. I gained a new appreciation for the ingrained skill and reflexes of my stolen body in the frenzied few moments it took to cut through the final rank of Merchant soldiery. Sho Tsai's ability with a blade was at least the equal of mighty Obvar's, and what he lacked in brute strength was compensated for by his speed and precision. Foes fell away from my path with a rapidity that made me glad I had never had to face the general in my prior life.

A thud of colliding flesh and armour brought me clear of the disordered ranks where I found Kehlbrand reined to a halt atop the crest of a hill. A few bodies lay around him but the surrounding ground was clear, at least for now, creating a surreal sense of calm as I halted at his side. He gave no response to my exhausted request for orders, continuing to sit in quiet contemplation of the country to the south-east. Beneath his helm his blood-spattered features were possessed of a curious, almost wistful expression and I heard him murmur, "Why couldn't you have seen this, Luralyn?"

"Kehlbrand!" I said, adding when he failed to answer, "Darkblade!"

He glanced at me with a faint smile before removing his helm to run a hand through his hair. "Yes, old friend?"

"The battle," I said. "The horde needs its commander . . . its god."

"What battle?" he enquired, returning his gaze to the view beyond the ridge.

I bit down on an exasperated sigh and turned to the field behind us, my next words dying on my lips at what I saw. He was right. There was no battle now, just slaughter.

The entire cohort we had just cut our way through was gone, dissolved into a few isolated clusters of die-hard fighters amongst a sea of Redeemed. They surged up the slope in a dark tide, a hungry growl rising from every throat as they slashed and tore at every Merchant soldier they could lay hands on. I could see a line snaking through the chaos, its progress marked by occasional gouts of flame or the sight of men tossed into the air. As it came nearer, the blank faces of Kehlbrand's small coterie of Divinely Blooded became clear, wan, pale youths paying little heed to the havoc they wrought in their compulsion to reach their god's side.

To the east and west the Heavenly Host's line bowed under the pressure of yet more Redeemed, soon to break apart and herald yet more slaughter. A stream of fleeing soldiers cresting the ridgeline to pelt away into the flat country beyond soon became a torrent. Soldiers cast aside weapons and armour in their panicked desire to get away from this horde of maddened monsters. Off to the west the great mass of mounted Stahlhast was wheeling around the valley to rampage across the fields, cutting down scores of fleeing men. Turning my gaze east I saw a growing pall of dust rise to enshroud a vicious struggle between the Tuhla and the conscripts. Curiously, this mob of pressed men was putting up a far more impressive fight than their veteran comrades, but then, they hadn't had to face the Redeemed. Their valour, of course, was wasted. The Stahlhast rode around the ridge before veering south, thousands of armoured warriors slamming into the fray at full gallop. Yet more dust rose to obscure the result, but the outcome was no longer in doubt.

Throughout it all, Kehlbrand continued to sit at ease, hands rested on his helm and gaze still fixed firmly on the horizon. "How far to Muzan-Khi from here, would you say, General?" he asked when the din of battle began to fade into the familiar groans and screams of the wounded.

"Between one hundred and eighty-five and eighty-eight miles," I said, my uncanny eye for numbers having discerned a great deal from captured maps of the region. "Depending on the route. Nine days' march."

"For the entire horde, perhaps," he said. "Four days for the Stahlhast, wouldn't you say?"

"We should pause here," I said. "Consolidate, count our captives. The ranks of the Redeemed will grow . . ."

"In time, but not today. This must be a complete victory, a judgement upon those who would raise arms against the Darkblade." He glanced over his shoulder at the corpses and wounded littering the slope. "I will ride to Muzan-Khi with the Stahlhast and my Divinely Blessed. Tell the Redeemed to leave no soul alive on this field. The Tuhla will hunt down the runners and make whatever sport of them they care to. Follow as soon as you can, old friend. I'm very keen for the Merchant King to meet his general one last time."

He donned his helm once more and set off towards the distant capital at a steady canter. Although no order had been sent to them, the Stahlhast quickly detached themselves from the aftermath of the conscripts' demise and followed in his wake, the small coterie of blessed children trailing behind, all drawn by the unspoken will of the Darkblade.

CHAPTER ELEVEN

The day after Vaelin's ascent to the fifth tier every denizen of the Temple of Spears gathered in the courtyard to have their head shaved. They all knelt in ranks as a small group of brothers went about shearing away their long hair before shaving what remained down to the scalp. Vaelin and Cho-ka stood watching as each bald head was revealed to bear an extensive tattoo from brow to nape. They all seemed to be different, though their form resembled the ancient script he had seen in Mah-Shin's tomb.

"Crimson Thorn," Zhuan-Kai said, bowing to reveal the intricate pattern inked into his scalp. "My war name, chosen for me by the temple when first I came here. We all have them, though for many years few were required to reveal them."

He had evidently recovered his cheerful disposition and smiled as he raised the shears in his hand, snipping them an inch from Vaelin's nose. "Shall we, brother?"

"No, thank you," Vaelin told him. He expected the large monk to insist but instead he just laughed and turned to Cho-ka. "Just you then, new brother."

Cho-ka eyed the shears with a doubtful eye. "I . . . don't know my war name," he said.

"No," Zhuan-Kai agreed, clamping a large arm around Cho-ka's shoulders and guiding him firmly towards the host of kneeling Servants, "but the temple does, and brother Jah Lin over there is very capable of using his needle to discern its wishes."

Spying a slender, freshly shorn figure rise from the ranks, Vaelin moved to intercept her as she started towards the dwellings. "What does it mean?" he asked. Mi-Hahn's tattoo was the least elaborate he had seen so far, formed of a single symbol that resembled an elongated teardrop. With her hair gone she should have appeared yet more vulnerable, but Vaelin felt the opposite to be true. Her back was a little straighter today and any pretence of timidity had vanished. Even so, he didn't like the obvious reason why she hadn't been spared this ritual.

"I'm told the literal translation means 'truth,'" she said. "Though how that pertains to war, I've yet to discover."

"Truth is hard to find in war," he said. "And it's no place for you."

"I am not helpless. I've climbed all five tiers, just like you."

He couldn't keep the baffled tone from his voice or face as he asked, "How?"

"Because the temple wanted me to. How else?" She stepped around him with a smile of apology. "If you'll excuse me, I have to pack."

"War drove my sister to the point of madness," he said, catching hold of her arm. "I do not want that for you."

"You talk as if we have a choice." Mi-Hahn shifted, the movement slight but swift, breaking his grip with ease as she stepped away. "And your sister is not me."

With the heads shaved, the products of Dei-yun's forge were distributed, each Servant taking possession of their weapon of choice. Zhuan-Kai was the one exception, his only weapon being a newly crafted plain wooden staff. Next the horses were led from the stables and Vaelin found himself reunited with Derka. The stallion's nostrils flared as Vaelin rubbed a hand over his snout, sensing a rebuke when the horse lowered his head to deliver a hard shove to his shoulder.

"Bored, were you?" Vaelin asked, receiving a loud snort in response. "Don't worry," he added, moving to check the straps on the saddle and bridle. "I've a notion we'll soon have plenty to do."

When each brother and sister had been given a mount and supplies packed onto a brace of sturdy ponies, the abbot climbed onto the back of his horse and trotted towards the gate. The great doors were open now and the battlement above bare of sentries. The abbot paused before the gate, turning to his brothers and sisters in wordless, expressionless regard. When he bowed his head they all followed suit and for a moment silence reigned in the Temple of Spears.

"All right," the abbot said, turning his horse towards the open portal. "Let's get on, and no pissing about on the trail. We've a long way to go."

Vaelin lingered to watch them troop through the gate, just over five hundred men and women of varying ages and stature somehow rendered uniform with their black robes and shorn heads. Reaching inside his tunic, Vaelin extracted the bottle the abbot had given him. A small murmur of disquiet sounded from the black-song as he contemplated the clear liquid within the glass. Although muted by whatever power resided in this place, he could still discern some meaning in the song; *drink it*, it seemed to sing, *and I will no longer be of use to you*. However, deep within the tune, he could also detect a small note of deceit.

"You're lying," he said aloud, removing the stopper and drinking half the contents. The taste was slightly acidic with a faint floral tint, but neither pleasant nor unappetising. At first he felt no effect then sensed a dim warmth spreading from the base of his skull. The black-song's murmur lost its ugly edge as the warmth spread, the tune rendered completely neutral save for an impetus to follow the brothers and sisters from their refuge to whatever waited in the world beyond.

"Not coming, brother?"

Cho-ka sat atop his horse beneath the gate, his gaze expectant if a little quizzical. The former outlaw had stopped addressing him as "lord" since their ordeal on the fifth tier, something Vaelin found he appreciated greatly. He could see Mi-Hahn waiting just beyond Cho-ka, her expression far more guarded, as if she worried he might actually opt to stay behind.

"That must have hurt," Vaelin said, gesturing to the freshly inked tattoo covering Cho-ka's head and urging Derka into motion. The symbol resembled an intertwined spiral of two snakes, light and dark hues overlapping to form a complex knot.

"It did," Cho-ka said with a frown that turned into a pained grimace as the flesh of his freshly inked scalp creased. "So much I wasn't really listening when they told me what it means. Something to do with the dual natures of man."

Vaelin fell in beside Mi-Hahn as they followed the rest of the Servants of the Temple down the misted mountainside. "Wouldn't it be prudent to leave a guard?" he asked her, inclining his head at the empty temple.

"We have never been the temple's guardians," she replied. "Only its servants. It will be here when we return."

"Is there any point in asking where we're going?"

"Nuan-Khi, where the heir will be."

"It's like Daiszhen-Khi only a good deal bigger," Cho-ka explained in response to Vaelin's questioning glance. "Sits atop the junction of the canals carrying goods between the Venerable and Enlightened Kingdoms."

"A lynchpin between two realms," Vaelin concluded. *Somewhere the Darkblade will be bound to strike sooner or later.* The notion stirred another murmur from the song, marginally stronger now but still maintaining the same neutral tone. It urged his gaze towards the north-east where he could see only the vague forms of mist-shrouded mountains whilst the song left no doubt that something terrible was happening far beyond. The ominous tune and occasional discordant notes spoke darkly familiar things: *battle and murder.*

He turned to Mi-Hahn as she let out a thin sigh, fine features tensed in discomfort as a measure of trepidation crept into her gaze. "*That* is your blessing?" she asked, her tone marked by sympathy rather than envy. "What a burden you carry."

"Thank you," he said with a final glance back at the temple, its summit now swallowed by drifting cloud. "But it's a good deal lighter now."

◆ ◆ ◆

The abbot set a pace that would have taxed even veteran cavalry, leading them on a winding course from the base of the mountain into the foothills to the south-west and through successive valleys beyond. Come nightfall, sentries were posted and fires lit but no tents were raised. It seemed the Servants of the Temple were required to shun such comforts. Despite the hard wind sweeping down from the mountains, they seemed both cheerful and resolute, although their conversation remained as muted as it had been back in the meal hall. Cho-ka, unsurprisingly, proved to be the exception.

"Only been to Nuan-Khi once," he said, hands raised to the fire and brow frowning with a chill-born ache. "The local gangs got together to kick out the Green Viper Link that had a hold on the smuggling trade. Me and a few dozen others were sent to win it back." His frown became a humourless smile. "We failed. The Dien-Ven and the town garrison joined in the fight and we were lucky to get away with only a handful gutted and strung up as warning not to come back. Folk there are not fond of outsiders, that's for sure."

"They will welcome us, brother," Zhuan-Kai said with an assured grin. "The Servants of the Temple of Spears need fear no door closed against them."

"Is that a prophecy?" Vaelin asked.

"Prophecy and custom both." The big monk's grin broadened, revealing a white flash of teeth. "This is not the first time the temple has sent forth its Servants. When the land under Heaven's gaze grows troubled, the people know we will ride to their protection."

"Did you ride out when the Emerald Empire fell?"

Vaelin saw Zhuan-Kai's smile falter a little, though his eyes still shone with good humour. "It was before my time. But no, the temple did not see fit to send us forth."

"Because the old empire had to end? How many died in its ending?"

"All empires end." The abbot's tone was curt as he stepped from the shadows, face half-lit by the fire. With his hair gone he appeared both older and more threatening than before, the bones of his face and skull thrown into stark relief. His appearance put Vaelin in mind of a wild cat, a being of muscle and predatory lethality. *A wretched and unworthy soul*, Vaelin recalled the abbot's description of himself when he had fetched up at the temple. However wretched this man had been, Vaelin suspected the intervening years had crafted him into something very different, if not worse in some ways.

"Empires can fall in a storm or a slow tumble, brick by brick, death by death," the abbot went on. "The Emerald Empire's end was a mix of both, and all of it came from within, not without. We could have done nothing to prevent it." He turned to Cho-ka, jerking his head at the gloom beyond the firelight. "Take a turn on sentry duty; might teach you to still your tongue for an hour or two. No dozing." His tone reminded Vaelin of many a sergeant, making him surmise that this was not the abbot's first experience of war. "The rest of you get to sleep," he added before slipping back into the shadows. "There's likely to be killing soon. Best be fresh for it."

◆ ◆ ◆

True to the abbot's prediction, the next day brought the Servants of the Temple their first taste of combat, albeit brief and one-sided. Outriders reported
a band of deserters assailing a village three miles to the south and the old
man's reaction was immediate. Small contingents were sent to cover the
approaches to the village before the main body rode in at a gallop. The
small settlement was already a chaos of plundered houses and murdered
villagers. The deserters, fully drunk on looted rice wine, were capable of
no more than feeble resistance. The few who managed to draw a sword or
brandish a spear were swiftly disarmed, and those who took the wiser
course of fleeing into the surrounding fields were promptly captured. Vaelin watched one particularly fleet-of-foot soldier vault an irrigation ditch
only for Zhuan-Kai's staff to catch him in midair, whipping around his
neck and dragging him through the muck of a paddy field to lie gasping at
the monk's feet. Another deserter, a large man with a face spattered by both
blood and his own vomit, began an ungainly charge at Mi-Hahn, waving his
sword as he voiced a stream of barely coherent obscenities. She sidestepped
a clumsy sword thrust, hands blurring as she took hold of his wrist and
elbow. A loud crack of breaking bone and the drunkard fell to his knees, his
diatribe descending into piteous sobs. Within moments every deserter had
been disarmed, bound and gathered in the village square, kneeling with
heads bowed, many sobbing in terror or sagging in exhausted acceptance of
their fate.

"Stop begging, you worthless fucker," the abbot told the leader of the
deserters as the man gabbled out a plea for mercy. His tattered clothing and
uncared-for armour marked him as a corporal, though his youth and lack of
scars meant he was hardly a veteran.

"Five killed, six wounded," Zhuan-Kai reported after consulting with the
surviving villagers. "They were arguing over which women to take when we
got here."

"Fetch a rope," the abbot told him, pointing to the sturdy postern that
marked the southward road.

"Wait," Vaelin said, moving to crouch at the weeping corporal's side.

"I'll have no tedious moralising from you," the abbot warned. "The Servants of the Temple will not shirk from setting an example . . ."

"A minute!" Vaelin snapped, meeting the abbot's baleful eye for a second before turning back to the corporal. "You will die here," he said, voice flat but soft. "You have done murder and will pay for it. You know nothing you say will change this."

The man continued to weep, apparently incapable of voicing a reply. After a few more sobs, however, his head bobbed in acknowledgement.

"You had rank," Vaelin went on, tapping the insignia on the deserter's armour, "which means you were favoured, picked out and promoted. Such a man is not worthless. You were not always as you are."

The corporal's sobs faltered as he drew in a breath, craning his neck to meet Vaelin's gaze. "The Merchant King's soldiers came . . . to our town," he said, voice ragged but possessing the resolve of a man aware he was voicing his last words. "Told us we all had to join them . . . for the Merchant King had commanded it . . . All must fight the horde, they said. I was the only one to speak in support of the king. So the officer put me in charge. We . . ." His eyes closed tight as he fought down another sob, lowering his gaze again. "We marched . . . we met the horde . . ." His voice died as he began to weep once more.

"There was a battle," Vaelin said, recalling the black-song's tune when they departed the temple. "A great battle in the north, yes?"

"Battle?" The corporal's voice was shrill with near-hysterical mirth. "No . . . a slaughter. The Darkblade came . . ." The man's eyes snapped open again and Vaelin saw as much madness as terror in their moist sheen. "We didn't believe it. What they said he was. How can a man truly be a god?" His voice fell to a whisper and he leaned close, speaking with fierce sincerity. "But he is! One man cutting his way through an army. Only a god could do this."

"So you shit yourselves and ran?" the abbot enquired, voice weary with impatience.

"We fought!" the corporal snarled, reeling towards the abbot, features red with sudden defiant anger. "Whilst the regulars ran, we fought. But there were so many . . ." His anger fell away as suddenly as it had arrived, his head slumping once more. "And not all were barbarians from the Steppe, but Venerable subjects filled with the Darkblade's fury and led by a traitor general."

"Traitor general?" Vaelin asked, a murmur from the black-song stirring a sudden swell of unease. When the corporal said the name there was no surprise, only grim mystification.

"Sho Tsai," he said. "The defender of Keshin-Kho is now the Darkblade's truest servant."

"Liar!" the abbot spat, reaching down to grasp the man's hair, jerking his head back. "Don't die with a lie on your lips, cur!"

"I saw him!" the corporal spat back, clearly now beyond fear. "We all did. If a man like that can be swayed by the Darkblade's power we are all lost."

"He's telling the truth," Vaelin told the abbot as the old man's hand went to the knife on his belt. For all the abbot's abrasive ways, there had been an odd serenity to the constancy of his mood distinctly at odds with this sudden rage.

"There were a thousand men in our regiment when we marched into line," the corporal went on, his defiance slipping away when the abbot released his grip and stepped back. "This is all that remains. We only survived because the barbarians were so busy torturing the wounded to death. Many miles we walked, hunger growing by the day. At first we asked for food, but fear and hunger change a man . . ."

The corporal's voice dwindled to silence and his gaze strayed to the dozen nooses dangling from the postern. "I'll make no defence, claim no rights," he said. "At least now I'll know an untroubled sleep."

"The Darkblade's horde," Vaelin said. "Where is it?"

"Making for Muzan-Khi, last we saw. That was two weeks ago. In all likelihood, the capital has already fallen."

Vaelin rose and stood back as Zhuan-Kai stepped forward to haul the corporal to his feet. He walked to the postern on steady legs, keeping his face rigid and eyes open as the noose was tightened around his neck. The other deserters reacted with far less stoicism, vainly struggling against the hands dragging them to their death, or stumbling or crawling as they wailed in misery. When two monks hauled on the rope to drag the corporal aloft, Vaelin felt a lurch of sickness in his gut, a nauseous sense of recognition that urged him to look away even as he forced himself to watch. How many times had he ordered this done in the Reaches? A dozen? More? *Lawless scum, the lot of them*, he told himself but the thought was hollow. Perhaps it was his acceptance of Ahm Lin's song that no longer allowed him to take refuge in authority and notions of balanced scales, or just the realisation brought on by a long and difficult journey. In either case, he now knew he had spent the years since Dahrena's death finding worthless men to kill in the hope that it would vent the rage still boiling within him.

No more of this, he decided, gaze lingering on the corporal's feet as they performed a familiar midair dance. In the event that he somehow managed to return to the Reaches, the fate of any outlaw would be decided by the queen's appointed magistrate. *Leave slaughter to the likes of the Darkblade. I will never be him.*

CHAPTER TWELVE

Another five days' ride brought them within sight of the Western Canal, an arrow-straight channel cutting through a vast patchwork of green and gold fields. It would have reflected the blue of the mostly cloudless sky but for the sheer number of barges filling it as far as Vaelin could see, all moving in the same direction. As they drew closer, he saw that each barge was heavily laden with people and goods, many sitting dangerously low in the water. They were either propelled by oars or drawn by huge dray horses plodding alongside the waterway amidst a thick crowd of yet more people. The horses were frequently impeded by the crowd, leading to numerous shouting matches and more than a few scuffles. One particularly violent argument was raging as the Servants drew alongside the northern bank. The densely packed occupants of a barge were assailing a group of people on the far bank with insults, raised fists and an increasing number of missiles. The walkers began to retaliate with their own barrage of stones, a few leaning over the gap between barge and bank to lash out with sticks and fists. The burgeoning fracas came to an abrupt end, however, when one of the people on the barge caught sight of the Servants.

An instant hush settled over the barge, soon spreading to the banks and surrounding boats. Vaelin saw a mingling of hope and desperation amongst the grimy, emaciated faces, mostly women, children and older men. Here and there he picked out a few shamefaced younger men in filthy armour, many with bandaged wounds. Silence reigned as the abbot halted his horse on the bank, all heads lowering as his gaze tracked over them.

"They tried to steal our horse, brother!" one man on the barge called out only to be shushed to silence by those around him.

"They're probably hungry," the abbot replied. He grimaced as he cast his gaze along the length of the canal. "It'll take a month or more to reach Nuan-Khi at this rate. Best if you take only what you can carry and walk."

He moved on without waiting for a response, the Servants falling in behind as he spurred his mount to a steady westward trot. Vaelin lingered at the rear, watching the people in the barge, their argument now forgotten, use poles to push the craft to the bank where they began to disembark. The barges in front and behind soon followed suit and within a few minutes most barges in sight had begun to empty.

"The word of the Temple of Spears carries a great deal of weight." Vaelin turned to find Zhuan-Kai a few yards ahead, his usually affable features drawn in sympathy as he surveyed the beggared throng swelling on both banks of the canal. "Would that we could do more for them than just offer guidance."

"If you never leave your temple," Vaelin said, "how do they even recognise you?"

"Not all of us spend our lives in seclusion. Many are sent forth to do the temple's bidding, alone or with one or two companions. I myself have done so several times."

"The temple's bidding?" Vaelin nudged Derka into motion and fell alongside Zhuan-Kai as they followed the track of the Servants. "What did it have you do?"

"Some missions were . . . dark in nature." Vaelin saw Zhuan-Kai's gaze stray to the Servants, settling on one slender figure in particular. "Others, less so."

Mi-Hahn, Vaelin thought, his eyes slipping back to the monk as the song conveyed a tune rich in a particular combination of emotions. The desire to protect was the most salient but shot through with something far more heartfelt and fundamental.

"She said she had assistance in getting to the temple," Vaelin said. "I take it the journey was perilous."

"A long and interesting tale." Zhuan-Kai smiled again and hefted his staff. "But one for another time."

◆ ◆ ◆

It required the better part of a week before they came to the outskirts of Nuan-Khi. At times the stream of people they passed would thin to just a trickle before swelling into a disordered mass a few miles on. As with the incident on the canal, Vaelin noted how calm seemed to follow in the Servants' wake. Burgeoning arguments and brawls quelled and the combatants shuffled aside, eyes downcast. He also noted how the numerous deserters began to group together, forming companies that asserted a modicum of control over the unruly throng. When the Servants made camp, various officers and sergeants would present themselves to the abbot. Vaelin found it odd how the old man's often caustic judgement on their cowardice and a few curt words of advice seemed to fortify these men rather than sink them deeper in shame.

"Did you shit on your armour or have you been hiding in a dung-pile?" the abbot enquired of a particular officer, the captain of a horseless cavalry company whose besmirched appearance matched that of the forty or so soldiers he had collected.

Instead of taking offence, the captain straightened, Vaelin recognising the habitual response of a lifelong soldier to the voice of a superior. "The road was long and we've had little time for the usual ablutions," he said in clipped tones, receiving only a hard stare from the abbot in response. "But that's a poor excuse," the captain added. "I'll reinstitute the proper regimen tomorrow."

"Do that," the abbot said. "Your new commander waits in Nuan-Khi and I'd prefer not to present him with a host consisting of slovenly soldiers."

The captain straightened yet further, surprise and a small measure of hope on his face. "New commander, Servant of Heaven?"

"Heaven has chosen its champion. One who will defeat the barbarian horde and the liar who pretends to godhood. The age of the Merchant Kings may be over but this war is not." He dismissed the officer with a jerk of his head. "Be sure to tell your men so and spread the word. Soldiers who wish to regain some honour should make their way to Nuan-Khi."

By the time the Servants drew near to the city, a contingent of about two thousand soldiers in mismatched livery marched at their back in reasonably good order. Koa Lien, the formerly besmirched and now comparatively clean captain, being the most senior officer yet encountered on the road, had taken charge of this composite regiment. A strict disciplinarian, he ensured tight formation on the march and forbade any drunkenness or thievery on pain of immediate execution. As yet, no such measures had been required, as the soldiers seemed content, even grateful, for a return to some measure of military normalcy. They were mostly regular infantry or cavalrymen who had lost their mounts, with a small number of youthful conscripts. Many marched without weapons, a situation partially rectified when the captain sent a number into the woods with instructions to return with bamboo spears. Vaelin knew these would be of scant use against the well-armoured Stahlhast but the mere fact of once again holding a weapon did a great deal to restore the morale of men still suffering the sting of defeat.

"No walls," Vaelin observed as they drew closer to the city. The small, mostly empty villages they passed had begun to coalesce into a continual sprawl of houses and walled gardens, soon thickening into tight-packed streets. As yet he had seen no fortifications, but plentiful signs of conflict. Many doors and windows were smashed and cobbled streets strewn with shattered crockery and discarded wares. He also glimpsed several houses that had been gutted by fire, although the absence of smoke meant whatever storm had ravaged this neighbourhood had passed days ago.

"The city outgrew them decades ago," Cho-ka replied. "The Merchant Realms were not immune to war, but it never came here. The place is too valuable." He glanced at a looted house and gave a rueful sigh. "Or it was."

They encountered few people as they made their way through the winding streets, mainly the old or the infirm. "Fighting started two weeks ago," Cho-ka reported after pausing to quiz an elderly couple stoically daubing fresh paint onto the blackened wall of their garden.

"The Darkblade's horde is already here?" Vaelin asked, thinking it unlikely. Even the Stahlhast would be hard-pressed to cover such a distance so quickly.

"They're fighting each other, not the horde. Seems the garrison split when news of the defeat in the north arrived. The governor wanted to close the city to outsiders. Too many mouths to feed, he said. It's also rumoured he'd been bribed to hand the place over to the Enlightened Kingdom. Seems the more loyal soldiers had different notions. Two days of fighting, a lot of looting then a stalemate. The governor's holed up in his mansion and the mutineers at the docks. Everyone's expecting an invasion force to come across the southern border any day."

"And where will the heir be amongst all this?" the abbot wondered.

"The docks," Vaelin said without hesitation. The black-song, still lacking malice but also insistent, drew his gaze towards the west. "I doubt he or my friends would have had much sympathy for refusing aid to starving people."

The abbot turned to Captain Koa Lien who had been listening to the news with stoic calm until now. "You've a choice to make here," the abbot told him. "Throw your lot in with the governor and complete your disgrace or follow us to Heaven's chosen and regain your honour." He kicked his horse into motion without waiting for a reply. Vaelin saw no hesitation in the captain's demeanour as he barked out an order for his men to follow.

◆　◆　◆

The streets surrounding the docks had suffered the greatest destruction seen so far, many gutted by fire and others collapsed into ruin. The devastation had created a semicircular ring of comparatively open and defensible ground between the docks and the rest of the city.

"It might be better to wait here," Vaelin suggested to the abbot. Before them lay a demolished street, he assumed as a result of deliberate design rather than random action, as it provided a killing ground for any defenders waiting in the undamaged warehouses opposite. "Send an emissary under a banner of truce . . ."

"The heir knows his own," the abbot cut in. "And no denizen of these lands will raise a hand against the Servants of the Temple . . ."

The old man's words were abruptly stilled when Vaelin's hand lashed out to clamp onto his shoulder, jerking him from the path of the arrow that whistled within an inch of his nose. It juddered as it sank into a blackened beam. Vaelin noted the black gull-feathered fletching and let out a small grunt of recognition.

"No need for anger," he told the scowling abbot as he guided Derka forward. "It didn't come from a denizen of these lands."

He trotted Derka from cover and out into the brick-strewn ground, the black-song guiding his gaze to a triangular shadow created by a mound of rubble some thirty paces ahead. "Not like you to miss, my lady!" he called out in Realm Tongue.

It took a second for the archer to appear, rising spectre-like from the rubble clad head to toe in a dust-covered cloak. The figure lowered the bow she held, the cloak slipping away as she came forward, revealing dark curls, cut much shorter now he noted, and youthful features drawn in both hope and admonition.

"Uncle . . ." Ellese began, coming to a halt. Her voice caught and she looked down, Vaelin hearing a sharp intake of breath. He hadn't seen her cry before and found it very disconcerting. Climbing down from Derka's back he went to her, pulling her close.

"It's good to see you too," he said.

She sniffed and pushed away from him, palming moisture from her eyes. "Where've you been?" she demanded, admonition now winning out over hope.

"A longer story than we have time for at present," he told her, casting a pointed glance over his shoulder at the Servants of Heaven now emerging into the open. "I need you to take us to Tsai Lin." He locked his gaze on hers, freezing the no-doubt-scornful reply on her lips. "Now, Ellese."

◆ ◆ ◆

The headquarters of what Ellese termed, with a roll of her eyes, "the Guardians of Nuan-Khi" were located in what had been the guardhouse of the city's Dien-Ven contingent. A solid three-storey structure, it sat at the end of a jetty protruding into the waters of the artificial lake around which the docks were constructed. Ellese had insisted that only Vaelin and the abbot accompany her to Tsai Lin's presence, stating baldly that a battle would surely erupt should the other Servants and soldiers attempt to follow. Dozens of people, most bearing arms of varying description, emerged from improvised strongholds and barricades as Ellese led them through the district, Vaelin finding three familiar souls amongst them.

"I told them," Nortah said, clambering over a pile of bricks to enfold him in a tight embrace, "no matter how hard you try, you just can't die."

He drew back, looking Vaelin up and down before settling a searching gaze on his face. Although Vaelin bore no visible wounds, it was clear from Nortah's cautious squint that he saw a difference in him. "Something . . . happened?" he ventured, his gaze tracking to the abbot and back again.

"A great many things."

"Ahm Lin?" Nortah sighed when Vaelin shook his head. "Sherin will take it hard."

"I know." The prospect of facing her had begun to weigh on him as they neared the city, for he had more grief to impart than the death of her longest-standing friend.

"My lord."

Vaelin turned to regard the youth who had sunk to one knee close by. "Get up, Master Sehmon." As the lad straightened, Vaelin wondered how he had somehow managed to grow both taller and older in the space of a few weeks. There seemed to be a new breadth to his shoulders and a steadiness to his gaze that hadn't been there before. *Some are worn down by war*, he thought, recalling Sehmon's bravery at Keshin-Kho, *others it forges into something new.*

A yet taller figure moved past Sehmon to rest a large hand on Vaelin's shoulder, teeth bared in a relieved smile. "I worried that the path to the children might be lost," Alum said with a shamed grimace. "I wanted to hunt for you, but your brother assured me you would follow soon enough. If you didn't, then you were surely dead and a hunt would be pointless."

Vaelin raised an eyebrow at Nortah. "I thought I just couldn't die."

Nortah gave a sheepish grimace, his answer cut off by an impatient cough from the abbot. "Tsai Lin?" Vaelin asked. "Am I wrong to assume he's in charge here?"

"As much as anyone is. Come." Nortah started towards the former guardhouse. "We'll see if the daily bickering has died down a bit."

The two brawny stevedores barring the door moved aside at Nortah's curt order, voiced in poorly phrased Chu-Shin but possessed of the kind of authority that needed little translation. Following him inside, Vaelin was greeted by a chorus of overlapping voices, all raised in heated argument. Nortah led him into what had once been the guardhouse's meal hall where about a dozen people were all speaking, or shouting, at once. They wore clothing that marked them as occupying various places in the Far Western pecking order. Peasants and artisans, a couple of merchants and a pair of soldiers, one clad in the blue enameled armour of the regular Merchant Realm soldiery, the other Dien-Ven. Despite the volume of the debate, Vaelin's gaze instinctively went to the smaller but silent contingent standing at the far wall, another familiar face amongst them.

Chien stood at the forefront of four men, all bearing weapons and clad in scavenged armour. Her reaction upon seeing him consisted of a raised eyebrow before she made her way through the raucous throng to greet him with a shallow bob of her head. "You're alive," she observed.

"I am," he said, returning the bow. "And glad to see you are too." He angled his head to glance at her companions, all now viewing their exchange with varying degrees of glowering suspicion. "New friends?"

"Old friends." Her usually inexpressive features betrayed a small smile. "Of my father's. The Crimson Band had many dealings in Nuan-Khi, alliances going back generations. It's thanks to them that we were given refuge here, before . . ." Her face soured a little as she turned to regard the argumentative crowd. "I advised that we stay out of all this. The Dai Shin and the Grace of Heaven had other ideas."

She stiffened as she turned back, falling silent as she caught sight of the abbot for the first time, as did every other person in the room. A few whispered, "Servant of the Temple," but otherwise all voices remained stilled until a door at the rear of the hall opened. Like Sehmon, Tsai Lin seemed to have aged in the space of weeks. But, whereas the former outlaw had gained some vitality in the process, the only survivor of the Red Scouts had become a grave-faced man with a haunted cast to his eyes. Sherin followed him into the room, clutching a bundle of documents and rolled maps, some of which fell to the floor when she saw Vaelin.

For a second the gravity seemed to lift from Tsai Lin's face, his lips widening into a genuinely joyful smile that froze as his eyes happened upon the abbot and narrowed into instant hostile recognition. For what felt like a considerable stretch of time no sound was heard until Vaelin cleared his throat.

"Dai Shin Tsai," he said, stepping forward to offer Tsai Lin a bow of deep respect. "I bring news."

◆ ◆ ◆

"My father is alive?"

Vaelin's eyes shifted from Tsai Lin to Sherin. She hadn't yet offered any greeting, instead choosing to stand at a window, her face turned out to the placid waters of the harbour. He saw her shoulders hunch a fraction when he gave his reply to Tsai Lin. "So it seems."

"And serving the Darkblade? *This* is what you're telling me?"

Tsai Lin stood in the centre of the hall, which had been cleared on his order save for himself, Vaelin, Sherin, and the abbot. A few amongst the fractious crowd had protested at the dismissal, but with half-hearted petulance rather than genuine outrage. Vaelin suspected the abbot's presence had a great deal to do with the relatively meek compliance they displayed upon trooping from the hall.

"So it seems," Vaelin repeated. "I'm sorry."

"It's impossible," Tsai Lin stated in a rasp. His voice took on a desperate note as he swung towards Sherin who continued to maintain her unspeaking vigil of the harbour. "He would never . . ."

"There are those with powerful gifts in the Darkblade's ranks," Vaelin broke in. "You know this. He also has an artefact in his possession, an ancient stone the Stahlhast dug from the earth centuries ago, a source of what my people call the Dark. Such power can twist a man . . ."

"Not him!" Tsai Lin insisted. "He would die first!"

"He would." Sherin's voice was flat as she turned from the window, arms crossed, face wary but determined. "He has. Someone . . . something else now wears his face. That much is clear." She closed her eyes and took a deep breath before speaking further, forcing the words out. "Our grief is as true as his death. Hold to that, remember it should you have to face him."

"The Grace of Heaven speaks wisdom," the abbot said. "You should heed her."

Tsai Lin's gaze slid from Sherin to the old man with a predatory slowness, the hostility shining brighter although the abbot either failed to see it or didn't care. "We have much to plan," he went on briskly. "It's time the people knew their emperor is reborn. I'd've preferred somewhere more historically significant to make the proclamation, but this dump will have to do . . ."

"Get out."

Tsai Lin's words were spoken softly but possessed a profound sense of loathing. Vaelin also saw the potential for violence in the younger man's balled fists and unwavering stare.

"A man can't hide from his destiny," the abbot said, his own voice mild and lacking fear.

"I told you I want no part of your insane scheme." Tsai Lin bore no weapon but the capacity for lethal action was evident in his stance as he started towards the abbot. "Now, get out."

The abbot raised his chin, refusing to move until Vaelin stepped between him and the advancing youth. "Best if I talk to him alone," Vaelin said, inclining his head at the door.

The old man's lean features gave a fractional twitch of frustration before he turned and walked from the room at an unhurried pace.

"Why have you allied yourself with him, with *them*?" Tsai Lin demanded once the door closed. "Do you know what they did?"

"I ascended to the final tier," Vaelin said. "So I understand your anger."

"Who did they make you kill? If you ascended then you must have killed someone."

"I was certainly willing to kill the abbot, but no, I killed no one."

"Then you are fortunate. I spent years attempting to climb the temple. For as long as I could remember it was my sole ambition, and what did I find at the top? Murder. He made me kill my best friend, my brother since childhood. I threw him from the top tier because that old man told me to. The Temple of Spears is a liars' haven. Nothing good comes of it."

"Yet you returned there after Keshin-Kho," Vaelin pointed out. "As your father commanded."

Tsai Lin said nothing. The muscles of his face bunched as he ground his jaw, averting his gaze.

"He knew what they would tell you," Vaelin continued. "He knew it was time. The Merchant Realms are lost and cannot be saved. But perhaps they can be remade."

"Into what? The temple's vision? Would that be any better than the Darkblade's design?"

"Into your vision. Into something your father would take pride in. I rode past many thousands of people to get here, people with nothing save the faint hope of salvation, a hope that will burn bright if they are given something to believe in."

"I am the adopted third son of a traitor." Tsai Lin's shoulders sagged as he sank into a chair. "Captain is the highest rank I held, in an army that no longer exists, serving a king now most likely dead. You imagine they would believe in me?"

"Why wouldn't they? With every victory the Darkblade provides us a lesson, one we should heed. He builds his horde, yes, but he also builds his legend. He is not just engaged in conquest, he is writing scripture. He chose me as the villain, his own sister he cast as the great betrayer, all to build the epic of the Darkblade. He knows simple conquest is not enough, not if he is to truly reign as a god. To defeat him, we need to craft our own tale, the tale of the reborn emperor, hailed and blessed as such by the Servants of the Temple of Spears."

"You think people would follow me on the basis of a lie?"

"It's not a lie," Sherin said. "The Servants of the Temple have proclaimed your legitimacy and who would dare to call them liars? Besides, people are already willing to follow you. Half the garrison of this city and most of its people rallied to your banner when you declared rebellion against the governor. Nuan-Khi will shortly be yours. Perhaps it can be a foundation stone for something greater."

Vaelin stilled his tongue at that. He had already formed a conclusion as to the fate of this city but, seeing the conflict on Tsai Lin's face, sensed now was not the time to voice it. "There is something else to consider," he said instead. "Your father knew of your bloodline, did he not?"

"He did. The abbot told him when he summoned him to take me in, although I didn't know it at the time." His brow creased as the notion led to an inevitable conclusion, the words emerging in a weary sigh: "And now the Darkblade knows what he knows."

"The living god pitched against the reborn emperor," Vaelin said. "A fine climax to the epic of scripture. I doubt he'll be able to resist it, as his sister will surely attest. I take it she's here somewhere?"

"She is," Sherin said, standing back from the window and gesturing to a fresh column of smoke rising above the rooftops in the city's western quarter. "Doing us a particular service at this moment. We were going to announce it to our ever-verbose council of fellow rebels. All being well, this struggle, at least, should now be over."

◆ ◆ ◆

He found Luralyn amidst the ashes of what had been the cherry orchard belonging to Nuan-Khi's governor. Smoke rose from the blackened and twisted tree stumps as he made his way through the scorched remnants of the mansion. The Stahlhast woman's auburn hair trailed in the breeze as she stood regarding the corpse at her feet, the only one he could see amongst the devastation. He saw no burns on the dead man's face, which was partially obscured by a growing drift of ash that had begun to pile up like snow. However, large red streaks stained the sleeves of his fine silk robe.

Luralyn betrayed no surprise at Vaelin's arrival, offering only a faint smile before returning her gaze to the dead man. "The governor of Nuan-Khi," she said. "He ordered his guards to surrender, then cut his wrists."

"In shame at his defeat or fear over a traitor's fate? Rumour has it he was intending to sell the city to the Enlightened Kingdom."

"Both, I suspect. He had been negotiating with an emissary from the Enlightened Kingdom, it is true, but my dream revealed his true intention was to hold the city long enough for the horde to arrive."

"Another agent of your brother's, then?"

Luralyn shook her head. "No, just a man with enough wisdom to sense a shift in the winds of power. He hoped to ingratiate himself with the Dark-blade by surrendering the city intact. He had even composed his own oath swearing fealty to his new god. Still"—her voice took on a faint note of admiration as she angled her head to view the governor's empty eyes—"he found courage enough to grasp a shred of honour at the end. All this"—she gestured to the growing blanket of ash—"was unnecessary."

"Jihla's work?" Vaelin enquired.

Luralyn nodded, glancing at two girlish figures visible through the haze. Jihla and Eresa were at play, gathering the ash up into missiles to assail each other as they laughed and teased. "Don't think them too heartless," Luralyn said. "Being raised under the sting of a Stahlhast whip does much to harden the spirit."

She turned back to him, offering a broader smile now. "I'm glad you survived, Vaelin Al Sorna. I wasn't sure. I tried to seek your fate in the True Dream, but no vision came."

"Your brother . . ."

"Has defeated the armies of Lian Sha and taken Muzan-Khi," she finished. "That, the dream did consent to show me, though I wish it hadn't. He made the old king watch, you see? He had so many children and grandchildren, killing them all took such a long time."

Vaelin recalled his meeting with Lian Sha in the private park at his palace. The only glimmer of true humanity he had seen in the old man came when he looked upon his granddaughter at play with her dolls, a child Sherin had delivered, now most likely one of many corpses. "You know he will come here next," he said. "To claim you and to destroy the man who has risen to oppose him."

"I know. I feel his eyes on me sometimes, the touch of his gift. There's a hunger in it, and a great, desperate need to have me at his side once more. I never truly understood it before, but I know now that I was my brother's only real kin, his only true friend. Without me he is a desolate god. There is nowhere I can go, no distance I can travel that will place me beyond his sight."

"That," Vaelin said, taking the leather purse from his belt, "is not quite true."

Luralyn's brow furrowed in bemusement as she peered at the small pieces of gold he extracted from the purse. "My people have little use for this metal," she said. "Shiny though it is."

"I found another stone," Vaelin replied. "Once owned by a long-dead emperor." He went on to describe the tomb of Mah-Shin and the properties of the gold taken from the shattered stone.

"This will shield me from him?" Luralyn's hand was hesitant as she touched a finger to the gold.

"I rode many miles without pursuit, I suspect because I carried these. They may also be the reason why your dream couldn't find me. Here." He grasped her wrist and placed the nuggets in her palm. "Now you are beyond his sight."

"And you?"

"I've kept some." He jangled the purse before tightening the string and returning it to his belt. "I suspect even one may be enough."

"This will . . . anger him," she murmured, closing her fingers over the gold. "Now he will be lonelier than ever." Vaelin found he didn't like the sadness on her face; it looked too much like sympathy.

"Your brother is a madman who has murdered thousands," he reminded her, voice growing hard. "I have to kill him and you have to help me. That was the Jade Princess's design, was it not?"

"In truth, I'm not sure I ever fully understood her design." She met his gaze, the sadness slipping away as her features became a hard, resolute mask. The steellike resolve in her eyes reminded him that this woman, for all her learned compassion and insight, was still of Stahlhast blood. "I've known my brother has to die for years," she said, "and never since swayed from that mission. I won't now."

"Good. I have some hard truths to tell a reborn emperor and will need your support for what happens next."

"And what will happen next?"

Vaelin cast a parting glance at the governor's body before turning to survey the ruins of his mansion. "A great deal more of this, I fear."

CHAPTER THIRTEEN

T he proclamation announcing the ascendency of Emperor Tsai Lin, Heaven's Chosen Heir to the Emerald Empire, took place in the market square close to the docks of Nuan-Khi. The courtyard of the governor's mansion, as the largest official building in the city, was usually the preferred site for any significant public event. However, since it was now a smoking husk, the abbot felt it made a poor backdrop for such an auspicious moment. In any case, the market offered the only space large enough to accommodate so many onlookers. The city had turned out in their thousands to watch as a young man in captain's armour knelt before an aged monk to receive the endorsement of Heaven.

"Know that Heaven's sight is upon this man!" the abbot intoned, his voice carrying well in the morning air. "Know that the blood of emperors past runs in his veins!"

Tsai Lin's expression remained utterly blank as the old man spoke, and Vaelin could sense the palpable resentment roiling behind the mask. It had taken many hours of persuasion, mainly from Sherin, before he had agreed to take on this mantle. With the local civil war resolved and an entire city looking to him for leadership, a city that had already suffered several near riots as inhabitants quarrelled with new arrivals, his reluctance had finally been overcome. Tsai Lin had his own preconditions, however, chief amongst them a complete refusal to accept any counsel from the abbot or any other Servant of the Temple. As a result, Vaelin found himself cast in the role of intermediary, a role that allowed him to discard the abbot's wishes whilst promoting his own. As yet, he found little in the arrangement to trouble his conscience.

Despite the clarity of the abbot's words, the crowd was so large not all could hear, and monks and trusted soldiers had been placed throughout the throng to relate every word of the proclamation. A great many rice paper pamphlets containing an abbreviated version had also been handed out. Vaelin noted the bafflement and often outright incredulity displayed by many townsfolk as they read the block-printed characters. Others seemed heartened by the words and the ceremony, keen to cling on to some vestige of authority in a time of successive crises when dire rumours flew like pestilent starlings. However, fear and uncertainty were the predominant emotions on most faces. Although these people, like most in the Venerable Kingdom, had been deliberately starved of information for much of their lives, the rumours and an instinctive sense of normality being overturned left few in any doubt that their former lives were in the process of being irrevocably changed. The rise to emperor of a youth they had never heard of until a few weeks previously was not about to allay their fears nor win their loyalty.

Their loyalty doesn't matter. The thought rose unbidden in Vaelin's mind, rich in a hard certainty he would have ascribed to the black-song. But he had taken the elixir that morning and his gift retained its neutral tone. This, he knew, came from a different and more basic place. War had been his province all his life and he knew victory was never achieved without facing hard choices.

"Know that the reign of the Merchant Kings is over!" the abbot went on, stirring an uncomfortable murmur from the crowd, although the presence of so many soldiers, aligned in neat ranks at the edges of the square, proved sufficient to quell any outspoken dissent. Captain Koa Lien's two thousand deserters had been joined by local mutineers and Dien-Ven to create what had been dubbed the Imperial Host. At just over five thousand strong it was hardly a mighty force, and Vaelin knew it would have to grow considerably should they have any hope of contesting the horde.

"A new age dawns!" The abbot's voice became shrill as he raised his arms, Vaelin finding himself struck by the absence of habitual cynicism in the old man's expression. "A bright age! An age of justice and the banishment of greed!" His eyes gleamed with unalloyed belief as they tracked across the crowd, Vaelin taking grim satisfaction in recognising it as the face of a true fanatic. "Rise now, Emperor Tsai Lin, Chosen of Heaven and Blessed for all the Ages!"

Cheers began as Tsai Lin rose from his knees to face the throng. The monks and soldiers in the crowd led the shouts of acclaim, followed quickly by their neighbours. Surveying the cheering faces, Vaelin saw little in the way of genuine enthusiasm, many casting cautious glances in the direction of the soldiers even as they raised their voices.

"Remember the queen's speech after Alltor?" Nortah said. They stood in the shadow of the platform with the other foreigners in the new emperor's retinue, save for Sherin who, as the Grace of Heaven, had been afforded a privileged place at Tsai Lin's side. Nortah arched an eyebrow as he turned from the crowd to Vaelin, a sourly amused grin on his lips. "When she spoke that morning the people screamed themselves hoarse. Sometimes I think it was that speech that won the war."

"Blood and sacrifice won the war," Vaelin replied.

"And do you see any great desire for either here?" The ironic lilt faded from Nortah's voice as his expression grew intent. "The army we built to crush the Volarians was fuelled by a fierce hunger for vengeance." He paused, letting out a sigh and shaking his head. "So fierce it terrified me to think of what we might have unleashed upon the world. All I sense here is fear. Vengeance might win a war, but fear alone won't."

Recognising the set jaw of one caging his words, Vaelin prompted, "If you have something to say, brother, I'd like to hear it."

Nortah's brows were heavy with reluctance but his words free of doubt. "We've had an interesting journey, met many fine people, killed some others and found what we came for." He gave a pointed glance at Sherin. "The coast is not so far away. Let's bundle her on a ship and be gone."

"You know she won't leave."

"Why give her the choice?" Seeing Vaelin's flat, unyielding stare Nortah moved closer, speaking in a low but urgent whisper. "The Merchant Realms will fall, brother. Nothing you, me or her does here will stop that. I've seen enough kingdoms burn and . . ." He trailed off for a moment, a part-rueful, part-joyful smile playing over his lips. "And I'm sober now. I'm keen for my children to look upon a father who isn't a drunk."

"Sherin won't leave," Vaelin insisted. "And neither will I. This man, this creature who thinks himself a god needs to be stopped. If we don't stop him in the Far West I've little doubt we'll find his horde on the shores of the Northern Reaches soon after."

He watched Nortah's eyes take on the same shrewd appraisal he had shown at the moment of their reunion. "What happened to you? A few weeks apart and you're as you used to be, years ago when we were still killing for the lies the Order told us. Are you telling yourself lies now, or just hungry for another chance at the Darkblade? Trying to reclaim a name you never wanted to begin with? It's just a name, brother."

"A name that binds me to him, and him to me. I'm supposed to be here." Vaelin fell silent as the cheers dwindled, and turned to see Tsai Lin straightening as he prepared to speak. "Perhaps you aren't," he told Nortah in a murmur. "Go if you wish. I'll think no less of you for it. Just know any time you have with your family will be brief."

He stepped away as Tsai Lin's voice rang out, ragged at first. "I stand before you a stranger to many," he said, the monks and soldiers once again relaying his words to the crowd. Vaelin saw Tsai Lin's throat constrict as he swallowed a cough, his pale features making him appear very young, but when he spoke his voice had gained in volume and surety. "But I also stand here as a soldier, one who fought atop the walls of Keshin-Kho and knows well the mettle of our enemy. One who made common cause with the people of this city to preserve them from the actions of a traitor. One who asks not for your loyalty, but your trust. Be sure that the Darkblade will ask for neither. In truth he will ask for nothing. He will only take. If not all you possess then all you hope for. If not your lives then your souls. To die in battle against such evil is to know death but once. To live beneath the Darkblade's lash is to know death every day. If you would know life, then trust in me!"

This heralded more cheers, largely of the same mixed temper as before, but Vaelin detected a marginal increase in enthusiasm. After pushing through his initial hesitancy, Tsai Lin was proving a commanding speaker, although his delivery lacked the perfectly pitched solicitation and exhortation Vaelin had seen from Queen Lyrna. Even so, all eyes were now on Heaven's Chosen Heir and none seemed inclined to look away.

"I stand before you blessed by Servants of the Temple of Spears," Tsai Lin continued, "raised in Heaven's sight as your emperor, but know that I lay no claim to the Emerald Throne." He paused to allow a puzzled murmur to ripple through the crowd. Vaelin, having watched Sherin and Tsai Lin craft this speech, had worried over the reaction to what came next. Still, the new emperor had been insistent upon it. "The Emerald Empire died decades ago," he said. "As the Merchant Realms are soon to die. A corpse should stay in its tomb for no good can come from trying to raise the dead. Today, in the Sight of Heaven and blessed by its Servants, I proclaim the birth of a new empire, to be known hereafter as the Jade Empire, named in honour of she who embodied Heaven's favour. The Jade Princess gave her life so that this day could dawn. Join with me and fight for her!"

Tsai Lin raised his arms as the crowd cheered once more. Whilst there were those whose shouts and waves were perfunctory, even reluctant, Vaelin discerned more spontaneity to their acclaim now, seeing many faces rapt in genuine fervour.

"Well," Nortah said, surveying the crowd with a critical eye. "It's a start, I suppose."

◆ ◆ ◆

"No!"

The cup scattered wine across the maps arrayed on the table, propelled by Tsai Lin's fist to explode in clay shards against the far wall. His nostrils flared as he stared at Vaelin, furious and implacable in his refusal.

"There is no other choice," Vaelin stated, maintaining a calm, measured tone. "Except to stay here and craft a heroic death, which will do little but bring about the end of your Jade Empire before it's even begun."

"Cowardice is not a choice!" Tsai Lin growled. "To abandon a city I have spilled blood to secure. To run like a dog . . ."

"We have already abandoned one city and run faster than any dog," Vaelin pointed out. "Keshin-Kho fell and it had strong walls and an army to defend it. This city has neither and any attempt to fight here means certain defeat for us and death for its inhabitants."

Tsai Lin gritted his teeth, both fists resting on the table as he lowered his gaze. "Are these your words or the abbot's?" he grated.

"My words alone," Vaelin said. "The abbot wishes to stay here and send out emissaries calling for all those who trust in Heaven to rally to your banner. He's wrong. All reports indicate people are already fleeing south in the Enlightened Kingdom and its king is facing rebellions in the outlying provinces. A troubled land is not fertile ground for new recruits, and fortifying Nuan-Khi against siege would be the work of years, not weeks. We have to move on, and I've little doubt if he were here, your father would advise the same course."

Tsai Lin's eyes flashed at him for a second before he turned away, taking a calming breath before glancing at Sherin. "I know nothing of military matters," she said. "But I trusted your father's judgement in such things and"—her mouth hardened in reluctance as she looked at Vaelin—"this man knows war better than any other. If he says the city can't be held, I believe him."

"You would have me march away and leave these people defenceless?" Tsai Lin asked, gaze switching between them both. "And where would we go in any case? The north is under the sway of the Darkblade. Go west and we face miles of empty plains beyond which lie the Kishan-Vohl mountains, which no army has ever managed to traverse. South lies the Enlightened Kingdom, and troubled or not, they will hardly welcome an army under the command of a man who proclaims himself emperor, and we have a fraction of the numbers required to fight our way through."

"Fight? No." Vaelin went to the table, wiping away some of the spilled wine from the largest map, an extensive rendering of the southern canal system that had been unearthed from the archives of the Dien-Ven. "But we do possess numbers and the means to move them." He spread his hand over the myriad waterways spreading south from Nuan-Khi like a spider's web. "Control of this region is entirely dependent on command of the canals. Our scouts tell us the army of the Enlightened Kingdom is concentrated here." He pointed to the west where the canal network was particularly dense. "Reasoning, no doubt, that the ground is so rich in bridges and roads it makes the most likely avenue of advance for the horde, and for any mass of people fleeing before them. Instead"—he traced his finger east where the matrix of canals at first broadened then constricted before meeting the irregular course of a river—"we take the more difficult route."

"The Yi Ming River," Tsai Lin mused, his own finger moving to a point where the meandering line met the coast. "The port of Huin-Shi lies here. A small place but by all accounts well fortified."

And sure to have ships capable of sailing south, Vaelin thought. He had decided not to enlighten Tsai Lin regarding what he had learned in Mah-Shin's tomb. Having already heaped one hard decision upon his shoulders, he doubted the new emperor would be amenable to talk of visions experienced in the tomb of his ancestor. However, since leaving the Temple of Spears the black-song had become more insistent with each passing day. Something of great importance lay far to the south, and there was no chance of finding it whilst being mired in a hopeless battle in this doomed city.

"You spoke of numbers," Tsai Lin said. "Where are we to find them?"

"Not every member of an army need be a soldier." Vaelin shuffled through the various papers on the table to find a scroll neatly inscribed with an extensive schedule. "The last census of Nuan-Khi puts the population at just over sixty thousand. We can estimate the number has swollen by at least a third in recent weeks. Amongst them, perhaps a fifth will be of fighting age. With the soldiers already under your banner, that's a good-sized force, one we'll need if we're to seize Huin-Shi."

"You intend to press the young folk of this city into service, cram them onto barges and simply sail away?" Sherin enquired, Vaelin finding himself struck by the clear suspicion in her gaze. He had sensed a marginal lessening of resentment ever since their escape from the Stahlhast, but it seemed her attitude had once again hardened in the aftermath of Sho Tsai's capture.

"I thought you knew me better, my lady," he said before turning to Tsai Lin. "Some soldiers may fight for a reborn emperor blessed by Heaven, but if trained and led well, they'll certainly fight to defend their families."

"You suggest we take so many with us?" Tsai Lin frowned as he surveyed the map.

"We have barges enough for about two-thirds. The rest can be built whilst we train our new troops."

"That will take months."

"It can be done in three to four weeks, if all available hands are put to the task."

"By which time the Darkblade's horde will be within striking distance."

"Yes." Vaelin reached for another map, this one more detailed and of a larger scale. It charted the northern canals to where they terminated in a hard lateral line amidst a set of hills. "I certainly hope so."

CHAPTER FOURTEEN

Tsai Lin oversaw the training of the recruits himself, promoting Koa
Lien from captain to general with orders to organise the newly raised
regiments. A core of five hundred veterans was formed into a body-
guard named the Emperor's Spears whilst the remainder were split up to
form the nucleus of the Imperial Host. Sergeants found themselves elevated
to officer status and placed in charge of companies and battalions, spending
each day drilling their youthful charges under the harsh tutelage of corporals and private soldiers made sergeants. Their regimen was set down by
their emperor who would train alongside them for hours every day. Morning
drills were followed by marches in the afternoon and a final hour or two of
sparring with weapons come evening. Whilst Zhuan-Kai and the other Servants took part in training, Vaelin and the other foreigners were excluded at
Tsai Lin's insistence.

"There are many already looking askance at an emperor taking foreign
counsel," he said after Nortah offered to lend his experience to the army's
contingent of archers. He gave a slightly apologetic grimace as he spoke, but
his tone was firm. "Long has it been believed that Heaven's sight rests only
upon these lands and its people."

He proved equally deaf to suggestions that the city's young women be
offered the opportunity to join the host, laughing despite Ellese's disapprov-
ing scowl. "Any such notion would raise this place in revolt," he said.

"I fight," she pointed out in her halting Chu-Shin before nodding to

Chien. "So does she. Many dead Stahlhast at Keshin-Kho to prove it. My people beat an empire because women fight."

"Your people, your customs," he replied, his laughter fading. "Not mine. With the blessing of the Servants I may convince this city that an emperor walks amongst them, but no blessing will convince them to arm their women."

Overseeing the construction of the barges needed to transport the city's population was placed in the hands of Chien's comrades in Nuan-Khi's criminal fraternity. Since the various loosely allied outlaw groups had enjoyed unofficial control over the docks and principal canals for many years, they were best placed to marshal the various artisans to the task and ensure the work was efficiently done. Tsai Lin had made no secret of the plan, issuing a proclamation stating that the city would empty at the beginning of the succeeding month and those loyal to their emperor were welcome to join his host. Not all were keen to accept the offer, and a second southward migration soon began. The abbot had initially railed against the departure of those he termed "ingrates and defilers of Heaven's blessing," insisting to Vaelin that the emperor post soldiers to prevent the outflux. Vaelin hadn't bothered to pass on the message, knowing Tsai Lin would prove deaf to the suggestion and also reasoning that every inhabitant who fled was one less mouth to feed and one less place to find on the growing but still incomplete fleet of barges.

He had expected any reduction in the pool of recruits to be made good by the constant arrival of more refugees from the north. However, only a week after Tsai Lin was proclaimed emperor, the steady stream of beggared people began to slow. Within days the stream had become a trickle that faded to nothing a few days later. Questioning new arrivals produced talk of rampaging barbarians rounding up those they found on the roads, killing some to make an example before herding the survivors back to their homes.

"Used whips to keep us moving," one emaciated, hollow-eyed woman said. Vaelin had led a patrol into the farmlands north-west of the city, finding this woman staggering south amongst a dozen-strong group of similarly bedraggled people. "Didn't care if we starved on the way. If you fell out on the march they'd stick you and leave you to die by the road. 'S'how I got away, see?" She lifted her shirt to reveal a puckered, poorly stitched scar above her hip. "Fell down in a ditch and the bastard speared me. Didn't find a vein nor an organ though, so I just laid still until he fucked off."

"Did they tell you anything of the Darkblade?" Vaelin asked. "Where he is?"

"Still laying waste to the dead king's palaces they say. Killing all those with royal blood. I heard he bleeds them dry then drinks it." The woman bared yellowed teeth in a near-hysterical laugh. "They told us we should be grateful to him, for sparing us, see? Said we needed to go back to our farms and grow crops for the Darkblade's armies."

He gave the woman's group some food and told them where to find the makeshift healing house Sherin had established in Nuan-Khi. "The Darkblade is jealous of his subjects, it seems," Zhuan-Kai observed as Vaelin climbed onto Derka's back.

"What is a god without believers?" Vaelin nudged Derka into motion. "Let's see if we can find some of these whippers."

He let the black-song guide him, feeling its music flare loudest when his gaze turned north. They passed miles of empty fields, at first finding one or two corpses on the roadside, either having succumbed to hunger or wounds. As the day wore on and the sky assumed a deeper shade of blue, the corpses grew more frequent and almost all were the victims of murder rather than starvation.

"Bastards," he heard Ellese mutter as she gazed down at the bodies of two children, a boy and a girl embracing in death, both skulls shattered. Catching sight of Vaelin she closed her eyes and took a calming breath. "Those who attack in anger are already defeated," she said, repeating one of the many lessons from their days on the *Sea Wasp*.

"Not always." Vaelin gazed at the horizon, picking out a distant column of smoke rising into the darkening sky. The black-song gave a sharp, ravenous snarl at the sight, momentarily regaining some of its viciousness before subsiding back into its neutral state. Some measure of alarm must have shown on his face, for Ellese nudged her horse closer, frowning in concern.

"Uncle?"

"Anger can be a fuel as well as a disadvantage," he said, forcing a smile. "It always served your mother well, as I recall."

◆　◆　◆

The village sprawled across the lower slope of a shallow, bowl-shaped valley, a collection of cottages and storehouses overlooking a stepped expanse of paddy fields. It would have been picturesque but for the blackened, hollowed-out state of the buildings, the flames that had destroyed them gone but the smoke still gusting across the valley in acrid grey clouds. From his vantage point atop the opposite slope Vaelin could see numerous figures moving amongst the destruction, gathering grain sacks onto a train of carts. As they worked they stepped over dozens of bodies scattered amongst the houses. Unlike the drunken revels of the deserters found south of the Temple of Spears, these murderers were quiet and efficient in their looting.

"Perhaps the Darkblade doesn't desire believers after all," Zhuan-Kai commented, his habitual humour replaced by grave determination as he eyed the many corpses through the smoke.

"They may have rebelled," Vaelin said. "Or voiced sentiments taken as blasphemous, requiring an example to be made."

"Just under a hundred, my lord," Sehmon reported, moving to Vaelin's side in a crouch. Vaelin had sent him and Alum to scout the village from the western approaches, trusting the Moreska's skills to keep them hidden. "Some Tuhla, mostly Redeemed."

"That's three times our number," Nortah pointed out. Vaelin had originally intended to patrol with just his friends, but Zhuan-Kai and Mi-Hahn insisted on accompanying them with a score of Servants, claiming boredom as the emperor had forbidden them any part in training his army. Vaelin was glad he had agreed, but the odds were still longer than he would have liked. Casting his gaze to the sky, he decided they had less than an hour before full dark.

"It's a quarter moon night," he said, "which works in our favour. Circle round to the eastern road," he told Zhuan-Kai. "Kill any sentries you find but be quiet about it. When you hear a tumult from the village, launch your attack."

He half expected the monk to object to being given an order rather than a request, but he merely responded with a nod before slipping away with the other Servants, save for Mi-Hahn. "I'm curious," she said in response to Vaelin's questioning glance. "How do you intend to attack without being seen?"

"I don't." Vaelin took the purse of gold from his belt and tossed it to Ellese. "Hold on to that for me." He rose and started down the track that skirted the valley's edge and led to the village gates; by the time he reached them the Servants should be in place. "I need one alive," he told the others over his shoulder before drawing his sword. "Just one."

◆ ◆ ◆

The Redeemed was a man of average build and studious appearance. From the way he squinted at his captors, Vaelin deduced his eyesight to be poor but that didn't prevent him glowering in implacable defiance. "You'll get nothing from me!" he snarled at Vaelin, reeling about to hurl passionate invective at the others who stood watching in disgust or bafflement. "Worthless wretches! Those who refuse the Darkblade's love will know only suffering! Kill me and I die in the service of a worthy god!"

"You couldn't've spared anyone else, sister?" Cho-ka enquired of Mi-Hahn who sat atop a nearby cart, charcoal moving rapidly over the unfurled paper on her lap. She replied with only a raised eyebrow before returning to her work.

"I who have heard his voice!" the Redeemed ranted on. "I who have looked into his very eyes . . ."

Vaelin closed his ears against the diatribe and turned to survey the village. A dozen Tuhla lay near the village gate, half brought down by Nortah's and Ellese's arrows as they mustered for a charge. The reaction to Vaelin's approach had at first been more curious than aggressive, the plainsmen gathering to regard him with either amused anticipation or puzzlement. Vaelin had no knowledge of their language so responded to their shouted challenges in Chu-Shin.

"The Thief of Names!" he called back, pausing to offer a bow. "I've come to deliver a message to the Darkblade."

This appeared to generate some modicum of understanding, for all the Tuhla immediately began to reach for their bows or draw their long-bladed sabres, at which point Ellese and Nortah rose from the shadows at the side of the road to unleash their first arrows. Vaelin charged into the resulting chaos with Sehmon and Alum close behind. The fight had been brief but loud enough to gain the attention of the remaining Tuhla and Redeemed. A few Tuhla managed to gain the saddle, but the oncoming mob of Redeemed impeded their charge. Several fell to Nortah's and Ellese's arrows before the battle was joined in earnest. Vaelin allowed the black-song to guide his sword as he fought, his blade parrying frenzied thrusts and laying open exposed flesh. The tone was mostly serene but he could feel the black-song's hunger beneath it like the growl of a caged beast. It grew with every Redeemed he cut down, never managing to blossom into the unconscious rage from before, but still proving loud enough that he felt a swelling of relief when he cut down the last Redeemed. The song guttered like a flame in the wind for a second then faded into quietude as he surveyed the scene.

The Servants had evidently moved with skilful alacrity, charging through the few Tuhla defending the village's eastern flank before falling upon the rear of the mob at the gates. He saw Zhuan-Kai grimace in distaste as he tightened the wooden whip of his staff around a Redeemed's throat. Beyond him the other Servants were finishing off the few remaining opponents with efficient strokes of their swords and spears. As at Keshin-Kho, none of the Redeemed made any effort to flee despite the obvious disparity in skill. It was Mi-Hahn who had taken the only captive, dragging his senseless form across the paved courtyard at the centre of the village and dumping it at Vaelin's feet.

"Just one," she had said.

"Assail me with your tortures!" the studious fanatic railed now. "I'll show you how a true follower of the Darkblade dies!"

"We've already seen it," Cho-ka said, crouching to grasp the Redeemed's head in both hands, turning it towards the pile of corpses surrounding the village gates. "Don't worry, you'll be joining them soon enough."

"Brother Cho," Vaelin said, shaking his head. The former outlaw gave the Redeemed's face a final squeeze before jerking his hands away, eyes dark with disgust as he retreated a few steps.

"Where were you taken?" Vaelin asked the Redeemed. "Did the Darkblade lay his holy sight upon you at at Muzan-Khi perhaps?"

The Redeemed snarled again before closing his eyes tight, head lowered and face quivering.

"You're no soldier," Vaelin went on, moving to inspect the man's hands, which were bound behind his back, the flesh showing the rawness of recent labour but lacking any callouses. They did, however, feature an ingrained blue stain on the fingers. "A scribe, then?" Vaelin shifted his gaze back to the Redeemed's reddening features, once again letting the song guide him. "A bookkeeper," he realised as the tune gave a confirmatory murmur. "Therefore a man with a fine head for numbers and an eye for detail. I'd wager you made a very accurate count of every sack of grain looted from the people you murdered today. Such a man would have a shrewd notion of the current strength of the Darkblade's horde and where they might be situated."

A mingling of mucous and blood came from the captive's nose as he snorted, eyes closed and face still rigid with refusal. Vaelin rose and went to Mi-Hahn, looking over her shoulder at the fruits of her gift. It was more of a picture than a map, rendered in elevated perspective complete with mountains and rivers, but he had no difficulty discerning the shape of the coastline as the eastern shore of the Venerable Kingdom.

"Half are still concentrated here," she said, her charcoal stub circling Muzan-Khi. "But a third captured this port three weeks ago." She drew another circle around Hahn-Shi. "It's where he was taken, and commanded to do this." She underlined a small diagram she had drawn in the corner of the map, a series of columns comprised of small lateral lines.

"What is that?" Vaelin asked.

"A fleet. One of his tasks was to count all the ships captured at Hahn-Shi and calculate their carrying capacity."

"What happened to the city?"

Vaelin looked up to find Chien staring at Mi-Hahn. The outlaw's features were possessed of a demanding, almost desperate aspect Vaelin hadn't seen before. *I have sisters*, she had said when he asked how the Merchant King had compelled her loyalty.

"Flame, smoke and death," Mi-Hahn replied simply.

"They barred the gates to the Darkblade!" the bound bookkeeper blurted out. His eyes were open now and Vaelin saw a jarring mix of unalloyed belief and despairing regret in his gaze. "Professed loyalty to a dead tyrant. In decreeing only half the city burnt the Darkblade's justice was both righteous and merciful."

Chien's staff parted to reveal its blade as she started towards him, speaking in a low, grief-choked groan. "I have mercy for you. The mercy of the Crimson Band."

"I have need of this one," Vaelin said, halting her in mid-stride. He moved to her, speaking in a low voice. "Before long, you'll have chances aplenty to balance the scales. And we don't yet know your sisters' fate."

"They're dead." She turned to him with empty eyes, the colour leeched from her skin. "I know it. I feel it." Her gaze slid back to the bookkeeper, voice flat as she said, "I hope you live long enough to watch me kill your god."

She walked away, ignoring the barely coherent babble he cast at her.

Watching the spittle fly from his lips, Vaelin was forced to the conclusion that the Darkblade's ability to twist souls to his will also meant twisting their minds beyond the point of madness.

"The other thing?" he said, turning back to Mi-Hahn.

"A strange subject," she said, producing a scroll from her satchel. "Her mind was like a sea in a storm, but her face was serene."

Vaelin took the scroll and returned to the kneeling captive whose babble had finally abated into exhausted sobs. "Look!" Vaelin instructed, unfurling the scroll and taking hold of the Redeemed's hair to jerk his head up. He stared at the face of the woman captured in the paper with wide eyes that showed no sign of recognition. "This," Vaelin told him, "is the Great Betrayer. Luralyn Reyerik, the Darkblade's sister, last of his blood. Take this to him. Tell him it was given to you by the Thief of Names. Tell him we both await him at Nuan-Khi."

Chapter Fifteen

The old woman stood in the doorway to her home, arms crossed and face unmoved by Sherin's attempts at persuasion. The house was a well-appointed two-storey building in the city's merchants' quarter, its formerly well-cared-for garden unkempt and overgrown, presumably due to the departure of the gardener some weeks ago. The interior of the house was also absent of any sound, indicating that this lady, attired in a robe of fine embroidered silk with silver chimes dangling from her ears and bejewelled pins adorning the grey mass of her hair, was entirely alone.

"Please understand," Sherin said. "You cannot stay. The emperor has decreed the city must be abandoned."

The woman blinked, stating in a voice that told of a lifetime of unquestioned authority, "I haven't left this house in thirty years. The worthless swine I employed for years may have fled, but I will not."

Vaelin stepped forward as Sherin began another entreaty. He met the old woman's gaze squarely, speaking in a tone that matched hers. "Within days this house will be a ruin. And if you stay, it will be occupied only by a corpse."

"It will be occupied by the spirits of my husband and the three children I lost to the plague." She cast a brief glance at a small monument in the garden, the gold that gilded its roof partly obscured by a growth of weeds. "As long as their ashes reside here, so will I." Her tone grew colder as she raised her chin, eyes averted in dismissal. "I do not allow foreigners on my property. Please leave."

She turned and disappeared back into the house without another word, closing the door firmly behind her. "Don't bother," Vaelin said as Sherin raised her hand to knock. "She's decided her course. We should respect it."

He saw Sherin bite down on a retort as they retraced their steps from the garden to the street. "That makes a dozen," she said, consulting her list. It had been compiled by the former Dien-Ven officer given the onerous task of clearing the last souls from the city. The fleet of barges was almost complete and the emperor had ordered the great migration to begin in two days. Not all, however, were willing to follow his order and Sherin had taken it upon herself to persuade them, so far with a complete lack of success. Most were old and stubborn, like the wealthy merchant's widow. Others were resigned to infirmity and unable to face an arduous journey. Sherin, of course, remained undaunted. Her willingness to allow Vaelin to accompany her had surprised him, although her demeanour was largely unchanged.

"Another city brought to the brink of destruction," she observed as they made their way into the less salubrious neighbourhood south of the merchants' quarter. "It seems to be a habit of yours."

The streets were empty save for a few prowling cats. The bulk of the city's inhabitants, those that hadn't joined the general exodus towards the uncertain welcome of the Enlightened Kingdom, were gathered in a huge encampment on the banks of the eastern canal. All told, it consisted of just under fifty thousand people. Half were soldiers in the nascent Imperial Host with their families and dependents comprising the remainder. Tsai Lin had expressed concern that these were paltry numbers compared to the might the Darkblade would surely bring against them, but Vaelin felt it a manageable host. Thanks to an assiduous, even ruthless scouring of the city's storehouses they had provisions enough for the journey to Huin-Shi and even some barges to spare should they encounter willing recruits along the way.

"Linesh wasn't destroyed," he pointed out in response to her barb.

"It surely would have been if the king hadn't ordered your surrender. I've often wondered, did it irk you so to be denied a final sacrificial battle?"

"Not the slightest. And it was Lyrna who ordered my surrender. King Janus had succumbed to illness by then and she agreed to the Alpiran ambassador's terms in his name, not that you'll find a history of the war that says so."

"Princess Lyrna gave you to the Alpirans?" Genuine puzzlement creased

Sherin's brow. "I never knew that. I only spent a short time in her company, but her . . . regard for you was obvious."

"She's never been one to shirk a hard choice. And they had captured her brother."

"Yet you continue to serve her, despite it all?" Sherin's voice regained a slightly caustic note. "Out of duty, I suppose."

"Necessity. The Realm needed a queen, great and terrible in her vengeance, kind and loving in her governance. She is all that, and more."

"She can't be so terrible if you risked her ire to sail across the ocean." Sherin came to a halt before the gate to a house of such reduced dimensions it was more of a hut. "You are here without her leave, I take it?"

"I am." He met her gaze and held it. "And you know why."

She returned his gaze in full measure, eyes both hard and critical, though also not without some measure of fresh understanding. "I need to ask you for something," she said. "A promise."

He knew before she voiced it. "Sho Tsai."

"Yes. I know there'll come a time when you have to face him. I want you to deliver him to me alive and unharmed."

"That may not be possible . . ."

"Then make it possible!" Her stare grew fierce as she stepped closer. "You sailed across an ocean to save me, I know. I also know you owe me far more than that. Do this for me, Vaelin, and I'll consider all debts settled."

"You told Tsai Lin to consider his father dead, that what wears Sho Tsai's face is no longer him. You were right."

"I told Tsai Lin what he needed to hear." She raised her hands, spreading the fingers wide. "You know I am not as I was. The stone gave me a gift. I intend to use it well."

"I doubt Sho Tsai can be healed. Not in the way you want. I suspect what lives within him will be beyond any healing."

She lowered her hands but her eyes retained the same fierce demand. "We'll see. I need your promise."

"I promise to try. Anything else would be a lie and you've heard enough of those from me."

They regarded each other in silence for a moment longer, then she gave a slow nod, unfolding her list. "Captain Ohtan Lah," she read, turning to the diminutive house.

"An old soldier, then?"

"A sailor, apparently."

Her knock was answered with far more alacrity than that shown by the merchant's widow, the door soon swinging wide to reveal a stocky man, one hand gripping a gnarled walking stick, and back bent and stooped to a low angle. His silver-grey hair was cropped short in the manner of Far Western seafarers, the many lines on his leathery face creasing into a smile. When he spoke it was in near-perfect Realm Tongue, possessed of a deep, vibrant timbre that belied his age. "Well, ain't you two a long way from home?"

"We are," Sherin agreed with a formal bow. "Captain Ohtan?"

"Not for a long stretch, m'dear. Been more than a ten-year span since this crook-backed old bird trod a deck. Well"—his eyes narrowed as he peered up at them, lingering longest on Vaelin—"'spose yer'd better come in, then."

He turned and hobbled back inside, his walking stick thumping the bare floor of his house. Upon entering, Vaelin found it consisted of only two rooms and every available space was taken up by some form of artefact or ornament. He recognised porcelain from the Alpiran Empire and bronze figurines that could only have come from Volaria. However, his attention was soon mostly captured by the maps that adorned the walls, dozens of them, so many they overlapped. As his gaze tracked from one to the other, the black-song gave a low but insistent murmur. *There is something of import here.*

"You'll have to forgive the lack of hospitality," the captain said, groaning as he sank into a chair. From the way his aged but lean features tensed, Vaelin could tell he was concealing a great deal more pain than he displayed. "Could never abide tea, and the last drop of grog went days ago. You're welcome to join me in a puff of five-leaf, though." His bony hands reached for a long-stemmed clay pipe on a nearby table. "Helps soothe me aches, y'see."

"No, thank you," Sherin told him with a smile. "We have come . . ."

"To persuade my old carcass out of this house and onto the new emperor's barges." The old man's cheeks bulged and smoke billowed as he puffed on his pipe. "You're the Healing Grace of Heaven and he's the one the Alpirans called the Killer of Hopes."

"Hopekiller," Vaelin corrected in Alpiran before resuming his inspection of the maps.

"That's it. Been too long away from the empire. Must say, I always preferred their ports to your lot's. More civilised and a better chance of sneaking a little extra cargo past the excise men."

"Captain," Sherin said, "this city will soon fall to the northern barbarians. It is the emperor's wish that none of his subjects be left behind to face their cruelties."

"Cruelties, is it?" Ohtan Lah barked out a laugh. "More like mercy, I calls it. Sorry, m'dear. You seem nice and all, but this old bird's sailed his last voyage."

Vaelin's eyes alighted on one particular map, showing a forbidding coastline of numerous inlets and small islands. It was marked in a mix of Far Western script and Realm numerals, all neatly hand drawn rather than the more irregular result of a block print.

"Like my handiwork, eh?" the old captain asked.

"You drew this?"

"Drew 'em all. Always had a talent for charts and such. Good skill for a sailor, means you'll never be short of a berth."

Vaelin tapped a finger to the map. "This is the upper shore of the Northern Reaches. You've been there?"

"Few corners of the world I haven't been, lad. Did my best to draw them all too."

Vaelin stepped back, scanning the array of charts. "I have a friend in North Tower who would pay a great deal for these."

"Take 'em." Smoke trailed from Ohtan Lah's pipe bowl as he waved it. "With my blessing, if it means you'll not trouble my door again."

The black-song gave another murmur, bringing a question to Vaelin's lips. "Do you have any that depict the southern seas? What lies beyond the Free Cantons."

The old man's voice took on a cautious note as he nodded, inclining his head to the most cluttered corner of the room. "Over there."

Vaelin rummaged amongst the piled waxed paper charts whilst Sherin tried again to convince Ohtan Lah of the wisdom of leaving. "I don't think you understand what will befall Nuan-Khi when we leave," she said, her tone soft with solicitation but also laced with dogged sincerity.

"A whole bundle of death and destruction, I'd guess," he mused in response. "Quite a spectacle to witness before I shuffle off to Heaven's embrace."

Vaelin unfurled map after map until the song gave a note of harsh, triumphant certainty. The chart he held depicted an archipelago in fine detail, hundreds of islands, small and large spread out in a chaotic crescent. Like the map of the Reaches, this one bore numerous annotations, symbols and numbers presumably stating the relative depths of the various channels. However, he noted that they grew less frequent as the map progressed south, the islands depicted in fainter ink, some incomplete. It was as if a fog had settled over the southern portion of the chart, the region where the song left little doubt he needed to go.

"Why didn't you finish it?" he asked, moving to hold the chart in front of the old man's eyes.

Ohtan Lah dragged some more five-leaf into his lungs, the many lines on his forehead forming a web of deep furrows as his eyes flicked from the chart to Vaelin. "The lower climes of the Opal Isles," he said. "Believe me, lad, that's nowhere you want to travel."

The Opal Islands, where the long-dead Emperor Mah-Shin spoke of sending a fleet in a vain search for a stone. "You would be wrong," he informed the old sailor. "You've been here, you know the waters?"

"Well enough. But it's a dark memory. Lost a good mate in those isles. S'pose that's why I never finished it."

"Lost them how?" The demand in his voice brought a hard glint to the old man's gaze and a reproachful glare from Sherin. Vaelin took a breath, looking around until he found a stool. "Forgive me," he said, dragging the stool to Ohtan Lah's side and sitting down. "But this is important."

"All you'll find in those islands is torment and death. The beasts there"— the captain paused to shake his head, face dark with ugly memories—"aren't like other beasts."

"There is something here, a place I need to go," Vaelin insisted, presenting the map once more. "Can you finish this?"

"Maybe, if I had time to ponder, and time we ain't got, have we, lad? As this lovely says, the barbarians are coming."

"Then I have to insist you come with us."

"Insist all you want, but I'm stopping here. I know a big strong fellow like you could drag me out of here, but unless you're willing to flog me to it, I won't be drawing any maps if you do." He drew on his pipe again, huffing in annoyance as the last embers flared in the bowl. "Bugger it," he muttered, reaching for an ornate lacquer box on the table, stubby fingers crushing the dried leaf inside. "Bastard Stahlhast better get here before this runs out."

"Why are you so determined to die here?" Sherin asked as the old man refilled his pipe.

His eyes flashed at her in sudden anger and he jerked forward in his seat, grunting in pain as he lowered his head to show her his back, pulling down the collar of his tunic. "See this, do you, lovely?" he demanded, and Vaelin saw how his spine was twisted below the neck, coiling like a snake beneath his wrinkled skin. "Lost an argument with a wayward crossbeam ten years ago. Didn't kill me but there's few days I don't wish it had. Feels like a dozen knives stabbing into me every waking hour. I ain't known proper sleep in years and what money I had's gone on five-leaf or poppy balm."

He jerked his tunic back in place, eyes moist as he returned to lighting his pipe. "Barbarians'll be doing me a favour," he said in a hoarse whisper.

Seeing the insistent question in Vaelin's gaze, Sherin briefly closed her eyes in resignation before rising and addressing Ohtan Lah in brisk tones. "Do you possess any gifts? Beyond your facility for mapmaking, I mean."

The old man squinted up at her. "Gifts?"

"The Dark," she said before adding in Chu-Shin, "Blessings of Heaven."

"No." Ohtan Lah shifted in discomfort that Vaelin suspected had little to do with his back. "Once dreamt the wife had died when I was at sea and, right enough, she had. But that may have been more hope than premonition. If I'd had to suffer both her tongue *and* my back I'd've probably sliced me wrists by now."

Sherin turned to Vaelin and gave a small nod.

"I know pain," Vaelin said to the old sailor. "So, I know why you'd rather stay here than face another voyage. But that doesn't need to be." He got to his feet and moved to the door. "I'll wait outside. The choice will still be yours when it's done."

◆ ◆ ◆

"Can you do it?"

Zhuan-Kai frowned as he surveyed the massive oaken beams that formed the dam's sluice gate. It had been constructed so as to allow only a controlled amount of water through each day, creating a regular flow to feed the canal network. It spread out below like an elongated, oddly regular spider's web, stretching away towards Nuan-Khi ten miles east. The dam itself was a curved wall of sheer granite situated in the dip between two mountains. Eyeing the precision of its construction, Vaelin experienced a pang of regret that Ahm Lin would never see it. The mason would have spent hours in fascinated study of the interlocking stone blocks that formed the smooth edifice. It had stood here since the latter days of the Emerald Empire, holding back the waters of three lakes that had merged into one, starving the plain below of water and allowing the construction of the canals.

"Wood is wood," the monk said, rubbing his chin. They stood on a stone platform positioned to the side of the gate, presumably used by those charged with maintaining the dam. Although the workmen had all fled in recent weeks the gate remained in disappointingly good condition, allowing not the barest trickle through from the vast weight of water beyond. "But to command it"—Zhuan-Kai reached out a hand to the closest timber, face tensing in concentration—"you have to know it. All its strengths, all its flaws."

"Why not just set fire to it?" Nortah asked. "Douse it in pitch and throw a torch."

"This has to happen in an instant," Vaelin said. "No telling how long it would take to burn enough to burst."

He watched the monk hold his hand in place for a while longer before grunting and moving back. "It can be done," he said. "But these timbers are ancient and thick. I'll need a day to get to know them a little better."

"You talk like they're alive," Nortah observed.

"Wood doesn't die just because it's cut." Zhuan-Kai cast a slightly judgemental glance at Vaelin. "It only truly dies when you burn it."

"You found a new one," Vaelin pointed out, nodding to the monk's staff.

"I carried his brother for many years; he was an old friend."

"Then I'm sorry."

"The temple required that you ascend." Zhuan-Kai shrugged, turning back to the gate. "As it requires me to sunder these old fellows. Still, they'll have a long sleep in the moist earth when it's over."

A shout from above drew Vaelin's gaze to the top of the dam. "Patrols came back!" Ellese called down, leaning over the parapet, hands cupped around her mouth. "Stahlhast in large numbers twenty miles north!"

"We may not have a full day," Vaelin told Zhuan-Kai.

"I'll manage," he said with a resigned wince. "It will be . . . taxing, however."

"Watch for the beacon," Vaelin said, making for the stairwell. "Ride for the meeting point when it's done."

◆ ◆ ◆

The fleet began leaving in the early hours of the morning, led by the emperor himself, resplendent in burnished, gold-lacquered armour unearthed from the late governor's extensive wardrobe. The original family crests had been removed and replaced with the motif of the Jade Empire, which consisted of a four-spoked wheel encircled by spears. Each spoke symbolised one of the four principal regions of the empire, once sundered now reunited, in name if not in fact. The spears signified the blessing and protection of the Servants of the Temple. Tsai Lin had initially balked at wearing such garish attire but yielded in the face of Vaelin's advice: "You have to be more than just a man. We need to craft a legend that will rival the Darkblade. He is the shadow, so you must be the light."

At his request, Tsai Lin appointed Ohtan Lah to command one of the barges as a sop to the old man's pride. In truth, Vaelin wasn't sure the captain could still be described as old. He kept hold of his walking stick but wielded it more like a baton, apparently having no need of support as he harangued his crew to get the casks of provisions stored all neat and proper. The stoop that bent his back was gone completely as were many of the lines creasing his face. His voice had a deeper timbre to it but the cheerful authority remained unchanged, even in the face of the many curses hurled at all aboard by the merchant's widow. She squirmed in her bonds at the stern of the barge, face painted a continual shade of red by her apparently inexhaustible fury.

"Kidnapper!" she railed at Vaelin. "Villain! I demand immediate release, you vile foreign scum!"

"Now, now, Madame Shek," Captain Ohtan said, wagging a finger in her crimson face. "That's no way to address your saviour, is it? Don't forget this man carries the emperor's seal."

"Emperor?" Madame Shek delivered a glob of ignoble spit to the deck between the captain's feet. "Some boy from nowhere raised by monks determined to unseat the rightful king."

"The rightful king's dead, you daft old cow," Chien told her, climbing aboard with her retinue of outlaws. She maintained a hard glare as she moved to take a seat at the widow's side. Some instinct for survival must have risen in the woman's breast, for she fell to an abrupt, sullen silence.

"I thought we were going to respect her decision?" Sherin asked, clutching her chest of curatives as she paused at the gangway.

"I suspected a voyage would broaden her mind," Vaelin said. In fact, he wasn't entirely sure what had caused him to march to the widow's house that morning and bind her hand and foot before slinging her over his shoulder and carrying her to the docks, suffering her increasingly voluble curses along the way. Perhaps it had been retribution for her foreigner-hating prejudice, or more likely the recurring image of her formerly prideful features bleached and bloated in death. Either way, from the simmering glower she continued to cast at him, he felt it likely he would soon come to regret the impulse.

"I've asked Chien to watch over you once again," Vaelin told Sherin. "At the emperor's insistence."

She nodded and glanced around at Nuan-Khi, a keen note of regret in her voice. "This city has stood for at least a thousand years."

"Stone and wood can always be gathered and built into something new," Vaelin replied. "Corpses can't."

He found Luralyn bidding farewell to Eresa and Jihla at the gangplank of the neighbouring barge, both of whom displayed a deep aversion to leaving her side. "Stop that!" Luralyn snapped at Jihla, spying a tear welling in her eye. Seeing the hurt on the girl's face she sighed. "Apologies, sometimes I forget I'm no longer Stahlhast," she said, reaching out to clasp their hands. "Should we part forever today, be strong and trust in each other. The emperor's course is now yours."

"You could have gone with them," Vaelin said as they watched the barges make their way along the eastern canal.

"My brother is more likely to bring his whole strength if he knows I'm here," Luralyn replied. Like Vaelin, she had given her gold nuggets to Ellese for safekeeping. "I feel his eyes upon me again," she added with a tight grimace that told of a great deal of controlled fear within.

"And I." It had begun soon after the skirmish in the village, long before the freed bookkeeper could have reached the Darkblade's side, a dark murmur of song from the north. It grew with each passing day, building into a constant growl rich in both fury and envy. "He doesn't like our alliance."

"It was always this way with us on the Steppe. Two souls entwined so close no other was allowed in. Even Obvar was never truly his brother." Her expression grew tighter still, Vaelin reading grief as well as fear in her eyes. "The only love he ever shared was with me."

Then let's hope his love kills him today. He didn't say the words but saw Luralyn's eyes widen at the accompanying flare of ugly desire from the black-song. It had become less muted lately, although he remained scrupulous in the doses he drank of Brother Kish-an's elixir, making him conclude he would ask him for a stronger dose when they reunited.

"Come," he said, turning and striding towards the rowboat sitting incongruously atop the wharf. "We'd best be at it."

Chapter Sixteen

They carried the boat to the base of what had once been the watchtower of Nuan-Khi. Successive decades of peace had seen it fall into disuse until an enterprising merchant purchased it from the governor for service as a grain store. The grain had all been carted away in recent weeks, leaving an empty tower of cracked stone held together by flaking mortar. After tethering the boat to the tower's door with a length of sturdy rope, Vaelin sent Ellese, Sehmon and Alum north with the horses. "Wait for the signal before you light it," he reminded Alum, handing him a spyglass. "Then ride hard for the high ground to the south. We'll meet you at the eastern locks." Before entering the tower he paused to rub a hand over Derka's snout. "Behave yourself."

The roof that covered the tower's summit had withered away years ago, ensuring they were greeted by a chill northerly wind as they emerged from the stairwell. The powerful spyglass that had once stood here had long since vanished but Vaelin suspected they wouldn't need it today. The Darkblade's song had steadily grown in volume all morning, leaving little doubt that when he appeared, his accompanying host would be hard to miss.

"It won't be long," Luralyn said, face tense with anticipation. "He's driving them hard, probably has been for days."

"Did your True Dream reveal anything about the outcome today?"

She swept a mass of wind-tossed auburn curls from her face, shaking her head with a very small, rueful grin. "No, though I sought it out last night. It showed me . . . something else."

"Something of import?"

"A boy." Her grin faded into a reflective frown. "A boy playing with a toy ship. I watched him grow into a man."

"What does that mean?"

"I don't know yet, but the dream never shows me anything I don't need to see."

"Brother," Nortah said, pointing north, voice urgent. His brother had always possessed better eyes so it took a moment longer for Vaelin to make out the dark shimmer on the horizon to the left of the great southern canal, growing broader and thicker with every passing second. The lead riders came into view soon after, Stahlhast in their dark armour on the right with a greyish brown mass of Tuhla to the left. They all came on at full gallop with no sign of military cohesion. The dense throng of riders behind was similarly disordered, a roiling multitude a mile wide beneath a growing pall of dust. The distant thunder of their approach soon rose to a storm as the vanguard reached the outskirts of Nuan-Khi. Vaelin saw a few rear up in apparent puzzlement at finding no one to fight, the air free of the expected hail of arrows. However, most continued their headlong charge through the streets.

"Can you sense him?" Vaelin asked Luralyn as more and more warriors poured into the city.

"He's here . . ." She trailed off, grimacing in confusion. "But where pre-cisely, I can't tell."

Vaelin waited until the main body of the horde had begun to infiltrate the outskirts before turning to Nortah. "Now."

Nortah placed a shaft on the parapet and struck a flint, sending sparks onto the oil-soaked rag encasing the arrowhead. Nocking it to his bow he raised it high, drawing the string fully back before loosing. The flaming arrow soared into the clear sky, trailing smoke and reaching a height of over a hundred feet before arcing down. Vaelin stared towards the west, counting the seconds until a dim orange glow appeared atop the rooftops a mile away. Alum had seen the flare and lit the beacon, a process that would be repeated by Servants of the Temple for the next four miles, carrying the signal to the dam in the space of a few heartbeats.

"Are you sure this tower is strong enough?" Nortah asked, his tone possessed of a slight tremor as he ran a hand over the weathered stonework of the parapet.

"The foundations go deep," Vaelin replied, turning once more to view the host now streaming into Nuan-Khi. They slowed as they advanced, constricted by the narrow maze of streets. The plain beyond the city was covered by the horde, and Vaelin searched the charging mass for anything that might betray Kehlbrand's presence. His song was as loud as a shout now, so filled with the rage and jealousy it sent flashes of pain through Vaelin's skull.

Luralyn let out a hiss, and he turned to see her staring at the horde with tears beading her eyes. "Unseen preserve me," she whispered, her distress sufficient to make her pay homage to gods she no longer held to. "He's truly gone mad."

The roar began to build in the west when the advance elements of the horde had reached the docks. Many were on foot now, forsaking their mounts to ransack houses in search of victims or plunder, emerging soon after in baffled frustration. Vaelin tracked a band of Stahlhast from the harbour to the base of the tower, stepping forward to meet their upturned gaze in the faint hope he might find the Darkblade amongst them, but seeing only a dozen frowning faces. They quickly dismounted and started towards the tower entrance, then paused as the roar grew to deafening volume.

Vaelin switched his gaze in time to see the wave engulf the western half of Nuan-Khi, streets and houses disappearing beneath a raging wall of white. Dark specks tumbled amidst the oncoming fury, Stahlhast and Tuhla torn from the ground to be swallowed by the wave. It struck the tower with a disconcerting boom, shrouding them in displaced dust from centuries-old stonework. The impact sent the three of them sprawling, the grind of granite and powdered mortar mingling with the ongoing roar of the wave. Vaelin began to question his faith in the structure's foundations as it swayed and water lapped over the parapet for one alarming instant. Then, amidst a chorus of scrapes and groans, it settled.

"Faith!" Nortah breathed, rising to survey the spectacle below.

The city of Nuan-Khi was gone, replaced by a turbulent lake seeded by the twisting bodies of drowned or drowning warriors. Vaelin could see over a hundred close by, some struggling vainly in the current, others already dead, all soon to slip beneath the churning spate. The water had risen to within a yard of the tower's summit but soon began to subside, the rushing torrent losing much of its violence to reveal the mass of corpses it had claimed. They were crushed together in ugly clumps at the junctions of streets or impaled on trees, horses and riders entangled in death. Counting them with any accuracy was impossible, but Vaelin knew he had killed more foes today than in any other battle, all without drawing a sword.

He turned to watch the wave sweep east, flooding the network of canals as far as he could see. The emperor's fleet would be beyond the locks now and already traversing the Yi Ming River to Huin-Shi. The water covering Nuan-Khi settled and reduced in volume, the destruction beneath mostly concealed by a vast cloud of mud and detritus from so many destroyed buildings. The roofs of some of the taller buildings jutted above the surface of this new inland sea, but it otherwise remained an expanse of brown water stretching away for at least two miles in all directions. The bodies were no longer visible but he could make out a mass of survivors on the northern shore. He could also hear nothing of the Darkblade's song.

"Do you . . . ?" he began, the words fading at the grief on Luralyn's face. Her people considered her an outcast and betrayer of their living god, but she was still of their blood.

"Kehlbrand was supposed to bring them to destruction," she whispered. "Not I."

"They invited their own destruction when they chose to follow him," Vaelin said. "Besides"—he pointed to the far shore where a great throng of riders milled about—"it seems there are many left. I doubt more than a fifth of the horde died today."

"You sound disappointed." Luralyn's face hardened, eyes lingering on his as he felt himself being reassessed. He wondered what she had imagined him to be before now. A noble warrior from across the sea, perhaps? A hero summoned by her visions to put right her brother's wrongs? In truth, they were both victims snared in the web spun by the Jade Princess, and he knew there would be no escaping it with clean hands.

"This war ends when the horde is exterminated or your brother dies," he said. "What I need to know from you is whether we did that today."

She shifted her gaze from him, staring out across the ugly sea at the distant host. "No," she said in a small, hoarse voice. "I still feel him."

Vaelin watched the surviving horde convulse with sudden purpose,

Stahlhast and Tuhla war bands reforming and striking out towards the east. At first, the Darkblade's song remained elusive but then he heard it once more, muted and less enraged, possessed of something that Vaelin found stirred his own anger, small and grudging but still discernable: respect.

I don't want your regard, he replied silently as the horde faded from the northern shore. *I only want your death.*

◆　◆　◆

Vaelin and Nortah worked the oars whilst Luralyn steered the tiller. The boat had suffered some scrapes in the flood but its hull remained intact, for which Vaelin was thankful. The prospect of swimming through an expanse of water so rich in corpses was far from agreeable. They passed more bodies the further south they rowed as the newly crafted sea became shallower, revealing warriors entangled in trees, limbs and torsos twisted to impossible angles. It seemed to Vaelin that, despite the outrages inflicted upon their flesh, the torrent had somehow contrived to spare their faces, all of which seemed to be turned in his direction. He kept his gaze fixed on the boat's stern, but could still feel the weight of so many empty eyes staring in silent accusation.

After two hours' rowing, the boat grounded amidst a mass of tumbled brickwork where the flood had destroyed Nuan-Khi's southern districts. "Already starting to stink," Nortah complained, nose wrinkling as they abandoned the boat and began to wade through the waist-high waters.

"The sewers will have flooded," Vaelin said, blinking his eyes against the stinging odour. He started to slosh in his brother's wake then paused, seeing Luralyn halted next to the boat. She stood in silent and expressionless regard of what at first appeared to be a jagged bundle of mud-covered wreckage. Looking closer, Vaelin saw it to be two corpses, one much smaller than the other and both impaled upon the spokes of a shattered cart wheel. Further inspection revealed the larger body to be a young woman, the manner of her impalement making it appear as if she had been reaching out to the dead infant at her side.

Did they invite their own destruction? a small but insistent voice asked Vaelin. He wasn't sure if it came from himself or some vestige of the black-song, but the truth contained in its question was inescapable. *You saved a crippled sailor because you needed him, and that unpleasant old woman because she tweaked your guilt. Did you imagine there were no other victims here besides the horde?*

Luralyn, however, said nothing as she turned away from the corpses and began to labour through the water. For some reason he found the blankness of her face and avoidance of his gaze worse than if she had raged at him. *No clean hands*, he reminded himself. *This is a crime we share.*

They found Alum and the others waiting with the horses atop the crest of a hill an hour's march from where the floodwaters finally met dry land.

"That was quite a show, Uncle," Ellese enthused, handing him Derka's reins. "I'd say it was worth the journey just to see that."

Her smile faltered and faded at the hardness in his eyes as he took the reins and held out his hands. "The purses I gave you," he said, tossing one to Luralyn when Ellese handed them over. It pleased him to imagine the Darkblade's sudden rage at finding them both lost to his song, but it was a small flowering of comfort in a mind still crowded by the staring corpses and the impaled mother and child.

"The Servants?" he asked Alum.

"No sign yet," the Moreska replied.

"We shouldn't tarry here," Nortah advised. "Best if we push on, catch up to the fleet. The Servants will be sure to follow along soon enough."

"No, we need to find them." Vaelin climbed onto Derka's back and turned him about, allowing the black-song to guide him. It had begun to sing ever louder since they departed the tower, and his supply of the elixir was down to its last few drops. The music told of trouble, the notes as rich in anticipation as warning. "Be ready," he said, spurring the stallion to a gallop. "There may be fighting to be done today after all."

◆　◆　◆

In fact, the fighting was almost done by the time they came upon the Servants. A few miles south of the city they began to find riderless horses, their tack of Stahlhast manufacture. The first bodies appeared soon after, a trail of armoured corpses leading them to a farmhouse where the Servants were busy despatching the few survivors of a Stahlhast war band. Surveying the bodies, Vaelin estimated they must have numbered well over a hundred, and the few black-robed figures lying amongst them told of a fierce encounter. A dozen surviving Stahlhast were clustered against the farmhouse wall, all dismounted and fighting with the desperation of the doomed. Vaelin could see the abbot in the thick of it, ducking under the axe of a tall warrior to slash his sword through the man's leg, instantly whirling away to lay open the neck of another. The other Servants closed in, displaying similar skills in cutting down the rest, all of whom died with shouts of defiance and no request for quarter.

Vaelin had led the others in a charge towards the farm but reined to a walk as the fighting ebbed, halting Derka in a ploughed field where a slender figure knelt at the side of an older monk. Mi-Hahn glanced up at him with moist eyes, her hand still holding a blood-soaked bandage to the monk's neck, although it was clear that wound had already claimed his life.

Dismounting, Vaelin crouched, reaching out to draw her hand back. "So," she said in a thin, choked rasp. "This is the truth of war."

"Yes." Vaelin reached out to close Dei-yun's eyes, recalling the time spent in his forge at the temple. The blacksmith had been sparing with words but patient in his forbearance of a foreigner's presence. "Good men die, along with the bad. I'm sorry, sister."

"Marvellous fucking plan you had, Battle Lord of something or other!" Vaelin looked up to find the abbot advancing towards him, lean features mottled by anger. "These bastards were all supposed to drown today. I've lost ten Servants to this farce."

"This was an advance scouting party," Vaelin said, rising to face the abbot, speaking with neither anger nor contrition. "Most likely they skirted the city to the west before the dam broke. If you're going to lead people in war you should know there are no certainties." He looked down at Dei-yun's lifeless form for a moment before turning away. "And you'll lose a great deal more than ten lives before this is over. If you haven't the stomach for it, make way for one who has."

"Don't tell me what I can stomach!" The abbot moved to bar his way. "I've known war since I was a child. It's why the temple called to me, to lead its Servants in this time of need . . ."

"It called to me too," Vaelin pointed out. "Perhaps because it knew you were not equal to the task."

"Brother Abbot," Mi-Hahn said, stepping between them as the old man's face took on an even deeper shade of crimson. Her voice was soft and mild but Vaelin noted how the abbot immediately retreated from her, the anger on his face quickly replaced by chagrin. "We have wounded," she added, her gaze slipping back to the slain blacksmith at her feet. "And dead to care for."

◆ ◆ ◆

"This was supposed to last you a week." Brother Kish-an's features formed a judgemental scowl as he regarded the empty vial.

Vaelin had sought him out after they made camp following an arduous ride from the farmland south of Nuan-Khi to the banks of the Yi Ming. The black-song had raised its voice with increasing and aggravating persistence with each passing mile, diminishing only slightly when he gulped down the last of the elixir. Its music was something of a contrast to the previous, often dirgelike chorus of bloodlust. Now it held a triumphant note, blaring with the force of many trumpets whenever his thoughts strayed to the corpse-choked waters covering Nuan-Khi. Its approval was coloured by a darker urge, made dangerous by how tempting he found it: *Turn around. He's waiting. We can finish this.*

"It didn't," he told the monk. "I need more."

He moved to his saddlebags and returned with another small bottle. "Go easy on it," he said, handing it over. "I'm not sure when I'll manage to mix another batch."

"The Grace of Heaven knows much of curatives. She could help . . ."

"She doesn't know this one." Kish-an's tone was curt, causing Vaelin to assume he had delivered an unintended barb to his pride. "This is a gift of the temple, not some concoction of herbs and sundry fluids squeezed from the balls of a goat." He jerked his head in dismissal and returned to stirring the bubbling stewpot suspended over his fire, not glancing up as Vaelin walked away.

They rode for a day and a half, keeping close to the southern bank of the broad river without catching sight of the rearmost barges of the emperor's fleet. The surrounding country remained a curiously empty expanse of untended fields and recently abandoned farms. They also passed through a number of small fishing villages, finding them all deserted and the boats vanished.

"Gone with the morning tide, I'd say," Cho-ka surmised, emerging from a hut with a bowl of gruel in hand. "It's cold," he said, spooning some into his mouth, "but still worth eating."

"They most likely answered the emperor's call and joined the fleet," Nortah said. "Means they can't be too far ahead."

Pressing on until evening, they encountered the more ominous but familiar sight of people fleeing with what meagre possessions they could gather. They were only a few dozen, and most wore the garb of the city rather than peasants or fisherfolk.

"They're from Huin-Shi," Cho-ka reported after questioning a family pushing an ox-less cart along the road. "Seems an army landed by ship a mile from the city a few days ago, a great mob of ravening fanatics calling out prayers to the Darkblade as they hurled themselves at the walls, at least as far as these folk tell it. They managed to get out before the place came under siege."

"The ships taken at Hahn-Shi," Vaelin realised, recalling the map Mi-Hahn had plucked from the head of the captured bookkeeper. He bit down a sigh of frustration at failing to anticipate this move on the Darkblade's board. *He took his horsemen to Nuan-Khi to claim his sister, but packed his Redeemed onto ships to invade the Enlightened Kingdom by sea.* His self-reproach was heightened by the knowledge that the black-song hadn't raised any warning of this outcome. The reason was obvious, even though he tried to suppress the urge to ponder it. The black-song, however, felt no such restraint, voicing a caustic tune, reduced to a whisper by the elixir but still potent enough to leave a sting: *Because you caged me. Let me free, or he wins.*

"Brother?"

He found Cho-ka staring at him, features bunched in puzzlement, as were those of his companions. Vaelin realised he had been sitting motionless in the saddle with his head lowered for a protracted interval as he fought the urges left in the black-song's wake. "Has the city fallen?" he asked.

"The garrison was putting up a pretty good fight when they fled. The governor's a former admiral in the Enlightened fleet, but who knows how long he'll hold out? They did have a crumb of good news to offer. The emperor put his host ashore just a few miles further on. Last they saw he was marching to save the city. Looks like the Imperial Host is about to fight its first battle."

CHAPTER SEVENTEEN

The battle was already raging by the time they rode within sight of Huin-Shi. The city resembled a miniature version of Keshin-Kho, being formed of a roughly conical settlement atop a hill overlooking the natural harbour beyond. Unlike Keshin-Kho, it featured only one outer wall, which had been breached in three places. Smoke drifted in ugly grey clouds across the scene, preventing Vaelin from gaining a clear picture of events, but he could see a sprawl of disordered infantry assailing one another on the western slope whilst two columns advanced in good order up the eastern slope, making for the two largest breaches. Although the smoke lay thick over the battlefield, even from this distance the continual din told of an unabated struggle.

"Where is the emperor?" the abbot demanded, surveying the scene with near-desperate eyes. Clearly, the prospect of losing his Heavenly chosen monarch so soon weighed heavily on his mind.

Vaelin sought guidance from the black-song, receiving a grudging eastward mutter in response. Squinting, he managed to make out a banner waving at the forefront of the more advanced column. It marched with a steady purpose towards the widest breach in the wall. "There," he said, pointing. "It appears he sent skirmishers to draw off the rear guard before launching his main assault. A decent plan . . ."

The abbot was already spurring his horse forward, snarling at the

Servants to follow. They charged off towards the eastern slope, swords drawn and lances levelled.

"Do we follow, my lord?" Sehmon asked.

"No." Vaelin nodded at the confused and frenzied infantry melee on the western slope. The mismatched armour of the Imperial Host made it difficult to gauge the weight of numbers on either side, but it seemed to him the darker garb of the Redeemed was markedly less evident amidst the chaos. The dark mass of Redeemed was thickest in the most narrow breach and appeared to be gaining ground, albeit slowly. Once they fought their way into the city, he had no doubts about the kind of slaughter they would wreak on its inhabitants.

"Stay together," he said, drawing his sword and pausing to meet Ellese's eyes. She held the sabre he had given to her atop the walls of Keshin-Kho, the blade once carried by Varnko Materk, Skeltir of Ostra Skeld who had deserved a better end. Vaelin knew she was deadly with a bow and lethal at close quarters with a knife, but this was battle.

"Wasting time, Uncle," she told him before he could voice any cautionary words. The smile she tried to form emerged as more of a grimace, and he took some comfort from the knowledge that she at least had learned enough to be afraid.

He nodded to Nortah who placed his horse alongside as they set off, cantering for the first hundred yards then accelerating into a gallop, the others falling in behind. Derka tossed his head and whinnied in anticipation when they started up the slope towards the smoke-covered city, the drum of hoof-beats swallowed by the tumult of combat. The haze grew thicker as they ascended, the incline gentle enough to allow the horses to maintain a decent pace. The combination of speed and smoke ensured the first Redeemed they encountered were smashed aside before they had time to raise a weapon in defence. Vaelin slashed at any within reach of his blade, their thinning numbers and lack of cohesion ensuring an uninterrupted charge all the way to the base of the city walls. The smoke parted as they neared the struggle, allowing Vaelin to make out a mass of Redeemed thronging the ragged gap of the breach, somehow prevented from moving into the city whilst a growing number of Imperial Host soldiers assailed them from the rear.

He steered Derka towards an unmolested section of the Redeemed mob, reining him to a halt. The breach was too crammed with combatants to allow for a successful charge, but not immune to the rage of a Steppe-born stallion bred for battle. Derka's snorts and whinnies betrayed a deep exultation as he reared, lashing out with his forehooves to crush skulls and pound men and women into the earth. A few Redeemed turned about to face the new danger, launching themselves at Vaelin with jabbing spears and flailing swords. He cut down two with a left and right slash of the Order blade, another falling to Nortah's sword and a fourth falling dead with Alum's spear buried in his chest.

The Moreska's face formed a snarl of frustration as he tried to tug the spear free of the Redeemed's ribs. Cursing in Alpiran, he leapt down from the saddle, stamping onto the corpse's chest to draw out the spear in time to parry the thrust of another Redeemed then whirling to deliver a blinding slash to the man's eyes. Never fond of fighting on horseback, Alum made no attempt to remount his mare, instead joining the growing but ragged line of Imperial soldiers in thrusting their spears into the scrum of Redeemed.

"Who's in charge?" Vaelin demanded of a nearby corporal, receiving a look of mingled shock and bafflement in response.

"Aren't you, lord?" the soldier asked, Vaelin noting how young he was under the accumulated grime and gore covering his face. "Our captain got ran through back there, and the sergeant got his head bashed in." He looked around in abject confusion. "Can't find my men, see?"

"*They* are your men now." Vaelin pointed his sword at a group of soldiers nearby, all leaning on their spears and sagging in exhaustion. "Form them up on the right flank."

The corporal gave a sketchy salute and hurried off, shouting orders. Vaelin turned Derka back towards the fray, seeing Sehmon had also dismounted to fight at Alum's side. Nortah and Ellese were wheeling about, hacking down a group of Redeemed who had sallied from the breach.

"Draw back," Vaelin told them. "Gather all the archers you can find amongst this lot."

After they galloped off, Vaelin rode back and forth, haranguing straggling soldiers into some semblance of a formation. The small number of surviving sergeants and officers, all dazed and drained by the ferocity of the recent fight on the slope, soon recovered their wits at the sound of an authoritative voice. Within a few moments he had managed to put together a reasonably cohesive force about two hundred strong. The Redeemed in the

breach were responding to the attacks against their rear with increasing violence, showing customary disregard for their own lives with successive
rushes at their tormentors.

Vaelin ordered his scratch force into a crescent formation before calling
out to Alum and Sehmon to pull back to the new line. The Moreska despatched a charging Redeemed with a spear-thrust to the belly before he and
Sehmon backed away, the other soldiers following their example. A number
of Redeemed attempted to charge in pursuit but were cut down by an arcing
volley of arrows and crossbow bolts from the two dozen archers Nortah and
Ellese had managed to scrape together.

"Hold!" Vaelin called out, steadying the line in expectation of a larger
charge. The Redeemed in the breach, however, were still mostly concerned
with fighting their way into the city. He heard no shouted orders and saw no
rallying banners, but they all seemed possessed of the same unifying purpose. He saw several turn their backs on the assembled ranks of Imperial
soldiers to once again hurl themselves into the crush of the breach. A thick
pall of smoke and steam clouded the air above the Redeemed, making it difficult to see whatever defences lay beyond. From the way the Redeemed were
now inching forward with rhythmic collective shoves, heedless of the continuing rain of bolts and arrows loosed at them by Nortah, Ellese and their
collection of archers, he concluded this breach was about to fall. Although
he could still hear nothing that resembled a commanding voice from the
Redeemed, they were far from quiet, calling out the same prayer-chants he
had heard at Keshin-Kho.

Their god has decreed they take this city, Vaelin surmised. *And so they will
or die in the trying. But*, he reminded himself, *their god's scripture has an
enemy.*

"Stand ready!" he barked out, trotting Derka forward. "No man takes a
step back!" He came to a halt midway between the Redeemed and the crescent of soldiers, raising his sword high and calling out in his loudest voice.
"Will you cower from the Thief of Names?!"

An immediate hush fell on the nearest Redeemed, which soon spread to
the entire throng. Their prayer-chants died away as they abandoned their
heaving advance. The entire close-packed mass turned as one, the same
frowning incomprehension showing on each face. They were all of Far Western origin, the youngest in their mid-teens, the eldest close to sixty. Their

weapons and armour the same non-uniform collection he had seen before. However, the suddenness with which the puzzlement on each face switched to enraged bloodlust told of a unity of purpose. It appeared the Darkblade had imbued all his Redeemed with a deep desire to kill the Thief of Names.

The sound that rose from the Redeemed was scarcely recognisable as human, a snarl of ravenous fury that signalled their attack. They streamed from the breach like water unleashed from a shattered barrel, clawing at one another to get to him, eyes blazing with hate. He had intended to return to the ranks of soldiers, but there was no time as the Redeemed came for the Thief of Names with inhuman haste.

Vaelin dragged on Derka's reins, causing the stallion to rear once more, hooves lashing out to send the first few Redeemed to the earth. The onrushing crowd filled Vaelin's sight as he allowed the black-song to guide his blade, the sword hacking down to shatter the hate-filled faces on either side. Derka gave a shrill scream of anger as he dipped his head to bite at the Redeemed and Vaelin's sword became red from point to hilt. The throng had almost surrounded him now, and would surely have borne him down to be crushed and rent to pieces if the soldiers of the Imperial Host hadn't surged forward to halt their charge.

Spears and swords stabbed with frenzied energy as the soldiers matched the Redeemed's fury with their own. Veterans sought retribution for past defeats whilst youthful recruits vented their rage at abandoned homes and slain relatives. The two sides may have been matched in ferocity, but the Redeemed still held the advantage of numbers, despite the dozens falling to the soldiers' blades each passing second. Such a weight of flesh and steel might have buckled and broken the soldiers' ranks if Vaelin hadn't been the focus of their assault. Some Redeemed ignored all distractions in their desperation to get at him, seemingly oblivious to grievous wounds suffered in the process. The soldiers were even able to surround them as they clustered in the centre, Vaelin seeing several disappear under the seething mass to be trampled underfoot.

Still they came on with undiminished fury, heedless of the many faces he cleaved or limbs he severed. He gritted his teeth against the lure of the black-song as it rose in dissonant joy with every life taken. Although he allowed it to guide his sword, he refused to surrender to it completely, even as the crowding Redeemed before him swelled and forced him back. Clawed hands lashed out to snare Derka's bridle, whilst another Redeemed, bleeding from numerous wounds and scuttling forward on hands and knees, managed to grip his stirrup. The wounded man hauled at Vaelin's foot with a strength that should have been beyond him. Vaelin swayed in the saddle and would have toppled from Derka's back if Alum hadn't forced his way forward to spear the Redeemed through the neck. Sehmon appeared on Vaelin's left, spear thrusting with furious energy.

The Redeemed, however, seemed to possess an endless well of strength, and two of them were borne up by the throng to assail him from the front. One fell when Derka's teeth bit deep into his throat, but the second managed to clamp a hand on Vaelin's neck, raising a dagger with his other. The man's snarling face froze as something sharp and red erupted from the centre of his forehead. Vaelin had time to recognise the barb of a crossbow bolt before the Redeemed tumbled away. The air became filled with the thrum of multiple bolts launched at once. The throng of Redeemed convulsed as the rain of missiles slammed home, Vaelin looking up to see numerous soldiers crowding the battlements on either side of the breach. Many were rapidly reloading their crossbows whilst others cast a constant barrage of stones at the Redeemed.

With so many fallen at once, the pressure of the assault slackened, and the soldiers responded to shouted exhortations from their sergeants and thrusted with renewed vigour. The diminishing throng was gradually forced back towards the breach, where they were greeted by a new rain, this one formed of oil from upended clay pots. Flaming torches soon followed, engulfing the surviving Redeemed in fire.

Vaelin shouted orders for the soldiers to withdraw and allow the fire to do its work, but still the Redeemed were not done. A few dozen charged from the midst of the inferno, armour, skin and hair alight, hurling themselves at the Thief of Names. All were cut down by swarms of crossbow bolts from above. Those too injured or burnt to fight returned to their prayer-chants, discordant voices shrieking their devotion until the flames finally ate away their tongues.

◆　◆　◆

Sherin knelt beside the body of a girl no more than thirteen years old. Small, thin and pale, and clad in simple garb with no scrap of armour, she lay outside the walls near the largest of the three breaches. The paleness of her skin was a contrast to the dark stain of accumulated dried blood that covered its lower half. Vaelin had seen this before and knew well what it meant.

"Gifted," he said.

Sherin glanced up at him with her typical compassion evident on her face, but also a new glimmer of anger in her eyes. "It was she who brought down the walls," she said, voice raspy until she coughed and continued. "Just one small girl with no weapons and no escort. Even when the battlements started cracking beneath their feet the archers couldn't bring themselves to kill her."

More likely they didn't understand what was happening, Vaelin thought. From what he had seen of the defenders of Huin-Shi they didn't strike him as overly sentimental. The Enlightened Kingdom had a much more ingrained tradition of professional soldiery than their neighbour to the north, maintaining a larger standing army organised around a core of experienced officers and senior sergeants. Also, all adult male citizens below the age of fifty were required to serve in reserve regiments, providing an additional well of trained recruits in times of war. Consequently, the local garrison of only five hundred men had swollen to over two thousand by the time the Darkblade's fleet hove into view.

The Redeemed army that swept ashore numbered close to twenty thousand, all that could be crammed onto the available ships. Even against such odds, Vaelin reckoned the defenders could have held out for weeks or even months given their discipline and the stoutness of their walls. Then this girl emerged from the ranks of the Redeemed and the wall collapsed in three different places. The governor had moved quickly to block the breaches with veteran companies, but against so many their fate would surely have been sealed if Tsai Lin hadn't chosen to intervene.

Vaelin scanned the expanse of sea beyond the city, unblemished by any ships and rendered a pleasing shade of gold by the fading sun. It seemed the Darkblade's fleet had disappeared with the evening tide, although he entertained few doubts that they would find Redeemed aplenty waiting to refill their holds in the northern ports.

He crouched at Sherin's side, noting the red stains on her sleeves and rawness of her hands, which told of recent and thorough scrubbing. Clearly, she had been tending wounded for some time. "He did the same thing at Keshin-Kho," he said, nodding to the girl. "A boy that time. It seems he now prefers to recruit children into the ranks of his Gifted. Easier to control and less likely to follow his sister's example in questioning the Darkblade's divinity. We'll see more like her before this is over."

He rose, offering her a hand. "Come, the emperor has called us to conference. It appears the governor is willing to talk."

◆ ◆ ◆

The governor of Huin-Shi was a trim man of small stature with the permanently salt-reddened features that told of a life mostly spent at sea. Although his hair was uniformly steel grey in colour and his complexion creased, the man's evident vitality and keenly intelligent gaze made it difficult to guess his age. Vaelin assumed he must be more than fifty, but the depth of experience in his voice told of a far older soul.

He received them in the main hall of the governor's residence, a place of wide, polished wooden floors and stout ancient beams of oak supporting a tall ceiling from which banners had been suspended. Vaelin couldn't decipher the Far Western script on display, but the martial nature of much of the symbology led him to the conclusion that these were regimental banners, some showing the black and brown stains of the recent struggle. He decided it said much of the governor's judgement that, despite such a display of military valour, he had chosen to meet them without any guards present. Whatever might be spoken or agreed to in this chamber would be best kept private, at least for now.

"Nuraka Shan," the governor said, greeting Tsai Lin with a formal bow. It was a precisely measured gesture Vaelin recognise as appropriate for dignitaries equal to one's own rank.

"It is my great honour to meet you," Tsai Lin replied, his own bow considerably lower. This, Vaelin knew, created a dilemma for the governor. To be shown more respect than that offered to a guest could be a source of great embarrassment.

Nuraka Shan, however, merely blinked in response, keeping his features impassive as he said, "On behalf of the Most Honoured Mah-Lol, Monarch of the Enlightened Kingdom, I offer thanks for coming to the aid of this city. Although I offer no assurances, I will request mercy when he passes judgement on your unlawful intrusion into his domain."

The abbot, whom Tsai Lin had permitted to attend the meeting only after Sherin's persuasion, gave a loud, grating laugh. "Oh, fuck off. This place would now be a smoking ruin but for this man. You should be on your knees, begging for your emperor's mercy . . ."

"Quiet!" Tsai Lin snapped. The old man sighed and fell silent but maintained a hard stare at the governor. In the immediate aftermath of the Redeemed's defeat, the abbot had led the Servants into the city's main square where he gave an impromptu speech to a loose gathering of local soldiery and townsfolk. Their dazed and besmirched faces betrayed mostly bafflement or scorn as he proclaimed the coming of the reborn emperor and the birth of the Jade Empire. To Vaelin's eyes, the governor's attitude to such pronouncements mirrored that of his people.

"Nuraka is a name from the Free Cantons, is it not?" Tsai Lin said, favouring the governor with a smile that he failed to return.

"My mother hailed from the Cantons," Nuraka Shan replied tonelessly. "My father was a captain in the Gilded Fleet of Lol-Than, father to our most honoured king."

"Who is to be commended in his choice of servants. Please know, Honoured Admiral, I come not as an invader. I come to defend the people of these lands as I have striven to defend those in the north . . ."

"I haven't been called 'admiral' for a long time," Nuraka Shan broke in. It was a considerable breach of etiquette but Vaelin was learning this man perhaps stood alone amongst the nobility of the Far West in not caring one whit for ancient formalities. "And your defence of the Venerable Kingdom would appear to be somewhat lacking, since you are here and the barbarians are there."

The abbot's stare turned into a glower and he would no doubt have voiced another profane retort if Vaelin hadn't spoken first.

"Your city has already fallen, to us."

The governor's gaze narrowed as it switched to Vaelin, rich in scrutiny but lacking the usual sneering disregard for foreigners commonly displayed by nobles in these lands. "You drew the mad ones back," he said. "They came within inches of breaking into the city but abandoned their assault when they were presented with the chance of killing you. Why?"

"Their god doesn't like me."

"You have met the Darkblade?"

"I have." Vaelin gestured to Sherin. "So has the Healing Grace of Heaven whose renown I'm sure has reached this far, so you know my words are true.

You think the Darkblade a conqueror, a lunatic pretending godhood at the head of a barbarian horde. In fact, he is a plague. One that will spread. This city may stand but its survival is temporary, an illusion. More ships will come bearing more mad ones and you will not stand against them. The Enlightened Kingdom will soon fall." Vaelin nodded at Tsai Lin. "Only this man can offer you the chance of salvation."

He saw the governor maintain a rigid composure, his doubts betrayed only by the smallest tightening of his jaw. "I have received firm assurances from the court of our king that reinforcements will arrive shortly. The Northern Division marches to our aid as we speak. The barbarians will be turned back."

Vaelin turned expectantly to the fifth person present who had so far remained silent. Luralyn greeted the governor with an incline of her head that he failed to return in any regard.

"This woman is Stahlhast," he stated, eyes flinty as he turned back to Vaelin.

"She is," he agreed. "I present Luralyn Reyerik of the Cova Skeld. She is also the Darkblade's sister and possessor of a singular blessing of Heaven. You would do well to listen to her."

Nuraka Shan's control began to slip then, a redness creeping over his face, matched by the heat in his voice. "You expect me to stand here and take counsel from this barbarian witch . . ."

"You made the king a ship," Luralyn said, causing the governor to fall into an abrupt silence. "Mah-Lol, when he was boy. You returned from one of your expeditions to the southern seas and presented him with the model you had crafted during the voyage. He cherished it, as he cherished you. No other member of the court was so honest, nor so willing to spend time in his company. His father was a stranger to him, little more than a living statue of silk and gold who deigned to speak to his sons no more than once a year. When Mah-Lol ascended to the throne, his father's courtiers were mostly pensioned off, the more ambitious and venal poisoned or commanded to commit suicide, but not you, his true friend. To you he gave a city, although you begged him for a return to the sea. 'I need a new hand on the tiller of the Gilded Fleet,' he told you. In fact, he wanted an admiral who saw no dishonour in using the fleet to transport slaves."

Vaelin watched the governor's face tighten, lips quivering but raising no objection as Luralyn continued. "Your king still plays with his toy ship, but now he has many others. He sits in his great bath for many hours a day fighting battles against enemies only he can see whilst his court descends into chaos around him. Rebellions have broken out in all provinces; the Northern Division is beset by disease, desertion and mutiny. They will march nowhere but to abject defeat when my brother finds the boats to carry his horde across the water, and he will."

She fell silent, offering another incline of her head to the governor and Tsai Lin before stepping back.

"This kingdom is lost," Tsai Lin told Nuraka Shan. "Come with me and build an empire. I have need of an admiral."

CHAPTER EIGHTEEN

T his is all?"

Nuraka Shan, recently promoted Admiral of the Imperial Fleet, gave a sombre nod as he gestured to the vessels in the harbour. "One of our scout ships brought two days' advance warning of the barbarians' approach. I packed all the women, children and old folk I could onto the available ships and sent them off to Lishun-Shi. The vessels that remain were mostly unfit for the voyage, but I did keep hold of a few seaworthy ships in case they proved useful."

The natural harbour of Huin-Shi was partially shielded by a wall that extended down the seaward slope to form two moles that served as both defense against the tides and waterborne invasion. The sight of the moles, substantial structures featuring tall defensive towers, caused Vaelin a pang of regret at having to forsake this city. With sufficient numbers it could have held out for a very long time. In addition to a hundred-strong fleet of fishing boats, there were a total of twenty-three ships in the harbour, all merchantmen save for the narrow-hulled, two-masted vessel that had brought word of the impending Redeemed assault. She differed from most ships of Far Western manufacture with a shape and rigging more reminiscent of a Meldenean design.

"The *Stormhawk*," Nuraka Shan said, seeing Vaelin's interest. "I took her as a prize years ago. Pirates they may be, but those far-off islanders know how to build a fast ship, I'll give them that. I once attempted to persuade the

Royal yards to copy her, but the shipwrights rioted at the mere suggestion. Undoing tradition is ever frowned on in these lands."

"But not by you," Vaelin observed, recalling the admiral's disregard for social custom. "Your king must have forgiven much over the years."

The former governor's face clouded at the mention of his king and he gave no reply. In the two days since voicing his taciturn agreement to Tsai Lin's terms, he had maintained rigid composure, any contemplation of his prior loyalties kept hidden behind an unchanging mask.

"I'll have need of a ship soon," Vaelin said, turning back to the *Stormhawk*. "Fast but capable of navigating the southern seas, particularly the Opal Isles. Is she up to the task?"

"I've sailed her all the way to Linesh and back, but she's not much good without a crew or a captain. I pressed every sailor into service as a soldier. There aren't many left, including the *Stormhawk*'s captain. He was a genius at gauging the stars and the wind, but useless with a sword."

"I have a captain." Vaelin turned to go. "And we'll find a crew."

"Lord Vaelin," Nuraka Shan said, making him pause. "There are only enough ships here to evacuate a few hundred people at most. Certainly not enough to carry an army."

"Then we'll have to march to where there are."

◆ ◆ ◆

This time Tsai Lin raised no objections to abandoning a recently seized city. The breaches in the walls would take months to repair and there were insufficient supplies to sustain the army and populace throughout a protracted siege. There was also little point attempting to hold a city without hope of reinforcement. As at Nuan-Khi, no one was forced to join the Imperial Host or follow it south along the coast to the capital. However, throughout the four days it took to prepare for the march, the abbot spent many hours proclaiming the emperor's divinely blessed ascension to any who would listen. The Servants' word carried a good deal of weight in the Enlightened Kingdom, but Vaelin suspected the willingness of so many to follow their governor's example in swearing loyalty to Tsai Lin owed more to a basic desire for survival than any devotional instinct.

"A drowning man will grasp at the thinnest rope," Captain Ohtan noted, shielding his eyes against the rising sun as he surveyed the long procession atop the cliffs south of Huin-Shi. Neat columns of soldiers marched ahead of a long line of people, a mingling of folk driven from two cities. They would follow the coast road south whilst the Imperial Fleet, such as it was, would protect the fishing boats as they laboured to keep the emperor's host fed throughout the journey. Some fishermen had vanished with their boats come the morning tide, much to Admiral Nuraka's annoyance, though he decided any attempt at pursuit would be pointless.

He had taken over the largest merchantman for service as his flagship after scouring the city and the Imperial Host for any souls with sailing experience. The results were poor, something Vaelin ascribed to the Far Western custom of rarely changing professions chosen or inherited at an early age. Consequently, the fishing boats were all left with half their usual complement and the other ships obliged to sail with the bare minimum required to work a ship at sea. Their crews had been augmented with two hundred soldiers in case any fighting might be required, but none seemed to know one end of a rope from the other and most were already disgorging their breakfast over the rails.

"Hardly the Gilded Fleet, lad," Captain Ohtan said, grimacing at the sight of a dozen soldiers busily heaving into the choppy waters.

"But it is a fleet," Vaelin replied. "One we didn't have yesterday."

"I suppose the plan is that we get to Lishun-Shi and overawe the entire city with the emperor's glory. The people come over to us and the Merchant King graciously steps aside so we can seize his fleet and destroy the barbarians before they land another army."

"Your shrewd insight does you credit, Captain."

"It's not going to work, you know."

Vaelin turned to the captain, finding a serious frown on his newly revitalised face. "Merchant Kings," Ohtan went on, "and those that serve them don't just give up power. Especially not to some boy from nowhere, regardless of what blessings the Servants heap on him. Mah-Lol may be as mad as a sun-baked dog, but those around him aren't. If we want Lishun-Shi, we're going to have to fight for it."

Vaelin looked to the south, seeing tall clouds rising above a steel-grey sea. He couldn't find fault with Ohtan's reasoning but the black-song told a different story. A full dose of Kish-an's elixir had denuded its underlying ugliness, producing a tune that told of chaos beyond the horizon, but no real danger. There was also a small, unusually light note that might well indicate opportunity.

"We'll see," he said, gesturing at the deck and the rigging. "How do you find your new ship?"

The captain's face brightened a little at the change of subject, although a few lines of concern lingered on his brow. "She's a wonder. Served on a few Meldenean tubs over the years and they're always a lick or two faster than most ships. This girl though"—he ran a hand over the smooth oak of the rail—"she's a real thoroughbred. With a decent wind she'll outpace anything else afloat." He winced as a newly recruited sailor let out a stream of curses when a rope slipped through his grip, burning his palms in the process. "Would've liked a decent crew to go with her, though."

"With you to whip them into shape, I've little doubt she'll fly fast enough for my purposes." He clapped the captain on the shoulder. "The admiral has given us permission to leave the fleet and scout ahead. Let's be at it, eh?"

◆ ◆ ◆

"Well," Captain Ohtan said as the shifting orange glow played over his shocked features, "seems we won't have to fight for it after all, unless the emperor's keen to hold dominion over a pile of ash."

The fire had clearly been burning for some time. The northern sprawl of Lishun-Shi was already a blackened ruin where smaller blazes lingered like embers in a scattering of charred logs. Beyond the docks, a sea of flames consumed the centre of the city, some rising to mountainous heights as they devoured the mass of housing below. The southern districts weren't yet fully ablaze, but the inferno, driven by a stiff northerly wind, was moving rapidly from street to street. Even above the distant roar of flame, Vaelin could hear thousands of voices raised in panicked flight.

"Stahlhast?" Nortah wondered, the brightness of the fire causing him to squint as he surveyed the dying city.

"Even they could never have covered so many miles so quickly," Vaelin said.

"Riot, then? A rebellion gone out of control?"

Vaelin frowned, shaking his head. "I don't think so." The black-song was singing louder now, due he supposed to the elixir thinning in his veins. The tune was the unmistakable music of recognition. *This is a product of the Dark.*

"We have to go ashore."

They both turned to find Sherin at the rail, staring at the burning city with fierce intensity, her tone hard with inarguable resolve.

"The place is a death trap, sister," Nortah said with an appalled laugh.

She ignored him, instead fixing her gaze on Vaelin. "Something comes back," she said before nodding to the city. "There is someone we need to find."

Juhkar, Vaelin recalled. The former Stahlhast slave with the tracking gift she had healed during the siege, only for him to die at the Darkblade's hand. But still, she had healed him. *Something comes back.*

"What is it?" he asked her.

"A soul in need of healing." She moved away, instructing Ohtan Lah to ready a boat. The captain, who tended to display an unquestioning regard, even devotion, for the woman who had healed him, moved immediately to comply.

"Stay if you like," Sherin told Vaelin as the boat was hauled over the side.

Vaelin smothered a sigh before joining her in clambering over the rail. He made no attempt to command or persuade the others but they all wordlessly followed them onto the boat, Ellese cursing as she slipped and had to be hauled aboard, half-soaked.

"Shut up, you!" she said, flicking water at Sehmon's smirking face.

"Oars," Vaelin told them both. He and Alum took the other oars whilst Sherin had charge of the tiller and Nortah positioned himself at the prow, bow in hand. Vaelin felt the skin on the back of his neck prickle as they neared the city, the growing heat provoking a slick of sweat down his spine. At Captain Ohtan's suggestion they made for the northern fringe of the harbour where a huge stone pier jutted into the water. It loomed above as they neared it, more an elongated town than a pier, with houses and shops clustered along its length. The buildings were mostly constructed of stone, meaning they had so far proven immune to the flames. As they neared the point at which the pier joined the docks, it transpired the local inhabitants had chosen not to take any chances. A twenty-yard stretch of buildings had been torn down to create a firebreak, and a large number of people were working relays of buckets to douse the ruins with seawater.

"What clever folk," Nortah observed, waving to the people on the pier. None waved back and those that noticed their passing just stared in blank incomprehension before returning to their labours.

"Who started it?!" Nortah persisted, cupping his hands around his mouth as he called out before pointing to the flaming shoreline.

Most of the bucket-hauling people ignored him, but one man momentarily left off from his labours to call back: "Buggered if we know! Whole northern quarter went up in flames at midday!"

"Don't worry!" Nortah assured them with another wave. "The emperor's coming!"

Vaelin saw the man onshore exchange bemused glances with his neighbours, his answer a distant fading call as they rowed on. "What fucking emperor?!"

◆ ◆ ◆

They moored the boat at a small jetty on the dock's northern edge, Vaelin setting Alum and Sehmon the task of guarding it. They protested at being left behind, but not with the fierceness he had come to expect. He sensed concealed relief rather than injured pride in their sweat-damp features as they eyed the flames rising over the rooftops.

"If the fire gets too close, put to sea," he told them before turning to Sherin, gesturing at the city in expectation. "Your gift, your hunt."

She replied with a faint frown of annoyance, most of her attention preoccupied with scouring the various streets beyond the docks. "This way," she said, making for the broadest thoroughfare, which seemed to lead into the heart of the city. She moved at a half run, maintaining the same concentrated frown that didn't waver at the sight of various horrors encountered along the way. Corpses lay in clusters at junctions or doorways, some burnt, others with the slack, openmouthed features that told of death by suffocation. Embers swirled in hot blizzards, driven by a gale that at times threatened to pitch them into one of the blazing houses. Sherin, however, seemed to be following a map only she could see, a route that allowed them to skirt the worst of the fire. Still, it wasn't without danger. Twice they had to sprint to avoid a cascade of burning timbers from collapsing houses. But, as ever in times of disaster, the greatest danger came from its victims.

Maddened people stumbled into their path, some rendered blank eyed and passive with shock, others driven to unreasoning violence by what they had seen. Vaelin was obliged to knock one man unconscious when he came charging out of the smoke, screaming about evil foreign magics with a cleaver raised high in his hand. Sherin barely seemed to notice when Vaelin's fist slammed into the crazed man's temple, sparing his unconscious form the briefest glance before squinting into the glowing haze. "There," she said, pointing to a tall, crenelated silhouette rising above the smoke ahead.

Following her, Vaelin sought guidance from the song as to what her quarry might be. Its sullen response was confined to a discordant tune that spoke of both danger and salvation, counterpointed by the same faint, hopeful note from before.

They soon came to a broad expanse of what appeared to be parkland. Once clear of the streets, the gale-like winds lessened, making it harder to see through the thickened smoke, although he could now see that the tall silhouette was a palace. As they drew nearer he gained a better impression of its size, proving to be only marginally smaller than the city-within-a-city from which Lian Sha had ruled over the Venerable Kingdom. A large portion of it was burning, tall flames licking over the eastern wall to feed the conflagration within. Sherin led them towards a bastion of the south-facing wall, Vaelin seeing no guards and finding the gate standing open. Bodies lay scattered about the courtyard beyond, all burnt with smoke still rising from their charred armour. Oddly, the cherry blossom trees that lined the winding pathway to the inner palace were all untouched by fire.

They made their way through a maze of shrines, gardens and statuary, Sherin never faltering in her course, nor pausing even at the sight of the bodies they encountered. Although this wing of the palace appeared untouched by fire, the corpses, like the guards at the bastion, had all been scorched to death. She finally came to a halt at the edge of a broad circular courtyard surrounding a large three-storey building. The corpses were most numerous here, more guards arranged in a loose circle around the building, causing Vaelin to conclude they had died trying to defend it. The wind was also stronger now, whipping at them with harsh ferocity and heated by the fire raging only a few hundred paces away.

"Uncle," Ellese said, voice heavy with unease as she nodded at a blaze consuming a garden on the other side of the courtyard. Having claimed what fuel it could from the garden, the blaze lurched towards one of the wooden posterns ringing the courtyard then abruptly reared back as the wind gusted with fresh energy. Looking around, Vaelin saw the fire being kept at bay to the north and the east, leaving the courtyard a partial island of order in a sea of flaming ruin. He doubted it was accidental.

"Wait," he said, the hardness of his tone enough to halt Sherin in place as she started towards the building. Ignoring her scowl, he drew his sword and stepped in front of her, Nortah and Ellese nocking arrows and falling in on either side. The black-song still sang the same uncertain tune, but louder now, the note of warning keener than ever.

They started forward, maintaining a steady, cautious pace. Vaelin insisted on circling the building once before entering, stepping over a score of armoured corpses but finding no obvious threat. They entered via the opulently carved main entrance to be greeted by more bodies. They lay together on the marble floor, Vaelin making out scraps of fine silk amongst the pile of blackened limbs and skulls seared down to the bone. *Courtiers*, he concluded before spying a long braid of silken black hair bound with ornate silver, somehow untouched amongst the charred remains. *And wives.*

They came to an abrupt halt as a sound echoed from deep within the building, so out of place amongst this scene of charred slaughter it took a moment to recognise it as the loud, delighted giggle of a child at play.

The laughter drew them on, Vaelin leading with deliberate slowness, eyes snapping from one doorway and corridor to the next, but seeing only more corpses. As they moved deeper into this miniature palace the air began to thicken, not with smoke, but steam. It was thin enough to provide a clear view of the large, high vaulted chamber ahead, and the pool it held. Sherin let out a choked gasp at the sight of more bodies lying at the pool's edge, her distress born of the fact that these were not soldiers, courtiers or wives, but children. There were four of them, two boys and two girls, Vaelin guessing their age at somewhere between ten and twelve. They wore ragged, threadbare clothes, unmarked by fire, and all bore the raw, red chafing to their wrists that spoke of having been recently shackled. Vaelin paused to look at one, a girl with the features of the northern border country. Although her face was untouched by flame, he had no difficulty in discerning the cause of her death. Red tears streamed from her eyes and fresh blood lay thick around her nose and mouth.

"Gifted," he muttered to Sherin. "She bled herself dry."

Another giggle drew his gaze back to the pool, the steam parting to reveal the sight of a small figure perched on an ornamental island in the centre. The larger form of a man stood in the pool itself, surrounded by a bobbing fleet of toy ships.

"And that one?" the small figure asked, pointing to one of the ships.

"*The King's Revenge*," the man replied, a note of pride in his voice as he plucked the model from the water. "She'll be the biggest in the Gilded Fleet when she's finished. With her and her sisters I'll carry my host north to smite the Darkblade and take the Venerable Kingdom. It should always have been mine, anyway."

The small figure's hands went to its mouth as it let out another giggle. "You're so funny!"

The man in the pool laughed along, although his humour faded into stern-faced anger as he caught sight of Vaelin and the others. "I summoned no attendants," he said, water splashing as he flicked a dismissive hand. "Get out."

Mah-Lol, Merchant King of the Enlightened Kingdom, was a man of impressive stature, his finely muscled torso belying his age, which Vaelin guessed to be well past his fiftieth year. He displayed no panic or particular alarm as Vaelin skirted the pool, merely a mounting sense of outraged dignity. "Foreigners, eh?" he huffed. "I no longer receive embassies from your lands. Take yourselves off and seek an audience with my chamberlain of trade."

Vaelin spared this patently deluded soul a brief glance before fixing his gaze on the child. He was a little younger than the corpses lying at the poolside, his features also betraying a border origin and streaked in blood, but much less than the others. His face formed a half-impish, half-delighted smile as Vaelin came closer. "You're the Thief of Names!" he exclaimed, hands clapping in excitement. "He said you might turn up."

"Thief, is it?" Mah-Lol's features darkened further and he reached for a small silver bell set upon a floating tray alongside a crystal decanter. "I'm a merciful ruler but can't abide thievery so it'll be a flogging before they take your head." He began to ring the bell, just a soft tinkle at first but growing in volume when no one came to answer it. After a few seconds' feverish ringing, the bell came apart and fell into the water, Mah-Lol instantly diving under the surface to retrieve the pieces, much to the boy's delight.

"We were supposed to boil him right away," he said, giggling again. "But he's just too funny. Then more of his guards turned up and my brothers and sisters had to play with them too."

"Do you have a name?" Vaelin asked him, causing the laughter to fade, though the impish grin remained.

"Mother and Father named me, but it was wrong." The boy puffed out his chest. "Saikir, the Darkblade named me. It means Wind Fox in Stahlhast."

Vaelin nodded at the dead children. "Did he name them too?"

"Oh yes." The boy extended an arm to point at each corpse in turn. "That's Dream Dance, he made people see whatever he liked. Their houses would burn down and they wouldn't even notice. My sisters, Candle and Torch, could make things burn just by looking at them. Tale Weaver could tell people anything and they'd believe it, like they needed to cover their neighbour's house in oil or the world would end, that kind of thing."

"And you?"

"Didn't you hear my name?" The boy's grin became a sneer. "Wind, stupid. Can't burn a whole city without a lot of wind, can you?"

Mah-Lol splashed back to the surface, face triumphant as he held up the disassembled bell. "Now then," he said, trying to fit the pieces back together then stopping as his face slipped into a mask of confusion. "Why was I doing this?"

Hearing the black-song's note of warning build, Vaelin's gaze snapped back to the boy, meeting his eyes. Under the weight of the song's music it felt like looking into a mirror and seeing a shadowy reflection, one only a little darker than his own. Fresh ripples appeared on the pool water as a chill breeze stirred the air.

"He told me to tell you," Saikir said, raising his arms, the breeze shifting into a hard driving wind that whipped the pool into a froth, "thank you for the picture. When he finds *your* sister he'll paint one of his own, in her blood."

"Nortah!" Vaelin hissed, turning to find his brother with bow drawn and arrow aimed. His face, however, lacked the expected hard, purposeful focus. Instead his eyes were wide with fear and indecision, staring back at Vaelin and shaking his head. *Keshin-Kho*, Vaelin recalled. *The Gifted boy who twisted the minds of the soldiers on the wall.* Plainly, his brother wasn't capable of committing the same crime twice.

They both staggered as a fresh gust blasted them, barely managing to keep their feet. Vaelin heard Ellese grunt as she released her shaft. In contrast to Nortah, her face was fixed in reluctant certainty. The arrow, however, covered only half the distance to the boy before being whipped away like a leaf in a maelstrom. Saikir laughed and the wind turned to a gale, the force of it sending Vaelin and the others tumbling into the pool. Luckily, it proved to be only four feet deep, though the weight of water that assailed him as he found his feet made him consider the possibility he might drown standing upright.

Snorting, he raised an arm to shield his face from the gale, fixing his gaze on the boy, now just a small, dim figure in the whirlwind he had crafted. Although Vaelin didn't try to summon it, the black-song blossomed into a deafening roar, dispelling the effects of the elixir with apparent ease born perhaps of a primal instinct to survive. Its music was unusually melodious, the notes formed into a coherent tune at odds with its typical discordant ugliness. The song it sang was one of command, an assertion of unquestioning authority and a statement of superior power, one Saikir apparently heard in full measure.

The storm he had raised died in an instant, water raining down in a brief deluge as he stood, staring at Vaelin with wide-eyed, openmouthed shock. The song's tune shifted, its note of command unaltered but shot through with a specific imperative: *KILL IT! Now, before it recovers!*

Vaelin thrashed through the water towards the island, the boy continuing to stare at him, arms still raised and seemingly frozen in the same pose. No sound came from him as Vaelin hauled himself free of the pool, not even a whimper raised when the hands clamped around his throat, dragging him towards the water. The black-song quieted when Vaelin prepared to force Saikir's head into the pool, sibilant with anticipation. *Yes . . . drown it.*

"Vaelin!"

The shout cut through the song like a knife, its sudden absence leaving him dazed and blinking into Sherin's wide, appalled eyes. Her hands were latched onto his, attempting to pry them away from Saikir's throat. His fingers slackened and fell away as he recoiled from the depth of disgust and anger in her gaze. He scuttled back to watch her raise the boy up, rubbing his back as he gasped for air. Vaelin saw Nortah and Ellese standing in the pool alongside the Merchant King. Mah-Lol had managed to retrieve one of his toy ships and played contentedly whilst Vaelin's brother and niece exchanged troubled glances. Vaelin shrank from the fear and distress they tried not to show on their faces.

"You are not well." Vaelin's gaze snapped back to Sherin, seeing her smooth a hand over Saikir's brow. "I can help you. Would you like that?"

"Don't," Vaelin grated, rising to his feet. He stepped closer but stopped when Sherin turned to him, face dark with a warning glower. "Something comes back," he reminded her. "You want no part of what's inside him."

"I have no need of your counsel today, Lord Vaelin," she replied, voice clipped and very precise.

"He was supposed to kill us," Saikir coughed, a certain petulant confusion marring his face. "At least one of us, anyway. You were supposed to see it. My other brother said it would be this way."

"Other brother?" Vaelin demanded, drawing another glare from Sherin.

"Uhlkar, it means Coming Dawn." Saikir coughed again, face brightening a little. "We touched the stone together, saw the tiger together. I thought he was the Darkblade's favourite because he sees so much. But, I knew he would like me best when you killed me." He started to strain against Sherin's grasp, features bunching in annoyance. "Get off! The Thief of Names has to kill me . . ."

"Sherin," Vaelin warned, feeling the black-song rise again as it sensed the boy's gift building once more.

"I know," she said, voice soft but determined. "I feel it."

Saikir let out a yell of protest as she pulled him close, wrapping her arms around him. Vaelin watched fury and terror play over his face, feeling the boy's gift roil against Sherin's. For a moment Vaelin feared Saikir's might be stronger as the air began to shift once more, but then Sherin clutched him tighter and the boy's yell became a scream. It was not a sound that should have come from a child's throat, so loud and shrill with pain Vaelin found himself clamping his hands to his ears. Nortah and Ellese did the same, whilst Mah-Lol only grimaced in annoyance before returning to his toy ship.

When the scream finally dwindled into a guttural rasp, Saikir's eyes rolled back into his skull as he slumped into a faint, lying slack in Sherin's arms. Her features were tight as she rose, bearing him up. From the tension in her jaw and temples, Vaelin saw she was attempting to conceal a substantial amount of pain.

"Are you . . . ?" he ventured, reaching out a hand to her.

"Leave me be!" she snapped, pulling her sodden cloak about both her and the boy in her arms. She stayed out of Vaelin's reach as she moved around him. "We need to get back to the ship."

She walked away without waiting for a response, Vaelin nodding at Ellese and Nortah to follow. He lingered for a moment, head and shoulders slumping as he regarded the deluded king still playing in the pool, muttering to himself as he guided his toy ship towards invisible foes.

"You may not remember," Vaelin said, "but there was a minor clerk in your father's court. A young man stolen from his home as a boy, his parents, his entire village killed at the Merchant King's order, all because he could hear the Music of Heaven."

Mah-Lol looked up from his ship with a good-natured smile. "My father had a lot of silly notions," he said. "Or so they tell me."

"Your father was poisoned by a Volarian assassin. The young man could have warned him, but he didn't, out of revenge. Your father died because of his cruelty and because he refused something the Volarians asked of him. I would know what it was."

"The trade agreement, probably." Mah-Lol shrugged, his attention distracted by the sight of a second ship bobbing nearby.

"Trade agreement?" Vaelin asked as the king splashed towards the second ship.

"Exchange of goods and slaves." Mah-Lol gave a pleased laugh as he retrieved the ship and began carefully aligning it alongside the other. "Father didn't like slavery, said it upset the peasants too much. But the Volarians were running short of labour and had a good deal of gold to trade. I restricted the sale of slaves to criminals and debt defaulters; it only seemed fair."

Vaelin's gaze returned to the dead children at the pool edge, lingering on their threadbare garb and the marks left by the chains they had worn. "They came here in the guise of slaves," he realised. "Your father's cruelty doomed him and your greed doomed you. I think the young clerk would have found some satisfaction in that."

"Mmmm?" Mah-Lol looked up once more and it was clear from his empty gaze he had no memory of their prior conversation. "It's unduly warm in here," he said, squinting at the smoke seeping into the bathhouse from the burning city outside. "Fetch chilled water and tell the chamberlain of coin I'll meet him tomorrow. I have more pressing matters to see to at present."

Vaelin stood watching the Merchant King of the Enlightened Kingdom play with toys for a moment longer before bowing low. "I shall, Highness," he said before striding from the bathhouse. Outside, he began to run at the sight of flames licking over the rooftops surrounding the courtyard. Mah-Lol, it appeared, was destined to boil in his bath after all.

CHAPTER NINETEEN

In the space of a single night, the city of Lishun-Shi, once the richest and most well-fortified port in all of the Far West, had been transformed into an expanse of ash covering a few miles of coastline, save for a few neighbourhoods in and around the docks. They had survived due to the exhaustive efforts of their inhabitants in tearing down buildings to create firebreaks whilst battling the flames with a constant supply of water. The death toll was incalculable. Close to a million people had lived here before the fire, and whilst many had fled, the blaze had moved with such swiftness many more had never had the chance. Most of the survivors had formed into disorderly makeshift camps fringing the blackened remnants of the outskirts, whilst thousands of others began a trek towards the imagined safety of the Transcendent Kingdom to the south. Rumours abounded regarding the origin of the fire, from fiery otherworldly beasts descending from the skies to the last insane act of the Merchant King. In all cases, the only thing the rumours agreed upon was that the Darkblade's hand surely lay behind the destruction, either through his magics or having somehow driven their king to madness. For once, Vaelin was forced to conclude rumour born of disaster had found a semblance of truth.

"So," Tsai Lin said, casting a sidelong glance at the abbot, "this will be the jewel at the heart of my empire."

They stood atop the raised headland south of the city from where the great grey swath of the destroyed port could be viewed in its entirety. Besides

Vaelin and Luralyn, Tsai Lin had summoned only the abbot to counsel. Vaelin suspected it wasn't out of a desire to hear the old man's sage words of wisdom.

"I never said it would be easy, did I?" Vaelin replied.

"No," Tsai Lin acceded. "But you did say the blessing of Heaven was upon me and those who follow me. I see little evidence of any blessing here."

"We came for ships. There they are." The abbot pointed to the harbour where a sizeable number of merchant vessels were moored together with much of the Gilded Fleet of the Enlightened Kingdom. The fleet had been gathered at Lishun-Shi weeks ago on Mah-Lol's command, with instructions to prepare for a grand expedition to the north. However, the order to sail had never come, and it appeared the fleet's admiral, a long-standing sycophant of the Merchant King with little in the way of maritime experience, had fled south with the morning tide aboard the fastest ship available. Tsai Lin had wisely sent Nuraka Shan to parley with the now-leaderless captains, although negotiations were proving to be a protracted business. Nuraka Shan still enjoyed great respect amongst the fleet but even he found it a difficult task to persuade so many crews to swear fealty to a previously unknown emperor.

It was a similar story amongst the surviving soldiery of Mah-Lol's army. Many had perished fighting the fire, but a thirty-thousand-strong contingent of veteran regiments remained. They were commanded by a general with an attachment to loyalty that would have done him great credit at any other time. So far, the Servants' pronouncements regarding the new emperor's divine blessing had met with a flat statement that these soldiers served only the Monarch of the Enlightened Kingdom. The fact of the Merchant King's demise, along with all of his heirs, proved insufficient to move the intransigent general who continued to refuse all requests for a personal meeting with Tsai Lin. This vestige of the Enlightened Host remained camped along a line of hills north of the city, its hastily raised fortifications arranged to ward off attacks from all directions.

"To fight the Darkblade's horde I need an army as well as a fleet," Tsai Lin replied. "And so far, few in these lands appear keen to join our ranks."

"So we sail to other lands," Vaelin said, inclining his head at the grey expanse of sea to the south. "The Free Cantons lie but a few days away, and I'm told they still follow the old imperial ways."

"And it's the most devout region in all the Far West," the abbot added.

"The word of Heaven will carry more weight there than in this greed-infested realm."

"Traditionalists they are," Tsai Lin agreed. "And devout, by all accounts. Also, their ruling houses spend much of their time in a constant state of feud. Hardly a year goes by without a notable assassination or bloody massacre."

"Then the common folk will welcome the unifying presence of a reborn emperor," Vaelin said. He spoke with more certainty than he felt. In truth, he had little knowledge of the Free Cantons beyond what Erlin had told him, nor any faith that the people there would be amenable to throwing their lot in with the Jade Empire. However, sailing there would bring him one step closer to the Opal Isles. He continued to resist telling Tsai Lin of his ultimate goal, instinct warning against the emperor's reaction to his trusted advisor soon having to leave his side. The duplicity sat uneasily on Vaelin's shoulders but he didn't shirk it. *Many a war is won with lies*, he thought, recalling his queen's frequent obfuscations and outright falsehoods during the Liberation War.

Tsai Lin swallowed a sigh and turned to Luralyn. "And do your dreams have any guidance to offer?"

"I'm sorry," she said, shaking her head. "But I can offer the judgement of the Darkblade's sister and one born to the Stahlhast." She gestured to the great smear of ash below. "Had it been taken whole, this city might have stood against my brother, but now there is nothing to stop him sweeping to the sea. I've little doubt your host will fight bravely, as will those men over there on that hill, but it would be wasted bravery. The people who chose to follow you did so out of hope of salvation, not a desire for sacrifice, however noble."

The young emperor closed his eyes and raised his face to the sky. It was darkening with cloud, and a few drops of rain had beaded his skin by the time he lowered his gaze. "Is this Heaven's jest, I wonder?" he said as the rain began to fall in earnest. He let out a bitter laugh, turning to gaze at the grey ruin of Lishun-Shi, the ashen sprawl darkening under shifting curtains of rain. "They couldn't have sent this just one day sooner."

He stood straighter, meeting each of their gazes in turn. "We shall sail to the Free Cantons," he said. "But know that this is my final retreat. When the Darkblade next comes against us we will defeat him or meet our end trying. Tell all who choose to follow me this: From the moment we land in the Free

Cantons our every effort will be bent towards just one task, the defeat of the Darkblade and the destruction of his horde. I've had my fill of running."

◆　◆　◆

"Stop doing that!" Chien snatched a tangle of knotted rope from the deck and cast it at Mi-Hahn. The sister sidestepped the flailing missile easily, her face maintaining the same concentrated stare in the outlaw's direction as her charcoal moved across the paper board she held. Chien's face flushed in anger as she hefted her staff, starting towards Mi-Hahn with a determined glint in her eye before Vaelin stepped into her path.

"She does no harm," he said.

"The faces of the Crimson Band are never captured!" Chien snapped, trying to edge around him. "Not even by the Servants of Heaven." He saw a pulsing vein in the outlaw woman's temple, indicating a sudden, unexplained headache, which meant Mi-Hahn's charcoal was capturing more than Chien's face.

"Sister," Vaelin said, barring the outlaw's path once more as he turned to Mi-Hahn, shaking his head. She gave a small grimace of annoyance but duly lowered her paper and charcoal before wandering off towards the *Stormhawk*'s bows, her attention captured by the matrix of rigging above.

"I want that picture," Chien said, starting in pursuit.

"No," Vaelin told her, his tone sufficiently emphatic to halt her in place. "You don't."

She scowled and stepped back, lowering her staff. "This would be easier without them," she said, jutting her chin at the Servants. They sat in a quiescent cluster around the mainmast, thirty in all and lacking the abbot, who preferred to stay at the emperor's side, or at least as close to his side as he was permitted. Instead, leadership of their mission had been entrusted to Zhuan-Kai, who Vaelin had noted enjoyed greater success in preaching word of the emperor's return than his abbot. The large monk exuded an aura of cheerful trustworthiness, his sermons more inquisitive than declamatory. *Consider the course of your lives,* he would tell his audience. *Think on how different it would have been if not beset by the avarice of the Merchant King. Heaven has ordained that the Jade Empire be a land where opportunity is not just the province of those born to wealth.*

"They have many skills," Vaelin told Chien. "And the Free Cantons need to be prepared for the arrival of their new emperor."

"They're not all grovellers to Heaven," she returned. "Despite what this lot might tell you."

"So I've heard. Why else would I be sending you with them? The Servants have no need of another blade, but the emperor will have need of those with other skills, your skills."

Since learning of the fall of Hahn-Shi and the likely death of her sisters, Chien's demeanour had been one of perennial, poorly contained rage. In accordance with Vaelin's request, she had remained close to Sherin, but a series of ill-tempered outbursts directed towards the "pathetic, ungrateful wretches" in the healer's care put an end to their association. Fortunately, the advent of the evacuation to the Free Cantons provided a useful avenue for the woman's talents.

"The Crimson Band has contacts there," she said, brow furrowing in contemplation. "But not allies. Every thief, smuggler and cutthroat in the Cantons owes allegiance to the Orchid Dealers. It's a bland name for the oldest criminal society in all of the Far West, and the most feared. I'm sure they'll receive me with all politeness, and I'm also sure they'll be polite about slitting my throat if it pleases them to do so."

"They must know of the Darkblade, and what his conquest of the Cantons would mean. Tell them the emperor will sign pardons for all crimes committed by those who enlist in his service. If they require any further persuasion, give them this." He handed her a folded document bearing two wax seals, embossed not with the emperor's sigil, but that of the Northern Reaches and the Greater Unified Realm. Although exquisitely inscribed in formal Chu-Shin courtesy of Mi-Hahn, the contents had been translated from Realm Tongue and constituted yet more lies from the Tower Lord of the Northern Reaches.

"It had better be a substantial bribe," Chien said, consigning the document to the inner folds of her jacket.

"It is," Vaelin assured her. "One quarter of a year's gold and bluestone receipts from the Northern Reaches."

"Tempting, but you know they'll ask for more. Outlaws always do."

"Then I trust you to strike a suitable bargain; just try not to bankrupt my realm in the process."

◆ ◆ ◆

Nuraka Shan was ultimately successful in persuading two-thirds of the Gilded Fleet to join the emperor's cause, although many captains did so on condition that they would not be required to swear an oath of loyalty. Those that refused the chance to join what was now named the Jade Fleet sailed away the following day, most ploughing a southward course whilst a few set their bows towards the Alpiran Empire. Whatever direction they chose, Vaelin found it significant that banners signifying allegiance to the Enlightened Kingdom had disappeared from every mast.

The many merchant vessels at anchor in the harbour were equally resistant to persuasion, but for different reasons. Most had empty holds thanks to the chaos caused by the war, and those that did have cargoes could find no merchants to buy their goods. Even so, their captains, all well attuned to the concepts of financial risk and unsecured debt, were unmoved by promises of future payment from the yet-to-be-established Imperial Treasury. Eventually, after two days of fruitless bargaining, Vaelin was forced to issue a promissory note signed on behalf of High Queen Lyrna Al Nieren guaranteeing generous payment to every captain and sailor who volunteered their service. Of all the lies he had told since leaving the Northern Reaches, the notion that he was here on the queen's orders and had authority to make promises in her name was undoubtedly the most outrageous, if not treasonous. Fortunately, the merchant captains, whilst fully aware of the queen's renown and wealth, possessed little knowledge of her temperament, and the note proved sufficient to sway several dozen to the cause. Consequently, they now had ample capacity for both the Imperial Host and those noncombatants that followed it.

Success in the seaborne arena, however, was not matched by their efforts on land. Just over a thousand younger men amongst the dispossessed former residents of Lishun-Shi were persuaded by the Servants' constant preaching to enlist in the Imperial Host. Far more opted to join the continual stream of people fleeing south whilst the great majority continued to linger in their increasingly fetid camps.

"What are they waiting for?" Ellese wondered, her baffled gaze tracking the mass of people squatting in makeshift shelters. "Running off I can understand, but why just sit here amongst all this stink?"

The camp lay at the foot of the hill where the remnants of the Enlightened Army had established themselves. Vaelin assumed these people expected their proximity to offer some measure of protection. If so, it would surely prove an illusion when the horde arrived.

"They've been told what to do their entire lives," Cho-ka replied, contempt in his voice as he surveyed the settlement. "Now they're just waiting for the next king to do the same. Servile idiots, the lot of them."

"They're afraid, that's all," Nortah said. "Everything they owned, everything they knew went up in smoke a week ago."

"They'll know a great deal more when the Darkblade gets here. In truth, feeding them seems wasteful." Cho-ka nodded at Sherin and her growing band of healers and helpers doling out soup to a long line of people. Vaelin found his gaze preoccupied by the boy at her side. Saikir had woken on the *Stormhawk* several hours after Sherin's healing embrace and maintained an absolute silence since. She ascribed it to the many traumas he had suffered, but the keen intelligence and awareness Vaelin saw in the boy's eyes made him wonder if his wordlessness wasn't a deliberate choice. *Questions he doesn't want to answer*, he surmised. *Crimes he doesn't want to admit.*

The black-song, partially muted by a fresh dose of elixir, remained quiet on the subject. Still, Saikir made Vaelin uneasy, especially in his refusal to stray more than a few feet from Sherin. As yet, she seemed unchanged by her contact with whatever lurked inside the boy, but Vaelin remembered the pain on her face. Saikir turned to him then, brows furrowed as he moved protectively in front of Sherin. *He still has his gift*, Vaelin knew, raising the uncomfortable question of what gift the boy had left in her. *Her soul could never be turned*, he thought, his conviction arousing a sleepy but mocking response from the black-song, the tune provoking an uncomfortable question: *So certain, are you? Like you were about Barkus all those years ago?*

"You seem to have a harder heart as a monk than you did as an outlaw," he observed to Cho-ka, looking away as Saikir continued to scowl at him.

"Can't help those that refuse to hear the message of Heaven, brother." They both raised their gazes to the hilltop above at a sudden tumult; the thrum of many bows loosed at once accompanied by the drumbeat of a horse at a gallop. "Speaking of which."

"Disrespectful fuckers!" the abbot fumed as he drew his horse up nearby, a volley of arrows falling onto the hillside to his rear.

"The general said no?" Vaelin asked.

"Bastard wouldn't let me get close enough for his soldiers to hear the words." The abbot turned his reddened face to the hill's crest and filled his lungs before shouting, "Stay here and die then, you unbelieving shitheads!"

Wheeling his horse about, he jerked his head at Cho-ka. "Come on. I'm done wasting time here."

He and Cho-ka set off at a steady trot back to the ruins of the city and the waiting fleet. "Brother?" Nortah asked when Vaelin lingered.

"They've been up there for nearly four days," he said, returning his gaze to Sherin and the people lining up before the steaming cauldrons of soup. "They must be hungry."

◆　◆　◆

"So, the usurper sends foreigners to do his bidding, now?"

The general was much younger than Vaelin expected, a year or two shy of thirty and possessed of the kind of swaggering surety rarely found in older men. He was close to Vaelin's own height with an athletic frame and a broad handsomeness to his features that stirred a note of familiarity.

"Vaelin Al Sorna," Vaelin said, offering a bow appropriate to one of equal rank. "Tower Lord of the Northern Reaches . . ."

"I know who you are, foreigner. Our spies brought word of your presence in these lands months ago."

"Then you have the advantage of me, sir," Vaelin replied, maintaining the bow.

The general's face flushed in mingled anger and embarrassment, casting a brief gaze at the stern-faced officers arranged at his back. Like their general, they all wore recently cleaned armour, although from the dull sheen of their bronze-coloured breastplates, they hadn't managed to get their hands on any polish. Their faces had a uniform leanness mirrored in the many soldiers viewing the meeting from behind their barriers of sharpened logs and entrenchments. Despite their evident hunger, Vaelin was impressed by their discipline, not one stepping out of line or raising a voice as the carts bearing copper urns filled with freshly made soup followed Vaelin up the hill.

"Duhlan Sai," the general said, returning the bow with stiff formality. "Commander of the Amber Regiments of the Enlightened Host. If you are here to plead for an alliance, you may as well leave now before I give my archers more target practice."

"Plead? No." Vaelin gestured to the carts drawing to a halt nearby, the breeze carrying the richly scented steam rising from the soup across the hilltop. More carts followed behind, all laden with bread and freshly boiled rice. "I just thought your men would appreciate a meal."

"Why feed your enemy?" Duhlan Sai asked. "Except with poison?"

Vaelin went to the nearest cart, climbing aboard to lift the lid on the copper urn, raising the ladle to his lips and taking a hearty gulp. "We are not enemies," he informed the general before raising the ladle and bowing to the troops clustering in greater numbers at the barricades. He had expected some form of mutiny by now, or at least a measure of discord. Even the best soldiers fall victim to ill discipline in the face of starvation. Instead, the soldiers' only response was a low murmur of hunger that swiftly faded when their general cast a single backward glance. *Still respected, despite their hunger and the destruction of their capital,* Vaelin concluded. *This is not a man to let go to waste.*

"I've met your true enemy," he told Duhlan Sai, jumping down from the cart. "I'd advise against facing him with a starving host."

The general insisted on tasting the soup and the rice himself before ordering the barricades parted to allow the carts through. The men were swiftly formed into lines by their officers and sergeants, moving with a disciplined alacrity Vaelin had only seen in the best Realm Guard regiments, and even they couldn't have matched the uniform cohesion he saw here. The soldiers all seemed to be much the same height, their armour painted with the same dark golden enamel and each breastplate featuring an amber stone in the centre.

"These are chosen men," he commented to Duhlan Sai. "Elite troops."

The general's response was spoken as a toneless statement of fact, lacking any puff-chested boasting. "The finest in all the Far West, if not the world. Only veterans who have tasted battle can volunteer for the Amber Regiments, and even then it requires half a year of training and tests to be permitted to serve." He paused before adding in a grudging tone, "You have a keen eye, foreigner."

"I've seen a great deal of war. Enough to know that these men will not prevail against the Darkblade's horde, no matter how brave, well trained or well led. And I've a sense you've seen enough of war to know that too."

The general's face hardened at this, turning to regard the ruins of Lishun-Shi. Two days of rain had washed away a good deal of the ash whilst the seaborne winds raised what remained into a shifting grey shroud. When he spoke, Duhlan Sai's voice was low and well controlled, though Vaelin heard the pain in it nonetheless. "An oath doesn't die with the man you gave it to.

A man who honoured you all your life. Such a man at least deserves loyalty in death."

"Fathers should honour their sons."

That earned a sidelong glance but no obvious anger. "Found a turncoat courtier to tell you the tale of Mah-Lol's favourite bastard, then?" Duhlan Sai shrugged. "It was never a secret. And favourite I may have been, but I earned my place at the head of these men, in battle."

"There are no courtiers left to tell tales of royal bastards, favourite or otherwise. You have his face, that's all."

The general's eyes narrowed, his voice becoming hoarse as he asked, "So you saw him, before the end?"

"I did."

"How did he meet it?"

Vaelin felt a momentary temptation to lie, craft a story of how the Merchant King shrugged off his madness at the last instant and spent his final moments marshalling his troops to fight the blaze engulfing his city. But, seeing the wary insistence on Duhlan Sai's face, he felt his loyalty deserved the truth. "He sat in his pool and played with his toy ships. I doubt he knew what was happening."

The general closed his eyes, head lowering a fraction before he reasserted his composure. It wouldn't do to show emotion in front of his men. "He wasn't always so . . . eccentric," he said, reopening his eyes to view the city again. "I believe it was when my mother died that his mind began to slip into daydreams. In time, daydreams became delusions. I know some say the Darkblade had a hand in unseating his mind, but that's the blather of the ignorant. His chamberlains ruled in his name, some good men of conscientious character, others greedy to the point of folly. They intrigued against each other constantly, a war within the palace that left us leaderless when the first reports of the Darkblade's invasion came from the north. This"—he gestured to the ruins—"is the ultimate result. Do you know how it was done?"

"The Darkblade has a means of placing the blessing of Heaven in children. When he captured Hahn-Shi he put some on a merchant ship disguised as slaves. They sailed ahead whilst his Redeemed attacked Huin-Shi in what I now realise was an elaborate but effective diversion."

"Children did this?" The general shook his head. "Now I begin to understand why so many say the Darkblade cannot be defeated."

"He can."

Duhlan Sai turned then, frowning quizzically at the hard certainty in Vaelin's voice. "So speaks one who has run very far to escape him."

"Sometimes you have to run before you can find the ground to stand on. I spoke true when I said I have met the Darkblade. I have looked into his eyes and, whatever claims to godhood he makes, I saw only a man. Clever, certainly. Ruthless too. But also, in his own way, just as mad as your father ever was. A god might be invincible, but not a man, especially not one with a fractured mind."

He stepped closer to Duhlan Sai, speaking with quiet intensity. "Loyalty is one thing; revenge is another. Come with us to the Free Cantons and I promise you'll have it."

"I won't swear fealty to your emperor; neither will my men."

"If you stay here you and your men will die. Oh, I'm sure the battle you'll fight will provide all the glory you could ever want. Thousands of the Darkblade's followers will fall, but there will be no victory, and when it's done he most likely won't even spare a glance for your corpses. As for fealty, keep your banners and fight in your father's name if that's your wish, or fight in the name of the Enlightened Kingdom. It matters not. You will retain command of these regiments and have a seat at all councils of war. Also, my queen will see that your men are paid for their service."

"And when this war is won? What then?"

"I don't know," Vaelin replied honestly. "But I do know what will happen if it's lost." He started back down the hill, speaking over his shoulder. "Think on it. The fleet departs in two days. If you choose to stay, we'll leave sufficient provisions to sustain you until the horde arrives."

He descended a few more yards before the general called after him, "Only a fool ever promises victory in war, foreigner."

Vaelin paused to turn and offer a parting bow. "And only a fool sticks his head in a noose when no one is holding the rope."

CHAPTER TWENTY

The smoke blossomed over the crest of the hill like an ugly black flower, the sight of it causing Vaelin to rein Derka to a halt with Nortah and Ellese drawing their mounts up close by. They had set out in the morning to scout the country north-east of Lishun-Shi, ranging out in a wide arc to guide any wayward fugitives towards the emperor's embrace as the fleet made its final preparations for departure. So far they had encountered only a few bedraggled souls, all of whom bore witness to recent travails, meaning the horde could not be far behind.

"Has he sent more little horrors to plague us?" Nortah wondered, drawing his sword as the smoke thinned in the sky.

Vaelin could hear only a dull murmur from the black-song that told of no enemies nearby. "I don't think so," he said, spurring Derka up the hill.

"That's enough!" Luralyn's voice greeted him as he took in the sight below. She and Eresa sat atop their own mounts at the edge of a stretch of blackened pasture some twenty paces wide. Streams of grey smoke rose from the scorched grass, obscuring much of the scene, but Vaelin could make out several mounds amongst the ash, his experienced eye alighting on the charred and stiffened limbs, both human and horse.

"This one's still moving," Jihla's voice called back, unseen amidst the drifting smoke until her diminutive form was abruptly silhouetted by a fresh blossoming of flame. She emerged from the black fog a second later, face besmirched and blood seeping from her nose but her eyes glowing with a cheery sense of satisfaction. "All done," she said, taking the reins of her horse from Eresa and climbing into the saddle.

"How many?" Vaelin asked, trotting Derka closer. The fire had been so fierce he couldn't make out the full number of those who had died here.

"About a dozen," Jihla told him, wiping the blood from her face. "All Tuhla. None got away. There's probably more further north." She turned her mount in preparation to gallop off, pausing with an annoyed frown when Vaelin reached out to clasp the reins.

"That'll do for now," he said before shifting his gaze to Luralyn. "Best get back to the city."

"She still weeps for her brother," Luralyn said a short while later, falling in alongside Vaelin as they followed the coast road to Lishun-Shi. "Every night. Eresa and I have to hold her until she finally falls asleep. Grief compels her to . . . excess."

Vaelin watched Jihla as she cantered ahead with Ellese and Eresa, their mingled laughter sounding absurdly girlish with the sting of smoke still tainting the air. He found he didn't like to ponder how many lives they had taken between them, with more to come.

"Excess will have its place before long," he said.

He halted Derka at the edge of the ruins, dismounting and telling the others to go on ahead. The stallion gave an inquisitive snort as Vaelin unfastened his bridle before undoing the straps of his saddle. "I doubt you'll take to life at sea," he said, raising a hand to rub Derka's muzzle. "You'll be at home here. Plenty of open country."

Derka bared his teeth, forehoof stamping as he prepared to rear, then calmed when Vaelin looked directly into his eye. "I don't know what song she sang to you," he murmured, smoothing his palm over the stallion's head. "But I've a sense we're not done. Wait for me if you want. Run free if you don't."

He held Derka's gaze for a moment longer, seeing some flicker of comprehension there before letting his hand drop. The stallion gave another snort, Vaelin sensing a glimmer of reproach along with acceptance in the animal's eye. Then he was off, hooves pounding hard on the gravel of the road before finding the soft earth of the pasture beyond. He galloped to the top of the nearest hill, paused briefly to whinny and kick his back legs, either as a farewell or a parting insult, then was gone.

◆ ◆ ◆

"They're not coming, brother." Nortah gave a sympathetic grimace before moving back from the rail. "You tried, at least."

Vaelin surveyed the wharf where the merchant ships waited at anchor, the quayside empty of all but a few prowling cats that had somehow contrived to survive the inferno. The residents of the dockside district had been amongst the most enthusiastic new subjects of the Jade Empire, many of them former sailors with less ingrained reluctance to forsake one land for another. Those who looked askance upon a voyage to the Free Cantons, a place that aroused decidedly mixed attitudes amongst people born to the mainland, had faded away to the camps or the last few groups straggling south. Consequently, Lishun-Shi was now an empty, wasted husk. In recent days the ash had reduced, revealing many of the fire's victims and subjecting those who walked shadowy lanes that had once been streets to the empty stares of countless blackened skulls.

Vaelin turned to regard the many masts crowding the eastern horizon. The Jade Fleet had begun its departure at the first swell of the morning tide. The previous day Vaelin's report of the Tuhla scouting party compelled Tsai Lin to refuse Admiral Nuraka's request for another week to gather supplies and recruits from the surrounding country. Instead, he permitted only another two days, but even that allowance had to be abandoned when Koa Lien arrived after a reconnaissance mission to the north. The former captain had been promoted to the grandiosely titled general of cavalry, despite the Imperial Host possessing only a few hundred horsemen worthy of the name.

"The Northern Division is destroyed, Heaven's Chosen," he said, sinking to one knee before Tsai Lin. "Surrounded and wiped out in two days of battle a hundred miles south of the border. We captured a Redeemed who was happy to tell the tale before we took his head."

"Where?" the emperor asked.

"He was part of a scavenging party picking over a village only three days' ride from the city, Heaven's Chosen. The horde can't be far behind."

And so the Jade Fleet had sailed come the dawn after a night of frantic labour to gather all possible supplies. Admiral Nuraka acceded to Vaelin's request to leave sufficient ships for the Amber Regiments but, as yet, they remained conspicuously absent.

"Pass the word to cast off," he said to the captain of the *Southern Star*, the merchant ship he and the others had chosen for the voyage. The fellow gave a relieved nod and began to bark out orders to raise the appropriate pennants. However, his voice faded at a shout from the crow's nest. Vaelin looked up to see the sailor atop the mainmast pointing to the city, and followed his outstretched arm to a rising pall of dust beyond the intact streets ringing the docks. A few seconds later came the familiar rhythmic tramp of a large body of men marching in unison. The first companies of the Amber Regiments filed through the streets to form up on the wharf in neat ranks, their number swelling by the second as the entire complement followed suit. Once every regiment had been assembled beneath their banner, General Duhlan Sai appeared. He was mounted on a tall black warhorse that appeared to Vaelin to have been trained to embody the stern aloofness of its rider.

The general halted his mount at the foot of the *Southern Star*'s gangplank, sitting in silent regard of his men. Each soldier stood to perfect attention, eyes locked forward, every back and spear unwavering in their straightness. "Companies!" Duhlan Sai called out, his voice echoing across the docks. "To your ships, fall out!"

As the regiments transformed into orderly lines leading to the gangways positioned along the quay, the general dismounted, handing the reins of his horse to a sergeant before striding up the gangway. "For revenge," he told Vaelin shortly, sparing him only a brief glance as he stepped onto the deck. "And a one-fifth increase in pay. If we're to be mercenaries, it may as well be lucrative. I will require a private cabin."

◆ ◆ ◆

The *Southern Star* was the last ship to leave harbour, by which time morning was giving way to the midday sun. It was as the ship cleared the moles and angled her bows south that another cry came from the crow's nest.

"Just in time again," Nortah observed as they stood watching the dark figures appear on the receding dockside. "They must've ridden their horses near to death to get here so fast."

Despite the distance, Vaelin recognised the form and surety of Stahlhast riders. Several dozen reined their mounts to a halt on the wharf whilst a great deal more were boiling over the crest of the hill where the Amber Regiments had been encamped only hours before. "Looks like they were expecting a battle," Nortah added to Duhlan Sai with a raised eyebrow.

The general maintained a rigid expression and didn't deign to answer; however, the twitch to his features and narrowing eyes told of a deep frustration. Contrary to his request, he had been obliged to make do with a sectioned-off corner of the hold, which offered only marginally more space and privacy than that afforded his men. The indignity clearly did little to improve his mood. His features twitched with yet greater animation when the Stahlhast on the wharf began hurling insults at the departing ships. Their voices were lost to the wind but the intent was clear in their gestures, many dismounting to bare their backsides in contempt.

"The thousands I could have slaughtered," Duhlan Sai said, his voice a soft hiss uttered through clenched teeth.

"And died for it," Vaelin reminded him. "You'll get your chance in the Cantons."

He began to turn away then paused at a murmur from the black-song, a dull pulse that found its way past the barrier created by Kish-an's elixir. Although faint, the note of recognition was strong and confirmed when he saw the Stahlhast on the docks suddenly abandon their gesticulations. Mounted warriors swiftly climbed down from their saddles to join their fellows in forming a disorderly line. Every head bowed in quiescent respect as a tall figure in silver and black armour trotted a fine stallion along the quayside. As at Keshin-Kho, Kehlbrand Reyerik wore no helm, and although his features were indistinct, Vaelin knew the man's stare matched his own.

"*That* is the Darkblade?" the general asked.

"That's him," Nortah said. "Nice of him to see us off personally." He grinned at the dubious frown on Duhlan Sai's face. "I suppose you were expecting something more impressive."

"He's supposed to be a god." The general gave a humourless laugh, shaking his head. "How could a mere man have wrought so much destruction?"

"Because he found those willing to destroy," Vaelin replied. "As long as they heard the right lies."

He watched the figures onshore fade into the blackish-grey mess of Lishun-Shi, hearing the black-song swell several times to voice an ugly snarl, like a dog warding off the inquisitive stare of a stranger. *His own song, trying to find me*, Vaelin realised as the snarl sounded a final time. He was sorely tempted to hand his pouch of gold to Nortah and allow Kehlbrand's song to latch onto his. The moment of realisation when the Darkblade understood that the Thief of Names now possessed a song of his own would have been sweet indeed.

Always keep your last knife hidden. One of Master Sollis's lessons, proving sufficient to suppress the urge. *He's confused over why his song can't find me, and confusion works to our advantage now.*

"He's mine."

Vaelin turned at the sound of Duhlan Sai's stern voice, finding the general's strong, handsome features were now rendered ugly by a forbidding implacability. "This must be understood between us, foreigner. The Darkblade dies at my hand."

"Your hand, the hand of the emperor or the spear-point of the lowliest soldier." Vaelin shrugged and stepped back from the rail, moving to the stern to gauge the mood of the seas they faced. "I don't care, as long as he dies."

◆ ◆ ◆

Nakira was the largest of the main islands that comprised the heart of the Free Cantons, but not the most populous. That distinction belonged to the northernmost island of Askira, which was also by all accounts the wealthiest due to its proximity to the mainland trade routes. However, the decision to make Nakira the site of the Jade Emperor's landing was due to the abbot's insistence that it possessed the largest number of temples of any island in the region. It naturally followed that the inhabitants would be the most receptive to the arrival of Heaven's Chosen in their hour of need. As yet, a day of sailing the island's rocky and mostly beach-free coastline had revealed little evidence of any local enthusiasm. They caught glimpses of people clustered atop cliffs to watch the fleet pass by, but none felt moved to offer more than a cautious wave by way of greeting whilst others fled inland at the first sight of the ships.

"Likura Bay," Admiral Nuraka said, pointing to a mist-covered headland a few miles off the starboard bow. "One of only two places on the whole island with a beach broad enough to land an army. It's also closest to the regional capital."

"Meaning the enemy will have concentrated his forces there," General Duhlan said with a note of disapproval. "We should make for the alternative site, less chance of encountering opposition."

Tsai Lin turned slowly to the general, his features mostly impassive, but

Vaelin could see the well-hidden anger beneath his gaze. Upon being called to conference aboard the flagship of the Jade Fleet, the general had offered Tsai Lin a bow appropriate to one of only marginally higher rank. He also continued to avoid addressing the emperor with any honorific beyond those required by basic politeness when conversing with the nobility.

"Enemy?" Tsai Lin enquired, his voice as passive as his face.

"The Canton-folk are notoriously warlike, honoured sir." The general gave a patient smile, as if explaining the obvious to a bright but ignorant pupil. "Whatever this one may have told you"—Duhlan Sai's smile slipped into a grimace as he glanced at the abbot—"they are not simply going to allow you to invade their islands and proclaim yourself overlord. Today," he sniffed, straightening his back, "we face battle. It might be best if we accepted that now and acted accordingly."

"The only other suitable landing site is on the southern shore of the island," Admiral Nuraka said. "Meaning a sixty-mile march over mountainous country to reach the capital. I know this land, Heaven's Chosen. The mountain passes are well fortified and can be held by a comparatively small force. It would take weeks to fight our way through. If we don't land here, I advise we don't land on Nakira at all. Askira has a less forbidding coastline and fewer mountains."

"Here is where the blessings of Heaven are most cherished," the abbot stated. "I sent our Brother Zhuan to preach the word of the emperor's coming to this island for a reason. The people will be expecting his arrival, so here is where we land. Unless you fuckers want to contradict the word of the temple."

"Since we appear to be in the gutter," Duhlan returned, "I welcome the opportunity to say that I couldn't give ten sties worth of pig shit for the word of your temple, old man."

"Enough," Tsai Lin said as the abbot's face reddened in preparation for an obscene retort. The emperor glanced at Luralyn, who stood alongside Vaelin on the periphery of the gathering. It had become custom for them not to speak at council unless directly addressed. The sight of the Jade Emperor heeding the advice of a foreigner and a Stahlhast apparently made a poor impression on newer recruits to the imperial cause. He asked no question, instead raising an eyebrow and receiving an apologetic shrug in response. Once again, Luralyn's True Dream had no guidance to offer here.

Tsai Lin's mouth twitched in disappointment but he maintained a tone of calm surety when he asked the admiral, "Best sailing time to Askira?"

"The distance is not great, but navigating the currents that swirl around the Cantons is never easy. Three days if the winds are kind. Another two at least to get in a position to land."

"I have learned that, in war, the most precious commodity is not gold, nor soldiers, it's time. Five more days at sea means more men and horses lost to illness, and more children and old folk suffering in the bowels of these ships. I promised them refuge and a place to make a stand. It's time their emperor proved he is no liar."

He stepped back to address all the gathered officers, voice raised to a pitch of command that Vaelin found chilling in its similarity to that used by Sho Tsai at Keshin-Kho. "We will land in Likura Bay. If we are opposed, we fight. General Duhlan, the Amber Regiments will have the honour of landing first. Secure the high ground beyond the beach and hold it whilst the main body disembarks."

"An honour indeed," the general said with a bow fractionally lower than before.

"Admiral"—Tsai Lin nodded to Nuraka Shan—"issue your orders accordingly and let's be about it."

◆　◆　◆

Tsai Lin insisted on the flagship being at the head of the formation when the fleet rounded the headland and turned towards the bay. By then the mist had thinned and faded under the midday sun to afford Vaelin a clear view of the host awaiting them onshore.

"So," Duhlan said with a note of grim satisfaction, "a fight it is."

The force had been arranged in a wide, irregular crescent along the hills ringing the bay. They were grouped into formations that possessed a basic orderliness but lacked the dense cohesion Vaelin had seen in other Far Western soldiery. Also, upon borrowing the admiral's spyglass, he discovered an odd lack of conformity amongst the assembled warriors. Some carried spears, others only swords. They wore armour of similar design to that found on the mainland but with a great deal of variation in colour, whilst each helm appeared to bear a different crest. He also noted that the many archers present stood amongst the swordsmen and spear-bearers rather than being clustered into cohorts. Their weapons bore a vague similarity to a Cumbraelin longbow in being over four feet in length, but with a much thinner stave.

"Any notion of the range of those bows?" he asked the general, handing him the spyglass.

"Fifty paces further than a crossbow and a great deal more accurate," Duhlan said, pressing his eye to the glass. "The Sehtaku spend their whole lives perfecting the use of their favoured weapons."

"Sehtaku?"

"The warrior caste of the Free Cantons. Small in comparison to the population as a whole, but not to be underestimated, even if they don't have any idea of how to organise a battle line. War is all about glory and honour to them, you see. They look upon battle as an opportunity to win personal renown. Today will be an interesting one to be sure." He tracked the spyglass along the length of the bay and back again, letting out a small grunt of puzzlement as he focused on the beach. "That's odd."

As the flagship drew nearer to shore, the object of his puzzlement became clear: a man in full armour sitting on a stool beneath a fluttering rectangular banner. Two more armoured men stood to the rear of the sitting man whilst a dozen or so people were clustered some twenty paces off to the left. Vaelin recognised the various coloured robes of monks and nuns with one darker exception. Chien strode from the midst of the group with Zhuan-Kai at her side, making their way through the sand to the edge of the shifting surf. Vaelin climbed atop the ship's rail and waved to get their attention, receiving a beckoning gesture from the outlaw in response.

"The banner is in Canton script, Heaven's Chosen," he heard Admiral Nuraka advise Tsai Lin. "It proclaims an invitation to personal combat, addressed to you."

"In what terms?" Tsai Lin enquired.

The admiral hesitated before replying. "'If he has courage, let the Pretender come forth and take my head, for it is the only bow he will receive in the Free Cantons.'"

"Pretender, eh?" Tsai Lin's lips formed a sardonic smile. "A slight improvement on 'Usurper,' don't you think?"

"The original phrasing is less . . . complimentary, Heaven's Chosen."

"I see. And the man on the stool?"

"The crest on his helm belongs to the Urikien Clan. Word reached me in Huin-Shi they recently gained control of the island after a long feud with various rivals. I recall hearing that the feuds were all settled in the same manner."

"Personal combat, I assume."

"Quite so, Heaven's Chosen."

"Is some measure of formality required before the challenge commences?"

"It's customary to appoint two seconds to make formal introductions and ensure only agreed-upon weapons are used."

"Very well, Admiral. Prepare a boat to take us to shore. Yourself and Lord Vaelin will do me the honour of acting as seconds."

"A moment, Heaven's Chosen," the abbot said, stepping close to the emperor, lowering his voice with a glance at Vaelin. "Not sure if having a foreigner at your side when you step ashore is the best idea. I shall be happy to . . ."

"No," Tsai Lin stated flatly, dismissing the abbot with a jerk of his head. "If I'm to die today I'd prefer to do it with a friend at my side."

◆   ◆   ◆

"I offered to fight him in your stead, Heaven's Chosen," Zhuan-Kai said after exchanging brief formalities with Tsai Lin once they waded ashore. "He said his blade is too pure to be stained with a Servant's blood."

"Very pious of him," Tsai Lin observed, tightening a strap on his breast-plate. "Does he have a name?"

"He calls himself the Whispering Blade, Heaven's Chosen," Chien said. "Proclaimed as the finest swordsman in all the Cantons, mostly by his own clan, it should be noted. His real name is Baron Urikien Shori and he's a vicious, devious bastard, by all accounts. Don't expect him to fight fair."

Tsai Lin nodded, and Vaelin thought it a measure of the change in him that he now accepted the counsel of a woman he once looked upon with nothing but judgemental disdain. "I'm told he has lordship of this island."

"So he claims, Heaven's Chosen. But in fact his clan's control is restricted to the capital. The Sehtaku in the other districts refuse to recognise his authority. The nobles here certainly like to fight amongst themselves; everyone else just gets on with things and leaves them to it. By which I mean to say, when you kill him, no one besides his own clan is going to care that much."

"Including all these many warriors?" Tsai Lin inclined his head at the host arrayed on the surrounding hills.

"Come to watch the show, for the most part. Only a few hundred belong to the Urikien Clan."

"So, control of this island will truly be decided by just this duel."

"I have been given assurances that this will be so, Heaven's Chosen."

"Assurances, eh? By whom?"

Chien gave a cautious glance in Vaelin's direction and, receiving a nod in response, replied, "As I said, the nobles pursue their feuds whilst others do the important things."

Tsai Lin's gaze lingered on her for a moment, causing Chien to retreat a respectful distance, keeping her head bowed. "I can see we will need to have a long talk when this is over," he said, turning and striding up the beach with Vaelin and Nuraka Shan in tow.

Before following, Vaelin paused at Chien's side to ask, "Can I assume our new friends have some responsibility for this farce?"

She replied with a short nod.

"How much did it cost?" he asked.

"Double the suggested amount." She gave a chagrined frown. "The baron's clan was amenable to negotiation, after suitable encouragement from the Orchid Dealers, but being a prideful idiot, he was insistent on a challenge. When this is done our new friends expect a personal meeting where you will put your mark on a document confirming our arrangement. They put a lot of stock in such things here."

Another lie spoken in the queen's name. Another crime to answer for. Vaelin smothered a resigned sigh and afforded her a smile. "Your efforts are appreciated," he said before following in Tsai Lin's footsteps.

The two warriors flanking the seated baron stepped forward when they drew within a dozen yards. "I, Urikien Sikaru, speak for my cousin Baron Shori," the man on the right said. He spoke a heavily accented form of Chu-Shin that Vaelin could follow easily, although his strident tone was muffled somewhat by the half visor that covered the lower portion of his face. "Who speaks for the Pretender?"

The admiral stepped forward, speaking with carefully placed emphasis. "I, Nuraka Shan, Admiral of the Jade Fleet, speak for *Emperor* Tsai Lin, Heaven's Chosen and rightful overlord of the Free Cantons. State your terms."

The dark eyes above the visor glared for an instant before the warrior snorted a response. "Swords only. No quarter. All possessions and titles of the defeated fall to the victor."

Vaelin's gaze slid to the seated man. Unlike his appointed second, he wore a full-face visor, a lacquered bronze mask that had been moulded into the snarling face of some kind of cat. Although the baron maintained a rigid posture, the muted tune of the black-song sang of mingled fury, fear and ambition beneath the mask. *A man gambling all for the greatest reward*, he decided, pondering what manner of nation would contrive to make him a leader. *Not truly a leader*, he reminded himself, recalling Chien's words to the emperor. *Merely the head of a faction engaged in a feud that never ends. This is a show intended to place him at the pinnacle of this land's nobles, the climax to the legend of the Whispering Blade.* Vaelin lowered his head to conceal the faint, piteous smile that came to his lips. *His arrogance blinds him to the fact that he is but a player in someone else's story.*

"Accepted," Nuraka Shan said after receiving a confirmatory nod from Tsai Lin.

"Custom dictates a pause for meditation and final entreaties to Heaven's mercy," Sikaru said, crouching to scoop a handful of sand from the beach. "The contest begins when the final grain falls from my hand." He and the other second retreated several paces whereupon he extended his arm, opening his fist to allow a trickle of sand to drift away on the sea breeze.

Tsai Lin nodded to the admiral and Vaelin. Nuraka Shan bowed and backed away, whilst Vaelin lingered a moment, addressing the emperor in softly spoken Realm Tongue. "Killing this fool avails us nothing. Remember what I said at Nuan-Khi. The Darkblade writes his scripture in blood and conquest, therefore the Jade Emperor must write his in mercy and wisdom."

Bowing low, he followed the admiral's example and retreated. Vaelin watched Tsai Lin regard the baron in silence before striding forward, pausing only a few paces away to offer a respectful bow. "They call you the Whispering Blade," he said. "A name worthy of honour. You do not honour my name and for that I forgive you, for you do not know me. But, before we spill our blood upon these sands, I would ask you, noble baron, why do you raise your sword against me?"

The seated warrior gave no reply, the snarling cat's face of his visor betraying nothing, not even a glimmer from the eyes within its shaded sockets.

"Is it to defend this land, its people?" Tsai Lin asked, standing back to cast his arm at the hills and the onlooking warriors. His words were probably lost to most of them but not to the cluster of monks and nuns nearby, all of whom could be counted on to relate them once this particular chapter in the Jade Emperor's story had been concluded.

"Or is it your own pride?" Tsai Lin swung back to the baron. "Your own ambition. I beseech you in Heaven's sight, noble sir, put aside such things. For I am not your enemy. I do not come to the Free Cantons to conquer, but to save them from a conqueror."

He pointed to the sea beyond the assembled ships in the bay. "You think a mere stretch of water will protect you from the Darkblade? It will not, and when he brings his horde to these shores there will be no challenges, no honour shown to the noble clans. In the world he is building, you worship him or you die."

Vaelin looked to the outstretched fist of the baron's kinsman, seeing the wispy stream of sand begin to thin. The snarling cat, however, remained unmoved.

"Join me," Tsai Lin said, stepping closer to proffer his hand to the baron. "Join me! The Whispering Blade and the Jade Emperor will fight side by side for the salvation of this land and the world entire. If, when the war is won, you still wish to settle this challenge then settle it we will. Until then"—Tsai Lin turned his back, unbuckling his sword belt to allow the weapon to fall to the sands—"I will not fight you, for you are not my enemy."

Vaelin felt no surprise at what happened next. A wiser man than this self-named Whispering Blade would either have sunk to his knees and pledged allegiance to the Jade Emperor, or let the last grains of sand fall before drawing his sword. But, whatever his virtues may have been, Baron Urikien Shori plainly did not count wisdom amongst them.

Whilst the sand still ran through Sikaru's fingers the baron surged to his feet with an angry roar. His sword flashed from its scabbard with a worrying speed, surely the product of a lifetime's practice. Had the emperor stood only an inch closer it would have severed his head from his shoulders, but Tsai Lin, who had climbed to the top of the Temple of Spears when still a boy and fought many a battle since, possessed a very keen eye for the reach of an opponent's arm.

He ducked his head only a few inches to avoid the stroke, turning with a deceptive absence of haste to evade the follow-up downward slash that would have cleaved his shoulder. Sand blossomed as the baron's blade missed its target, a muffled curse emerging from the mask before he lunged, attacking once again with an expert's speed and precision. Tsai Lin barely seemed to move, fractionally angling his torso to allow the sword point to miss before clamping his hands on the baron's outstretched arm.

"Enough!" he said, voice pitched with an urgent need for understanding. "Stop this! Join me and win the greatest glory!"

Before now Vaelin had thought this man mostly incapable of artifice, thinking him a mirror of Sho Tsai's peerless rectitude. But the ease with which Tsai Lin moulded his features into a part-dismayed, part-determined frown, eyes bright with compassion, told a different story. *Whatever power resides in the Temple of Spears chose well*, Vaelin concluded. *All rulers need to know how to lie.*

A raspy, barely coherent snarl came from the mask as Tsai Lin continued to hold the baron in place. "Fuck your glory, boy! I'll make my own . . ."

The snarl abruptly transformed into a choked, wet gurgle. Blood spouted from the baron's mask, followed an instant later by the reddened point of a sword. He jerked and collapsed onto the sand as Urikien Sikaru withdrew his blade, flicking the gore from the steel before returning it to the scabbard at his side. He and the other second both immediately sank to their knees, bowing low to Tsai Lin.

"The last grain had not fallen," Sikaru said. "He dishonoured our house, which now belongs to you"—the Sehtaku's head bowed lower—"Heaven's Chosen."

Tsai Lin spared a brief, sorrowful glance for the slain baron before stepping forward to place a hand on Sikaru's helm. "His dishonour is washed away by your actions. Your house will remain in the hands of your clan, for I did not come here to steal. Will you fight alongside me, Urikien Sikaru? Will your house join its banner to mine?"

The helm moved under Tsai Lin's hand as Sikaru exchanged a glance with his fellow second, receiving a hesitant nod in response. "For now and forever, Heaven's Chosen," he said. "House Urikien pledges its service to the Jade Emperor."

"And it is gratefully received. Rise now. Go and tell your kin and your fellow Sehtaku that their emperor makes them only two promises: honour and glory."

"Honour and glory, Heaven's Chosen!" Vaelin heard a genuine fervour in Sikaru's voice as he rose and backed away, his words echoed by his kinsman. "Honour and glory!"

The monks and nuns nearby soon took up the cry and rushed to share it with the ranks of warriors, casting their voices high. It spread like wildfire through the ranks of the Sehtaku, discordant at first but quickly taking on a rhythmic cadence as every voice shouted out the same three words, "Honour and glory! Honour and glory!"

"Another chapter written," Tsai Lin observed as Vaelin moved to his side.

He confined his response to a tight approving smile that belied a sudden unease stirred by the ardency of the emperor's new subjects. Vaelin's disquiet deepened when the chants of those onshore spread to the ships in the bay. The collective cry of thousands of voices inevitably recalled the prayer-chants of the Redeemed as they charged to their deaths, making him wonder if, in seeking to bring down one false god, he may have helped create another.

PART III

In war, only the final victory should be celebrated.
All others are just bloody footprints on a road best untravelled.

—QUEEN LYRNA AL NIEREN, *COLLECTED SAYINGS*

Obvar's Account

The final, degraded end of the Merchant King Lian Sha would once have aroused mighty Obvar to contemptuous laughter. Now, bearing the stolen name of General Sho Tsai, commander of the Redeemed Host and most trusted hand of the Darkblade, I felt only piteous repulsion at the sight of an old man forced to kiss Kehlbrand's boots. He wept as he knelt and shuffled forward, words babbling from his drooling lips, an utterly broken vestige of a man who once held sway over millions. Yet not a hand had been laid upon his flesh. No whips nor blades had brought the Merchant King to this ebb. It had all been wrought by the blood of his family.

They lay around this absurdly ornate park in varying states of dismemberment or mutilation, all meted out at Kehlbrand's whim. Sons, daughters, grandchildren, great-grandchildren, anyone with a direct bloodline to Lian Sha's dynasty. At first, the old man watched them die in silence, face and form moulded into a dignified posture, seeming more a statue than a man. He had refused to speak a single word to Kehlbrand, barely acknowledging his presence, even when his eldest son was dragged forth and disembowelled before his eyes. The statue began to crack as the killings wore on, tears trickling down his cheeks to mat carefully coiffured silver whiskers. He began to sob when the executioners moved on to his daughters, but it was when the grandchildren started to die that his composure evaporated. Sinking to his knees, he begged Kehlbrand for mercy then fell once more to choking silence when the Darkblade extended his boot. It was only when the last grandchild was led forward, a girl of no more than five with a doll clutched in her arms, that Lian Sha consented to press his lips to the foot of his vanquisher.

"Pathetic, isn't he, Obvar?" Kehlbrand commented, shoving the old man away with a hard nudge of his boot. "A Stahlhast Skeltir would have watched me murder every kin he had and never once consented to kneel. This is why you lost, old man." He loomed over Lian Sha's prostrate, cowering form. "This weakness." He flicked his hand at the guards flanking the little girl. "Drown her in that ridiculous lake. Have him watch then cut his throat."

"A moment, Darkblade," I said. The words were immediate, delivered without pause for thought. I would later contemplate the notion that Sho Tsai's remnant had surged forth to briefly resume command of this stolen body, but knew it to be false. Obvar had killed many, even murdered a few when enraged or drunk, but never a child.

"I am not in a merciful mood, old friend," Kehlbrand said wearily, turning away. "And we have another campaign to plan."

"This child may still have use, Darkblade," I persisted. "She was delivered by the hand of the Healing Grace."

"Really?" Kehlbrand paused to regard the girl, offering her a kind smile. She stared back with wide, unblinking eyes, small fists grasping the fabric of her doll. I recognised it as Koan-Tai, the legendary messenger of Heaven said to have the head of a tiger and the body of a man. I had noticed throughout the horde's rampages that children didn't always cry when faced with horrors that would have driven an adult mind to madness. Blank incomprehension was often the norm, though who could tell what inner wounds lurked behind those bright, staring eyes.

"You imagine this child will be sufficient to bargain for the healer's loyalty?" Kehlbrand asked. "I find that unlikely."

"Her loyalty? Probably not. But recall that Sho Tsai loved her, and she him. Were I to stand before her with this child in hand . . ."

I trailed off as Kehlbrand let out a hearty laugh. "The ghost inside you must truly retain some influence. Obvar was never so devious. Keep her." He waved at the girl again. "I'm sure your nun would appreciate another brat to fawn over. Best make sure she doesn't get too attached, though."

He paused to afford Lian Sha a final glance. The old man was shuddering now, more, I suspected, in relief than sorrow. "On second thought," Kehlbrand said, "a throat slitting is too merciful. Take his eyes and his tongue then he can wander this park amongst the corpses of his kin until he starves. Let it be known that the Darkblade punishes weakness as he punishes greed."

◆　◆　◆

"And this one?"

Uhlkar blinked his overlarge eyes as he followed the track of Mai Wehn's brush upon the rice paper. I was no expert in letters, but even my untutored eye could tell she possessed a fine, flowing hand that would have been the envy of many a calligrapher. However, I had severe doubts that Uhlkar was capable of appreciating or even understanding such things.

"Tree," he said after a moment's doleful consideration of the freshly inked character.

"That's right." Mai tweaked his nose with the end of her brush, a gesture that might be expected to arouse a giggle or at least a smile from a normal child. The other Divinely Blooded horrors sat around the opulent garden practising their letters with varying degrees of success, quieter than most children but still prone to occasional squabbles and outbursts of laughter or temper. Not so Uhlkar who just blinked again, continuing to sit in expressionless expectation of his next lesson.

They had begun to cluster around her after the fall of Muzan-Khi, perhaps drawn by some primal childhood instinct, a need to seek out an island of kindness amongst the sea of indifference or fanatical cruelty that the horde had become. Although I no longer used her previous title, she had now truly become a mother of sorts. She fed them, cared for their various maladies and saw to their education. My opinion on the danger inherent in such selflessness was, of course, completely ignored.

"You try," she said, handing Uhlkar the brush after glancing in my direction. "Whilst I talk to Obvar, see if you can copy all these characters and then tell me what it says."

Uhlkar nodded and turned his attention to the paper, for once taking on a childlike aspect as his tongue poked between his lips and brows furrowed in concentration.

"Please don't look at him like that." Mai's gaze was steady with warning and resolve. Her fears hadn't faded during the long march through what had been the Venerable Kingdom, but when it came to these children, she had all the courage in the world.

262 · ANTHONY RYAN

"Like what?" I asked, voice made truculent by the events I had witnessed that morning.

"Like he's a rat," Mai said. "Something you'd like to stomp on."

She spoke softly but not so much that Uhlkar couldn't hear, if he cared to. But the little terror betrayed no interest at all in me, continuing to form his letters on the paper with unusually focused determination.

"This is Nai Lian," I told Mai, gesturing to the girl at my back. She still clutched her doll tight, something she had done as I carried her to this smaller palace on the edge of the Merchant King's park. The sound of her grandfather's mutilation had followed us for the first few dozen paces, and her eyes retained the same unblinking stare.

"Is she . . . ?" Mai ventured after greeting the girl with a wide, welcoming smile.

I shook my head. "Lian Sha's only surviving kin. He spared her at my request."

Mai's brow showed only a brief puzzlement before she crouched to smooth a few wayward black tresses from Nai Lian's forehead. "Aren't you such a pretty thing? Your name means blossom in winter, did you know that?" For the first time, some animation returned to the child's face and she gave a slow nod. "And who is this?" Mai asked, nodding at the doll in the girl's hand. "Koan-Tai, if I'm not mistaken."

"Ko," the girl said in a small voice. "I just call him Ko."

"We have a lot of dolls here." Mai rose, taking the girl's hand and leading her towards the other children. "Let's see if we can find Ko a friend."

I stood for a moment, watching Mai play with the last remnant of Lian Sha's dynasty, marvelling somewhat when she actually brought a smile to the girl's lips.

"You should have let him kill her."

My gaze snapped to Uhlkar. His words had been little more than a sibilant mutter, heard only by me. He didn't look up from his letters, which, I noticed with discomfort, were just as perfectly formed as Mai's, and yet I felt certain he had never touched a brush until this morning.

"What?" I demanded, stepping closer.

"She'll come to hate you even though you will love her as a father loves a daughter," he said, inscribing another symbol I recognised from engravings adorning the gallows present in every town in the Merchant King's realm.

Obvar didn't know the full meaning but Sho Tsai did: Just execution has been done. *"She will grow to beauty and greatness," Uhlkar added as he crafted another symbol, the wheel-like shape that signified passage of time. "Her cunning matched only by her cruelty. Her vengeance will be terrible."*

The brush stopped and he sat back, the focus fading from his skull-face to be replaced by faint puzzlement. "Do you know what this says?" he asked, holding the paper up for me to see.

My gaze snapped from him to the now-laughing little girl and back again, jaw clenching as my heart lurched in my chest. "It says you're a little shit who should learn to shut his mouth," I growled before turning and stalking from the palace.

◆ ◆ ◆

"Ah, how the Unseen have blessed me with the Thief of Names!" Kehlbrand laughed and shook his head in appreciation. "I had thought him merely an irritant, but every time I worry the Darkblade's tale might descend into tedium, he writes me another chapter."

The muddy, debris-choked sea covering the city of Nuan-Khi lay before us, a placid, brownish grey expanse extending several miles in each direction, broken here and there by the occasional rooftop or spire. I didn't like to think how many Stahlhast lay dead beneath those waters, but my unnatural gift for calculation made it inescapable. Twenty-six thousand, nine hundred and forty-three. The warriors of four entire Skeld drowned and smashed in a few moments. It was the greatest defeat ever suffered in Stahlhast history, and yet Kehlbrand found it a cause for celebration.

"Here," he continued in a sombre, contemplative tone, "did I look upon the evil wrought by the Thief of Names, vile servant of the Jade Emperor, and here did I swear that I would pursue them unto every corner of this world so they may know the Darkblade's justice."

Watching him smile, I wondered if his Divine gift allowed him to feel the anger roiling inside me, or was it that he simply no longer cared what thoughts his favoured dog might harbour? "You've no doubt this was his work, Darkblade?" I asked.

"None at all. He is like a void moving across the earth, leaving no trace save the obstacles he places in my path, for which I am grateful. And yet, old friend, I find I hate him, for he made my sister a void too." He reached for the leather case on his saddle, undoing the ties to extract the rolled canvas within,

something I had seen him do many times during the ride south. The likeness on the canvas was uncanny in its accuracy, leaving me little doubt it had been crafted by a Divinely Blooded hand, and Kehlbrand never seemed to tire of gazing at it. "I used to have some sense of her," he said, smiling at Luralyn's eerily lifelike face. "A brief glimpse now and then, the sorrow she feels, the love for the family she made. At times I even saw the world through her eyes. It made me imagine we were still joined, as we were on the Steppe for so many years. But he took that from me, and thereby earned my hate. I refused his challenge twice before. I won't again."

Looking again at this new unlovely sea to ponder the corpses it concealed, I wondered at my own absence of hatred for Al Sorna. He had orchestrated the deaths of so many Stahlhast, not to mention killing my former body. I should have been enraged, and yet all I felt was a weary sorrow at the knowledge this war was far from over. To think mighty Obvar would ever tire of war.

"We should scout the northern banks of the Yi Ming," I said. "Find the best site for a crossing. The Jade Emperor has a few days' lead on us, but if we move swiftly enough we may be able to cut off his line of march."

"Why bother," Kehlbrand asked, "when I intend to leave him with no destination for his march?" He turned his stallion, gesturing for his saddle brothers to fall in alongside. They did so with unspeaking, blank-faced obedience. Ever since Timurik's ignoble end, these men, these pinnacles of Stahlhast warriordom, behaved as no more than whipped hounds in the presence of a harsh master. As do you, I reminded myself in a voice that held a taint of Sho Tsai's accent.

"I leave you with half the horde, General," Kehlbrand said. "Build or seize whatever craft you need to cross this sea then destroy the Northern Division of the Enlightened Host. Be sure to take as many captives as you can. We have losses to make good."

He spurred to a gallop without another word, riding hard towards the east with his whipped dogs trailing behind. It wouldn't become apparent for a number of weeks that he had a hidden purpose for leaving his most trusted general behind to command a campaign that could have been left in the hands of any half-competent Skeltir.

◆ ◆ ◆

"He took them!" Mai clutched at me with frantic, desperate hands, eyes wide and wet. Her hollow, reddened face told of a woman who had been lost in sorrow for days. "Saikir, Kistrik, Haityra. All of them save Uhlkar and Nai Lian. Where are they?"

She rushed to meet me at the entrance to the tent we shared, enlarged recently thanks to her growing brood but now mostly empty. Uhlkar and Nai Lian sat in a corner, the girl orchestrating some kind of farce with her dolls whilst the boy looked on in silent incomprehension. The horde was encamped on the plain south of Huin-Shi. The Tuhla had been the first to reach the port and, finding it mostly empty of people and loot, proceeded to burn it to the ground after slaughtering the few old folk who had unwisely chosen not to follow the Jade Emperor.

That morning I had led my force of Stahlhast and Redeemed to the huge encampment with eight thousand captives, the survivors of the Northern Division. They had been a well-led and disciplined foe, establishing themselves on a low ridgeline and holding out for longer than I would have expected against repeated assaults. A constant rain of Stahlhast arrows, weight of numbers and Redeemed fanaticism had eventually sundered their ranks after a day and a half of battle, and the paucity of captives told of a determination amongst these men, regulars all, to die fighting.

I confess to a trepidation regarding Kehlbrand's reaction to being presented with so few new recruits to the Darkblade's ranks, but it slipped into steadily mounting anger at the sight of Mai's stricken face.

"They're in Lishun-Shi, old friend," Kehlbrand told me. "Having fulfilled the sacred duty of those who accept the love of the Darkblade."

I had sought him out at the Huin-Shi docks, or what was left of them. Piers had been rendered into blackened stumps jutting from waters crowded with scuttled hulks. The hulks had been left behind by the Jade Emperor to delay our use of this port, but the destroyed piers were the work of the Tuhla and not appreciated by their god.

"I let him choose," Kehlbrand said, nodding to the line of kneeling Tuhla warriors arrayed on the soot-streaked wharf. There were a hundred in all, the first dozen already decapitated by the weeping, stumbling man dragging a bloody tulwar across the cobbles. I hadn't seen much of Heralka since the fall of Keshin-Kho. He was rarely summoned to Kehlbrand for counsel, and it wouldn't have surprised me to hear the Tuhla chieftain had fallen victim to one of the many blood feuds that his people continued to delight in, even in the midst of war. Never an admirable man, he had at least possessed an impressive vitality. Now, he seemed to have shrunk, both in size and character. His leather armour was besmirched by weeks of drink and mingled effluent, his cheeks sunken and an unruly mass of greying hair sprouted from his head. I watched him sob as he placed a tremulous hand on the bowed head of one of the kneeling warriors, whispering something in the Tuhla tongue before raising the tulwar for the killing stroke.

"A destroyed port is no use to me," Kehlbrand said as another head rolled on the wharf. "I love the Tuhla as I love all my brethren. But they are still like children in many ways, and children need correction."

"Sacred duty, Darkblade?" I said. At another time I would have taken the lead from his change of subject and let the matter drop, but not today.

"Yes," he said, apparently unperturbed. "A great and sacred duty that has, in one stroke, delivered the Enlightened Kingdom into our hands whilst also denying refuge to the Jade Emperor. When we get to Lishun-Shi I will raise a fine monument in their honour. Your nun can pray at it. I'm sure she'd like that."

He kept his back to me as he spoke, apparently keen to watch the administration of his justice. Myriad notions churned within me as my hand tightened on my sword, gaze fixed on the muscles of his neck, thick but not so thick as to resist a blade. One stroke and he's just another head littering these docks. Not a god. Not my brother. Just a corpse like any other.

"I'll have the Redeemed rape her to death," he said, without turning.

For a second my hand froze on the sword, the wire that covered the handle drawing blood as it dug into my palm.

"The city had to burn, Obvar," Kehlbrand added in a more sombre tone, coloured by a small note of regret. "And the Merchant King along with it. Besides, you were getting overly sentimental. Mighty Obvar was never made to play the father." He glanced over his shoulder, eyes slipping from my face to the blood seeping through my fingers still clutching the sword handle. "Muster your captives, General," he said, turning away. "It's time I met my new followers. And make sure the horde is ready to march in two days."

◆　◆　◆

Over the course of the months since my last encounter with Babukir Reyerik he seemed to have grown taller in stature whilst being reduced in any other way that mattered. His once muscular but finely honed frame now possessed the knotted muscle and sunbaked appearance of one set to hard labour without benefit of a decent diet. It also bore more than a few marks that told of the whip. His face was the most changed aspect of his appearance, however; the smooth handsomeness of youth rendered into hollow-cheeked angularity. He stared at his older brother with eyes that gleamed bright in dark sockets, not with anger, but the same worship I had seen on the faces of a thousand Redeemed.

A dozen Stahlhast escorted him to the centre of the sprawling ruins that had been Lishun-Shi. I assumed they had been his guards and tormentors ever since the Darkblade pronounced penance upon his brother for failing to return Luralyn to his embrace, fleeing from the Thief of Names into the bargain. These were all hard-bitten veteran warriors of the Iron Steppe with the scars and booty to prove it, but they seemed strangely innocent to my eyes. The long march through the Venerable and Enlightened Kingdoms had wrought many changes in the Stahlhast who had survived it. Their armour was often augmented by captured gear, and many had been forced to replace lost mounts with southland breeds. More than that, it was the absence of weariness and grief in the eyes of these newcomers that made them resemble callow youths. Conquest brought many rewards, it was true, mainly in loot and renown, but I was beginning to understand that a conqueror can suffer almost as much as the conquered.

"Brother," Kehlbrand said, moving to enfold Babukir in a tight embrace. I saw the younger man shudder at the Darkblade's touch, his face taking on an expression that mingled bliss with terror.

"Come, Obvar," Kehlbrand said, standing back and extending a hand to me. "Greet my reborn kin."

I saw doubt and suspicion in Babukir's eyes as he exchanged a brief nod with the southland general regarding him with all the disdain his brother's champion had shown him in his prior life.

"Oh, he's greatly changed, I know," Kehlbrand said, seeing Babukir's confusion. "But then, so are you, eh?"

"I am reforged by the Darkblade's hand," Babukir replied, his adoring gaze snapping back to the living god before him. His tone spoke of a habitual, almost obsessive repetition but was no less ardent for it. The selfish, often sadistic and cynical youth I had known was gone now and, I suspected, fashioned into something far worse.

"You are the Darkblade's hand now, brother." Kehlbrand laid both hands on Babukir's shoulders, speaking with soft conviction. "For your blood remains true. Our sister has betrayed me. You know this."

"I do." The glimmer in Babukir's dark sockets grew brighter as his eyes widened. "She must die for it."

"No, brother!" Kehlbrand's voice rose as his grip tightened, fingers digging into Babukir's flesh although he seemed not to feel it. "She must be reclaimed by her people," Kehlbrand went on, voice softening as his grip relaxed. "She must be returned to me. Only then can the lies that drove her to treachery be washed away. Will you do this?"

"I am the Darkblade's hand."

"You are. It was not anger that had me set you hewing ore from the Great Tor under the cruelest of guards; it was love. Your failure to reclaim our sister and kill the Thief of Names was a measure of my weakness, not yours. Long had I allowed your education to be neglected. Long had I allowed your vices and indulgences, but no more. Now you are Babukir Reyerik in blood and in name. Failure has been burned out of you."

"It has!" The words hissed from Babukir's lips, as fierce as any prayer.

"Do you understand your mission, Hand of the Darkblade?"

"Reclaim our sister," Babukir said in the same implacable hiss, rising in volume as he continued. "Kill the Pretender to the Emerald Throne . . . and the Thief of Names!"

"Yes. Three goals of equal import. I give you ten thousand Stahlhast and twice that number of Redeemed for this task. A mighty fleet you will have, also, ships enough to ravage the Free Cantons. You've heard of this place?"

"I have, Darkblade." Babukir spoke with a fierce, hungry anticipation. "Their warriors have a fearsome reputation, one I will disprove in your name."

"You will, though the cost will surely be high, which is no bad thing." Kehlbrand smiled at his brother. "It wouldn't do for the first task of the Darkblade's hand to be too easy." The smile slipped away along with all vestige of humour as he stepped close to Babukir, his words spoken with slow deliberation. "She must not be harmed. Not even the slightest scratch, brother."

Babukir closed his eyes and sank to his knees, pressing his forehead to the ash-stained flagstones. "I am the Darkblade's hand."

"Go now." Kehlbrand guided Babukir to his feet. "Review your forces, prepare them for battle. You sail within the week."

"I should go with him," I said after Babukir strode away, he and his escort *filled with enthused purpose. Their faces were all lit with the anticipation of battle and the renown that would surely follow. I entertained little expectation of ever seeing them alive again. Even so, the prospect of sharing their fate was preferable to remaining in Kehlbrand's company for one more week, or even a day. "This face gives me an advantage over the heir . . ."*

"It gives more of an advantage to me," Kehlbrand cut in, waving a dismissive hand. "One I'll make full use of in time."

"He'll fail. The ships we've gathered can carry his force, but hardly any are warships and the folk of the Free Cantons are as famed as sailors as they are as warriors." I knew such persistence to be dangerous but Kehlbrand just laughed.

"Of course he'll fail. Failure is the one thing I can always count on my brother to produce."

"Then why . . . ?"

"Because, old friend, the Darkblade's epic of conquest must have a crowning glory, a final act in which he retrieves victory from the ashes of defeat, avenging his fallen brother in the process."

"You expect him to die, then?"

"I'd be very disappointed if he doesn't. But then, even before ascending to godhood I spent many years feeling much the same. Capture or death, either will suit us very well."

He turned his attention to the mass of stone being carted and dragged to the heart of what had been the palace of the Merchant King Mah-Lol. A small army of masons and labourers was hard at work crafting the foundations of a structure that would stand higher than any ever raised in the Merchant Realms. He had ordered me to scour the horde for those with the requisite skills, artists and sculptors being particularly prized. The designs they produced in response to his often outlandish demands resembled a macabre, twisted spike of gigantic proportions, decorated from base to tip with statues depicting the Darkblade's epic of conquest.

"I told you I'd give them a fine monument," he said. "My wonderful children." He raised a hand to point to the as-yet-unbuilt summit of his grand folly. "They will sit there, Obvar. Alongside me for all time, as will you, and my sister."

I said nothing, as was now my custom whenever he made one of his more grandiose statements. At every meeting since that day at the Huin-Shi docks I would utter fewer formal expressions of respect. I had even stopped referring to him by his godly title. My anger hadn't been assuaged by the fact that he either hadn't noticed or didn't care.

"You've been scrupulous in your search, I hope," he said, turning back to me. "Uhlkar is getting lonely."

I doubted that Uhlkar understood the concept of loneliness, but Kehlbrand's concern stemmed, of course, from more practical considerations. "We've only found a handful with the Divine Blood so far," I said. "They seem to be more scarce the further south we travel, or more skilled at concealing their abilities. Also, no children amongst those we have found."

"Keep looking. Take the ones you found to the stone. Bring any that survive to me. Your preparations for the next march proceed well, I trust?"

"The horde has regained most of the strength we lost taking the Enlightened Kingdom. Scouts report the Transcendent Kingdom massing three armies on its eastern frontier. Captured prisoners tell different stories. Either the last Merchant King will invade to crush us or destroy us when we attempt to cross his borders."

"A confident foe, then. But is his confidence justified?"

"Like every other army we have faced, the Transcendent Host is rich in infantry but poor in cavalry. It's also the most peaceable of all the Merchant Realms so its soldiers and commanders have little experience of battle. It will be a costly victory, but still a victory."

"Requiring months of campaigning, I'm sure, since I no longer have any wonderful children to ensure a swift conclusion." Kehlbrand's eyes took on the unfocused cast that told of inner calculation, the formulation of a stratagem I had little doubt would succeed. This had been his true gift in life, long before he touched the stone: a remarkable ability to fight an entire war in his head before the first arrow had ever been loosed.

"Send two-thirds of the Redeemed horde within ten miles of the border, keeping to the coastal roads," he said once the focus returned to his gaze. "The Tuhla will range north, rounding up any unwise enough to flee the Darkblade's love. No one is to cross the border in either direction until I decree otherwise. We'll wait a while for Babukir's failure then send an embassy to this confident Merchant King, who, I suspect, is merely another coward mired in greed, and I never met a coward who could resist a bribe."

◆ ◆ ◆

That night I listened to Mai cry herself to sleep. This was our new ritual. The nightly question had fallen silent for a time during the march when the children began to cluster around her. Ever since the day I returned to find them gone a new question had risen between us, unspoken and confined to her cold, accusing eyes: Why didn't you stop him? *The tears I could bear, after a fashion, but the question I could not.*

Before Kehlbrand took all but two of her charges away, I would watch her sleep when my own slumber proved elusive. Nightmares still troubled her then, but she usually slept without waking, often with Saikir or one of the others snuggled close to her side. Nai Lian was the only one who slept beside her now, and even she would wait until the tears stopped before clambering onto the mats. Uhlkar, of course, never seemed to sleep at all.

"She will forgive you," he said that night, breaking my vigil of Mai and the orphan princess. "Or she won't."

Turning to regard his small, shadowed form in the corner of the tent, I felt the habitual rage he provoked flutter and then die in my breast. For all his renown, I no longer entertained any illusions that mighty Obvar was any less worthless a soul than this cursed child.

"Or she won't?" I asked, keeping my voice to a whisper as I moved to stand over him. He betrayed no alarm, continuing to stare into the cloth and bead features of Nai Lian's tiger-headed doll.

"Yes," he replied in his uninflected mutter. "Together you'll make children of your own. Or you won't. Nai Lian will stand at the head of the greatest host ever raised in the Heaven Blessed lands. Or she won't."

I took a deep breath, quelling another flush of anger and sinking to my haunches before him. "You see what will happen. How can there be more than one future?"

For the first time I actually saw him exhibit something that resembled amusement, his skull-face becoming almost impish as it managed to form a smile. "More than one. More than a hundred. More than a hundred hundreds. More than a hundred, hundred . . ."

"All right." I reached out to clasp his stick of an arm, forcing myself to maintain only a light grip. His flesh felt cool but not the corpse chill I expected. "But one must be more likely than the others."

The smile slipped from his face, replaced by a frowning concentration that told me he was actually trying to form an answer I might understand. "The future is a . . . web. Many, many threads all joined together. Some shine bright, others are dim. They flicker like candles, even break and fade to nothing. But sometimes there are two that are just as bright as each other." His overlarge eyes flicked towards the sleeping woman and girl. "You and Mai will make children together. Or you won't."

"And Kehlbrand, the Darkblade. What of him?"

"He will feed this world to the tiger in the stone. Or he won't."

My hand tensed on his arm, gripping hard enough to bruise the flesh. Gritting my teeth, I forced my fist open and withdrew it. Whether Uhlkar felt any pain, I couldn't tell as he continued to stare at me in silence, though it seemed as if his eyes were now somehow brighter despite the gloom.

"No more riddles, boy," I said, voice hoarse. "We need to stop him; you know this. For your brothers and sisters lost to the flames. For Nai Lian. For Mai. Tell me how."

He blinked and returned his gaze to the doll, fingers tracing over the orange and white fabric of its face. "I saw the tiger," he said. "So did you. So did he. *Now, he needs to see the wolf."*

◆ ◆ ◆

It was not an easy thing to arrange but I was helped by Kehlbrand's preoccupation with his grotesque monument. It had become his obsession the longer we remained in Lishun-Shi. The ruins of the palace were transformed into a huge work camp where the din of hammer and chisel formed an ear-straining refrain beneath a constant pall of dust. The monument grew with alarming swiftness, a testament to human skill and ingenuity when driven by blind worship and terror. By the end of the first week it had grown to twenty feet in height, every inch of it overseen by Kehlbrand himself. He was particularly concerned with the creation of the many statues, especially those intended to represent his sister and his most detested foe.

"No, no, no!" he said one day, tipping over a near-complete marble version of the Thief of Names, its constituent blocks breaking apart as it toppled to the ground. "He's taller than that by at least an inch." The mason who had carved the offending statue cowered on his knees, weeping as piss darkened the dust beneath. I had little doubt Kehlbrand would have killed him then and there, but skilled hands were hard to find. "Do it again," he said. "Get it right and the Darkblade will show his mercy by only taking one of your fingers."

With the monument's rise, I felt his attention slip from me, the sense of mutual recognition that swelled whenever his gift touched mine lessened then faded. Kehlbrand, for the moment at least, felt no particular need to keep close watch on his favourite dog. As a result, I retained almost complete command of that part of the horde that hadn't been sent to menace the border with the Transcendent Kingdom, plus the many captives it had taken over recent weeks.

"Traitor!"

I turned to regard the stocky man being dragged from the midst of the captives by two Redeemed. This particular group of prisoners were those who had proven immune to the Darkblade's love, spared due to the need for hands to hew stone from this quarry for the monument. It had required a day and a half of wandering the fringes of this ragged mob before one defiant soul consented to reveal himself. His face was dark with uncaring fury, and he continued to assail me with curses even as the guards beat him to the ground. "Treacherous filth!" he gasped, spitting blood onto my boots as I moved to stand over him. One of the Redeemed drew a dagger and grasped the captive's greying hair, dragging his head back to expose his throat.

"Leave him," I said, waving her back.

She hesitated, squinting at me in puzzlement. "General?"

"Open your eyes." I inclined my head at the other captives. All work had stopped and they stood regarding the scene with varying degrees of anger and burgeoning defiance. Some crouched to fill their hands with rocks as a low, ominous growl built in their ranks.

"We've more than enough blades and arrows to slaughter the lot of them," the Redeemed said, gesturing to the archers arrayed along the crest of the quarry.

"The dead can't work," I pointed out. "And the Darkblade wants his stone. Would you like to explain to him why you failed to deliver it?"

The woman's face paled as she immediately bowed her head, keeping it lowered as she rapidly backed away.

"Hah!" the captive taunted, spitting again but in the Redeemed's direction this time. "Your god rules only through fear. 'Fear is the only recourse of the tyrant.'"

A quote from a source unknown to me, but not Sho Tsai's memory. "So, you've studied Kuan-Shi," I said, sinking to my haunches in front of the captive. "A scholar, are you?"

His brow furrowed as bafflement mingled with defiance. He had evidently expected to have received a swift execution instead of a conversation with a traitor. "A teacher," he replied in a grudging mutter. His face and neck bore a plethora of scars, some more recent than others, evidence of the Redeemed's unsophisticated means of encouraging reluctant labour. It said much for this teacher that his spirit remained unbroken, but I had noticed this was often the way with those resistant to Kehlbrand's gift. Courage and resolve, it appeared, were an antidote to godly seduction.

I looked again at the unwashed, rag-clad throng of captives, every face filled with the same glowering, almost eager anticipation. This was no mob of slaves; it was a tinderbox awaiting a spark.

"When the work here is done you will all be killed," I told the teacher. "You know this, I assume. There is no place in the Darkblade's world for those who refuse his love."

"Then kill us now, traitor. I'd prefer death to life in whatever pestilence your god makes of this world."

"I don't offer death today. I offer life, or a chance at it." I leaned fractionally closer, voice lowered to a rapid but precisely spoken murmur. "You have no reason to trust me, but no hope if you do not. Two nights from now guards will be withdrawn from the eastern perimeter. You'll find weapons in the well near the stables. It won't be much, but it should be enough to slit some throats and gather more. Take as many horses as you can. You'll be tempted to ride south—don't. Head for the hill country to the north." I met his gaze, seeing mostly incomprehension, but also a small, desperate glimmer of hope in his eyes. "Most of you will die," I added with a grimace of apology. "Some of you won't. But know that by this act you will bring about the Darkblade's end."

He began to voice a question, which I choked off by grabbing him by the throat, dragging him to his feet. "Work will wash away your blasphemy!" I said, propelling him back to the throng of captives with a hard shove before turning and striding away. "Cut their rations for a day," I told the Redeemed woman, who still bowed low as I passed by. "But no more floggings. They can't work if they're bleeding their strength away by the hour."

◆ ◆ ◆

Finding a suitable vessel and the hands to crew it proved a harder challenge. Most of the surviving sailors in our fleet of mismatched ships were Redeemed converts. However, careful questioning and judicious use of my special ear for lies eventually led me to a half-dozen who possessed the wit to pretend adherence to the Darkblade's love. They were also keen and grateful for a chance at freedom, albeit with a typical seaman's eye for enriching themselves in the process.

"The Jade Emperor will see you amply rewarded," I assured the wiry Meldenean captain. I had used my authority to requisition a small but fast one-masted sloop under the pretence it would be employed in a covert reconnaissance mission to the Free Cantons. The Meldenean and his five crew were sufficient to sail her the required distance and, I hoped, sufficiently greedy to ensure their arrival.

"You sound pretty sure in speaking for a man you've been fighting for months," the Meldenean replied. His lean features bore scars that told of a less-than-peaceable career, stirring the strong suspicion that I was placing Mai and the children in the hands of a pirate with little attachment to scruples.

"Deliver your cargo and receive payment," I told him, stepping closer to gain a clear view of his face in the gloom. "Don't and there is no corner of this world that will hide you from me. Say that you believe me."

The Meldenean scowled, features tensing in anger, but nodded nonetheless.

"Say it," I repeated.

He bared his teeth in a half smile rich in anger and forced amusement. "I believe you."

Hearing the truth in his words I nodded in satisfaction, turning to Mai. She stood close by on the jetty with Uhlkar and Nai Lian clutched to her side. The girl's face was bunched and on the verge of tears as she sensed Mai's obvious distress. Uhlkar, of course, simply stared at everything with the usual doleful lack of surprise. "It's time," I said.

"Please come with us," Mai said, face pale and eyes bright in the grey pall of dusk.

My gaze went to the bright orange glow silhouetting the hills to the northeast, the site of the quarry that I knew to currently be in uproar. It was too far away to hear the din of conflict so I had no difficulty in detecting the clatter of ironshod hooves echoing from the city ruins. Seven, I counted with an ear tuned since infancy for the tumult of horses at the run. He sent his saddle brothers.

"You know I can't," I said, moving to take her arm and urging her to the gangway. "Remember, the Transcendent Kingdom . . ."

"I know." She ushered the children aboard then halted before stepping onto the deck. "I never thought you were a beast," she said. "Obvar . . ."

"Our time is done," I told her, kicking the gangway to send it tumbling into the harbour waters. "Take care of the children."

We both might have said more had I lingered, but I could see my former saddle brothers racing along the wharf now. The shameful fact is that I preferred the prospect of facing them to voicing what I knew would be the unvarnished truth if I spoke another word to Mai.

I moved to my stallion, a tall Hast-bred mount with an ingrained liking for battle, and climbed into the saddle. I bit down on the reins and drew my blades, a Stahlhast sabre in my right hand and Sho Tsai's preferred straight sword in my left. I spared one more glance at the sloop to ensure it was pulling away from the jetty, catching a final glimpse of Mai standing at the rail flanked by the children, before tearing my gaze away and kicking the stallion into motion.

We pelted along the jetty, meeting the first rider where it joined the wharf. His name was Laiskir, the youngest of Kehlbrand's guards, as renowned with a bow as he was with a blade. Neither skill availed him now. I leaned low in the saddle as we closed, Sho Tsai's sword sweeping up to slice through Laiskir's reins and the hand that held them. Despite the pain and shock, he showed considerable fortitude in trying to counter with an overhead slash of his sabre, but my stallion carried me clear before it could land. My parting stroke laid open Laiskir's spine with a wound that would allow him to linger in agony for several days.

Johtrahn came next, a brawny warrior of famed appetite and impressive strength who favoured the axe over the sabre, which he proved by trying to bury his in my stallion's skull. I angled my hips to steer him clear in time, although he let out a shrill enraged whinny as the axe lopped off the upper part of his ear. Drawing parallel with Johtrahn, I gave free rein to Sho Tsai's skill. The hand holding the straight sword moved with blurring speed and precision to deliver an inch-long cut to Johtrahn's neck, a small wound that nevertheless showered me in a considerable amount of blood before I spurred on.

Navrok and Lialkar, two brothers from the Lutra Skeld, charged at me side by side. Given that most of their Skeld now lay amidst the drowned streets of Nuan-Khi, it occurred to me they may well be the last of their kin still drawing breath. It failed to stir any merciful impulse. I followed Johtrahn's example *and killed their horses first, riding between them to lash out with both blades, slicing deep into the necks of each mount. The brothers were veteran warriors, however, and had little difficulty diving clear of tumbling horses.*

Navrok rolled clear and brought his lance around in a wide arc, slicing deep into my stallion's haunch. He reared, screaming in alarm, straining my teeth and jaw as he threatened to tear the reins free. Lialkar took advantage of the momentary distraction to hurl his own lance at my head, forcing me to duck. Off-balance by the move and my mount's stumbling attempts to stay upright, I allowed the reins to slip from my mouth and leapt from the saddle. Navrok attacked before my boots met the ground, bringing his sabre down in a two-handed grip that would have split me from skull to neck if my crossed blades hadn't blocked it. I pushed him back a few feet with a kick to the chest, bent low to avoid his brother's slashing sabre, and whirled, both arms extended to deliver cuts to their legs.

Navrok got the worst of it, screaming in unmanly panic as he clutched at the blood pumping from his near-severed right leg. I ended his ignoble display with a sabre thrust through the eye before turning to confront his brother. Lialkar spat curses as he hobbled towards me, apparently uncaring of the blood streaming from his own wound. I recognised the word "traitor" amongst the enraged babble and thought it odd that I should be regarded as such by both the Darkblade's followers and his victims.

"Something I always wanted you to know, Lialkar," I said, sidestepping his thrust before running him through, Sho Tsai's straight sword finding the small gap in his armour above the base of the spine. I held him upright as he shuddered, smiling into his wide, shocked eyes, their light fading fast. "I fucked both your wives the night of the Third Question," I told him. "And they both wept in gratitude."

Hearing the creak of a bowstave, I dropped and dodged away, leaving the straight sword buried in Lialkar. His suffering, however, abruptly ended when an arrow skewered his skull. More arrows followed, steel-headed barbs sparking on the cobbles as they chased me across the dock. The row of warehouses nearby offered some measure of cover but I ignored them, instead charging towards the three remaining saddle brothers arrayed before me. Sho Tsai's reflexes allowed me to evade two arrows as I sprinted towards the rider in the centre. Next to the now mortally wounded Laiskir, Kralkir had always been the best archer amongst us and therefore presented the most potent threat at this moment. His eye proved itself irksomely keen and unperturbed by my apparently irrational charge. I bit down on an agonised shout as one of his arrows slipped between my shoulder guard and breastplate, the arrowhead making it through the mail beneath to find flesh. A spasm flashed through my arm, sending the sabre clattering to the cobbles. Mighty Obvar would surely have kept charging but lacked the strength to leap and catch hold of Kralkir's bridle. Sho Tsai, however, possessed both the litheness of frame and speed to do so before Kralkir could nock another arrow.

I swung my leg up in a perfectly placed kick, slamming the toe of my boot into Kralkir's temple, he having unwisely neglected to don a helm that morning. The hard crack of shattered bone sounded before he slipped from the saddle, face slack and eyes rolling back in his skull. I might have taken control of his mount if it hadn't reared, dislodging my grip on the bridle. I succeeded in landing on my feet only to suffer the breath-stealing force of Sigrik's mace slamming into the centre of my breastplate.

Blood spouted from my mouth as I landed a half-dozen paces away, a sound like a rusted saw on steel escaping me as I tried to drag air into my lungs. I made several vain attempts to rise, only to collapse onto my back as overstrained muscles failed me. For a time the world slipped into reddish fog as I flailed and fought for the smallest scrap of air.

"It would be a mercy," I heard a voice say, the fog clearing a little to reveal two vague figures standing over me.

"You heard the Darkblade," another voice replied. "Take him alive if we can. Besides, look at what he did to our brothers." The figure on the left loomed closer as I at last managed to draw a faltering breath. The fog dissipated sufficiently to reveal Sigrik's face, a mask of scars and stubble riven by disgust and hate. Of all the saddle brothers, he had always taken the most delight in slaughter, usually when the fighting was done and there were wounded to torment.

"To think," he said, "the great Obvar of the Cova Skeld, who made the waters run red at the Three Rivers, champion to the Darkblade, reduced to this. Trapped in the body of a lesser man and selling his life for some southland whore."

"He was our brother once," the first voice said, the other figure's face coming into view as he crouched at my side. Kivar, I thought with a weary sourness.

He always was a tiresome prig when it came to custom. *"Many times he has saved us in the midst of battle,"* Kivar said. *"By all rights the least we owe this man is a swift death."*

"We owed Obvar," Sigrik insisted, still staring into my pain-dulled eyes. *"But our brother was killed by the Thief of Names. This is just his corrupted shadow."*

"I . . ." I began, the words choking into a crimson plume. Sigrik squinted and shuffled closer, watching me labour to gather more air into my lungs.

"Something to say, wretch?" he enquired. *"Is Obvar's remnant about to beg?"*

I took a long, grating breath, Sigrik's features swimming into full focus as I regained strength enough to speak clearly. "I . . . was the lesser man."

I waited for him to turn his amused face to Kivar before clamping my hand on the arrow shaft jutting from my shoulder, dragging it clear in time to thrust the barb under his chin. My other hand gripped his neck, holding him fast whilst I forced the arrow up through bone, muscle and vein until it found his brain.

Kivar, his adherence to Stahlhast custom abruptly forgotten, immediately drew a dagger and launched himself at me. Once again, Sho Tsai's reflexes proved my salvation, my good arm flashing out to block his thrust, stopping it just shy of impaling my throat. My weaker but still usable arm drove an extended thumb into his eye, digging deep. Kivar snarled in animalistic fury, clawing at me as he tried vainly to pull his knife hand free. We rolled away from Sigrik's corpse, flailing in his blood as we fought, biting and scratching. There was no art to this fight, no room for Sho Tsai's skills but plenty of opportunity for Obvar's brutality. Sensation slipped away amidst the frenzy of this last, desperate struggle for life. Even now I remember only red-tinged glimpses of it: tearing Kivar's eye from its socket, his teeth worrying at my arm like a dog, clasping his skull between my hands and pounding it onto the cobbles, again and again and again.

There was little left of Kivar's head by the time my reason chose to reassert itself. I sat astride him, hands filthy with gore, my chest heaving and vision clearing to reveal the fact that I was not alone on the docks. The Redeemed stood on all sides in dense, silent ranks, every face dark with the hate-filled judgement the fanatic reserves for those who have defiled their god.

"Well, then," I said, flicking the remnants of Kivar's brains from my hands in tired disgust. "Best get on with it. But before you do, know this: The Dark-blade is just a man . . ."

They screamed as they closed in, drowning my words as their hands dug into my flesh.

CHAPTER TWENTY-ONE

Vaelin!"

The hardness of Sherin's voice, accompanied by repeated and insistent shoving, stirred him from the dream, for which he was grateful. Since partaking of regular doses of Kish-an's elixir, his dreams had been rare and only dimly recollected. This had been different, hundreds of people, their flesh grey and bloated, rising from the waters that had drowned Nuan-Khi to regard him with opaque eyes, all filled with dire accusation.

"Get up!" Sherin hissed, shoving again until he consented to sit and swing his legs from the bed. "We have to find him!"

Looking up he saw her features were pale and stricken with worry. Beyond her Ellese and Sehmon peered through the open doorway. He hadn't asked them to guard his room, a modest chamber in the east wing of the principal mansion owned by Clan Urikien, but that hadn't stopped them taking up position in the corridor outside. However, it appeared their protective urges didn't extend to forbidding Sherin's entry.

"Find who?" he asked, blinking grit from his eyes and reaching for a shirt. The previous day had been a long one filled with instructing new recruits to the ranks of the Imperial Host. Tsai Lin's injunctions against having foreigners train his army remained in place, but it transpired that Nakira was home to a large number of immigrants. They consisted of merchant families with a wide disparity in both origin and wealth. The Alpirans were the most numerous, and the richest, merchant dynasties with three or four generations' worth of investment in lucrative local trade. There were also sizeable contingents of Meldeneans, Realm-born and even a few Volarians. These tended to be the poorest, thanks to the collapse of the slave trade following the conquest of their homeland. The scions of this disparate lot were prone to a good degree of squabbling born of decades-old disputes, squabbles that often escalated into violence in a curious mirroring of the Sehtaku's love of feuding. Consequently, they were a difficult group to mould into soldiers in so short a time, requiring many hours of drilling and a judicious use of physical correction. He had gone to bed that night with bruised knuckles and a keen anticipation of untroubled slumber.

"Saikir," Sherin said. "He's gone. We need to find him."

"You have more than one gift now," he pointed out. "Juhkar could track anyone . . ."

"I'm unpractised with it," she cut in, a slightly defensive tone creeping into her voice. "Just possessing a gift is not the same as using it."

"Children wander . . ." he began, then paused as the black-song gave a small but urgent pulse. It appeared that Saikir's sudden absence might hold some significance.

"He doesn't wander. You know that." Sherin cast about until her gaze alighted on Vaelin's trews. "Get dressed," she said, shoving them at him and striding from the room. "And be quick about it."

"And to think," Sehmon muttered to Ellese as they exchanged smirks, "'The Ballad of the Young Hawk' calls her the kindliest soul ever born in Alltor."

Their amusement vanished at Vaelin's growl. "Get your gear and meet me downstairs. If I don't get to sleep tonight I don't see why you do."

◆　◆　◆

"The little bugger can't have got far." Nortah let out a weary sigh and tightened his cloak against the stiffening breeze sweeping across the bluffs. He lowered his voice to evade Sherin's ear as he raised an eyebrow at Vaelin, adding, "And is finding him really such a good thing?"

Vaelin ignored the question and continued his squinting survey of the shoreline below. The song's muted but purposeful tune had led them here after a two-hour trek from the mansion. Alum and Nortah had consented to join the search whilst Chien, before yawning and returning to bed, agreed she would ask around amongst her outlaw contacts in the morning. Her indifference to Saikir's fate made Vaelin ponder if she had possessed a deeper reason for forsaking Sherin's company beyond a resentment of ungrateful patients. The boy's ability to disconcert those around him had barely diminished since his apparent healing.

It took a good few moments of scouring the wave-battered rocks of the darkened shoreline before the song flared again, Vaelin making out a small figure standing atop one of two outcrops forming a narrow cove. Saikir gave no reaction when Vaelin called his name, nor even when Sherin did the same.

Navigating the steep slope to the cove was a tedious and tricky business, made worse by the repeated need to stop Sherin rushing ahead. "Get off me!" she snapped, jerking her arm clear of Nortah's restraining hand.

"Won't do him much good if you break you neck, sister," Nortah replied, maintaining a calming tone that only partially soothed her mood.

"Stop calling me sister," she muttered, resuming her descent, albeit at a reduced pace. "Hasn't been true for years."

Vaelin had to restrain her once more when they came to the base of the outcrop, holding her wrist tight as she tried to twist it free. "Wait," he said. "Can't you feel it?"

Her struggles stopped and she frowned, no doubt sensing the same thing he did. Even without the warning born of their gifts, the burgeoning strength of the wind told the tale clearly enough. "I felt nothing from him, until now," she whispered. "He said he lost it."

"Evidently, he lied." Vaelin released her and started up the rocky incline towards the boy. He briefly considered telling Sherin not to follow but knew it would be pointless. An inability to resist a soul in need had always been both her best quality and greatest weakness.

The wind rose to buffet Vaelin as he moved to stand in front of Saikir, though it hadn't yet taken on the gale-like force he knew the boy could conjure. "What are you doing here?" Vaelin asked.

Saikir's response was slow in coming; his gaze, wider and more frightened than Vaelin had seen before, remained locked on the rough seas beyond the cove. "Waiting."

"For what?"

The boy's gaze flicked towards him, his lips trembling as he spoke. "Uhlkar. I met him in a dream. He'll be here soon."

Vaelin staggered as a hard gust of wind raised a dense cloud of salted spray from the waves pounding the surrounding rocks. "And when he gets here?" he shouted over the wind and surf. "What then?"

Saikir's face took on a defiant glower, his bottom lip jutting out and eyes blinking to banish tears. *Just a child,* Vaelin thought amidst a rising tide of shame. *Not the Darkblade's creature. Not something twisted into evil never to be healed. Just a scared boy.*

"Drown him!" Saikir shouted back in a strained half sob that drew Sherin to his side. He shrank from her touch at first but surrendered when she enfolded him in her arms, pulling him tight against her. Saikir shuddered as he buried his head in her shoulder, the gale he had crafted fading to irregular gusts.

"Why would you want to do such a thing?" Sherin asked, gently easing Saikir back, smoothing the damp hair from his forehead.

"Because I don't know," the boy replied, voice laden with tears. "I don't know if he's going to tell you to kill me or not. The Darkblade killed the others . . . sent us to die, just because of what Uhlkar said."

"Uncle."

Vaelin turned to find Ellese pointing out to sea. Following her outstretched arm he saw a small dark sail through the dissipating rain. Ships had been arriving and leaving for days, either warships answering the Jade Emperor's summons or merchantmen making for safer ports. However, a warning murmur from the black-song told him this was neither.

He shifted his attention back to Saikir, crouching alongside Sherin and reaching out to turn the boy's face to his. "If Uhlkar can do what you say, you're right to be afraid. But I'll make you this promise: Regardless of what he tells us, I won't harm you." He met Saikir's wet eyes, holding his gaze until he saw a fractional nod of understanding.

He caught Sherin's faint smile of gratitude before rising, fighting down the fresh welling of shame it provoked as the black-song trilled a taunting melody: *You won't kill him because his gift makes him too valuable.*

◆ ◆ ◆

The small sloop rode the tide into Likura Bay before weighing anchor in the shallows. Vaelin and the others had hurried to join the sizeable contingent of Sehtaku on the beach, all armoured with weapons in hand, the eagerness for battle clear on every face.

"The Darkblade sends spies," one said, Vaelin recognising Sikaru, cousin and executioner to the foolish Baron Shori. He and the other Sehtaku had spent the weeks since the emperor's arrival engaged in a punishing daily ritual of practise with sword, spear and bow. Suggestions that they might impart some of their skills to the growing number of conscripts were met with such appalled outrage Tsai Lin had felt it wise to drop the matter. Vaelin had noted that the division between nobles and those they termed "low-bloods" was so rigid the two groups spoke with markedly different accents and any direct communication between them was brief and highly formalised.

"I doubt spies would choose so conspicuous a landing site," Vaelin said, peering at the hazy silhouette of the sloop. Dawn was still a good hour away but he was able to make out the sight of a boat being lowered over the ship's side. It made a difficult passage to the beach thanks to the vigorous waves. Besides the man at the tiller and two others working the oars, the only other occupants were a woman and two children, all heavily cloaked. It was only as the boat grounded and the woman's cowl slipped as she leapt over the side that Vaelin recognised her.

"Mother Wehn!" he said, labouring through the water towards the boat. At first, the nun stared at him as if confronting a stranger, then she sagged in relief as he waded to her side. She clung to the boat's hull, head lowered and gasping out a series of hard sobs.

"You're the bad man."

Looking up, Vaelin found himself staring into a pair of very large eyes. The boy peered down at him, a single vertical line appearing in his otherwise smooth brow. The black-song's response was immediate and powerful, resembling the tolling of a bell, the sound deep and dark with foreboding. He didn't need to hear Mother Wehn's admonition to know the child's name.

"Don't be rude, Uhlkar." She straightened, using her cloak to wipe away her tears. "This is Lord Vaelin Al Sorna, and he is not a bad man at all."

"No," the boy agreed in a faint, almost singsong voice, the line on his brow deepening as he angled his head. Vaelin felt himself be captured by the boy's eyes, knowing they saw a great deal behind his own. "Not entirely."

"I need to see the emperor," Mother Wehn told Vaelin, the urgency in her tone sufficient to drag his gaze from Uhlkar's. "The Darkblade's brother is coming, and he brings a great many swords."

Vaelin's eyes went to the dim horizon beyond the bay, finding it empty. "When?"

"Within days. And not here." Mother Wehn reached up to retrieve another child from the arms of a sailor on the boat, a girl clutching a tiger-faced doll whom Vaelin had last seen playing in her grandfather's park. Mother Wehn, it was clear, had an interesting tale to tell.

"Then where?"

◆ ◆ ◆

"Askira, Heaven's Chosen." Mother Wehn kept her head bowed as she spoke, only consenting to raise her face when Tsai Lin came forward to gently touch a hand to her shoulder. "The invasion will fall there."

"You have no doubt of this?" he asked her.

Wehn glanced briefly at Uhlkar, who sat alongside Nai Lian in the corner of the large rectangular audience chamber once occupied by the governor of Nakira. The governor's seat had remained empty since the fall of the Emerald Empire but his mansion had changed hands numerous times over the intervening years, Baron Shori being its most recent and short-tenured occupant.

"The Darkblade will know of my escape, Heaven's Chosen," Wehn replied, turning back to the emperor. "And so may have changed his plans. But I am given to believe he won't. His brother's invasion is expected to fail, thereby providing justification for the vengeance he will reap when taking the Cantons. He believes it will be the crowning achievement in his rise to godhood."

Tsai Lin cast a questioning glance at Luralyn who replied with a sombre nod. "Kehlbrand always had little use for Babukir. This attack will be mostly theatre, but for the lives it claims."

"Theatre or not, it must be opposed. I will not leave any part of the Free Cantons undefended." Tsai Lin turned to Nuraka Shan. "Is our fleet ready for battle, Admiral?"

"As ready as I can make it, Heaven's Chosen. With the ships we have gathered in the Cantons it represents a far more potent force." He hesitated, eyes slipping momentarily to Sikaru and the dozen other Sehtaku present. "However, maintaining discipline amongst the fighting parties is proving challenging."

"It is injurious to Sehtaku honour to stand in file when there is glory to be won," Sikaru sniffed, regarding the admiral with a disdainful eye. "Such things are best left to low-blood half-breeds, like you."

"This war won't be won by ambition for personal glory," Nuraka replied, face darkening. "But it may be lost because of it."

"I'm sure," Tsai Lin cut in as Sikaru bridled, fist tightening on the hilt of his sword, "there will be glory for all when battle is joined. Admiral, you know these islands perhaps better than anyone. Where are we most likely to find our enemy?"

"Askira's coast is a good deal less forbidding than Nakira's, Heaven's Chosen. There are at least a dozen places where an army could be got ashore. It may be best to send scout ships ahead to identify their landing site before massing to attack once they're at anchor."

"Allowing them time to get a great many troops ashore." Tsai Lin frowned, shaking his head. "I'm keen to prevent a landing if possible."

"They will face battle wherever they land, Heaven's Chosen," Sikaru put in. "Long have we fought the Sehtaku of Askira, and whatever their faithlessness in matters of honour and business, they have never been lacking in skill or courage."

"How many swords can they muster?" Tsai Lin asked.

Sikaru paused for a murmured consultation with his fellow Sehtaku. "Perhaps six thousand, Heaven's Chosen. Assuming they're willing to put aside their grievances and fight side by side."

"Six thousand against thirty," General Duhlan commented with a doubtful grimace. "I don't give much for their odds. Still"—he gave the emperor one of his precisely measured bows—"with the Amber Regiments in the vanguard, honoured sir, the matter should be quickly resolved."

"Emperor, I must protest!" Sikaru stepped forward as angry mutters rose from the warriors at his back. "The honour of leading the assault must surely fall to the Sehtaku. To be denied the right to take first blood—"

"Rest assured, good Baron," Tsai Lin interrupted, moving to rest a hand on Sikaru's shoulder, "I would have it no other way. And know that your emperor will be at your side when you spill the first drop."

The abbot cleared his throat at this, mouth opening to voice a protest then shutting at a glare from Tsai Lin.

"We still need to know where, Heaven's Chosen," the admiral said. "If we take the wrong course . . ."

"My brother will choose the site closest to the capital of Askira," Luralyn stated in a tone that mingled surety with resignation. "Seeking battle being his intention. Also, he was never capable of subtlety in any aspect of life."

"Then it's almost certain they'll land at the Ivory Sands," Admiral Nuraka said. "It's a mile-long stretch of beach at the most northern point of the Tokira Peninsula. From there, an army could reach the capital after only a day's march."

"So the Ivory Sands will be our destination," Tsai Lin stated. "General Duhlan, whilst I lead the vanguard, you will take charge of the Imperial Host. I leave their disposition in your hands. Admiral, ready the fleet. We sail as soon as possible."

◆ ◆ ◆

It took two full days of preparations before the Jade Fleet was ready to sail, each ship laden with Sehtaku, Imperial soldiery and locally raised conscripts. General Duhlan revealed a surprising facility for collaboration in his willingness to consult Admiral Nuraka on how his army should be distributed throughout the fleet. The warships carrying the Sehtaku were all gathered in the centre to form the vanguard whilst the Amber Regiments were crowded onto the bulkier merchantmen to form a division on their right. Imperial soldiers and Canton conscripts found themselves crammed onto a mass of smaller coastal freighters and fishing junks on the left flank. Once clear of Likura Bay the fleet resembled a huge inverted crescent that managed to maintain an impressive cohesion until a darkening of the western horizon signalled the onset of bad weather.

"You might want to skip supper, my lord," Captain Ohtan advised Vaelin, squinting at the gathering clouds with a practised eye. "That's a proper storm, that is."

The next few hours provided opportunity aplenty for Vaelin to regret choosing to take his company of barely trained foreigners aboard the *Stormhawk*. Fast and capably handled as she was, her size made for a stomach-straining voyage as she pitched her way up and down waves that seemed to have taken on mountainous proportions. Vaelin, well used to sea travel, managed to contain his gorge but his companions were less fortunate.

Desert-born Alum had the worst of it, spending much of the night with his head poked out of a porthole whilst a less considerate Ellese contrived to shower Vaelin's boots with the contents of her guts.

"Sorry, Uncle," she gasped, eyes widening in alarm before she began a fresh bout of heaving. This time, Vaelin managed to swing his feet clear.

Morning brought clear skies and the sight of a becalmed but mostly empty sea. The carefully organised crescent that had stretched away off the port bow had been replaced by no more than two dozen small ships and fishing boats. The bulk of the fleet was nowhere in sight.

"Seems the storm swept the littler craft north, my lord," Captain Ohtan said, pointing to the irregular green line on the horizon. "By my reckoning we're only a few hours' sailing from the Ivory Sands. Do we wait for the rest of the fleet or press on?"

"Press on," Luralyn said. She had emerged from belowdecks paler of skin than usual. Like Alum, she had little liking for the sea. Jihla and Eresa, having fared marginally better during the storm, were obliged to keep close on either side of Luralyn to ensure she didn't stagger.

"We have barely a thousand soldiers," Vaelin said, gesturing to the nearby ships.

"Babukir won't wait; we shouldn't either." Luralyn blinked tired but determined eyes at him. A sleepless night of nausea had apparently done nothing to lessen her desire to confront her younger brother. "And I've little doubt the people facing slaughter and slavery on that island will welcome a thousand allies," she said. "Or even one."

Vaelin paused to consider the approaching shore, searching for some note of guidance from the black-song. However, it had nothing to offer beyond the small inharmonious murmur that always rose in anticipation of impending violence. *Wait for certain victory or plough ahead into chaos?* He let out a soft, resigned laugh as something he had realised long ago came to mind. *But then, war is always chaos.*

"Signal the other ships to close with us," he told Captain Ohtan. "Make best speed for the Ivory Sands."

◆ ◆ ◆

As the *Stormhawk* turned to lead their small fleet towards the Ivory Sands the burgeoning sun rendered them a shimmering white ribbon between the blue of the sea and the dense green of the tall grass and trees beyond. It would have made for a pleasing scene but for the ugly knot of smoking boats and corpses littering a two-hundred-yard stretch of the beach. A dense knot of ships was anchored a half mile offshore, the sea between them and the beach filled with boats ferrying troops to shore. Borrowing Ohtan's spyglass, Vaelin saw that the boats were heavily laden with Redeemed whilst most of the bodies bobbing in the surf or lying on the sands were Stahlhast. The veritable forest of arrows and the smoke rising from dozens of boats told of a fierce contest at the shoreline, one that had evidently moved inland. Through the acrid pall drifting over the scene Vaelin made out the sight of waving banners beneath a cloud of arcing shafts about a mile inland. The horde had forced their way ashore, but the battle for the island wasn't yet over.

Studying the terrain beyond the sands he saw it to be a procession of dunes crowned by long grass, meaning an advancing army would have trouble maintaining formation. It also meant an inland march could remain mostly unmolested provided they moved swiftly. The long grass, damp from the storm but now partly dried by the sun, also presented a tempting opportunity.

"Our course, my lord?" Captain Ohtan asked. Although Vaelin didn't doubt the man's courage, the way his gaze lingered on the clustered enemy fleet bespoke a considerable lack of enthusiasm for charging headlong into a very one-sided sea battle.

"The fight is on land," Vaelin said to the captain's obvious relief. "The Askiran Sehtaku are trying to block the horde's advance down the peninsula. We'll do what we can to aid them, at least until the emperor's arrival."

"There, my lord," Ohtan said after briefly scanning the shore. His finger pointed to a spot where the white sands disappeared into the rocky bluffs to the south. "The water remains deep until a few yards short of the beach. Means we can ground the ships and disembark without spending hours pissing about in boats."

"See to it." Vaelin handed him the spyglass and moved to the mid-deck where his companions waited at the head of two hundred soldiers from the Foreigner Company. "Once ashore, take charge of the company," he told Nortah. "Lead them inland until you find the Sehtaku battle line. If they're being pushed back, pitch in on the Stahlhast flank. If not, form up on the left. Alum, Sehmon, be so good as to guard Lord Nortah's back."

Nortah nodded. "And you, brother?"

Vaelin turned to Luralyn, meeting her still-determined gaze briefly before focusing on Jihla. "I have a fire to light."

CHAPTER TWENTY-TWO

Their passage from the ships to the beach was greeted by a brief shower of arrows from the Stahlhast in the dunes, felling a dozen soldiers, but the weight of arrows was too sparse to halt their advance. Once clearing the surf, Nortah, Ellese and their small contingent of archers and crossbowmen replied with a volley of their own, provoking the Stahlhast to forsake their bows and mount a charge. A series of barked commands had the Foreigner Company hurrying to form an uneven but still tight formation before a hundred or so Stahlhast threw themselves at it. Most were speared or cut down within moments but a handful managed to hack their way through the line before being met by Alum. The Moreska's spear whirled with its now-familiar deadly accuracy, causing the small band of Stahlhast to split apart. They were quickly surrounded by soldiers, the waves turning red as they disappeared under a frenzy of stabbing spears and swords.

"Form companies!" Nortah shouted, moving through the aftermath of the brief struggle, shoving and kicking soldiers whose faces were flushed either with triumph or the shock of first combat. "Shift, you lazy bastards! There's a war to be won and it's not on this beach!"

With the help of their sergeants and officers, Nortah had soon managed to get their command into a semblance of order and led them into the dunes.

"Ready?" Vaelin asked Jihla. As instructed, she had remained close to his side since climbing the ropes from the ship to the surf. Eresa and Luralyn had insisted on staying with her. Luralyn had her dagger in hand and wore a chain mail shirt as did Eresa, although given the nature of her gift, she felt no need to carry a weapon.

"I doubt I'll ever tire of setting the Stahlhast on fire," Jihla replied, sweaty-faced trepidation mixing with an unbridled need for retribution.

"Never stray more than a foot from my side," Vaelin told her, starting up the beach. Luralyn and Eresa kept close to Jihla as she hurried after Vaelin, whilst Ellese fell in on his right and Chien his left. They found only one Stahlhast upon cresting the first line of dunes, a hulking warrior hobbling towards them on a gashed leg, axe in hand. His garbled challenges, emerging from his mouth amidst reddened spit, fell abruptly silent when Chien nimbly ducked under a swing of his axe and slashed his throat open with a single stroke of her staff-blade.

Vaelin led them on until the grass cresting the dunes grew thicker, then paused to gauge the progress of the unfolding battle. The struggle had degenerated into a series of separate skirmishes, knots of Sehtaku attempting to hold out against groups of Stahlhast twice their number or larger. To the south he could see a disturbingly thin line of Sehtaku forming up under a series of clan banners. The archers amongst them kept up a steady rain of arrows, displaying all the accuracy General Duhlan had claimed, whilst the swordsmen and spear-bearers strung out in a loose formation in preparation for the Stahlhast. The few riders amongst the Sehtaku spent a moment raising their swords in a salute to whichever banner represented their clan before wheeling about and charging singly or in pairs into the midst of the disordered struggle. It was as impressive a display of naked courage as Vaelin had ever seen, but also a pointless sacrifice since none of the horsemen survived their first clash with the oncoming Stahlhast.

"Honour and glory," he muttered, shifting his gaze to the north. A growing number of Redeemed had advanced from the beach and begun to form a battle line on the uneven ground, moving with a well-drilled discipline Vaelin hadn't seen in them before. Apparently, during the course of his conquests the Darkblade had somehow managed to turn his horde of fanatics into a true army. Although the dunes made for difficult going, Vaelin's veteran eye told him this force would retain its cohesion all the way to the Sehtaku. They would undoubtedly display a remarkable courage in the few moments it took for them to be overrun. He could see the Foreigner Company moving at the run to join the left of the Sehtaku line, but knew they would only delay the combined Redeemed and Stahlhast for marginally longer than the Sehtaku.

Time, he thought, recalling Tsai Lin's words as he cast his gaze out to sea. *Always the most precious commodity in war.* At first he saw only drifting smoke and the dense cluster of the Darkblade's fleet, but then his gaze picked out a small dark square on the horizon, soon joined by more. There was still a chance this would work.

Turning to Jihla, he gestured to the nearest cluster of long grass. "Here's as good a place as any."

She nodded and stepped closer to the grass, gaze taking on a hard concentrated focus, the air between her and the grass shimmering with released heat. It would have been next to impossible for a torch to light the still-damp grass, but Jihla's flames burned fiercer than any natural flame. As Vaelin hoped, the dampness ensured a blossoming of thick grey smoke when the grass took light, instantly caught and swept inland by the seaward breeze.

"Come on," Vaelin said, tugging Jihla forward, pointing out where to birth her flames. Four fires were crafted within minutes, adding their smoke to the growing pall drifting in ever-thicker billows across the battlefield. Several times he had to restrain Jihla from rushing ahead as her enthusiasm for her task grew, the sight of three dunes bursting into flame at once bringing a harsh but delighted laugh to her lips.

Hearing the creak and snap of Ellese's bow, he turned in time to see another Stahlhast tumbling down the face of a dune with an arrow jutting from her shoulder. Four more followed, descending out of the smoke, battle cries rising from their throats, faces like hideous blackened and bloodied masks. Ellese put another arrow into one before they closed, Vaelin moving to stand in front of Jihla, sword driving aside the thrust of a Stahlhast sabre. Its owner appeared maddened by whatever horrors he had already witnessed that morning, the whites of his eyes bright and wide in the dark rictus of his face. He bared his teeth in a feral snarl and drew his sabre back for a slash at Vaelin's head, the snarl remaining frozen in place when Vaelin thrust his blade through the Stahlhast's open mouth.

Kicking the slain warrior aside, Vaelin saw Chien hack the legs from under a charging Stahlhast before reversing the blade to stab the point through the eye socket of his helm. Beyond her, Ellese was dodging the swinging mace of a warrior at least a foot taller, lashing out with her own sword to score cuts on his arms. Vaelin started towards her but stopped when Eresa darted forward to press a hand to the mace-wielder's mail-covered chest. A brief flowering of blue sparks and the Stahlhast was propelled off his feet, flying backwards to land lifeless on the sand.

Tearing his gaze away, Vaelin was obliged to jerk clear of the fourth Stahlhast who flailed about, wreathed in flame from head to toe, gaping mouth attempting to scream with a tongue that had been seared away. An arrow flicked past Vaelin's shoulder to bury itself in the burning man's chest, ending his agonies.

"You should've let him burn," Jihla snapped at Ellese.

She replied only with a disgusted scowl before nocking another arrow and looking to Vaelin. "Getting a trifle hot around here, Uncle."

"We've done enough," he said after a quick survey revealed a healthy blaze covering the left flank of the battlefield. The fires were spreading quickly, the summits of successive dunes bursting into flame to send yet more smoke into the eyes of the advancing Redeemed. It had also begun to create a barrier between the beach and the dunes, causing yet further delays to the troops still clambering from the dozens of boats on the shoreline. The grating stench of the smoke was laced with the sweetly sickening odour of burning flesh, meaning they had done more than just craft a useful diversion.

He started off towards the dimly visible Foreigner Company, now formed in ranks on the left of the Sehtaku line, the others following close behind. "Stay together!" he cautioned, blinking tears as the wind shifted to momentarily shroud them in smoke. Reaching out, he put a hand on Jihla's shoulder to guide her between two dunes, so when the blow fell, he felt her shudder.

She let out a small sound, the kind of sharp exhalation a child might make in response to a cut finger. Turning as Jihla came to a halt, he saw her head lowered, frowning in consternation at the knife protruding from her upper thigh. The arm that had wielded the knife was blackened and burnt from fingers to shoulder, its owner partially submerged in sand that stuck to his raw flesh as he tried to struggle free of it. Jihla gasped again as he jerked the knife free, birthing a jet of blood that told of a severed artery. The Stahlhast seemed to be laughing as he tried to rise, but his bared teeth were mostly due to the fact that the lower half of his face had been burned down to the bone. As Vaelin cleaved the Stahlhast's skull open with a downward stroke of his sword, the black-song lurched into deafening life, fed by the rage of knowing he had just done this man a mercy.

"Jihla!" Luralyn was on her knees, cradling Jihla's head in her lap whilst Eresa clamped a rag on the gushing wound in her leg. Seeing the skin under the soot staining Jihla's face turn white, Vaelin knew it to be a hopeless effort. He was aware of Luralyn screaming her name again, but it was a dim echo heard from far away. Jihla looked up into the eyes of the woman who had taken away her chains and given her a name, lips forming a small smile before her features slackened and all light faded from her eyes.

Feeling something tug at his arm, Vaelin jerked away, sword rising as the black-song rose to a crescendo. He stared into Ellese's face, watching bafflement turn to fear as she retreated, lips forming a word he couldn't hear. "Uncle?"

The song surged through him, filling every part of his body and crushing what remained of his reason into a small, ineffectual ball, making him little more than a spectator to what came next. His vision tilted and shifted, fading to red then returning to reveal a different ugly sight each time. Another burnt Stahlhast, too injured to do more than feebly wave a sabre at him. Vaelin severed both his arms at the wrist and left him thrashing, stumps staining the sand around him. Two more crawling towards the beach, smoke trailing from their blackened armour. He decapitated one and crushed the spine of the other. The further he walked, the more he found capable of fighting, showing them no more mercy than he did the wounded. The black-song exulted with every death, the discordant fury of it robbing him of all sensation save the joy it took in killing. The elixir's calming effect was still there but reduced to nothing more than a faint irritant, a lone note of harmony amidst the roar.

He was aware of moving with a swift lethality that he hadn't displayed since his youth, and even then the havoc he wrought now would have been beyond him, tempered by a humanity the black-song wouldn't allow him to feel. It didn't make him invulnerable, however; he suffered blows and cuts, but they were scarcely more of an irritant than the elixir. The only vital sensation he felt came when a tall Stahlhast woman drove a punch into his jaw, hard enough to slick his mouth with the familiar iron-tinged flush of blood. The fact that she had landed the blow despite being impaled on his sword made the feat doubly impressive, the act of a great and fearless warrior. Vaelin laughed and spat blood into her snarling face, twisting the blade to ensure it severed her spine. Dragging the sword clear he stooped to gather up her axe and strode on as the song sang out its sincere desire she suffer a prolonged death.

He leapt a flaming dune to land in the midst of Redeemed freshly arrived from the beach, axe and sword whirling to break their line apart. A nearby company saw the slaughter and surged towards him, Vaelin meeting them head-on, cleaving the skull of the Redeemed in front, cutting down those on his left and right. They attempted to mob him, leaping to wrap their arms around his head and chest, trying to bear him down. The song, however, brought ample warning before each attempt, allowing him to slip through their ranks, sidestepping and hacking at grabbing arms. His vision faded in and out again, bringing flashes of shattered faces as the axe rose and fell with tireless energy. But even the song couldn't overcome sheer weight of numbers. Sight returned to reveal the Redeemed crushing in on all sides, blades and clawed hands lashing in a frenzy. The song brought another laugh to his lips as he sank to his knees, sword and axe cleaving legs, sending those closest tumbling to the sand. He surged upright, whirling, only dimly aware of the cuts scoring his hands and outstretched arms as axe and sword reaped a bloody harvest.

The Redeemed, however, remained filled with the Darkblade's love, and whilst other soldiers may have fled, they continued to hurl themselves into the fray, again much to the black-song's delight. Its music became so all-encompassing that the nub of Vaelin's awareness found itself in complete blackness, denied all sight and feeling beyond an increasing pain to the chest that told of a body pushed beyond endurance.

Abruptly, Vaelin's sight returned as the song began to fade, the music descending into a faltering murmur of its previous all-consuming clamour. He found himself sitting amidst a pile of corpses, mostly Redeemed, their inert or twitching bodies pierced by a great number of crossbow bolts. Vaelin felt some pain, mostly stemming from the cuts to his hands and arms, but little else. His mind seemed mostly incapable of anything beyond basic comprehension save for a single thought, something he had decided after watching the Servants execute the deserters south of the temple, a once-sincere resolve that now felt absurdly hollow: *Leave slaughter to the likes of the Darkblade. I will never be him.*

The hiss of shifting sand drew his gaze to a hefty man in mismatched armour using a spear to push himself upright from the carpet of bodies, apparently heedless of the entrails dangling from the gaping wound in his belly. He glared at Vaelin in utter hatred, bloodied lips moving to voice a whispered prayer-chant to the glory of the Darkblade. Vaelin sat and watched the hefty man limp closer, stumbling over the corpses of his fellow Redeemed, gibbering his prayer with every painful step.

He came to a halt a foot or two away. Vaelin found he had neither the will nor the strength to prevent the Redeemed from raising his spear, watching with cold detachment as he staggered and prepared to thrust. "Thief of Names . . ." he sputtered, then stiffened when something fast and sharp flickered behind his head to unleash an instant blossom of red. Letting out an almost comical moan of frustration, the hefty Redeemed collapsed to the sand, Vaelin angling his head to watch his face spasm in concert with the last few beats of his heart.

"Not a good spot to choose for a rest, lord foreigner," General Duhlan advised, flicking blood from his sword. He frowned at Vaelin's unresponsive face before turning to bark at the soldiers cresting the surrounding dunes. "First Company, wheel right. Second to the left, sweep towards the road beyond the dunes. Crossbowmen form skirmish order and cover the northern flank. Move!"

His orders were greeted by a chorus of affirming shouts, and the Amber Regiments streamed past at the run, Vaelin noting the already tarnished blades of many. "Bunch've these mad bastards tried to stop us at the water's edge," the general explained. "Formed a decent enough line but didn't know how to deal with an envelopment."

When Vaelin replied with only a vague nod the general frowned again, stooping to offer his hand. Vaelin regarded it in puzzled silence for a moment before grasping hold and allowing himself to be hauled to his feet. "The emperor took his army of amateurs straight towards their centre," the general said, delivering a hard clap to Vaelin's shoulder before striding up the slope of the nearest dune. "By the sounds of things, this business is almost over. Be a shame to miss his moment of triumph."

"Emperor?" Vaelin asked, causing Duhlan to pause at the top of the dune.

His face betrayed a brief flicker of annoyance before he strode from view, adding, "No need to thank me for saving your foreign carcass, by the way."

◆　◆　◆

Babukir Reyerik lay beneath a makeshift awning on the beach where his army had landed before meeting its doom in the dunes beyond. His back was propped against a mound of piled sand, and he sat gazing out to sea whilst Luralyn ministered to his various wounds, of which there were many. She had been granted custody of her brother by virtue of the emperor's gracious act, given in recognition of her courage and loss on this, the day of his greatest victory to date. Vaelin could hear the shouted exhortations of the combined Askiran and Nakiran Sehtaku as they pledged their loyalty in a formal ceremony on the field of triumph. Fully half of the island's Sehtaku had died today, making the exultation and ardour of the survivors seem odd to Vaelin's foreign ear. But there was no doubting the sincerity of their allegiance to their new emperor. Loyalty won on the battlefield was always the fiercest.

"And they didn't tell you what's in this?"

Vaelin turned to find Sherin holding the vial of elixir to her nose, eyebrows arched as she tried to discern the contents. Despite being perhaps the emperor's closest confidant, like the other foreigners she had been advised to keep away from the ceremony. As the sun faded she came to share the meal Sehmon had prepared, having spent the latter half of the day tending to the wounded. Sehmon continued to prove himself a capable hand when it came to cookery, scrounging up various ingredients to make a tasty and hearty beef stew that most of them wolfed down despite the unpleasant miasma arising from the nearby dunes.

The fires were all extinguished but smoke continued to linger, laced by the charnel house smell unique to violent death. Vaelin had observed before how survivors of various battles gorged themselves in the aftermath. *Closeness to death breeds both hunger and desire*, he thought, watching Ellese clasp hands with Sehmon, cheeks bulging with meat. Noticing Vaelin's gaze she looked quickly away, releasing Sehmon's hand and returning her full attention to her meal. She had been scrupulous in avoiding him since he emerged alive from the drifting smoke. Whatever she had seen in his face after Jihla's death clearly hadn't been to her liking.

"No," he said, turning back to Sherin. "But, I believe its potency to be failing. Brother Kish-an claims to have only a limited supply and no means of concocting something more effective."

Sherin returned the stopper to the vial and angled it, studying the way the firelight caught the contents. "If I'm to make an improved version, I need to know what ailment it's intended to treat."

Vaelin matched her cautious but inquisitive stare for a moment before turning his eyes towards Eresa. She sat apart from the others, a hunched, small figure on the beach. They had laid Jihla's body alongside the many others fallen to the horde this day, long, neat lines of shrouded corpses awaiting burial or cremation according to the custom of their peoples or faiths. The Stahlhast and Redeemed still lay mostly where they fell, although a group of local peasants was busy rifling the corpses for valuables before dragging them off. Apparently, the traditional treatment of fallen enemies on this island entailed feeding them to the hammerhead sharks that crowded its many bays come evening.

"Today," Vaelin told Sherin, gaze still lingering on Eresa's lonely form, "I killed a good many people and have little memory of doing so, beyond the joy it gave me. These"—he raised his arm to display the dozen or so cuts he had suffered, some of them deep enough to have required stitching—"I didn't feel." He lowered his arm and face, unsure of how she would react to what came next. However, the chill indifference that seemed to be the norm after the black-song took its toll lingered enough for him to say it. "Ahm Lin suffered a mortal wound after Keshin-Kho. He implored me to drink his blood so I might regain my song. So I did."

Forcing his gaze to hers he found neither the surprise nor anger he expected, merely the sombre grimace of one hearing a suspicion confirmed. "Ahm Lin was always the most generous of friends," she said, coughing to banish the catch from her voice. "But his gift causes this"—she paused and he knew she was trying to avoid using the word "madness"—"difficulty?"

"I believe so. This song is not mine, or at least it doesn't feel like mine. The things it has me do . . ." He trailed off, glancing at the barely touched stew in his bowl before tossing it onto the sand. "The elixir they gave me at the temple helped, for a time, but it's growing weaker, whilst the song grows stronger."

"Very well." Sherin consigned the vial to the leather satchel at her feet.

"I'll need a day or two to study it. Divining the contents of a curative isn't always an easy matter."

"I will be grateful for anything you can do." He rose and started towards the shore before pausing as something occurred to him. "The boy?"

"His name is Saikir; it would be nice if you used it. And he's a good deal calmer, thank you. Although, he still won't go near Uhlkar whilst Nai Lian seems happy to play with anyone. Mai is watching over them."

"Mai?"

"Mother Wehn. It seems she has decided to forsake her vows and won't answer to her title any longer."

"War always was the greatest test of faith." His eyes lingered on Sherin's face. Mai's tale had included more than just intelligence on the Darkblade's plans. "Sho Tsai . . ." he began, only for her to cut him off.

"Died at Keshin-Kho." Sherin's face was tight, her voice clipped and void of emotion. "Something else wears his face and body. That is all."

"They can be driven out." Vaelin hesitated before speaking on, worried he might be offering false hope. "I've seen it done. Queen Lyrna had a Lonak concoction that could return a soul to a body claimed by the Ally's servants."

Her face remained closed and she kept her gaze averted as she replied, "Your queen is far away and this war far from won. I cannot allow distraction, Vaelin. Not now."

He nodded and turned away, moving to Eresa's side. She glanced up at him briefly before nodding to the sea. The evening tide was building, sending tall waves against the shore, beyond which lay the Jade Fleet. "They fled," she said. "The Darkblade's ships. As soon as the emperor hove into view, they all sailed away."

"A prudent decision," Vaelin said. "And one no doubt arrived at before they ever set sail for the Cantons. The Darkblade will have need of them when he returns. This attack was no more than a grand farce."

"So," Eresa's voice took on a bitter edge, "Jihla died for the sake of a farce."

"She died fighting an enemy she hated so that others might live. There's some comfort in that."

"Comfort." Eresa laughed, a small, faint sound quickly swallowed by the pounding surf. "A word that has no equivalent in the Stahlhast tongue. To them there is only pain or pleasure, with nothing in between. I think it was their smallness of mind more than their cruelty that made Jihla hate them so, even before our mistress came to break our chains, even before we beheld the Darkblade and knew him to be the greatest of frauds. We never felt it, you see? The lure of his love. To us, he was just the worst of the Stahlhast made flesh. It's always been a wonder to me that he let us live."

"He needed you, your gifts."

"As do you, as does the emperor."

"You are not a slave here. You fight because you wish to . . ."

"I fight for *her*." Eresa's tone grew sharp as she jerked her head at Luralyn, still tending to her dying brother beneath the awning. "And for the family I lost." Eresa's voice thickened, her shoulders hunching as she let the tears fall. Vaelin crouched at her side until her shallow, rasping sobs subsided.

"I had a family once," he told her. "A family of five brothers, and like you, I lost it. But"—he nodded to the fire where Alum, Ellese, Sehmon and the others sat—"I've been fortunate enough to find another. You should eat."

She took a deep breath, wiping at her eyes before nodding and rising, moving to join the meal. He watched Sehmon ladle stew into a bowl and Ellese make room for her, shooting a quick cautious glance at him as she did so. Her expression mixed uncertainty with a well-hidden twitch of fear, which did much to explain her need to avoid him. Of all things, she most hated being afraid.

"You're remembering it wrong . . ." he heard Babukir say in a low voice that was little more than a pain-filled groan. "Obvar stole the grey. I stole the white stallion. That's why Tehlvar tried to kill me . . . that first time, anyway . . ."

Vaelin came to a halt a few paces short of the shelter, drawing a forbidding glance from Luralyn. He had wanted to question her brother but, seeing the hard defiance on her face, decided she was owed this indulgence. Besides, he doubted Babukir had much to impart that he didn't already know.

"Kehlbrand wouldn't let him," Luralyn said, smiling as she tightened a bandage on Babukir's lower leg in a gesture Vaelin saw as comforting the-atre. Her brother's chest had been punctured by several crossbow bolts and his belly pierced through to the spine by a spear. No amount of stitching or bandaging would save him, and the fact that he still clung to life seemed miraculous.

"Why kill a dog," Babukir said, pausing to cough a dark wet glob onto his chest, "when it can still bite? That's what he said."

"That's what he said." Luralyn took a cloth to wipe away the red stain then soaked it in water before pressing it to his forehead.

"Did he ever . . . let you?" Babukir asked, a deep, needful glint in his eye as he stared at his sister.

"Let me?" she asked.

"Touch . . . the stone. He wouldn't let me . . . Though, I begged him."

She shook her head. "I never wanted to."

Babukir groaned, the faint jerk to his chest indicating an attempt to laugh. "Luralyn and Kehlbrand . . . always got given so much . . . just for being born. I only ever got shit . . ."

Vaelin saw a long-harboured resentment sweep over Luralyn's face before she forced another smile. "Not true, brother. There were always plenty of girls happy to give you all you asked for, if I remember right."

"Because of . . . him. His blood. That's what they . . . wanted. Lying bitches . . ."

His chest began to heave with increased energy as a series of hacking, blood-choked coughs wracked his body. Luralyn tried to pour a mix of wine and redflower into his mouth but he coughed it out before it could reach his throat. Exhaustion finally left him panting and incapable of more than a faint murmur. "Why . . . tend to me . . . now, sister?"

"Is it not tradition?" She reached for something behind her back, Vaelin catching a glimmer of steel as she gripped it. "Your enemies failed to kill you today. So it falls to me to ease your passing."

"Kehlbrand . . . made me . . . the hand of the Darkblade . . ." Babukir gasped out, lips growing redder with every word uttered. "The hand of a god . . . should not be afraid . . . But, I am . . . Luralyn. I always . . . have been . . ."

Vaelin turned away as Babukir's whispers turned to faint, piteous weeping. It continued for only a short time before ending in an abrupt choking gurgle. Vaelin stood watching the white-crested waves break on the beach until Luralyn came to his side. "The True Dream returned last night," she said, face expressionless as she wiped the blood from her dagger. "I don't think we're supposed to be here."

Chapter Twenty-Three

Vaelin felt sure that the ambassador from the court of the Most Esteemed Jeun Lah, Merchant King of the Transcendent Kingdom, must have owed his position to either bribery or familial connection, being so utterly lacking in both diplomacy and deceit. He should have made for an impressive figure, tall and elegantly attired in fine but not ostentatious silks, his face possessed of an angular, aristocratic handsomeness. However, the constant dabbing of a kerchief to his sweat-beaded brow and the uneven tone he tried unsuccessfully to banish from his voice combined to give the impression of a man forced into the presence of those likely to kill him. *In which case*, Vaelin conceded, *he's not a complete fool.*

"I assure you, honoured sir," he said, kerchief dabbing as he delivered another bow to Tsai Lin that was too low to match his chosen honorific. "I do not mean to denigrate the great victory you have scored over the barbarians. But, as is often said, one raindrop doesn't make a flood."

Tsai Lin merely raised an eyebrow in response, before allowing a prolonged silence to descend. He sat in a plain chair beneath a canvas roof raised in the gardens of the Temple of Winds. It was the largest building in Jaigan-Shu, the capital of Askira, chosen as the emperor's temporary palace on the abbot's advice. Whilst the Askiran Sehtaku had been quick to swear their allegiance in the aftermath of the Battle of the Dunes, the merchant and artisan classes, larger here than in Nakira, were more varied in their reaction to their new ruler. Placing the imperial seat at the heart of Heaven's authority was calculated to ensure none in the Cantons doubted that the Jade Emperor enjoyed divine favour.

"A flood," Tsai Lin repeated finally. "Much like the flood of barbarians currently encroaching upon the eastern border of your master's lands. Tell me, Lord Gau Yan, has the Transcendent Host met the barbarians in battle?"

"They avoid our host." The kerchief moved from the ambassador's forehead to his upper lip. "As well they might."

"Then you must have soldiers to spare, ships also. Both would be greatly welcomed in the Free Cantons, since we share an enemy."

"Would that we could forge some manner of alliance, honoured sir." Lord Gau Yan's broad but stooped shoulders moved in a shrug. "But with our own borders so threatened, Most Esteemed Jeun Lah could not countenance denuding our forces. However"—the ambassador coughed, Vaelin watching the kerchief bunch in his fist, clenched, he assumed, to banish a tremble—"my king might be more amenable should you see fit to abandon your"—another pause for a cough—"absurd claims to imperial lineage."

The scrape and grind of shifting armour and gripped weapons rose as the Sehtaku and Imperial officers arranged on either side of the emperor stirred, faces darkening. Tsai Lin, however, gave only a soft laugh. "Would you call yourself a learned man, Lord Gau Yan?" he enquired, speaking on when the ambassador could only manage a confused stutter in response. "I will assume, given your rank, that you would. That you have studied the sciences and the arts, as have I, for my education was both long and comprehensive. Whilst I found much of interest in all my varied studies, history was my principal fascination, particularly scholarship concerning the fall of the Emerald Empire and what rose in its place. For instance, did you know that the great-grandfather of the man you call king was a minor bookkeeper in the court of the governor of the Southern Prefecture, his principal duties being the allocation of stipends and pensions to the governor's many bastard offspring? It was a task he excelled at, it must be said, possibly because he counted himself amongst their number."

Lord Gau Yan could only offer the weakest of smiles in response, Vaelin seeing his throat bunch as he tried unsuccessfully to formulate a reply. Tsai Lin allowed him to shudder in place for a moment before continuing, his tone now entirely lacking in any humour or solicitation. "We know what your king has done, lord ambassador. We know he has agreed to provide use of his fleet to the Darkblade in return for half the lands of the former Enlightened Kingdom. In doing so he has forfeited all claims to honour and disgraced your people in the sight of Heaven."

General Duhlan stepped forward, face dark and mottled with rage, his sword already half-drawn. "Emperor," he grated, advancing towards the now-quailing Lord Gau Yan, "I humbly beg the honour of beheading this lying wretch!" The last word emerged in a shout as his fist bunched the ambassador's silks, dragging him to his knees, sword raised for the killing blow.

"Hold!"

The sword froze, twitching in the general's hand. Vaelin saw genuine outrage on Duhlan's face, grief too, for the mad king he had called father and the kingdom he had served, now lost and stolen. However, Tsai Lin's order was sufficient to stay his hand. *Lost a king but found an emperor*, Vaelin concluded, watching the general take a shuddering breath before mastering himself and stepping back.

"Get up, my lord," Tsai Lin told the still-kneeling ambassador. He did so with difficulty, fear having sapped much of his strength. Sweat now covered his face whilst tears of abject terror shone in his eyes. "Ancient custom dictates that no harm will be done to an ambassador received with proper ceremony," Tsai Lin said. "It is a custom I will observe, but not without regret."

He rose, clasping his hands behind his back to approach Lord Gau Yan at a measured pace. "Your master imagines himself a clever man, I suppose. Pitching one enemy against another whilst reaping a profit into the bargain. He also sends you to my court, a man in whom I assume he finds little of worth, in the full expectation that I will take your head, thereby proving myself no better than the barbarian who claims godhood. Your king is a fool. Should the Darkblade defeat us here he will take his horde across your borders and complete his conquest of the Heaven Blessed Lands, making sport of your king's death when he is done. But that will not happen."

Tsai Lin stepped closer to the ambassador, holding his gaze whilst the man dripped sweat and tears onto the ground. "It will not happen because I will defeat the Darkblade. Tell the dishonoured fool you serve that should he see fit to abandon his absurd claims to kingship, and beg forgiveness for his deceit, I might afford him a swift death when I come to take his realm."

The emperor turned about, waving a hand in dismissal. "Get this cur back on his ship and gone from here, for I find his presence offends my people."

◆ ◆ ◆

"A man raging in a cave," Luralyn said. "He spoke in curses and riddles that made little sense. It was clear to me he was mad, but he also had a stone. The image was vague, shifting, but I felt it. It was the same feeling as when I saw the stone in the priests' sepulchre."

Tsai Lin's gaze shifted from Luralyn to Vaelin, brows raised in an unspoken question. Apart from Sherin, there were no others within earshot as they toured the works. All along a twenty-mile stretch of the Tokira Peninsula's shoreline locals and imperial soldiers laboured to construct a wall. Whilst there were other landing sites on the Askiran coast, only the beaches here offered the prospect of landing an entire army. Luralyn also advised that its proximity to the island's capital made it the most likely point of attack. "He will want to succeed where Babukir failed," she said. "Vengeance and superiority demonstrated in one battle."

When completed, the Emperor's Wall would stand only ten feet high, there being no time to construct more elaborate defences. Even so, both General Duhlan and Vaelin agreed that any barrier capable of stemming the horde when it swept ashore, even for a brief time, was preferable to none. At the emperor's order, labourers had been shipped in from the other Cantons. Most were peasants released from obligations to their landlords now that the Sehtaku clans had all sworn allegiance to the Jade Empire. Added to these were the people who had followed Tsai Lin from the mainland, a great many artisans from Askira with necessary building skills and the entirety of the Imperial Host and the Amber Regiments. The Sehtaku, however, refused to demean themselves with physical labour, and Tsai Lin had pragmatically agreed they would undertake the role of guards and coast watchers.

The intensity of the work meant that much of the peninsula was now blanketed in dust, only partially thinned by the seaward winds. People laboured with scarves tied around their mouths, working ten-hour shifts, some driving themselves to the point of exhaustion. For weeks, ships had been arriving from the north with tales of horrors wrought by the Darkblade's horde. This, coupled with Tsai Lin's sudden arrival and ascendency, left few illusions about the scale of the approaching threat. When the horde came ashore they would face an army of close to eighty thousand people.

Only half could be said to possess decent arms and training, but Vaelin had little doubt most would fight when the time came, and fighting from atop a wall, however lacking in height, was always better than fighting on level ground.

"I told you what I experienced in Mah-Shin's tomb," he said, blinking as a gust of wind blew grit into his eyes. "There is a stone in the Opal Islands, a stone we need to find."

"From what I've experienced of them," Sherin said, looking down at her hands and flexing the fingers, "these stones are best left undiscovered."

"A sentiment I would normally agree with," Vaelin said. "If our enemy did not possess one of his own. With it he creates ever more Gifted whilst we lose ours with every battle. I'm certain we need to find this thing. I doubt that Luralyn's dream would have shared such a vision for any other reason."

He saw Tsai Lin's face darken, as it usually did at mention of the temple. "Your dream," he said to Luralyn after a moment's contemplation, "it told you where to find it?"

"I saw enough of the landscape to sketch a basic map," she said. "Lord Vaelin is confident his cartographer can locate it, once we have your permission, of course." She paused, clearly uncertain as to the wisdom of speaking her next words. "But, I will not lie. There is great danger in this. The man in my dream . . ." Her features bunched in mixed repugnance and rarely expressed fear. "He was not a good man. Although most of what he said was a maddening babble, it was clear he had wrought something terrible with the stone, losing his mind as a consequence."

"And yet you still wish to find it?" Tsai Lin asked.

"Lord Vaelin is right. My brother possesses an advantage, one he will use to its fullest regardless of the cost in lives and suffering. If this war is to be won, we need to take it away, or at least match it."

Tsai Lin turned to Vaelin, his lack of enthusiasm for this project evident in his face. "Your company fought well and bravely at the dunes. I am loath to deprive them of their commander on the eve of another campaign."

"Cho-ka and the Servants can lead and train them just as well as I," Vaelin assured him. "Besides, the war remains in a lull. The Darkblade will require weeks to rebuild his strength, regardless of how many ships he bought from the Transcendent Kingdom."

"Passage to the Opal Isles is notoriously hazardous. The seas are prone to storms and thick with pirates into the bargain, and there are a great many ugly, if fanciful, stories about what lurks in the unexplored heart of those islands."

"We will take only the *Stormhawk*. With decent winds and an expert hand on the tiller, the voyage need not be overly long."

"Long or short, it will still deprive me of my most able advisors whilst we prepare for the next assault."

"General Duhlan has all the military expertise you require, and you don't need Luralyn's dream to divine the Darkblade's next move. Besides"— Vaelin cast a glance at their escort, all Sehtaku of the Urikien Clan who pointedly avoided turning their gaze upon this gathering—"I suspect your new subjects will welcome the absence of foreign influence upon their emperor."

Tsai Lin accepted the point with a faint grimace. "Centuries of custom don't fade overnight, regardless of new threats." He paused to think for a moment longer before giving a reluctant nod. "Very well. But Sherin will remain here, without argument," he added, raising a hand to silence her rising protest. "This enterprise already risks much; I will not risk the Healing Grace as well. Your presence gives heart to my soldiers."

Vaelin half expected him to wilt under the glare Sherin directed at him, but he straightened his shoulders and met her gaze in a clear refusal to yield. The unspoken battle of wills continued for a few seconds until Sherin gave a stiff bow, speaking in a strained rasp, "As Heaven's Chosen commands."

◆　◆　◆

Uhlkar just stared at him with his large unblinking eyes, expression revealing no more than the words he spoke in response to Vaelin's question. "All the threads are just as bright now." He blinked and returned to Mai Wehn's side, saying nothing more.

"He always talks like that," Saikir said, squinting at the frustration on Vaelin's brow. "The Darkblade didn't seem to mind as much as you do."

"Go along with Mai, Saikir," Sherin told the boy. "It's time for your lessons." Vaelin caught the impish grin on his face before he scampered off in Mai's wake as she led Nai Lian and Uhlkar from the Jaigan-Shu docks.

"You don't beat him enough," Vaelin told Sherin, receiving a withering glance in return.

"I don't beat him at all. Here." She retrieved a clutch of vials from her satchel and placed them in his outstretched hand. "The recipe wasn't so hard to divine after all. It's a potent brew, however, so no more than one a day. You may get a trifle dizzy after drinking it, but that should fade quickly."

He held one of the vials up to the light, peering at the liquid inside. It seemed much the same as Brother Kish-an's concoction, but with a slightly darker hue. Given the black-song's relative quiescence after the Battle of the Dunes, he had hoped he might not need this any longer, but it had begun to sing again come the morning, perhaps stirred by the prospect of dangers ahead.

"Thank you," he said, consigning the vials to his pack.

"Tsai Lin spoke true," she said. "About the Opal Islands. I've been hearing stories of them ever since I came here. Some say the jungles are home to men with the heads of jackals, whilst others would have it that they're jackals with the heads of men. There are also said to be birds twice the height of any man with bills like axe blades, but I suspect you can ascribe those to long-embellished legend." The small welling of humour in her face faded as she nodded to the *Stormhawk* where the last barrels were being rolled aboard and ropes coiled in preparation for departure. "Are you sure this is necessary?"

"I wouldn't be going otherwise."

He watched her begin to say something more, then her jaw hardened as she bit down on the words. "Well," she said, turning to follow Mai and the children, "try not to die."

"Guard the boy well," he said, making her pause. "He's important."

"I'll guard them all as well as I can. But, rest assured, I know the value of Uhlkar's gift."

"Not him, Saikir. He has the most valuable gift now."

Sherin's face took on a now-familiar hardness, her normally smooth brow creasing in suspicion. "I won't let you use him. I won't let you place him in danger."

Searching her face, Vaelin knew himself to be looking upon a woman wondering how she could ever have loved one such as him. "He's already in danger," he said. "We all are. He knows that. I hope you do too. Should I fail to return, make sure the emperor also knows his value."

Before turning away he forced himself to meet her gaze, holding it until he saw understanding merge with anger. The knowledge that one failed to banish the other left a hard ache in his chest as he strode to the ship.

◆ ◆ ◆

"From the good lady's sketches, I put our destination here." Captain Ohtan tapped a spot on the map located in the eastern wing of the archipelago that formed the dense sprawl of the Opal Islands. Peering at the chart, Vaelin made out an island, unremarkable except for being marginally larger than those surrounding it.

"Does it have a name?" he asked.

Ohtan laughed, shaking his head. "The innards of the Opal Isles have only been sparsely mapped by a few ships, none inclined to stick around long enough to name much of anything."

"Too scared of the jackal-headed men, I suppose?" Nortah enquired, drawing another laugh from the captain. They had gathered in his cabin come evening to hear him lay out their course. Besides Luralyn and Nortah, Sister Mi-Hahn had taken it upon herself to join them, having boarded the *Stormhawk* just before she was about to sail. Whether she was here with the abbot's blessing or on her own initiative, Vaelin didn't know, but he found it significant that she seemed more interested in the various etchings decorating the cabin walls than the chart on the captain's table. Mention of the jackal-headed men, however, drew her eyes away from the art to settle on the captain with careful scrutiny.

"Never saw such a thing in all my years in the southern seas," he said, bringing a small frown of disappointment to the sister's brow. "No, my lord. It's true there's plenty in those isles that'll happily eat you if you're foolish enough to step ashore, but the real danger is the pirates. They keep to their ratholes in the northern fringes of the chain for the most part, but have been known to venture south if there's prizes to be had. Though I've been stuck on land for a good long while, my old mates occasionally came around to share news of recent voyages. Seems the pirates are a good deal bolder than they used to be. It'll be partly due to the war, I'd guess, but the way my old mates told it, they were already venturing further afield than usual even before the Darkblade came south."

Vaelin recalled his last meeting with Kerran before leaving the Northern Reaches, how she had related the intelligence gathered by the Merchants'

Guild regarding power struggles and new alliances amongst the pirate clans of the southern seas. "Can we avoid them?" he asked. "The swifter our voyage the better."

"Normally, I'd advise tacking east for a good stretch before heading south, but that's a voyage of months rather than weeks." Ohtan reached for another map, unfurling it to reveal a more detailed rendering of the seas surrounding the isles. The clarity of the lines and freshness of the ink made it clear this was his own work, and recently completed. "All I ever set down or can recall about the southern seas combined into one chart," he said, finger tracing a course already set down in faint charcoal. It proceeded south in a straight line before abruptly taking on a much more irregular course. "The reefs that fringe the north-east coast of the isles make for dangerous waters." Ohtan followed the line as it snaked its way along the shores of numerous islands before hooking into a narrow strait. "Pirates tend to stay to the less hazardous seas to the west, and I doubt there's a captain amongst them could navigate this course. With decent weather, I reckon we'll make your island within three weeks, sooner if the winds go in our favour."

Although the captain spoke with energetic enthusiasm, Vaelin still detected a faint tremulousness to his voice and bearing that told of well-concealed trepidation. "You fear them," he said. "The islands. Why?"

"Only a fool doesn't fear the unknown, my lord." Ohtan gave a forced laugh but sobered when he saw the insistence on Vaelin's face. "It was my third trip there," Ohtan said, "many years ago when I was a lowly third mate on a freighter come exploring. My captain had a sense there were new spices to be found in the Opal Isles, or at least a fresh source of molasses, the rum-fruit always commanding so high a price."

"No opals, then?" Nortah asked with a quizzical grin.

"The name comes from ancient times. Legend has it there was a prince from some long-forgotten kingdom who established a colony in the isles and, keen for more of his people to settle there, sent back word to the mainland that the place was so full of bounty that opals lay thick on the ground. In truth, I don't think a single precious stone has ever been found there. Nor did we find any spices or molasses.

"We sailed right into the centre of the chain, where the islands are biggest and jungle most thick, not more than a few miles from the island we're headed for, in fact. The captain resolved to lead a party ashore, harvest himself some plants that were sure to make our fortune. We watched the boat fetch up onshore, watched 'em all trek into the jungle. An hour or so passed then we heard . . . things." Ohtan lowered his eyes, brow furrowed and lips forming a grimace. "Sounds I never heard from the throat of man nor beast. We waited until the next sunrise but the captain never came back and not a man on board could be persuaded to go and look for him. After we sailed off I doubt any amongst that crew ever returned to the isles, save me. Could never quite shake loose of the place, went back dozens of times but never once set foot ashore." His lips formed a humourless smile. "Seems fascination doesn't make a man any less a coward."

"Seems more like common sense than cowardice to me," Nortah said, affording the captain a tight smile that faded when he turned to Vaelin, eyebrows raised in an unspoken question.

"The stone is there," Vaelin said. "Captain, set your course."

◆ ◆ ◆

The first glimpse of the Opal Isles came six days after setting out from Askira, just an uneven green line on the horizon. As the line grew thicker, Captain Ohtan ordered the *Stormhawk*'s sails trimmed to half their volume and took personal charge of the tiller. It was a testament to the power of Sherin's gift that he stayed at the wheel for several hours without rest, face set in hard concentration with only occasional glances at his charts. He would hold the rudder in place for a prolonged interval then abruptly spin the wheel to point the ship's prow in the required direction, sometimes causing her to rear and plunge as waves battered the hull. By the time the sky grew dark he had settled the ship into an eastward course and commanded the sails trimmed so that they barely seemed to be moving, although when Vaelin looked at the distant islands now passing off the starboard rail, the *Stormhawk* still appeared to be making decent headway.

"The current'll carry us the next thirty miles or so," Ohtan explained, letting out a relieved sigh as he relinquished the wheel to the hand of his helmsman. "The reefs are sparse here, different story further on." He squinted at the sky, features bunching. "Wind's getting up too. I recommend you enjoy the calm, my lord. Tomorrow, this will be a hard deck to stand on."

Once the sun had faded completely, Vaelin went to the prow to watch the jagged silhouette of the isles pass by whilst he drank his daily dose of Sherin's elixir.

"Too meagre an amount to drink."

Nortah, skilled from a young age in preventing his footsteps from being heard, stood with his arms folded and back resting against the forward anchor. "If you took more of it," he went on, eyeing the vial in Vaelin's hand with a critical frown, "I'd judge that our time apart had made you into a red-flower fiend. But you never have more than one vial a day. So if it's not a drug, or drink, what is it?"

Vaelin swiftly consigned the vial to his pocket, turning back to the shore. "One of Sherin's remedies," he said. "For the ache in my back."

"You don't have any aches these days, brother." Nortah unfolded his arms to move closer, eyes narrowing in cautious scrutiny. "Not since we found you at the Ghost Shacks and I beheld a man who had somehow become five years younger."

Vaelin didn't give an immediate reply, continuing to stare at the passing islands. The moon was high and the sky mostly cloudless, scattering blue light across the dense vegetation of the isles. Their course had brought them closer now, making it possible to discern some detail thanks to the moonlight. "So green here," he observed. "Haven't seen the like of these trees before . . ."

"You are changed." Nortah's voice took on a hard, insistent edge as he stepped closer still. "You never feared battle before, but neither did you relish it. Ellese told me what she saw at Askira. She said the man she beheld wasn't her uncle. And there are stories told by the emperor's soldiers of what you did that day. They don't sound like things my brother would do."

"This journey has changed us all . . ."

"That it has. But I don't fear the change in me, I welcome it." His voice became a whisper, concern joining the suspicion in his eyes as he clasped Vaelin's forearm. "I am grateful you brought me along, brother. For all the horrors I have seen, I wouldn't trade it. You helped me; let me help you."

Vaelin considered voicing more lies, attempting to placate Nortah with vague assurances. But this man, perhaps above all others, deserved some modicum of truth. "There is a . . . sickness within me," he said. "Something dangerous, to me and to others. The Servants of the Temple gave me a means of containing it."

"A sickness?" Nortah's brow creased, the concern in his eyes turning to fear. "You mean a sickness of the mind?"

"You could call it that. You remember how I found you at the Fallen City."

"The Dark, your gift. You said you lost it."

"I did. But after Keshin-Kho I got it back. However, it's different. It makes me different."

"Sherin can cure all ailments . . ."

"She has already helped me." He patted the pocket containing the vial.

"You know that's not what I mean."

"No." Vaelin's voice was sharp. "Not this. Her gift exacts too high a price, and I'll not have her pay it on my account."

"But this . . . potion keeps it at bay?"

"Mostly. It's been much quieter of late. But there may come a time when it isn't. It happened before, on the road to the Temple of Spears, at the dunes. Should it happen again . . ." He looked intently into Nortah's eyes, holding his gaze until understanding dawned.

"I will never . . ." Nortah began, drawing away.

"You said I should let you help me. This is how you can."

Nortah's features were pale in the moonlight; the way the shadows caught the planes of his face made him appear far older than his years. This was a man aged by grief, his own indulgence and the wars that had dominated his life, wars he had never sought out. He had always detested the act of killing, and clearly the very idea of what Vaelin asked of him was near impossible for him to contemplate.

"You know I left Caenis to die," Nortah said, voice soft but harsh. "You know he still haunts my dreams because of it."

"I saw Dentos die because I led him into a war that should never have been fought," Vaelin returned. "And I killed Barkus, because I had to, as you may have to do this. It has long been our lot in life, brother, to do what others can't." Seeing anger mix with the appalled refusal on Nortah's face, Vaelin sighed, the demand fading from his voice as he went on. "The Darkblade and I possess the same gift. He is what happens to a soul shorn of restraint and lost in ambition. He is the mirror that shows my future should this song claim me. Would you let another like him loose upon this world?"

Nortah retreated another step until the shadow of the mainmast obscured his face, so Vaelin was unable to read his expression when he said, "I would not. But you are not him and never will be. My Faith tells me so." He turned and started towards the hold.

"All I ask is that you stay at my side," Vaelin said, making him pause in mid-stride. "Throughout all that is to come. Keep a close watch. Will you do that for me at least, brother?"

Nortah remained still for the space of a heartbeat, then Vaelin made out the short nod of his head before he disappeared belowdecks.

CHAPTER TWENTY-FOUR

He was awoken by the black-song cutting through the elixir to push a hard, pulsating throb into his sleep-befuddled head. The tune was a demand rather than a warning, the tone less grating than usual. As he reached for his clothes, Vaelin even felt a twinge of recognition for the blood-song in the way it propelled him from the hold to the deck, eyes scanning the northern horizon. Whatever it expected to find, it didn't perceive it as dangerous, just highly significant. So it was with some surprise that his gaze alighted upon three sails cresting the distant waves as the cry of "Pirates!" went up from the crow's nest.

Thumping drums and whistles summoned the rest of the crew from slumber, although Vaelin only dimly heard the pounding of feet on the deck and the rattle and clatter of distributed weapons, the song commanding his full attention to the approaching ships.

"You forgot something, Uncle."

He turned to find Ellese with his sword in hand. These were the first words she had spoken to him in days, wariness continuing to cloud her face, but also a decisive resolution to meet his eye that made him wonder what Nortah had told her the night before.

"Thank you," he said, taking the sword and buckling the strap across his chest despite a growing surety that he wouldn't need it this morning. Nevertheless, he told her to take her bow aloft before moving to join Captain Ohtan at the port rail.

"Well," he said, cheek bunching around the eyepiece of his spyglass, "she's a big old bitch to be sure."

Vaelin squinted through the morning haze, noting the impressive dimensions of the ship in the centre of the approaching trio. She created at least twice the displacement of the other two, raising a tall wake around her bows as she ploughed her way through the choppy sea towards the *Storm-hawk*. Vaelin's sense of recognition deepened as the huge ship drew nearer, clearly guided by a hand just as expert as Ohtan's. She also bore a flag he had last seen on the voyage to the Far West, a white shield on a black background shot through with lightning.

"Not as fast as our own bitch though, nor her sisters," the captain added, lowering the spyglass and patting a hand to the rail before abruptly turning about, a stream of orders issuing from his mouth in a loud but precise torrent. "Unfurl all sheets and tighten all lines! Bosun, toss every empty barrel in the hold over the side! Helm, steer two more points to starboard!"

Within moments the *Stormhawk*'s wake had broadened, her deck tilting as Ohtan took over the tiller to ensure she caught the wind at precisely the right angle. Returning his gaze to the pursuing ships, Vaelin saw fresh sails blossoming on their own masts, but still they appeared to be falling behind. It was as he turned back to the deck that the black-song rose to its highest pitch, blaring loudest when Vaelin's eyes fell on Alum's tall form. The Moreska emerged from the hold with his spear slung across his back, grimacing in discomfort as he grappled his way across the pitching deck towards Vaelin.

"I would welcome a fight," he said, "if it meant an end to this. My feet were made for sand, not sea."

Vaelin's gaze slid from Alum to the pirate vessels, now growing dimmer as the *Stormhawk* sped on, the song's tune clear and unambiguous: *The Moreska followed you for this.*

"Captain Ohtan!" Vaelin called out, moving from rope to rope as he made his way to the tiller. "Trim your sails and heave to!"

The captain gaped at him. "My lord?!"

"You heard my order." Vaelin looked from Ohtan's wide-eyed, uncomprehending face to the fast-receding ships beyond the stern. "Trust me, there will be no fight today."

◆ ◆ ◆

"We'll kill the fucking lot of you!"

The pirate's laughing taunt was taken up by his mates crowding the starboard rail of the huge ship as she drew alongside. They were a mixed lot, the one who had shouted being a brawny Meldenean with a host of scars marring the tattoos covering his muscular arms. Alongside him stood a dark-skinned Alpiran almost the same height as Alum, beside him a Far Western woman with a shaven head clad in similar garb to the Sehtaku. As Vaelin's gaze tracked along them he counted people from five different nations, hearing a mélange of overlapping languages, much of it profane with anticipatory glee. His survey came to a halt as his eyes slipped from the pirates to the hull beneath the bowsprit where the ship's name had been emblazoned in ornate Meldenean lettering: *Sea Empress*.

His attention snapped back to the pirates as they all fell into sudden, uniform silence, the crowd at the rail swiftly moving aside to make way for a tall man with long blond hair. He had a handsome, familiar face drawn in an expression of resigned displeasure as he and Vaelin regarded each other across the few yards of sea that divided the vessels.

"She used to be named for our queen," Vaelin said finally, gesturing to the lettering on the hull.

Atheran Ell-Nestra, former Shield of the Meldenean Isles and dismissed Admiral of the Royal Fleet of Queen Lyrna Al Nieren, gave no response at first. The *Stormhawk*'s crew muttered and fidgeted in tense expectation as the silence stretched, Vaelin noting the contrast to the pirates opposite. Despite all being armed and primed in readiness for combat, they kept their mouths firmly closed, those closest to Ell-Nestra appearing cowed by his proximity. He had always enjoyed a good deal of loyalty from the Islanders who followed him, at least until Vaelin's blow had left him unconscious during their famously short-lived duel. Now, it appeared he had a crew who didn't even dare raise their voice without his consent.

"Lyrna is your queen," Ell-Nestra replied, voice clipped and hard. "And the name no longer suited her." He blinked and raised his gaze to the *Stormhawk*'s rigging, eyes narrowing as they focused on Ellese. She had secured herself to the mainmast with a length of rope and held her bow ready, half-drawn with an arrow against the string. Ell-Nestra's focus seemed to be more on the bow than its owner.

"Did you steal that?" he called out. "I hope for your sake you didn't."

Ellese scowled at him in baffled offence for a second before shouting back. "It was my mother's gift to me!" She paused, fumbling for a suitable insult. "So, fuck off, sea-rat!"

This drew a low chuckle from the pirates, although they once again fell silent at a glance from Ell-Nestra. "Her mother?" he asked, turning back to Vaelin.

"A lot has happened," Vaelin replied with a shrug.

"Clearly." Ell-Nestra's lips formed into something that was half grimace and half smile. "Once again," he said, shaking his head, "fate conspires to prove that there is no corner of this world where you will not appear to plague me."

"I'm not here for you."

"Then what?"

It was then that Alum rushed to the rail, shoving aside several sailors, his eyes wide and wet with sudden tears. "*Liambe!*" he called out, extending an open hand to the other ship, the fingers splayed wide. "*Su tehvu! Lem suetsu, Alum!*"

The language was that of the Moreska and very different from Alpiran. Although the words meant nothing to Vaelin, they clearly meant a great deal to one amongst Ell-Nestra's crew. The pirates moved aside to make room for a boy, almost as tall as a man but with a face that couldn't have had more than thirteen years. Like Alum, he had a series of scars marking the brows above his eyes, but not so many. He gaped at Alum in blank amazement, tears rising in his own eyes, before he too stretched out his arm, fingers splayed in the same manner.

"It seems I'm here for him," Vaelin told Ell-Nestra. "And his kin. My friend has come a very long way to find his family, you see."

Ell-Nestra raised a skeptical eyebrow. "And that's your only business in these waters?"

"As I said, a lot has happened, especially to the north, as I expect you know full well."

"Don't tell me what I know, Al Sorna!"

The angry snap of Ell-Nestra's voice aroused an instant response from his crew, voices raised once again as they brandished their weapons, although

Vaelin saw more than a few frowning faces for whom the name Al Sorna apparently held some meaning.

"Quiet!" Their captain's bark heralded another instant silence, save for Alum and the boy on the *Sea Empress* who continued to call to each other, arms still outstretched. "Liambe's a good lad," Ell-Nestra said with a weary sigh. "Far be it from me to sunder a family." He moved back from the rail, sending his crew scurrying to the rigging with a short series of orders before turning back to call to Vaelin a final time. "Follow our course, and don't stray."

◆　◆　◆

A dozen children waited alongside Liambe on the jetty where they moored up, five boys and seven girls. They flocked to Alum the moment he rushed down the gangway, clustering around him in a babble of laughter and tears. He opened his arms and gathered them to him, head lowered and bobbing as he gave vent to his feelings. The Moreska, it appeared, felt no shame in weeping openly.

In addition to the children, a large number of armed pirates also crowded the jetty, a stocky, bearded man of middling years standing at their head.

"Lord Belorath," Vaelin said, inclining his head after departing the ship. "Good to see you again."

"I've been called a lord only once," he said, a faint and not altogether unwelcoming smile on his lips. "Not sure it's a title I relish."

"Queen Lyrna named you a Sword of the Realm at the close of the Liberation War," Vaelin said. "There are lands and rewards to claim should you ever return to her dominions."

"Have a care, my lord," Belorath cautioned, "lest my king suspect you of trying to suborn the loyalty of his chamberlain."

"King?"

"Indeed." Belorath gave a formal bow, one hand extended to Vaelin, the other to the settlement beyond the series of wooden jetties that comprised the docks. The *Stormhawk* had followed the *Sea Empress* for two days before arriving in a sheltered bay on an elongated island Ohtan placed at the midpoint of the northern fringe of the Opal Isles. The settlement was small by Far Western standards but would be considered a town in the Realm. The houses were all of timber construction, forming a sprawl that ascended the slope leading to the island's highest point where a yet taller structure rose to an impressive height. It was fashioned from stone rather than wood, its flanks clad in scaffolding that told of an as-yet-unfinished grandeur.

"I bid you welcome to the Benevolent Kingdom of His Esteemed Majesty the Merchant King Atheran Ell-Nestra, First of His Name," Belorath said.

Vaelin confined his response to a raised eyebrow as he returned Belorath's bow. The Meldenean's polite visage, however, grew dark when Nortah let out a poorly concealed snort of amusement, muttering, "When pirates make themselves kings, the world truly has gone mad."

Belorath, clearly keen to maintain an appearance of courtly propriety, forced the politeness back onto his face before standing aside. "Allow us to escort you to your quarters, my lord," he said, bowing again and gesturing for Vaelin to proceed. "His Highness has decreed you receive all respect due your rank."

Vaelin turned to regard Alum, still fully engaged in the reunion with the Moreska children. "We found them on a slave ship headed to the southern reaches of Volaria," Belorath said. "Apparently, your queen's attempts to snuff out the old ways haven't been entirely successful."

"And their role here?" Vaelin asked.

"They work and are paid for their labour. Also, they are free to leave should they earn enough coin for a passage. Liambe, the eldest, has a growing share of prizes from his service aboard the *Sea Empress*. If you would, my lord." Belorath's voice took on an insistent note. "Your friend can berth with his kin, but you are *requested* to lodge at the palace."

Vaelin was unsurprised to learn that the palace of the Merchant King Atheran was the scaffold-encrusted stone building at the top of the slope. They made their way through the town past a great many staring onlookers, mostly wearing the mismatched garb common to pirates, but some dressed in finery that wouldn't have been out of place in the wealthier districts of Varinshold. According to Belorath, the settlement had previously held the inauspicious title of "Red Tahn's Clutch," named after the pirate chieftain who had first established a mooring in the bay. Over time it had simply become known as "the Clutch" until the ascendancy of King Atheran whereupon it became Margentis, the capital of the Benevolent Kingdom, named in honour of the greatest sea god in the Meldenean pantheon. Making his way through the broad central avenue, Vaelin saw how the town became progressively cleaner and more obviously wealthy the further they progressed up the slope. Hovels and smoke-shrouded drinking dens gave way to sturdy houses, which were in turn overshadowed by two- or three-storey mansions built in the Alpiran style. The palace, however, bore more familiar architecture.

"So," Nortah said, letting out another laugh as they came to the base of the tall, round-walled construction, "he wants to be a Tower Lord as well as a king, does he?"

Vaelin also found the resemblance to the tower he had called home for so long a little too close to be a coincidence. But for its height, about a dozen feet taller than Vaelin's North Tower, it was near identical in most respects, including a half-built barracks and outer defensive wall.

"Local stone is hard to quarry and often too brittle for building," Belorath said, stiffening a little. "Every brick has to be shipped in. It is simply a matter of common sense and efficiency to follow an established building pattern."

He pointedly turned his back to Nortah and bowed again, this time to Ellese rather than Vaelin. "Lady Mustor, despite appearances, the internals of the palace are complete and ready for occupancy. My liege has given the upper rooms over to your comfort. Servants will be provided to see to your needs. Lord Vaelin"—Belorath extended a hand to the barracks—"you and your companions will find adequate accommodation there. King Atheran has generously seen fit to invite you to share his table tonight." He spared a brief glance in Nortah's direction. "Please educate your retinue in the meaning of manners before then. My lady," he went on quickly, offering his arm to Ellese, "please allow me to show you to your rooms. We have a fine collection of dresses should you wish to change."

Ellese cast a half-amused yet puzzled glance at Vaelin and, receiving a nod, allowed herself to be led away. The large group of pirates that had escorted them from the bay continued to stand in loose but dense order close by, positioned so as to bar the road to the town.

"I don't remember that one being such a pompous arse during the war," Nortah said, nodding at Belorath as he guided Ellese into the tower.

"Why does she get a room in the tower and we bed down in there?" Sehmon asked, grimacing at the barracks. The building was mostly lacking a roof, and the interior seemed to be bare of any furnishings.

"Her mother saved the king's life in the Volarian arena," Vaelin said. "I imagine he feels he still owes a debt."

"More than one," Nortah said, his expression serious now. "Unless you think it likely he's going to let it drop."

"Didn't you let him live, my lord?" Sehmon asked. "After defeating him in fair combat. At least that's how the story goes. You'd think he'd be grateful."

Nortah laughed again, putting an arm around Sehmon's shoulders as they started towards the barracks. "You, my young, guileless friend, have a great deal to learn about heroes. You see, the only thing they're ever truly grateful for is a chance at a noteworthy death."

◆ ◆ ◆

"Mother said you were taller."

Atheran Ell-Nestra's lips twitched a little under his beard as he raised an eyebrow at Ellese. "Really?" he asked, taking a sip of wine from a silver goblet. He sat on a throne of finely carved mahogany, the back and arms decorated in motifs of a maritime nature. It matched the rich ornamentation that characterised the throne room of this self-proclaimed king. Statues from a great many cultures stood between the pillars, and fine tapestries hung from the walls alongside paintings of high quality, all presumably stolen from the holds of unfortunate merchantmen. Vaelin recognised two paintings as the work of none other than Master Benril Lenial, his sister's former tutor, held by many as the greatest artist of his age. Mi-Hahn, predictably, was fascinated by the collection, ignoring her place at the king's table to spend much of the evening wandering between the various treasures, eyes rapt.

"Yes," Ellese replied with a sweet smile. "Also, that you were an arrogant, conceited soul given to disparaging statements regarding the beliefs of others."

"Then, my lady," Ell-Nestra said, raising his goblet, "I am heartened to learn that she remembers me so well."

"In truth, I can recall hearing her speak of you at length on just one occasion, at the request of some historian who turned up at the governor's manse begging for her story. He was granted only a short interview, mainly because he came bearing an introductory letter from the queen. Mother isn't fond of discussing the Liberation War."

"No, I would assume she wouldn't be, or the Lord Marshal here." Ell-Nestra tipped his goblet in Nortah's direction. The banquet they had been treated to was laid out on a circular table, roasted boar and venison alongside piles of fruit and plentiful liquor, none of which Nortah had touched.

"Not keen on the wine, my lord?" Ell-Nestra nodded to the bottle sitting in front of Nortah, a fine Cumbraelin vintage with its wax seal still unbroken.

"I've always been picky as regards my drinking companions."

This sent a murmur of angry disquiet through the twenty or so pirates seated around the table, all captains dressed in silken finery that jarred with their often brutish, heavily scarred and tattooed features. Ell-Nestra, however, simply let out a laugh.

"Always brave to a fault, this one, and never shy in voicing an unwelcome opinion, even to the queen's face on occasion. He was there for every bloody step of it, you see? Alltor, Varinshold, the Beacon, the march to Volar. Unlike Lord Vaelin who, as I recall, disappeared on some mysterious jaunt to the northern ice on the eve of the invasion fleet's departure. Tell me, my lord, what exactly were you doing up there? I've always wondered."

"Freezing, for the most part," Vaelin replied. *Also, fighting a battle that would kill the woman I loved.* The thought stirred a resentful growl from the black-song, although Sherin's version of the elixir seemed capable of keeping it muted for the moment.

Ell-Nestra continued to regard him in expectation of further elaboration, letting out a faint sigh when it wasn't forthcoming. "Your sister is well, I trust?" he asked. "Still contriving her deadly mechanicals and such?"

"She has charge of the Royal College of Arts in Varinshold. Weapons are no longer her province, for which I am grateful."

"Those weapons did a great deal to win the war. I set my own small coterie of artificers to produce copies based on my recollections. So far, none of the bloody things work. Still, all the novelties in the world can't replace sound ships crewed by stout hearts." He raised his voice as he spoke, lifting his goblet. The response of the other pirates was so uniform and immediate Vaelin wondered if it hadn't been rehearsed.

"To stout hearts and the Merchant King!" they called out as one, lifting their own goblets in salute before drinking.

"My Council of Captains honours me with its loyalty," Ell-Nestra said, settling back onto his throne, voice lowered to a solicitous tone. "Borrowed the idea from my former people, with a few refinements. Kept the numbers high rather than just a few. Means they're always forming factions and bickering amongst themselves, none ever becoming strong enough to mount a challenge. Not that any are minded to. I made them all so very rich, you see. Before I came here they spent half their time pursuing feuds against one another rather than garnering the bounty of the very lucrative seas to the north. Unity, it transpires, breeds riches, when married to fair but firm leadership."

"What happened to your rivals?" Nortah asked. "I presume there were some."

"Can you name any kingdom not built on a foundation of blood as well as wisdom? Was it not barely two generations gone that the Unified Realm was continually mired in war? The great King Janus spilled blood for decades to build his kingdom. Your queen spilled a great deal more defeating the Volarians and claiming their empire. Whereas I fought skirmishes and duels for a few months, burning no villages or cities in the process."

"All so you could play the king amongst a cesspit of cutthroats and whores?"

Ell-Nestra's gaze narrowed as Nortah's words, spoken with a deliberate and loud forcefulness, heralding another murmur from the assembled pirates. This time it failed to fade, building to a constant and voluble animus. Several captains got to their feet, hands on the hilts of daggers and sabres. Their agitation quieted somewhat as Ell-Nestra raised a hand, but the simmering anger lingered, and several stayed on their feet.

"I do believe, Lord Vaelin," Ell-Nestra said, he and Nortah's gazes locked across the table, "your brother is trying to goad me. Why would he do that?"

Vaelin looked at the cold determination on Nortah's face, a determination that he knew had nothing to do with any animosity he might harbour towards Ell-Nestra. "He wishes to save me."

"From what? Does he imagine we are to duel again? And if we were, have your skills dulled so that he fears for your life?"

"Not my life. My soul. He fears what I will do if we fight."

This brought a faint purse-lipped smirk to Ell-Nestra's lips before he waved his goblet at the still-standing pirates. "Sit, brothers and sisters, eat. You know I'll have no blood spilled in my palace." He set the goblet aside, getting to his feet. "Lord Vaelin," he said, voice betraying more weariness than aggression, as if he were attending to a tedious but necessary chore. "I believe it's time we discussed terms for your continued presence in my kingdom."

◆ ◆ ◆

"So," Ell-Nestra said a short while later, "she truly didn't send you?"

He had led Vaelin from the palace along a paved pathway that traced the top of a cliff that formed the southern shore of this island. It plummeted towards the darkened sea for two hundred feet or more, breaking waves blossoming white in the gloomy depths below. Ell-Nestra hadn't felt the need to bring any guards, but nor had he left his sabre behind. Vaelin also thought it significant that he hadn't been asked to relinquish his sword when stepping ashore.

"Why would she?" he asked, continuing to follow Ell-Nestra's course. The moon was high and bright, making for sure-footed progress. The pathway's northern side was marked by a procession of rosebushes, the blooms appearing either black or white in the moonlight. From their obviously well-tended appearance Vaelin concluded they were the genesis of what would become Ell-Nestra's palace gardens.

"Our last meeting was somewhat acrimonious," Ell-Nestra said, glancing over his shoulder. "It occurred to me that she may have perceived some future . . . complication should I forsake her service, which, of course, I did."

"My niece may have heard you mentioned once, but when the war was done I never heard the queen speak of you at all. Besides, if she came against you, assuming she even knows of your continued existence, she would come with a fleet and an army, not a single ship bearing a man who left his tower without her leave."

"Isn't that treason?"

"I'm not entirely sure, though I've no doubt I'll soon find out when I return."

"She'd never hang you, you know that. In fact, not to be indelicate, my lord, but I confess myself surprised the Greater Unified Realm doesn't currently boast two monarchs instead of one."

Catching the undercurrent of resentment beneath Ell-Nestra's tone of taunting amusement, Vaelin said nothing for a time. For all his arrogance, this had never been a stupid man. He saw a great deal and understood what he saw, the indifference of the world's most powerful woman perhaps most of all.

"It's not in her nature to share power," Vaelin replied, keeping his own voice to a neutral pitch. "Nor should it be, given how well she wields it."

"Power," Ell-Nestra repeated softly, a note of agreement colouring his tone. "Yes, it's often been my experience that a woman's first love will triumph over all others."

He fell to silence, leading Vaelin up a slope to a wind-twisted tree rising from what appeared to be the island's summit. Ell-Nestra came to a halt beneath the tree's branches, stunted and malformed on the southern side, long and verdant on the northern. "I call him the Old Stranger," Ell-Nestra said, running a hand over the tree's craggy bark. "Being as he's so far from home, like me."

Looking closer at the leaves on the north-facing branches, Vaelin blinked in surprise. "An oak," he said.

"Yes, remarkable isn't it? Somehow a single acorn made its way across thousands of miles of ocean to fetch up here and take root. I like to think it was some lost sailor, perhaps from your Realm, stranded here by a wrecked ship and planting the acorn he had carried as a charm against ill fortune. Maybe he grew old and died here, watching the tree flourish as he diminished. If so, even his bones are vanished, but the Old Stranger remains." He slapped an affectionate hand to the oak's trunk, laughing again. "The true king, who'll be here long after I'm gone."

The humour slipped away quickly as Ell-Nestra's gaze shifted from the tree to Vaelin, his tone short and demanding. "What are you doing in my kingdom, Al Sorna?"

Vaelin steadied his gaze on Ell-Nestra's face, mostly concealed by the shadow of the oak. This man's ambition burned as bright as ever, he knew. Ell-Nestra could have stood at the head of the Meldenean Council of Captains but for his misbegotten attempt to avenge himself on the son of the man who had burned his city, and his family along with it. Now he saw a deeper hunger in this former Shield of the Isles, a desire for power that overshadowed all previous vendettas. *He made himself a king,* Vaelin thought, *for a mere pirate chieftain would be forever beneath the notice of a queen. Such a man will seize any source of power he can.*

"You know what has befallen the Merchant Realms?" Vaelin asked, deciding on obfuscation as his best tactic. Ell-Nestra had always been too perceptive for outright lies.

"Two of them have been conquered by a rampaging horde of barbarians bowing down to a living god. The Transcendent Kingdom has been spared due, my spies tell me, to a very pragmatic alliance. I'll save us both time by assuming you've chosen to oppose this godlike barbarian, throwing your lot in with the boy-emperor I've heard so much about. You always were fond of hopeless causes."

"Not every cause I chose was hopeless. We won the Liberation War, if you recall."

"I do. I've also had a great deal of time to ponder the rewards of victory. I find them small indeed."

"Life was our reward. As it will be when the Darkblade lies dead."

"Darkblade, yes. I recall asking if the translation was accurate when I heard that one." Ell-Nestra's mouth formed another smirk. "Don't tell me that didn't sting a bit."

"Not in the least. I never much cared for it. Reva's priests may have to reconsider the phrasing in their scripture, however."

"Clever." Ell-Nestra inclined his head. "Bringing her up to remind me of the debt I owe. Rest assured, I haven't forgotten it. But my debt is to her, not you."

"Send me and her daughter on our way and I'm sure she'll consider it settled."

"You are far too disruptive a personage to be permitted free rein in my dominion. There's many a Realm-born soul amongst my subjects. Some, I'm sure, would like to see you dead, but to most you're still the great saviour from the Liberation War."

"My business in these islands will be brief, and any complications are likely to be worsened by a prolonged stay as your guest."

"And yet, I note, you have been very careful to avoid elucidating the exact nature of your business."

"There's an island at the heart of the Opal Isles. There is something there that will help defeat the Darkblade."

"What manner of something?"

"I'll discover that when I find it."

"You're lying. I suggest you don't, if you wish to retrieve this mysterious something."

"We could settle this another way." Vaelin gestured to the hilt of Ell-Nestra's sabre. "But you won't."

"I won't?" Ell-Nestra's face was unreadable in the shadow, his voice also lacking inflection. The black-song could offer only a dim pulse of warning, either too drowned by Sherin's elixir or finding little of interest in this meeting.

"No," Vaelin went on. "Because you continue to wonder why my brother tried to tempt you into fighting him, and I think you know the answer."

"And what is that?"

"This time I won't spare you, which would greatly complicate our departure from this island."

Ell-Nestra remained still, a tall, broad-shouldered statue in the Old Stranger's shadow, but Vaelin saw how the hand resting on the oak's trunk momentarily spasmed into a claw, digging into the bark before he let it fall to his side.

"You call yourself a king," Vaelin went on, "but that is a title any outlaw can claim. You have no treaties, no laws, no borders recognised by anyone save yourself and the pirates who choose to follow you, for now. And, meagre though it is, all the grandeur you pretend will mean nothing should the Darkblade complete his conquest of the Merchant Realms. He will, I'm sure, find you amusing. If he thinks you'll be of use he won't kill you. Instead you'll become his creature. Perhaps he'll put you in charge of his fleet when he moves against the Alpiran Empire. But have no doubt, if he wins, whatever lies in your future, it won't be a kingdom. If you wish to be a king, act as a king would. Seek advantage through alliance."

Ell-Nestra let out a faint, derisive snort. "So, you wish to enlist me in your war. I've had my fill of fighting for others."

"Then fight for yourself, for those who bought the notion you sold, the notion that you are more than a pirate who won a few duels. Emperor Tsai Lin makes no claims to godhood, nor is he insane. Ally yourself with the Jade Empire and this kingdom of yours will become a reality. Tsai Lin will recognise you as a fellow monarch, proclaim your kingship for the whole world to hear. Is that not worth a war, Highness?"

"My subjects follow me because I promise what they crave above all, profit. The opportunity to die for an emperor they don't know is hardly profitable."

"Captured ships are profitable and the Darkblade has many. Also, I've little doubt the emperor will be generous enough to seal his grant of recognition with gold."

"Always the way with you." Ell-Nestra emerged from the oak's shadow, moving to stand within sword reach of Vaelin. "Every time I set eyes upon you, the course I've chosen goes awry and disaster follows soon after. No, Vaelin Al Sorna, not this time. This time I stay my own course. I told Lyrna I wouldn't fight another war for her, and nor will I fight one for you. But, I will, generously, allow you free passage through my domain to complete this oh-so-enigmatic mission. From what I've heard of the Darkblade, it might be best if his career comes to an end soon. If it doesn't"—Ell-Nestra shrugged—"then war it is, but at least it'll be *my* war. Besides, it's my hope you live to convey my respects to your queen. Please assure her I will be more than happy to welcome an embassy from the Greater Unified Realm, should she care to send one."

He stood in silence, regarding Vaelin with careful but determined scrutiny. His hand didn't stray to his sabre hilt, but Vaelin knew he itched for the chance to draw it. When Vaelin merely stared back, keeping his hands at his sides, Ell-Nestra gave a small sigh and stepped around him, starting back down the pathway to his incomplete palace.

"Begone with the morning tide," he said over his shoulder. "And don't feel obligated to call in on your return journey, should you survive to make one. My subjects avoid the interior isles for a reason."

CHAPTER TWENTY-FIVE

T hey are well-fed and cared for," Alum said, glancing back at the dwelling where the Moreska children had made their home. It was one of the older huts in the settlement, positioned just a short remove from the sea, a mean place with a sagging roof and warped planking on its walls. However, it also featured a garden with a burgeoning vegetable crop, and the walls, insubstantial as they were, had benefited from a recent coat of whitewash.

"Their skin bears the mark of the whip," Alum went on, "but they tell me the man who did most of the whipping was sliced across his arms and knees before the pirates gave him to the sharks, his crewmates following him soon after. Their king has no love for slavers and decrees none be spared when one of their ships is taken."

"As he should," Vaelin said. "Having known the sting of the whip himself."

A burst of giggling came from the beach where Sehmon was engaged in a game with the children, reminding Vaelin of his youth as Sehmon attempted to escape with a captive ball before allowing himself to be brought down, the children laughing as they swarmed over him.

"My cousin's word was true," Alum said. "As ever it was. The path to the children lay with you, my friend. The Protectors guided her vision, proving they have not forsaken the Moreska."

"So, you have more lines to add to your True Name," Vaelin said, glancing at the complex array of symbols Alum had carved into the sand.

"I have." Alum pointed to a set of swirling marks that hadn't been present in the pattern he had left on the soil of the Iron Steppe. The stiff morning breeze blowing in with the tide was already eroding the marks, although Alum seemed oddly pleased by this. "The Lord Sand and Sky has marked them well and given them to his brother the Lord of the Winds to carry to my people. Their rejoicing will be a fine and great thing. I wish I was there to see it."

"You'll see it soon enough." Vaelin waved to get Sehmon's attention and beckoned him over.

"My lord," he said, after struggling free of the giggling mob and tossing the ball far up the beach to send them chasing after it.

"Master Sehmon Vek," Vaelin said in formal tones. "It is my judgement as Tower Lord of the Northern Reaches that the debt incurred by your criminality is paid in full. I hereby release you from indentured service, subject to the approval of your master, Alum Vi Moreska."

Sehmon laughed then stopped, seeing Vaelin's serious expression. "I . . . understand, my lord," he replied, exchanging a puzzled glance with Alum.

"My people have no servants. I only allowed this as a courtesy to you." The Moreska shrugged before placing a large hand on Sehmon's shoulder. "Though, this one still has much to learn about the spear."

"Then he can learn it as a free man," Vaelin said. "In the Realm. Master Vek, it is my request that you accompany this man and these children to the Northern Reaches. From there you are free to do as you wish and go where you will." He took a sealed envelope from his belt and handed it to the former outlaw. "Letters signed in my name. One confirms your freedom under Realm law; the other is an introduction to Lord Commander Orven should you wish to enlist in the North Guard. If so, your service will be highly welcome."

"The North Guard?" Sehmon asked, his puzzlement deepening. "My lord, the war . . ."

"Is done, for you at least. And you, my friend," he added, offering his hand to Alum. "It's time for you both to go home."

"You have done so much," Alum said, taking his hand, the grip firm. He looked at the children now throwing the ball back and forth at the water's edge as the waves scattered foam into their midst. The Moreska's inner conflict was evident in the creases marking his usually smooth brow. "I feel more is owed. To you, and to the Darkblade for the crimes I have witnessed."

"Your obligation is to these children," Vaelin said, releasing Alum's hand and filling it with a purse. "Coin enough to persuade one of the captains here to take you to the Reaches. I'd recommend seeking out a Meldenean. They're the most given to piracy, but also the least likely to break a deal."

He nodded to both of them and turned to go, covering only a few steps before Sehmon burst out, "I can't leave, my lord." Turning, Vaelin saw the youth's gaze tracking from him to a spot further along the beach where Ellese was sparring with Mi-Hahn. "I believe you know why," Sehmon added.

Vaelin watched Ellese dance clear of Mi-Hahn's sheathed sword, replying with a swift backhand slash of her wooden blade that came close to slamming into the other woman's ribs. The blow said a great deal for how she had improved with the sword. *She can't return your love,* Vaelin thought. *This is what she loves, perhaps all she'll ever love. Besides, her mother would never approve. You hope for something you will never have.*

He left the words unsaid, instead replying with a shrug, "As a free man, you can make your own choices. We sail within the hour."

◆ ◆ ◆

The *Stormhawk* sailed west for another two days at a much reduced speed before Captain Ohtan, now almost a permanent fixture at the tiller, steered her south into a narrow channel between two steep-sided islands. As they progressed through the strait and into the myriad channels beyond, the sky became a perennially overcast murk of drifting mist that never fully faded regardless of the fierceness of the sun. It clung to the jungle-covered flanks of the passing islands like a form of ethereal mould. The aura of greyness and damp engendered a lingering atmosphere of oppression not alleviated by the sounds emerging from the jungle.

"When I was younger," Ellese said, wincing at the cacophony rising from a stretch of coastline only fifty paces distant, "I accompanied Mother when she gave alms to a home the church built for those left maddened by the war. It didn't sound near half as bad as this."

She gave a bland smile in response to Vaelin's judgemental frown then grimaced as a fresh chorus erupted from the jungle. It was a grating mélange of shrieks, chatters, clicks and a deeper sound eerily reminiscent of guttural laughter. "By the Father's arse, doesn't it ever stop?"

The fact that, beyond a few flocks of birds rising from distant treetops, they hadn't seen sign of anything, beast nor man, that might be the source of such a tumult, added to the growing sense of being observed. Vaelin's unease was deepened by the black-song's steadily growing volume. The music possessed an ominous tone, lacking the echo of his old song that had roused him at Ell-Nestra's approach. This was a constant and building thrum of unwelcome recognition. *There is something Dark here*, Vaelin knew. *Something more than the stone, if it's even still here.*

Captain Ohtan insisted they weigh anchor come nightfall, Vaelin ordering half the crew to remain on watch in relays of three hours. However, sleep proved elusive for those not on guard, as the jungle's raucous song seemed to grow louder in the dark, birthing a host of imagined menace. Several times crewmen called out alarms that set hands reaching for weapons and all eyes scouring the gloomy shore only to spend a prolonged interval in expectation of threats that failed to materialise. On each occasion the offending sentry responded to the ridicule and anger hurled their way by insisting they had seen something large prowling the far bank or something even larger break the surface of the deep lagoon where the *Stormhawk* lay at anchor.

As a consequence, Vaelin caught no more than two hours' sleep before dawn brought a thick mist that kept the Stormhawk in place until it thinned sufficiently for Ohtan to order the anchor raised. They proceeded at half sail for a time, the channels through which the captain steered becoming ever more narrow and winding. As the noon bell tolled, he commanded all sails furled and the *Stormhawk*'s two boats lowered over the side.

"No other means of steering a true course, my lord," he advised. "Not unless we want to risk running aground."

Vaelin took his place in the boats alongside the crew as they hauled oars and towed the ship onward. There was scant talk and little grumbling, the sailors all heaving in unison with determined vigour. Their keenness to be done with this voyage was evident in the brief but frequent glances they cast at the passing jungle. The steady rhythm, however, descended into the clattering chaos of colliding oars as the loudest cry yet erupted from the shore, a shriek powerful enough to pain the ears, shot through with a note of fierce challenge and warning, and this time there was no doubt as to the source.

The bird stood atop a large rock on the shoreline of the closest island, close enough for there to be no mistaking its size. Its broad, hooked bill gaped wide as it screamed, its dark, glistening tongue curling. When its cry ended, it snapped its beak, the sound echoing like a thunderclap. Vaelin stared at the bird as the sailors around him shrank from it, coming close to upsetting the boat in their panicked haste. The bird gave a shorter but still painfully loud shriek, its stubby wings flapping in angry agitation as the crest of vibrant green feathers sprouting from its head fanned out like a crown.

"He's a seven footer, wouldn't you say, brother?" Nortah wondered. He was in the other boat, regarding the bird with a delighted grin.

"Closer to nine," Vaelin replied.

The exchange seemed to enrage the bird, which angled its head to cast a baleful eye at them before snapping its beak again, causing all present to wince and mutter curses. The sailors' fear was giving way to fascination now, the boat righting itself as they relaxed, all eyes fixed on the bird.

"Not a soul in the Realm would believe such a thing," Sehmon breathed, shaking his head. Like Nortah, he seemed more pleased than scared of the beast, an attitude Vaelin didn't fully share. It was close enough for him to catch the scent of partially digested meat emerging with every cry and make out the dried gore along the serrated edges of its bill. For all its colour and majesty, this was plainly a deadly predator with territory to protect.

"And I'd hazard it's a she," he said, resuming his grip on the oar. "We're probably closer to her nest than we should be."

"She or not," Nortah replied, hefting his bow, "it'll keep us all fed for a week or more."

"No time." Vaelin settled his gaze on the sailors, gesturing for them to pick up their oars. "Besides, I doubt there's anyone here keen to venture ashore to do the butchering."

This brought a murmur of agreement as the crew once again began to work their oars, although Sehmon continued to stare at the bird in wonder. "We should name it at least, my lord," he said. "Since we saw it first."

Vaelin entertained serious doubts theirs were the only human eyes to ever see this beast, but had to concede that such a thing had never appeared in any book in his collection. He also suspected the same was true of every other library in the Realm. "The Third Order's custom is for the discoverer to afford a newly found beast a variation of their own name," he told Sehmon, gesturing for him to resume rowing.

"Vaelin's Hawk?" Sehmon suggested, provoking a laugh from Nortah.

"Didn't look like any hawk I ever saw," he said. "More of the chicken about it, I'd say. Vaelin's Chuck, perhaps?"

This engendered a lively discussion amongst the crew regarding the bird's similarity to a chicken or a goose, one sailor opining fiercely that it bore closest resemblance to a puffin. The bickering continued in the time it took to get the *Stormhawk* moving again, the bird assailing them with shrieks and thunderclap snaps of its beak all the while.

"Vek's Hook-bill," Vaelin said as they forged their way into a broader channel as the cries abated and faded away, heralding a relieved groan from the oarsmen. "That's what we'll call it."

Sehmon grinned in slightly abashed appreciation that became sullen when Nortah let out a derisive snort. "If an outlaw gets to name things, I'm having the next one."

"As you wish, brother," Vaelin assured him. "I'm sure there's an unfamiliar slug or two hereabouts."

He didn't join in the resulting laughter from the sailors; instead his eyes peered deep into the dense vegetation covering the shore. *Birds twice the height of a man with bills like axe blades*, he thought. Sherin's words from the dockside in Askira made him reconsider the likelihood of the other supposedly outlandish tales regarding this place.

◆ ◆ ◆

It was late afternoon when Ohtan's cry came from the *Stormhawk*. "Ship oars, lads! We're here!"

Looking around, Vaelin saw they had emerged into a wide, placid channel of lake-sized proportions. The north-east was dominated by the tallest island they had yet encountered whilst a series of small, forested islets lay to the south, one of them featuring a tall, narrow column of rock nearly identical to the one Luralyn described from her dream. The dense blanket of trees covering the larger island's flanks was so shrouded in mist as to obscure the summit, and Vaelin could see no cove or inlet on its shore that might allow for an easy landing. Fortunately, the captain had a keener eye for such things.

"There!" he called, pointing to a spot approximately midway along the island's coast. "Just a notch but it should offer enough purchase to ground a boat and get a party ashore. Just one, mind."

Vaelin opted to keep the party small; besides himself, Nortah and Sehmon, he brought Ellese, Eresa and Luralyn, plus two sailors to help work the oars. Mi-Hahn climbed down into the boat unbidden to sit at the prow, charcoal busy on the parchment in her lap as they made their way to shore.

"How long do we wait, my lord?" Captain Ohtan called after them, voice echoing loud across the water. It took Vaelin a moment to realise why. *No noise*, he thought, eyeing the quiescent wall of jungle ahead.

"Until you're certain we're not coming back!" he called in response before turning to Luralyn. She regarded the approaching island with intense, narrow-eyed scrutiny, brow furrowed. "You feel it, don't you?" he asked her.

She replied with a nod and a forced smile. "It would be hard not to."

A glance at Eresa's tense features confirmed that she felt it too; the sense of recognition experienced by all Gifted in the presence of the Dark.

Their arrival was met with a sudden and loud explosion of birds from the surrounding treetops; black feathered with red crests, they let out a chorus of high-pitched protest and circled above whilst the party clambered ashore. "Stay with the boat," Vaelin told the two sailors. Noting their faces, dampened by sweat despite the relatively cool air, with widened eyes that tracked continually over the jungle looming above, he added, "Feel at liberty to go back to the ship should the need arise. We'll light a torch to signal our return."

"Any notion of where we might be going?" Nortah enquired as they proceeded beneath the dense canopy of interweaving foliage. The gloom was broken by the occasional speckle of dull light, the air chill for want of sunlight and laced with the odour unique to rot. Tree trunks, thick and thin, ascended up a steep slope, the gaps between them rich in rocks, piled leaves and fallen branches.

"I could see a misted sky above treetops in the True Dream," Luralyn said. She kept her hand on her dagger as she spoke, her features drawn in the inevitable discomfort of one born to a vast open steppe confronted by the stifling confines of a jungle. "I had the sense of a high place."

"Then," Vaelin said, stepping over a moss-covered tree trunk to start up the slope, "it seems we have a climb ahead of us."

The going was hard and progress slow as they ascended through the trees, wariness of their surroundings giving way to irritated fatigue as the trek wore on. For once, Vaelin found himself grateful for the black-song, which had taken on a sharp, grating note that kept any tiredness at bay. Its note of warning was clear despite the effects of Sherin's elixir, and he suspected that, without its muting abilities, he may well have found it deafening. It was thanks to a sudden upsurge from the song that they found the first corpse.

"Careful!" Vaelin snapped as Eresa prepared to step off a large boulder. Moving around her, he leapt down, pushing aside a collection of overlapping, cobweb-covered branches, and Eresa smothered an involuntary squeal of fright at what he revealed.

The skeleton was partially clad in some kind of metal garment formed of plates of rough hammered bronze linked by copper wire into a vest. It lay across bones long denuded of flesh, either through decomposition or the attentions of scavengers. It was only partially complete, one leg and a forearm missing, and would have been easily identified as human remains but for the skull that crowned the rib cage. The eye sockets were jagged holes framing gaping nostrils above a set of sharp elongated teeth.

"Jackal-headed men," Nortah murmured, coming to Vaelin's side. They crouched to make a closer inspection, Vaelin's gaze taking in the multiple lacerations and fractures to the ribs and upper arms.

"Death by violence," he said. "And it wasn't quick."

"Maybe one of his brothers ate him." Nortah peered into the skull's eye socket and gave a soft, bemused laugh. "Or, perhaps not."

He clamped both hands to the skull's jaws, prizing them apart to reveal the very human but skinless face within.

"A shaman's mask?" Vaelin wondered. "Something worn for a ceremony."

"Worn for war," Mi-Hahn said, the first words she had spoken for several days. Turning, Vaelin saw her attention was fixed on something further up the slope. Rising, he went to her side, quickly picking out dozens of bones littering the ground between the thick trunks of the surrounding trees. A quick survey revealed skeletons in various states of disarray, many armless or decapitated, all wearing the same beast-skull mask.

"Too sturdy for a common dog," Nortah mused, holding up one of the masks. "Wrong teeth for a jackal."

"A wolf," Vaelin said. "A smaller breed than in the Realm. But still, a wolf."

"This was a battle, to be sure," Ellese commented, plucking a small item from the ground and tossing it to Vaelin. Holding it up to the meagre light he found it dirty and green with age but still easily identified as a bronze arrowhead.

"A battle fought so long ago everything else has rotted away," he concluded aloud.

"Left where they fell," Luralyn observed. "No one came to care for the dead."

"It might not have been their custom," Nortah suggested.

Or there was no one left to care, Vaelin thought, receiving an instant pulse of confirmation from the black-song. As he looked from one disarranged, long-dead warrior to another, the certainty grew that were they to scour this island from end to end, all they would find would be more scenes like this.

Keen to reach the island's crest before nightfall, he decided to press on rather than linger to ponder the mystery. Another hour's climbing revealed a sight that confirmed the humanity of those who had once dwelt here. The wall was formed of locally harvested stone and stretched away on either side, its ends lost in the jungle. Vines crept over and through the stone, obscuring much of the carving that marked it.

"They weren't savages," Nortah said, forcing aside a vine to peer at the marks in the stone. They were clearly pictograms of some kind, arranged in a neat rectangular pattern. "And knew how to write, at least. Though, I'd hazard there hasn't been a soul who could read it for centuries."

"It's their memory," Luralyn said, a deep sorrow colouring her voice as she pressed a hand to the wall. "There was something similar in the True Dream. This was not a fortification. It was how they marked their time upon the earth. This is a sacred place."

Finding no steps or other means of traversing the wall, they were obliged to scale it, hauling themselves up via the tangled vines to the comparatively bare slope beyond. From there it was a short climb to the ridge that formed the spine of the island. Vaelin blinked in the stiff wind sweeping the ridge, looking around at the mostly mist-covered land and sea below. He caught a glimpse of the *Stormhawk*'s mast through the drifting haze before it thickened once more. A glance at the sky confirmed the onset of night, a few stars already beginning to glimmer in the darkening blue.

"Does anything strike you as familiar?" he asked Luralyn, keen to find shelter rather than make camp in so exposed a spot.

She spent a prolonged interval staring at their surroundings, a frustrated frown on her brow. "It was different in the dream," she said. "Fewer trees . . . Wait." Her frown disappeared as she focused on something further along the ridge, starting towards it at a run. At first, Vaelin saw no obvious reason for her excitement, but followed to watch her circle a boulder that was mostly indistinguishable from its neighbours save for being a little broader and more conical in appearance.

"I saw this," Luralyn said, running her fingers over the boulder's surface. "The temple had no roof, just beams of stone. This stood atop it. A tall, perfect pyramid, edges straight as a razor."

Vaelin stepped closer, seeing numerous indentations in the stone. They were so weathered he would have taken them for just the depredations of the elements but for a vague similarity to the carved inscriptions on the wall.

"These were inlaid with mother-of-pearl," Luralyn went on, her fingers continuing their exploration. "The way they caught the sun was quite beautiful . . ." She trailed off, looking towards the sinking sun. "It was shining from the west. This way!"

Vaelin followed as she moved down the ridge's west-facing slope, hopping nimbly from boulder to boulder until she leapt to a bare patch of earth, turning about with a triumphant grin. "There," she said, pointing at what to Vaelin appeared to be just another pile of boulders. Jumping down to stand alongside her, he followed her finger to make out a narrow opening between two slabs of granite.

Not a ridge at all, he decided, moving to peer into the opening. *A ruin. A great structure stood here, something magnificent brought tumbling down to be worn away by nature.* The thought stirred inevitable memories of the Fallen City and the secrets contained within the grey stone that once stood at its centre. It seemed wherever they were to be found, their mere presence heralded a downfall.

Moving to the opening, he peered inside, seeing only blank shadow and smelling musty air that gave no clue as to what lay within. The gap was just wide enough to allow entry but he resisted the urge to delve into it immediately. The black-song had quelled a little, but the note of Dark recognition was as strong as ever. "Cut some branches," he told Sehmon and Ellese. "We need torches."

◆ ◆ ◆

The flickering flame of the torch revealed only bare rock as he scraped and struggled his way through the opening. Nortah, Luralyn and Eresa followed whilst Mi-Hahn, deaf to any orders to the contrary, brought up the rear.

Sehmon and Ellese, much to her scowling but unspoken annoyance, were ordered to light a fire and guard the entrance. The passage they entered was littered with tumbled stone, its sharp, unweathered edges contrasting with the exterior.

"More writing," Nortah said, playing his torch over a piece of fallen masonry. "Perhaps telling us to stay out."

"The Threshold of Ascension," Luralyn said. "That's what it means."

"You can read this?" Nortah enquired.

She shook her head. "*He* called it that. The man in my dream."

"Ascension to where?" Vaelin asked, his boots scattering a loose collection of rocks as they started along the passage.

"That wasn't made clear. He was quite mad, as I said. But I had a notion that this was once a place of pilgrimage. Much like the Great Tor for my people."

Vaelin was obliged to shove aside a good few blocks of varying sizes as he led them through the narrow channel until his torch began to gutter and a stream of chilled air caressed his face. The obstructions lessened as he pressed on, the torch scattering sparks into a broad chamber. Dim glimmers were visible in the ceiling, the light of the evening sky finding gaps between the tumbled stones above. They curved up and over Vaelin's head, creating the impression of a dome. The space it covered, however, appeared empty.

"This is it," Luralyn said, puzzlement mixing with disappointment in her voice. "I recognise this pattern." Her foot scuffed the dust-covered tiles on the floor, revealing a complex matrix of interlocking hexagonal shapes, some light in colour, others dark. "But it wasn't so empty. The stone was here." She moved to the centre of the chamber, pointing to a low platform a yard across, six-sided like the floor tiles, but bare of anything save a mound of dust. "He kept circling it, talking all the while."

"Did he touch it?"

"Not that I saw."

"He must have." He extended a hand to the space where the stone should have been, almost feeling its smooth surface under his fingers. "It would have held his memory, the essence of who he was. Waiting for us. We were supposed to talk to him."

"It seems, brother," Nortah said, coming to his side with a sympathetic grimace, "we came a long way for nothing much at all."

"I don't understand," Luralyn said, a frantic note creeping into her tone. "The True Dream led us here. Never has it set me on the wrong path."

Vaelin was about to embark upon a closer inspection of the chamber when his eye caught a small gleam amidst the mound of dust. Crouching, he saw it came from the dust itself, dust that was a shade of grey he had seen before.

"Yes!" Luralyn appeared at his side, a near-desperate smile appearing on her lips. "This must be it." She extended a hand to the dust mound. "All that remains . . ."

"Don't!" Vaelin said, reaching out to grasp her hand, but she was a trifle too fast, her finger dipping into the dust as his hand closed around her wrist and he felt a scrape of powdered stone brush his skin. In an instant, the chamber disappeared and light flooded his vision. And the black-song screamed.

CHAPTER TWENTY-SIX

The pain clutched at his mind like a claw, digging fiery talons deep into his being. He was aware of collapsing, unheard grunts emerging from his gritted teeth as he writhed on the floor. For a time all he could do was buck and jerk in agony as the black-song surged. It flooded his mind with urgent, frenzied music, its most ugly and discordant so far. Old nightmares were dredged up and married with the worst of memories, creating grotesque parodies of experience. Dentos looked up at him from the desert floor, his blood-spattered features forming a grin. Barkus begged forgiveness with inarguable sincerity before using his axe to sever his legs. And Dahrena . . .

"You killed us."

She stood atop the plateau in northern Volaria, as beautiful as she had been in life, as beautiful as the child she held. The infant boy pressed small hands into the flesh of his mother's face, a happy giggle emerging from his smiling mouth.

"Why?" Dahrena asked, her voice and face betraying only a sad sense of curiosity. "Why did you kill us, when we loved you so?"

His hands scrabbled on the hard ground, legs kicking as he tried to crawl away, pursued by her soft, inquisitive voice. "Was it so you could come here and play the hero? Rescue the woman you truly loved? Was I ever more than just a convenience?"

He clamped his eyes shut, pressed his hands to his ears, more pain than he ever knew he could endure coursing through him, the song raging with unbridled malice.

"Enough!"

The voice banished the song's rage in an instant, its sudden and complete absence almost like a new form of agony. Vaelin had borne its foulness for so long this silence felt utterly strange, but also, as the pain faded, brought a sensation of such release and liberation it left him gasping in helpless relief.

"Is he just going to lie there?" the same voice enquired. It possessed a deep note of authority laced with a faint, quizzical amusement.

Blinking, Vaelin found himself confronted by Luralyn's frowning, concerned features, a relieved sigh escaping her lips when she saw comprehension return to his gaze. "I felt it," she said, voice thick and tears welling in her eyes. "Just for a moment. I felt what you feel. I'm sorry, I didn't know . . ."

"If you're quite finished," the authoritative voice cut in, "we do have a task to attend to."

Luralyn moved aside to reveal a tall man with bronzed skin. His beardless features were angular and lined, Vaelin putting him somewhere late in his middle years. Long, silver-streaked hair swept back from his head into a complex overlapping braid, beaded with pearls. He wore a vest of bronze plates fastened with copper wire over a tunic of rough-weaved fabric that extended to his bare knees. The stern expression on his face was mixed with a frowning curiosity.

"Both so pale," he said. "Do you hail from a land without sun?"

"Occasional sun and frequent cloud," Vaelin said, getting to his feet. "And a good deal of rain."

The bronze-skinned man peered closely at him with a cautious, almost wary gaze. "There is something bad in you," he said. "A voice I didn't like, so I quelled it."

"For which I'm grateful." Vaelin turned to Luralyn. "This is him?"

"The man in my dream was different," she said, shaking her head. "Pale, like us, and mad. Whereas he seems very aware."

Looking around, Vaelin was unsurprised to recognise the hexagonal tiles on the floor, but the rest was startling in its unfamiliarity. The shadowed dome beneath the ruins was gone, replaced by an open-walled chamber formed of six arcing pillars. They rose in a curve to form an apex above Vaelin's head. As he angled his view he saw the pyramid Luralyn had seen in her dream atop the union of the pillars, smooth and sharp as a spear-point, sunlight gleaming on the inlaid symbols covering its flanks. Lowering his gaze, he saw blue skies through the arcing pillars, dozens of islands stretching away into the distance like emeralds on an azure blanket. However, all other distractions became irrelevant as his gaze alighted on the object sitting in the centre of the chamber.

For a moment, all he could do was stare at it, one thought coming into his mind. *How could it have got here?*

He realised his mistake almost immediately. This was plainly a memory from a great many years ago when the climate of the Opal Islands still permitted the sun to banish the morning mist. The stone wolf carved by Ahm Lin wouldn't come into existence for centuries. And yet here it stood, identical in every finely crafted line, but for the stone that formed it. The statue's surface glittered as he came closer, the form of the wolf unchanged from the day he had first seen it in the Urlish Forest all those years ago, albeit rendered in fur and flesh.

"It's not for you," the tall man said, a hard note of caution in his voice, although Vaelin had made no move to touch the stone. "At least, not yet."

Tearing his gaze from the wolf, Vaelin gave a formal bow. From the tall man's bemused expression he divined this was a custom he had never encountered before. "My name . . ." Vaelin began only to be waved to silence.

"Your given name doesn't matter. Neither does mine. Only the task we share matters here."

"Even so, I should like to know it," Vaelin persisted, continuing when the tall man replied with only a raised eyebrow. "Vaelin Al Sorna," he said, bowing again before nodding to Luralyn. "This is Luralyn Reyerik."

"She is 'Walks in Dreams,'" the tall man said, a note of correction colouring his voice. "Whilst you . . ." He paused for a moment, his face suddenly grave as if speaking words of great importance, and not without reluctance. "You are 'Child of the Wolf.'" He turned away, speaking on before Vaelin could voice a question. "Since you're so insistent on names, you can call me 'Keeper.'"

"And what do you keep?"

The tall man gestured to the wolf. "Isn't it obvious?"

A shuffling of nervous feet drew their gaze to a small group of people gathering between two of the pillars. There were six in all, three men and three women. Two of the men were young and matched the stature of Keeper in their broad athleticism. They also both carried spears and wore the same wolf-skull masks as the corpses found in the jungle. The three women, all similar in age and face, helped the third man as he stepped onto the tiled floor. He was considerably older than his companions, bent and stooped with age, but with bright, even eager eyes. He greeted Keeper with a smile, saying something in a language this memory chose not to translate.

"A moment," Keeper said, moving away to greet the old man. He matched his smile, taking hold of his hands to guide him forward as the three women stepped back. Vaelin saw a curious mix of emotion on their faces, tears and sorrow alternating with genuine joy. He noted how swiftly they retreated to the gap between the pillars, their eyes never once straying to the stone wolf.

Keeper and the old man exchanged a few words as they approached the statue, speaking with the easy familiarity of old friends, the taller man letting out a laugh at a cackled witticism. Their humour, however, faded when they came within reach of the statue. After a pause, Keeper spoke again and this time Vaelin understood the words. "Are you ready, my dear friend?"

"I am," the old man replied, the smile broadening on his lips. "I have been for a long time. They're waiting."

"They are." Keeper took hold of the old man's wrist and guided it towards the stone. "There will be no pain," he said as aged fingers trembled and splayed, "only ascension."

The old man let out a thin gasp as his fingertips met the stone snout of the wolf, his eyes rolling back in his head, and all the meagre strength remaining in his body fled in an instant. Keeper caught him before he fell, hefting his body in his arms and carrying it back to the three women. They slipped into vapour upon taking charge of the corpse, fading away along with the two warriors in the wolf-skull masks.

"Your people came here to die," Vaelin said as Keeper turned back to them.

"No," he said. "They came to ascend into the embrace of those they had loved in life and to embrace those who would follow, and they came to feed the wolf."

"Feed it?" Luralyn asked.

"The wolf is our saviour, our guide and our guardian." Keeper regarded the statue with sombre features. "So it has been since before the time of the grandfathers and grandmothers and the age of the one who carved it into being. It has given us so many gifts, empowered us to survive storms that would have scoured us from these isles and to defeat those who would steal them from us. All it asks in return is our memory at the moment of death, and even that is a blessing, for those we loved await us within."

A true Beyond, Vaelin thought, looking at the statue with fresh understanding. *Not a promise made in prayer or scripture. These people knew there was life beyond death. A precious thing indeed.* The notion stirred regret for what he was about to say, but he could see no alternative. They needed knowledge from this man, and that required mutual understanding.

"The statue is broken," he said. "In our time it exists only as dust."

"Of course it does." Keeper looked up at him with a frown of grim acceptance. "Nothing remains unchanged forever. All will be dust in the end. You, me, the people I love and cherish. That was its gift to me when I was chosen to touch it long ago, the ability to perceive the course of things." He went to look out at the splendour beyond the pillars. "I have seen what this place becomes. I know that one day a man will fetch up on our shores, a man my descendants will mistake for an injured soul deserving of succour, unsuspecting of the ill intent he harbours. I know that he will steal his way to this place and touch the wolf, greedy for the power it holds, little knowing that it will destroy his mind. For a stolen gift always demands a price."

As he spoke, the sky outside darkened, the familiar grey mist returning to shroud the many islands as the air took on a chilly edge. A man shimmered into existence in front of the statue, recoiling from it and clutching at his hand as if burnt. From the way Luralyn stiffened, Vaelin divined that this was the man from her dream.

"What he intended to do with his stolen power, who can say?" Keeper went on as Vaelin watched the newly arrived figure sink to his knees, a scream arising from his throat. He had been an impressive man in his time, arms thick with muscle and a face that may have been handsome if not for the distortions that twisted it now. Corded thews bulged and tendons strained to craft a mask of purest madness, eyes wide and threaded with veins around shrinking pupils. He screamed with all the strength his lungs could provide, a hideous cry that mingled utter confusion with the agony of a fractured mind. It continued on until, from outside, there came an answering call.

At first Vaelin wondered if this man's madness had somehow spread to the other inhabitants of this island, the rising tumult of voices being so discordant. Then, he realised these were not human sounds at all. Moving to Keeper's side he saw the jungle below the ridge was convulsing, the trees swaying with great energy even though there was only a soft breeze to the air. He could see the lights of many villages ringing the coastline, and on the shores of the nearby islands visible through the mist. It seemed as if the jungle reached out to snuff those lights, dark tendrils snaking out to claim the villages one by one, smothering them in darkness. A new note joined the awful chorus then, the unmistakably human sound of people dying by violence. Soon a roiling whiteness began to blossom at the shoreline, the result of hundreds of people fleeing land for water. He could make out individual figures swimming through surf, pursued by a great and obviously inhuman mass.

"Only a few amongst us were ever given the ability to compel beasts to our will," Keeper said. His voice had the dull, toneless quality of one who had witnessed a terrible event more times than he could count. "Why it chose to give it to him, I will never know."

Vaelin saw several giant, hook-billed birds amongst the pursuing throng, mighty beaks rising and falling to stain the water red. On the beach, large cats loped from the jungle to bring down running islanders whilst boars charged forth to gore flailing legs with their tusks. Out in the water fresh explosions of white broke the surface as some breed of long-jawed, snake-tailed reptile surged from the depths to claim yet more victims.

"This was not me!"

Vaelin turned back to see the maddened man on his feet now, railing at the indifferent stone wolf. "I didn't want to! This is your doing! Not mine!"

He began to circle the statue, a steady stream of babbled accusation issuing from his mouth. "You are the monster, not I! This was *never* what I wanted! I was promised the power to make the world anew! Not unmake it!"

The sounds of slaughter faded as he continued to pace, increasing in speed until he blurred, cracks appearing in the arcing pillars and rubble strewing the floor as the sky flickered with passing days and weeks. When time slowed once more the madman's endless circling hadn't stopped, although his once-impressive frame had become denuded to stick-thin emaciation. Vaelin saw half-consumed carcasses littering the ground beyond the pillars, both human and animal. Despite his thinness, this man had evidently retained enough comprehension to keep himself fed throughout the months or years since stealing his gift. Sustenance, however, hadn't improved the state of his mind. He croaked out his declarations now, the words rendered into incoherent babble.

"This is it," Luralyn said. "This is how he was in the dream."

The madman's stumbling circuit came to an abrupt end then, face twitching and head cocked as if he had heard her. But, if so, his attention soon became entirely fixed on the wolf. "I came . . . so far . . ." he slurred, sinking to his knees before it, continuing to address the statue's uncaring visage, his volume rising with every word. "So far . . . on the promise . . . The promise of what you . . . could give. But. It. LIED!" His hand scrabbled around on the floor, coming to rest on a brick-sized section of rubble. Vaelin took an involuntary step closer in response to the next words to gibber from his mouth. "The tiger . . . lied."

"What tiger?" Vaelin demanded, moving to stand between the madman and the statue. "What did it promise you?"

The madman hefted his piece of rubble in both hands, no more heedful of Vaelin than a buzzing fly.

"Promises . . . LIES!" Raising the boulder high, the madman lunged forward, moving through Vaelin's insubstantial form to bring it down on the wolf, scarring the fine, ancient carving and birthing a scattering of powder. He snarled and continued to pound away, shattering the statue's head.

"Where did you see the tiger?" Vaelin shouted over the rapid thud of stone on stone. "What did it promise you?"

Somehow the question penetrated the confusion dominating this memory of a long-vanished soul. His pounding ceased and he turned to regard Vaelin with eyes now so shot with blood they resembled rubies. "'Seek out my enemy,' it told me," he said in a hoarse, wavering rasp, head angled and brows raised, as if beseeching understanding. "'Find the wolf,' it told me. 'Then you will have it.'"

"Have what?"

The man blinked his ruby eyes, his voice gaining a vestige of coherence that almost resembled sane speech. "What all good and true souls in this world desire. Peace. It promised me peace."

He stared into Vaelin's eyes for the space of a single heartbeat, then all sanity fled once again and he returned to his work with a feral snarl. Further demands for answers met no response, and Vaelin could only stand back and watch as the wolf's destruction was completed. After delivering the last blow, the madman collapsed to his knees once more, chest heaving in exhaustion as he contemplated the mound of dust he had crafted.

"All will be dust in the end," Keeper repeated, the image of the madman slipping into mist and drifting away.

"Did he have a name?" Vaelin asked him.

"If he did, I never learned it."

"We found no bones here. Where did he go?"

"Perhaps he spent his days wandering the jungle in his madness, or gave himself to the beasts he commanded. Who can say? I have only this memory to share, captured in a vision towards the end of my days. I tried to prepare my people, leave a cautionary tale warning against giving safe harbour to strangers. It appears they failed to heed me."

"The tiger. Does it mean anything to you?"

"We only ever knew the wolf." Keeper gave an apologetic shake of his head. "The stranger's babble held little meaning for me."

The wolf and the tiger, Vaelin thought, recalling the vision he had been granted in the Temple of Spears. It was clear what had happened here was part of a contest between the two, a struggle that had been going on for a great deal of time.

"We came here for a stone," he said to Luralyn. "All we find is a pile of dust, and yet more questions with no answers."

"Dust, yes," Keeper said. "But that is not all. The stone may be broken but this memory persists, as does the memory of every soul who ever touched it. And the gifts they possessed, surrendered back to the wolf at the moment of their death, but enhanced, made greater. For that is the nature of life, to grow."

"He's right," Luralyn said, crouching over the dust to open her palm above it. "I can feel it. The power it holds . . ."

Her words died as the floor beneath them lurched, the air split by a deafening crack that accompanied the jagged fissure snaking through the tiles. The sky outside turned black as a hard gale swept through the pillars.

"What is this?" Vaelin asked of Keeper who could only reply with wide-eyed bafflement.

"This is not part of my memory. Something is happening in the waking world."

Vaelin rushed to Luralyn's side, taking her hand and preparing to press it into the dust.

"Wait!" Keeper said. "There was one other vision, one I kept hidden out of fear." A momentary shame crossed his face before he spoke on. "The gift the stranger stole was so powerful it couldn't be contained, not in one man. Perhaps that's why it drove him mad, why the killing started. Once set free it seeped into the fabric of these islands, into the soil and the blood of the beasts that dwell here, and it will never fade."

Another earsplitting crack sent a cascade of shattered stone into the air, the pillars collapsing into an overlapping matrix of rubble. Vaelin met Keeper's gaze one final time, seeing a need for understanding there, a message his shade had been waiting centuries to impart. As he grasped Luralyn's hand in his own and pressed both into the dust, Vaelin caught Keeper's fading voice amidst the tumult of ruin. "The Child of the Wolf must awaken it. My people cannot have died for nothing!"

CHAPTER TWENTY-SEVEN

H e snapped back into the waking world to be assailed by a hideously familiar chorus from outside; the sound of many beasts aroused into a frenzy. The sense of dislocation was heightened by the black-song's return, not the ugly flood of malice that had greeted him upon entering Keeper's memory, but still retaining enough strength to have him reach for one of the vials containing Sherin's elixir. He drank it down in a single gulp, uncaring of her injunctions regarding the dosage.

"Thank the Faith!" Nortah exclaimed. Looking up, Vaelin saw that his brother's torch had burned down to its last few embers.

"How long?" Vaelin asked, wiping his mouth and tossing the vial aside. The black-song gave a final growl before subsiding into its part-muted state.

"Hours," Nortah said. "We were starting to think you weren't coming back."

The beast chorus from outside increased in intensity, Vaelin hearing the familiar thrum of a bowstring followed by Ellese's voice, loud and strained. "Uncle!"

"Go!" he told Nortah and the others, taking the purse from his belt, extracting the gold nuggets and consigning them to his pockets. "Hold them off. I'll only need a moment."

"Hold off who?" Nortah asked, his face riven by alarmed bemusement even as he drew his sword.

"Not who. What." He jerked his head at the opening. "I'll be along shortly."

Luralyn hesitated as Nortah, Eresa and Mi-Hahn ran for the opening, watching Vaelin use his cloak to scrape dust into his purse. As he worked he could feel the power contained within the grains even through the cloth.

"Will it be enough?" she asked, eyeing the large mound of dust still remaining as he filled the purse to the brim and tightened the drawstring.

"We'll have to hope so," he said, getting to his feet. "For I doubt we'll get a chance to gather more. Come on."

He drew his sword before squirming his way to the outside in time to see Ellese bring down a charging boar with an arrow. It squealed and kicked until Sehmon ended its suffering with a stroke of his sword. Another boar, pierced by two arrows, lay nearby alongside the body of some form of diminutive ape that had been cleaved in two. Below the ridge the jungle convulsed, birthing flocks of birds into the night sky as the mingled screams of enraged beasts rose to a near-deafening pitch.

"Back to the boat!" Vaelin said, leading them in a scramble up the eroded ruins to the opposite slope. A small, swift shape streaked down at him from the sky, claws and beak trying to lash at his face. Vaelin hacked it out of the air and ran on, leaping down to the jungle's edge where he waited for the others to catch up. The cacophony was not so loud on this side of the ridgeline, the trees also not swaying with as much violence. Even so, the prospect of venturing into the darkened forest was far from appealing, if unavoidable.

"Stay together," he told the others as they formed up on either side. "Keep moving, whatever happens."

They advanced only a few dozen yards into the trees before the first attack came. A high-pitched growl accompanied the sight of three large cats leaping from the undergrowth, jaws gaping and clawed paws splayed wide. Ellese's arrow took one in midair, the shaft sinking into its open mouth to pierce through to the back of its skull. Nortah killed the second with a well-placed stroke of his sword as it landed in their midst. The third cat whirled and lashed out as they reeled back, its claws coming within an inch of Luralyn's flailing arm. With a shout, Eresa leapt forward, landing on the beast's back and clamping both hands to its skull. A bright flurry of sparks blinded Vaelin for a moment. When the reddish fog cleared he saw Eresa rising from the cat's smoking, lifeless body.

They moved on, stumbling often on the gloomy, uneven slope, but maintaining a rapid pace driven by the growing volume of shrieks to their rear. Birds struck at them with aggravating frequency, but also with a lack of coordination, meaning they could be swatted away or cut down individually, albeit not without injury.

"You little bastard!" Ellese cursed, squashing a parakeet against a tree trunk to dislodge its beak from her thumb. She hissed in relief as it came free, then let out a shocked grunt as Mi-Hahn delivered a kick to her chest, sending her flat onto her back in time to avoid the lateral slash of a huge hooked bill. The giant bird's beak rebounded from the tree trunk with considerable force, causing it to stagger, head shaking. It created sufficient delay for Mi-Hahn to dart forward and sever its left leg below the knee with a stroke of her sword. Vaelin moved in to finish the hook-bill with a two-handed cut to the neck before stooping to help a winded Ellese to her feet.

They came in sight of the boat shortly after, but their rush towards it was interrupted by the need to fight off a troop of a dozen or more monkeys that came screaming out of the trees. They leapt, clawed and bit with infuriating agility, immune to any fear even as they were hacked apart or rendered into shrunken, burnt dolls by Eresa's gift.

The only sign of the two sailors he had left to guard the boat was a thick pool of blood and some torn clothing on the nearby rocks. Fortunately, the craft and its oars remained unmolested. Clambering aboard, Vaelin, Sehmon, Nortah and Luralyn took up the oars whilst the others continued to fend off the dense cloud of birds swarming in pursuit. Ellese and Mi-Hahn hacked dozens out of the air whilst Eresa jabbed deadly sparks at any that managed to gain purchase on the stern. Even so, Vaelin suffered several bites and deep scratches to his face and arms before the assault faded.

"Don't slacken," he said, pulling on the oar with a steady and urgent rhythm, blinking to clear the trickle of blood from his eyes. Before the mist closed in, he caught a clear view of the horde now crowding the island's shore. Hook-bills gaped to scream their fury alongside growling cats and shrieking monkeys. None, however, seemed keen to take to the water to swim in pursuit, and Vaelin had a strong suspicion as to why.

He kept a close watch on the water as they continued to labour towards the vague bulk of the *Stormhawk*, seeing an unbroken, placid surface but for the ripple and splash of the oars. *It was long ago*, he reminded himself. *Perhaps they died out . . .*

Any such hope abruptly fled when his oar came to jarring halt mid-sweep and the water to the boat's starboard side erupted into white froth. Vaelin caught a glimpse of a long, jagged form whipping in the spray before the oar was torn from his grasp, the rowlock disappearing in a cloud of splinters along with a good portion of the hull. As the boat heaved and listed, another plume of displaced water blossomed to the port side and a gaping, many-toothed maw swept up and into the boat. Vaelin threw himself flat, the jaws coming together a whisker from his face with a bone-shaking snap. He found himself staring into a black slit surrounded by a yellow orb set within a socket of leathery scales. The eye regarded him for one frozen second then blinked before the jaws gaped wide once more.

There was a blur of black and Mi-Hahn appeared above the creature, sword raised in a reverse grip and face set in concentration. She brought it down in a swift vertical thrust, the point finding a spot precisely between the reptile's eyes, sinking through scaled hide and bone to skewer it through to the deck boards. Even in death, the creature thrashed, tail whipping and claws slashing as Mi-Hahn jerked her sword clear and the corpse slid back into the water. Vaelin was able to gauge its size before it sank from view, putting it at roughly eight feet from nose to tail. Also, from the interlocking matrix of ripples now surrounding the boat, it evidently hadn't been alone.

"Row, for Faith's sake!" Nortah shouted, heaving on his oar, Sehmon and Luralyn following suit. Water lapped over the damaged hull and the boat's list continued to grow as they ploughed an uneven course towards the *Stormhawk*. Ellese stood with one foot on the port rail, bow raised and drawn, the arrowhead panning back and forth across the water in search of a target amongst the now-churning water. A splash to the front of the prow immediately drew her eye and she loosed her arrow at the dark, glistening bulk surging from below. It was far larger than the one Mi-Hahn had slain only seconds before, its wide, flat body driven by a thrashing tail; two five-toed claws latched onto the prow, dragging it down. It jerked its head to dislodge Ellese's arrow from its snout, and Vaelin found himself transfixed by the creature's eyes. They fixed on him as it reared out of the water, seemingly possessed of a malign awareness far beyond any basic animal desire for prey. As the reptile's jaw gaped to reveal two triangular rows of tusklike teeth, head angled so it could still cast an eye at its target, Vaelin knew he was matching gazes with some vestige of the stranger's soul. The malice of the man who had wrought so much carnage in these islands somehow lingered in these beasts.

A deep, anticipatory hiss emerged from the reptile's throat, the jaws sweeping closer, the sound abruptly transforming into a gurgling rattle punctuated by a series of hard thwacks. A gust of foul air, rich in the stench of rotting meat, blasted into Vaelin's face as the beast subsided, the body shifting to reveal the row of feathered bolts protruding from its back. The creature gave a low, moaning rumble and slid from view, its claws slipping from the prow.

Hearing the clatter and rattle of a turning windlass, Vaelin shifted his gaze to the misted channel off the starboard bow just as another reptile broke the surface. A shout from an unseen source then a more rapid version of the windlass's tune. A line of tall waterspouts cut across the emerging beast, birthing a plume of red before its tail thrashed and it disappeared from view. More shouts and more mechanical clatters rang out as a large, broad-hulled shape resolved out of the mist.

The *Sea Empress* bore a great many torches along her rails, illuminating the devices fixed there and the sailors working them with well-drilled efficiency. They cast repeated torrents of bolts at the water, driving the reptiles, who evidently retained some instinct for self-preservation despite their blood-borne malice, down into the depths. When the ballistae fell silent, a tall figure appeared at the huge ship's bowsprit and tossed a weighted line into the centre of the boat with unerring accuracy.

"Debts are like the wind, Al Sorna!" called the monarch of the Benevolent Kingdom. "Very changeable according to the season!"

◆ ◆ ◆

"I thought you said you couldn't replicate them."

Ell-Nestra smiled and ran a hand over the boxy iron stock of the ballista. "I couldn't, not exactly. But my artificers came close enough. They don't loose as fast as your sister's version, but they'll do in a pinch. That flame-belcher of hers, however, still eludes me."

His humour faded as he met Vaelin's eye. The *Sea Empress* had carried them clear of the dense interior channels in the heart of the isles by sailing south into the open sea before turning east, the *Stormhawk* following close behind. "You're fortunate in your friends," Ell-Nestra said, casting a pointed glance at Alum on the mid-deck providing Sehmon another lesson with the spear. "A persuasive fellow with a fine memory for maps. I trust you'll reward his negotiating skills in due course."

"His children?" Vaelin asked.

"Packed off to the Northern Reaches in the charge of a trustworthy captain, also bearing formal greetings to your queen."

"A request for formal recognition, I assume."

"One she'll be most reluctant to grant, I'm sure. But she may have no choice once my realm receives the acknowledgement of the Jade Empire. Acknowledgement only, mind. I will not be a vassal and the Benevolent Kingdom will stand outside the empire. A faithful ally, but a realm in its own right holding dominion over the entirety of the Opal Islands."

"All achievable ambitions. There will be fighting ahead, a great deal of it. Are your subjects willing for you to lead them to war?"

"You doubt their loyalty?"

"I doubt the loyalty of any outlaw."

Ell-Nestra conceded the point with a raised eyebrow. "They'll fight if there's profit in it. Shares in all ships and cargos captured should suffice, plus a pardon from the emperor for all past crimes, regardless of severity."

"The emperor's mercy is famously boundless, Highness." He gave Ell-Nestra a formal bow and moved away, watching Alum spar with Sehmon for a time until the Moreska called a halt.

"You were supposed to go home," Vaelin told him, receiving a wide and unrepentant smile in return.

"Some wars can't be avoided," the Moreska said.

"I understand we have you to thank for this new alliance."

Alum's expression became more reflective as his eyes slid towards Ell-Nestra taking over the tiller from the helmsman. Even as a king, it appeared he still preferred to steer his own ship. "I think he was more open to persuasion than he pretended," Alum said. "Especially when I told him what I had seen at Keshin-Kho. Also, the prospect that you might never return from these islands seemed to weigh heavy on his mind."

"Most likely he worried he wouldn't get to kill me himself one day," Vaelin muttered.

"Did you find what you came for?" Alum asked.

"Part of it at least." Vaelin's hand went to the bulging purse on his belt, the power contained within stirring a snarl from the black-song. It had been subdued since leaving the isles, but proximity to the contents of the purse never failed to arouse its ire. Vaelin found the meaning of its tune difficult to parse, hearing an uneasy mix of both resentment and frustration, almost as if it regarded the gathered dust as some form of obstacle, but to what? He raised his face to Alum and forced a smile. "We'll just have to hope we return in time for it to make a difference."

◆ ◆ ◆

It took a week of arduous sailing to steer a course through the eastern wing of the islands before Ell-Nestra judged the water sufficiently deep to permit a westward turn. After that he worked his crew with a merciless hand, hounding them morning and night to gain every scrap of speed from the wind. It was a measure of the authority and respect he enjoyed amongst the mixed bag of cutthroats comprising his crew that none felt roused to mutiny, or even audible complaint. Such was the pitch of their labour, coupled with Ell-Nestra's skill at the tiller and facility for gauging the wind, the *Sea Empress* was able to keep pace with the *Stormhawk* throughout the five days' sailing required to reach Margentis.

The ruler of the Benevolent Kingdom had evidently sent word summoning his subjects before setting out in pursuit of the *Stormhawk*. The bay below the settlement was crammed with ships large and small, all flying the same shield-and-lightning flag that flew from the *Empress*'s mainmast. After weighing anchor on the fringes of the fleet, Ell-Nestra ordered another flag raised, a triangular red-and-green-striped pennant that apparently summoned the senior captains to council. They had all clambered aboard by late evening, twenty in all, hard-faced men and women of disparate origins. Most were in their middle years but a few were younger than Vaelin would have expected of those likely to win command of a pirate vessel. However, their uniform expressions of poorly suppressed suspicion worn on faces scarred by violence old and new told of characters for whom an imperial pardon would have some measure of appeal.

"All crimes, sire?" one asked, a sturdy young woman with the accent and look of one born to the Venerable Kingdom.

"All crimes," Ell-Nestra repeated. "Whoever you robbed, murdered or tortured in the past won't matter a thimble full of piss. Plus, you get to keep all the booty you capture."

"If we win," another said, this one a tall Meldenean with long, lank grey hair and lips bisected by an ancient scar that revealed his teeth in a parody of a half smile. Of them all, he seemed the least cowed by Ell-Nestra, although when his king turned to him he did quickly add, "Sire," in a suitably servile tone.

"*When* we win, Larith," Ell-Nestra said. "Our enemy is a mob of land-bound fanatics and horse-shagging nomads, both with no more ken of fighting at sea than a pig has of how to use a quill."

"Promises made by this man." Larith turned a baleful eye on Vaelin. The teeth revealed by his scar gleamed yellow in the torchlight so Vaelin couldn't tell if he was sneering, but the tone of his next words made it clear enough. "City Burner's spawn."

"The City Burner died many years gone," Ell-Nestra said. "And the isles that birthed us want no part of us now." He turned his gaze on the other captains, addressing them as one. "When you swore your ships to me I told you to forget your old allegiances. In return for your loyalty I promised we would have our own land, our own ports to call home where we need fear no law save what we make. Now that promise can be made real, but only if we fight for it. All kingdoms are forged in fire and quenched in blood. Why should our realm be any different?"

He drew his sabre, extending his arm to level the blade. "I'll fight no more duels to win your fealty. You all know me by now. I will not make an enemy of any captain who chooses to forsake this fleet, but neither will you ever again enjoy my friendship nor find a berth in my ports. Those who would be more than a pirate, touch blades with me now or get yourselves gone."

There was little hesitation before they all drew their various blades, even the suspicious Larith stepping forward to touch the tip of his falchion to Ell-Nestra's sabre. They stood in a circle with their heads bowed until Ell-Nestra flicked his sabre, breaking the wheel of steel. "We sail in two days," he said. "Provision your ships for a long voyage and set spare hands to crafting arrows. Any cowards or shirkers amongst your crews are to be put ashore. I'll have no tolerance for dead weight. For treasure and freedom!"

"Treasure and freedom!" Their response possessed an automatic and voluble enthusiasm that made Vaelin ponder the notion that there was much more to Ell-Nestra's kingship than useful playacting. To these scoundrels he was in fact a king. *But does he deserve a kingdom?* Watching him clasp hands with the captains before they returned to their boats, all easy smiles and shared jokes, it occurred to Vaelin that, in order to defeat a god, he had so far raised up two monarchs. All done with little regard for what future they might craft between them.

The necessities of war, he told himself, summoning a certain truth to mask the doubt that coloured the thought: *If the Darkblade triumphs there will be no future.*

◆ ◆ ◆

"City Burner's spawn?"

Mi-Hahn didn't look up from her parchment, hand blurring a little as she sketched, and Vaelin felt the disorientating tug at his mind that told of her gift at work. She had appeared at his side at the *Stormhawk*'s stern come evening. They had set sail from the pirate capital three days before, Vaelin and the others resuming their berth aboard Captain Ohtan's vessel before setting off. He had begun to feel Ell-Nestra's increasing agitation at his presence on the *Sea Empress*, despite the man's continual affability. His especially courteous attitude towards Luralyn had provided an added impetus to shifting berths. Although Vaelin recalled Ell-Nestra's fulsome charm whenever he found himself in company with an attractive woman, he sensed the pirate king's attentiveness now stemmed mostly from discovering Luralyn's shared blood with the Darkblade. It could have been no more than a desire to seek intelligence on his looming enemy, but Vaelin was too well acquainted with Ell-Nestra's facility for machination to see it as entirely innocent. Fortunately, from Luralyn's mostly baffled or indifferent reaction to his attentions, it appeared the man had made little headway on this particular course. Even so, Vaelin was glad to remove her from the *Sea Empress* to the more familiar if constricted *Stormhawk*.

"My father," he told Mi-Hahn. "He once served as general to the king of our homeland. The Meldeneans, the Pirate King's people, were fond of raiding our coast, so the king ordered my father to burn their capital. Many died, the Pirate King's family amongst them."

"He sought vengeance." Her charcoal came to a halt, and pursing her lips, she raised her eyes from the sketch. "You fought." She angled her head, frowning as Vaelin felt another tug at his mind. "He lost, badly."

"Yes," Vaelin confirmed with a sigh. "And has hated me for it ever since."

"He doesn't hate you." She lowered her eyes, the charcoal resuming its rapid course across the parchment. "He fears you. He envies you. A small part of him loves you, for he knows that without you in the world, his purpose would be gone. Also, you stripped away his illusions, the false pride with which he cloaked himself. He is grateful, if unable to acknowledge it."

Vaelin watched her charcoal for a time as it left what appeared to be meaningless scrawls on her parchment, knowing them to be far from meaningless. "Does it enable you to see everything?" he asked. "Your blessing."

"It offers insight, but only if I possess the wisdom to comprehend it. When I was young it was harder. I drew things I had never seen, events I had never witnessed. My family thought me mad or cursed. The notion that I might have been blessed by Heaven never rose to their minds, for how could this be a blessing? I do believe, if the Jade Princess hadn't sought me out in her dreams, my family may well have had me consigned to the White Cliffs."

"White Cliffs?"

"The place where the Merchant King's soldiers took those considered feebleminded or otherwise useless. They were set to hacking limestone from the face of a very tall cliff. Lime gets in the lungs. Most don't last more than a few months."

"A harsh fate for being different."

"Difference was never celebrated in the Merchant Realms. Stability was prized above all things, even innovation. It's why they were always doomed to fall. The Jade Princess foresaw it long before the first Merchant King ever sat upon a throne."

"The wolf and the tiger, did she foresee them too?"

Her charcoal came to an abrupt halt, scattering black grit across the paper. After a moment of stillness she shifted, reclining against the coiled rope at her back, meeting his gaze once again. "Do you have any notion of how old she was by the time she met her end?" she asked.

"Not exactly. I have a friend who has lived for centuries. He told me she was old long before he was born."

A faint smile passed across Mi-Hahn's lips. "Yes, I recall the memories she shared of him. Her young wandering friend, she called him, and he was but one amongst dozens of ancient souls she had encountered in her time. She had lost count of the empires that rose only to crumble. The great minds who scribbled peerless wisdom on pages that became dust within a few generations. The mighty heroes whose names were once exhorted to every corner of the world, names that are now forever lost to human memory. All this she had seen and yet, she told me, compared to the tiger and the wolf, she was but a child. She could not have foreseen them, for their kind walked this earth long before ours first took a breath. Whether or not they foresaw her, however, is another question."

"What is their kind?"

A small frown of consternation passed across Mi-Hahn's brow before she angled her gaze towards the deck, pointing her charcoal stub at a weevil crawling its way along the edge of a splintered plank. "When this one looks up at us do you think he wonders, 'What is their kind?'"

"Meaning you don't know."

"I mean I can't know what they are, neither can you and neither could the Jade Princess. But she did know two important facts, perhaps the most precious knowledge she had acquired in all her many, many years." She leaned forward, expression intent, speaking with simple, unvarnished honesty. "The tiger wishes us harm. The wolf wishes to prevent that harm. So has it ever been. So, as far as any can tell, it *will* ever be."

"That was her final vision for you? Endless conflict."

"She didn't have visions, not of what is to come. However, her accumulated knowledge enabled an ability to perceive a course amongst the myriad paths offered by the future. She could tell the tiger had woken from a long slumber and bent willing servants to its design. Her course was a chance to prevent its rise, for she could see only a minimal reaction from its eternal enemy. Whether the wolf had been diminished somehow or simply chosen to forsake us, she couldn't tell. She did know that certain events had to happen and certain important souls put in place to ensure her course remained true."

"Sherin, Ahm Lin, Sho Tsai." Vaelin paused, catching a glimmer of guilt in Mi-Hahn's gaze before adding, "You and me."

Her slim shoulders moved in a shrug, a gesture of indifference that didn't match the tear she thumbed from her eye. "Yes," was all she said.

"In the temple you said you were sure I would see my sister's face again. Are you so sure now?"

Mi-Hahn's voice caught on the word and she swallowed hard before it emerged, a soft, sorrowful whisper. "No."

"Did the princess tell you my fate?"

"She wanted you to know she regretted the price you would be required to pay."

Vaelin lowered his eyes to the parchment in her lap, seeing little more than a confusion of grey and black. "Is that it? My price?"

She shook her head, reversing the picture and holding it out to him. "No. I truly do not know your fate. But, hopefully this will be the final step on the course she set."

Taking hold of the parchment he initially saw little beyond his first impression of monochrome chaos. But the longer he looked at it, the more the swirls and lines formed into coherence, only for the meaning he had discerned to slip away when he tried to focus on it. "I see nothing . . ." he began, but she cut him off, voice sharp.

"Don't look. Feel. Listen."

He settled his gaze on the image once more, this time deliberately trying not to focus on any details. As for feelings, all her art seemed capable of arousing in him now was a deep sense of frustration, even a small welling of anger. Perhaps it was the anger that summoned the black-song, he couldn't tell, it being consistent only in its capriciousness. As the music swelled the swirling grey shifted and coalesced, forming a series of ghostly images. A roiling sea, waves driven to mountainous heights by the wind, carrying away dozens of ships as if they were mere toys. The sea swamped his vision, turning to a blank grey slate that darkened into something blacker than any night. For a second Vaelin felt himself lost in a void that stirred memories of his brief exposure to the Beyond, but then flames blossomed in the darkness. They were small, a dozen or more flickering like candles, but growing brighter as they drifted towards the centre of the page. He let out a grunt of discomfort as two came together, birthing a blinding flare of light. Then, as other flames slipped into the glow, it blossomed brighter still, forming a shimmering fiery globe. Tears streamed from his eyes as he stared into it, wondering why it hadn't burned his sight away.

Then he heard it, a low discordant roll of a distant drum, like the warning rumble of an approaching storm. The ball of flame roiled as the sound built, forming a recognisable shape, two eyes, eyes he had seen before, above a set of sharp bared teeth. The sound shifted in tone, thunder becoming a snarl as the wolf's mouth gaped. It lunged, jaws snapping with irresistible ferocity.

He reeled back, falling onto the deck, blinking away the salted water clouding his vision until it cleared to reveal a starlit sky, the view quickly obstructed by Mi-Hahn's face. Her expression mixed concern with grim and determined necessity as she asked, "Do you know now what you have to do?"

Vaelin got to his feet, letting the picture fall away as he had no desire to touch it again. He went to the rail, hands clasping the timber hard as he breathed deeply to calm his pounding chest. "Yes," he said. "I know."

CHAPTER TWENTY-EIGHT

He smelt the smoke before he saw it, a dark brown smudge rising into the early morning sky above the western horizon. The *Stormhawk* sailed alongside the *Sea Empress* at the head of the pirate fleet, arranged at their king's instruction into battle formation two days before when the outlying islands of the Free Cantons first hove into view. Ell-Nestra had insisted that the fleet skirt the Cantons to the east before turning west to Askira. Although the navigable channels bisecting the region offered a swifter route, he thought their narrowness would offer too much of an advantage to the Darkblade's ships, most of which were expected to be craft built for the coastal or river trade. The pirates' vessels, by contrast, were all oceangoing vessels, many captured products of the shipyards in the Meldenean Isles or the Unified Realm, all with crews experienced in fighting on the open sea.

"Inconsiderate of them to start without us," Nortah commented, the levity of his words negated by the troubled squint he focused on the thickening column of smoke.

"If there's smoke it means it's not yet over," Vaelin said before turning to Captain Ohtan. "Best tell your crew to rig for combat."

After a flurry of raised and lowered flags from the *Sea Empress*, the shape of the pirate fleet began to alter, grouping into three distinct divisions, each taking on a formation that resembled an arrowhead. Every sail was raised and white crests blossomed on the prows as they heaved through the swell at an increased pace. Vaelin climbed the mainmast to stand alongside Ellese on the platform she shared with the *Stormhawk*'s handful of archers. Peering into the distance he saw the smoke was rising mostly from the tip of the Tokira Peninsula, the sea to the north flecked with dark specks that told of many ships. Beyond them he could see the sun-dappled waters occluded by a larger mass of vessels, far more than he had ever seen in one place in fact.

He brought his whole fleet, he concluded. *Luralyn was right.*

"It's a nice day for it, at least, Uncle."

He turned to find Ellese regarding him with a cheery, if evidently forced smile. There was a new uncertainty to her gaze and a whiteness to her knuckles as she gripped the carved wych elm stave of her bow. *I asked much of her*, he knew. *Perhaps too much.* But now there was no sparing her, no way to get her clear of this, not that she would allow it. True courage was the ability to overcome fear, and in that he knew she would never be lacking.

"May I?" he said, gesturing to the bow.

She handed it over and watched him raise the stave, drawing the string back to his ear. It was not an easy draw, yet both Ellese and Reva had always made it appear effortless. "After the fall of Volar," he said, lowering the weapon and tracing a thumb over its exquisite carvings, "your mother allowed me to loose a few arrows with this. I wasn't particularly accurate, as I recall."

"She said you were always a better swordsman than archer."

"True enough, but that wasn't it. This bow doesn't sit well in my hands because it wasn't made for me. It's a bow of Arren crafted to be wielded only by the hand of a Mustor."

"I'm not a Mustor." He could hear a thickness to her voice, despite the cough she summoned to mask it. "Blessed Lady Reva's blood does not flow in these veins. I'm just the orphan child of a woman murdered by the monster who stole my father's body. I . . ." She took a deep, grating breath before forcing the words out. "I don't remember her face, Uncle. The woman who birthed me. I know she cherished me, loved me. But I can't remember her face. And yet I remember the face of the man who killed her as clearly as if he were standing before me right now. I thought by following you here, by tracking the steps of that monster to its master, I might . . . banish it somehow. Instead, all I have are a great many more faces to forget. So"—she let out a mirthless laugh, shaking her head—"I am not a Mustor. I am . . . damaged, broken. I always have been. I always will be. The Blessed Lady's strength does not reside in this unworthy vessel."

"And still, this bow doesn't seem to notice the difference." He took hold of her wrist and placed the bow in her palm, closing her fingers over it and letting his hand rest on hers. "The day we retook Varinshold for the queen I saw your mother kill at least a dozen Volarians with this bow's sister. She did that after she led your people through the siege of Alltor, and she would later be at the queen's side when she took Volar. If you think that throughout it all she never once knew a moment of doubt or weakness you are wrong."

He squeezed her hand and started towards the rope ladder at the platform edge, pausing to turn as she spoke, finding a more genuine smile on her lips. "A dozen? I'm sure I can give you thirty, at least."

◆   ◆   ◆

He set Sehmon and Mi-Hahn alongside Eresa with orders to guard Luralyn. The four of them clustered close to the base of the mainmast, the former outlaw gripping a spear whilst Eresa flexed her fingers and Luralyn clutched daggers in both hands. She gave an uncertain grimace as she watched Vaelin consign her gold nugget to the others in his purse.

"Allowing him to sense me may have the opposite of the desired effect," she said. "It could draw him to us."

"He'll know trying to claim you in the midst of a battle will risk your life. We'll just have to gamble on his love for you overcoming his lust for victory." Vaelin drew the bag's string tight, allowing it to fall alongside the other larger one on his belt.

"We do have an alternative," Luralyn pointed out, nodding to the larger purse.

"It's not yet time. I need to be sure of where he is, and we will require . . . assistance."

He moved to the foredeck where the *Stormhawk*'s fighting party was mustered. The half-dozen crewmen who could be spared to bear arms were joined by the fifteen pirates Ell-Nestra had insisted on placing on board. They were uniform only in their villainous aspect. Tall, short and in-between bearing sabre, hatchet or mace according to their preference, they regarded Vaelin with lean, weathered faces fixed in permanent scowls. Their leader was a heavily muscled man named Irvek who had been third mate aboard the *Sea Empress*. Around his bald head he wore a leather strap embossed in silver with a circular symbol of some kind. His skin was near as dark as Alum's and he possessed an accent Vaelin couldn't place, although he noted the fellow's profanity was spoken mostly in a coarse form of Volarian. His face differed from his fellow pirates' in being completely free of scars; however, the coiled muscles of his arms bore numerous marks that told of repeated exposure to combat.

"We'll most likely find ourselves fighting the Redeemed first," Vaelin told him. "Don't expect them to fear you as others might."

A very slight smile twisted Irvek's lips as a harsh snicker rose from the other pirates. "Any man who doesn't fear us is a fool," he said in his unfamiliar and somewhat jarring tones. "And fools die easily."

"They're not all men," Vaelin replied. "And as long as their god still draws breath you can be sure none will die easy."

He left them to their muttered scoffing and joined Nortah and Alum at the prow. "Not looking too good, brother," Nortah advised, handing him a spyglass. The pirate fleet was now only a mile east of the peninsula, forging ahead through drifting smoke that waxed and waned in its thickness. Focusing the glass on the northernmost tip of the peninsula, Vaelin saw ample reason for Nortah's concern. Many ships were clustered in an untidy knot at the centre of the Emperor's Wall, those on the fringes aflame. The sea to the north was littered with badly charred or sinking ships, their blackened masts leaking smoke into the air. Vaelin saw the newly minted banner of the Jade Empire fluttering from one mast as it sank beneath the waves. To the east and west other ships were locked in combat, casting flaming arrows at nearby enemies or drifting in an untidy dance with hulls jammed together as their crews battled on the decks.

"Fireships," Captain Ohtan said, appearing at Vaelin's side with his own glass pressed to his eye. "Looks to me like the Darkblade sent a mass of burning hulks ahead of his vanguard. Burned their way through Admiral Nuraka's fleet, cutting it in two. Seems they paid a hefty price for it though."

Vaelin's glass tracked across numerous bodies bobbing in the swell as he shifted his focus to the wall. A dark, ant-like mass was attempting to scale it from the ships clustered at its base. The Darkblade, or whichever cunning soul he had enlisted to plan this attack, had chosen their spot and their time well. They had waited for high tide to ensure the troop-carrying vessels following the fireships would reach the wall rather than ground on the beach, sparing them the inevitable arrow storm. It was hard to judge the course of the contest for the wall at such a distance, but he caught glimpses of the Amber Regiment's banners through the haze. Either the horde had been unfortunate in attacking at the point held by the stoutest troops in the Imperial Host or General Duhlan had been quick to shift them to meet the threat. In either case, this battle was still undecided and everything hinged on how swiftly the Darkblade could bring the bulk of his troops to bear.

Lowering the spyglass, Vaelin moved to the starboard prow to watch Ell-Nestra's fleet as it tacked towards the oncoming threat. As yet, he could discern no hesitation in the mass of ships heading for the peninsula. "Stay with the *Sea Empress*," he told Ohtan after a glance at Luralyn. His instinct was to steer for shore and assault the rear of the forces attacking the wall, but he knew that would achieve only a temporary respite if the Darkblade's fleet managed to fight their way through Ell-Nestra's pirates. To prevent that, the Darkblade needed to be given pause, and what better reason than a threat to the life of the sister he still cherished?

Captain Ohtan displayed his habitual skill at the tiller as he guided the *Stormhawk* in pursuit of the pirate flagship, calling out precise instructions to the sailors in the rigging as he spun and held the wheel. The smaller ship heaved and dipped through the *Sea Empress*'s wake before superior speed brought her alongside. By then the first few enemy vessels were already within arrow shot.

Ell-Nestra had judged the angle of his approach perfectly, sailing the most southerly division into the flank of the leading cohort of the Darkblade's fleet whilst the two others fanned out to engage those to the north. The ballista positioned on the *Sea Empress*'s hull voiced a familiar rattle and snap as they closed on the opposing ships, a stream of bolts fountaining into their heavily crowded decks. The pirate ships to port and starboard let loose with their own ballistae and a flurry of flaming projectiles cast by the catapults on their foredecks. Vaelin saw one of the fireballs arc down onto the stern of a horde vessel, birthing a bright yellow blossom of flame that sent a dozen or more burning Redeemed into the sea. The air between the pirates and the horde fleet became a blizzard of criss-crossing arrows and bolts as Tuhla and Stahlhast archers tried to contest with the ballistae. He and the others were obliged to crouch behind the bows to avoid a dense shower of arrows, the hard smack of their iron heads on the deck joined by a shout of pain from one of Irvek's pirates who found his foot pinned to the boards.

"Stop fucking whining!" Irvek chided him, stooping to grasp the man's ankle in both hands before jerking his foot free of the deck, bloody arrow and all. "And no shirking," he added, snapping the arrow then drawing out the shaft. "If you can hop you can fight."

They suffered two more sailors lost to enemy archers before the distance finally closed. From starboard came the hard grind and thump of the *Sea Empress*'s hull colliding with another, the huge ship shuddering to a listing halt as the *Stormhawk* surged past. The water beyond remained clear for only the barest moment before the tall curved prow of a coastal freighter slammed into their starboard hull. The freighter's deck was several feet lower than the *Stormhawk*'s, meaning Vaelin had no notion of how many troops she carried; however, the score of grappling hooks that sailed over the rail indicated a sizeable complement. The rhythmic thrum of Ellese's bow from the platform above as she methodically loosed arrow after arrow also spoke of a plentiful supply of targets.

"Cut the ropes!" Vaelin called to Irvek but the pirate and his comrades had already set about the task. Vaelin hacked the lines from two grapples before a challenging shout drew his gaze to the rail. A large Redeemed hauled himself half onto the deck, apparently uncaring of the arrow jutting from his shoulder, and managed to raise a sabre in a vain attempt to ward off Vaelin's stroke. The sword stabbed deep into the exposed joint between the Redeemed's shoulder and neck, Vaelin then drawing it clear before delivering a kick that sent the man tumbling onto his comrades crowding the deck below. A lithe, nimble woman bearing a wickedly curved dagger hopped onto the rail a yard to Vaelin's left, teeth bared in a feral snarl. Alum's spear caught her in midair as she lunged, spitting her clean through despite the light mail shirt she wore. Nortah appeared on Vaelin's right, sword blurring to send two Redeemed reeling back, blood trailing from blinded eyes.

Still more tried to claw their way up the wooden cliff, falling by the dozen as all spare hands aboard the *Stormhawk* laboured to hack them down. Bodies piled up on the freighter's deck, enabling the Redeemed to use them as a ramp with which to launch themselves upwards. One man, his torso bare of any armour but wearing an ornate helm, managed to leap high enough to clear the *Stormhawk*'s rail, twisting over the heads of the defenders to land in their rear. Wielding a double-bladed axe with impressive speed and skill he cut down a sailor and one of the pirates before Irvek's mace slammed into his helmet with sufficient force to shatter the skull within.

Pausing to regard the twitching corpse, Vaelin heard Irvek voice a bitter murmur in his roughly spoken Volarian. "Not easy enough by a long fucking chalk."

Feeling the deck pitch suddenly, Vaelin saw the starboard rail was now free of Redeemed. Leaning over the side he found the freighter's prow had been so borne down by the weight of dead and wounded it had slipped below the water, dislodging itself from the *Stormhawk* in the process. The freighter tipped as the sea covered the deck and filled her holds, fallen Redeemed sliding into the water when she capsized seconds later. However, her place at the *Stormhawk*'s side was not left empty for long. A squat, square-sailed junk, sitting low in the water thanks to the weight of troops crowding every inch of her, soon steered into the gap, driven by oarsmen on her lower deck.

The *Sea Empress* nudged forward then, having apparently bested any nearby foes, the massive bows pushing the junk aside, oars snapping against her hull as the ballistae resumed their deadly rattle. The hail of bolts was joined by volleys of fire arrows from the archers in the flagship's rigging as flaming firepots arced down amongst the storm of projectiles. Within seconds flames had blossomed along the length of the junk and Redeemed fell from her in a dark cascade. A loud splintering crunch sounded as the *Sea Empress* rammed the burning junk into the horde vessel on her starboard side, the flames immediately leaping from one vessel to another.

With his view of the sea to the north obscured by the *Sea Empress*'s bulk and a rising pall of black smoke, Vaelin hurried to climb the mainmast. "Already got my dozen, Uncle," Ellese told him as he moved to her side. She wore a tight smile under the soot and grime besmirching her face, a trickle of blood leaking from a small cut above her eye. "Not over yet is it?"

"I suspect it's only begun," he said, peering through the haze at the sea beyond the *Sea Empress*'s masts. It seemed as if a new road had been crafted to sit atop the water for a distance of at least a quarter mile, so close packed were the horde vessels. They were hemmed in to port by the pirate ships and to starboard by their comrades trying to maintain a course towards the battle still raging on the Emperor's Wall. It was hard to tell what lay beyond this long wooden island, but he caught a glimmer of open waves. It could mean the Darkblade had held back his fleet for fear of what might befall his sister, or he had directed them to another point of attack. Seeking guidance from the black-song, all Vaelin heard was a resentful grumble. The usual upsurge of lustful and discordant music that accompanied battle had failed to materialise today. He had briefly considered forsaking his daily dose of Sherin's elixir so as not to deny himself the song's insights, dangerous as they were. *There's more danger in setting it free*, he knew, but still this truculent refusal to offer a clue as to the Darkblade's intentions was frustrating, even worrying. *Does it want him to win?*

Feeling the platform tilt, he realised that the *Stormhawk* was being pushed yet again by the *Sea Empress*, the larger ship herself shifting under the weight of the compressed horde ships as the prevailing tide drew them towards shore. A fortuitous gust of wind banished the smoke for a moment, enabling him to gauge the state of the opposing ships. Many were burning, others sinking, all decks littered with the dead and dying as bolts and fireballs continued to rain down. Here and there groups of Redeemed a few dozen strong came together to try and contest the inevitable outcome. A few managed to scramble up keels and ropes to hurl themselves at the pirates, but most were cut down by ballista bolts or consumed by well-placed combinations of fire arrows and oil pots. The sea battle was over, at least for now. The battle ashore, however, was another matter.

Turning, Vaelin saw there was no longer a struggle atop the centre of the Emperor's Wall. Imperial contingents remained in place on either side, but the waving banners beyond the lip of the wall in the centre told of a continuing and fierce struggle inland. More Redeemed and Stahlhast were climbing up from the ships at the base of the wall. Although their assault had succeeded in gaining a foothold on land, without immediate reinforcements they were surely doomed. His confidence, however, evaporated when the black-song burst back into life. The force of its harsh, lacerating mix of warning and Dark recognition was enough to make him stagger. Vaelin gritted his teeth, letting out an involuntary growl of realisation. *He found more Gifted.* Beneath the recognition he heard a deeper note of warning, a signature tune he knew well from when he possessed a purer song; someone he loved was in danger.

"Uncle?"

From the uneasy caution on Ellese's face he could tell she worried she might be about to witness a repetition of what she had seen at the Battle of the Dunes. "I need to get over that wall," he told her. "Keep them off me."

He didn't wait for an answer before jumping down from the platform and climbing up onto the port rail. He watched the mass of overlapping and partially shattered decks drift closer, the black-song building all the while. It burned away any lingering protection instilled by Sherin's enhanced concoction, but somehow, this time it failed to claim him entirely. The world remained real and knowable around him, albeit now viewed with an impatient, hungry detachment.

"Vaelin?"

Glancing over his shoulder, he saw Nortah drawing up short a few paces away, his face a far more troubled version of Ellese's moments earlier. The song let out a faint, distracted trill of amused contempt, presumably more interested in the delights to come than his brother's concern, so Vaelin was able to find the resolve to speak. "Remember your promise," he said before vaulting over the side.

CHAPTER TWENTY-NINE

Redeemed sought to bar his path as he sprinted across the uneven field of compressed decks. Most were wounded, blood streaming from cuts or embedded crossbow bolts, but still they found the strength to stumble into his path. He killed them all, hardly breaking stride as the sword swept them away, guided by the black-song's exultant roar that swelled with every death. He was dimly aware of feet pounding in pursuit at his back, probably Nortah and Alum hoping to save him from a hopeless charge. A corner of his mind harboured a small concern that Nortah might present some form of obstacle, perhaps even a threat, but lost as he was in the throes of the song, he couldn't recall why, or even if it mattered.

A knot of Redeemed shambled into his path. They were led by a Stahlhast, half her face a charred ruin, although any agony she suffered didn't appear to diminish the strength with which she swung her sabre. It rebounded from his sword, the Order blade flashing up to parry the stroke then down to cleave the Stahlhast's neck. However, one of Ellese's arrows flicked past his ear to bury itself in the woman's remaining eye before his blow could land. He charged on, cutting his way through the Redeemed, sword lancing and slashing as he ducked and sidestepped their clumsy blows, leaving them bleeding and dying in his wake.

Reaching the base of a scaling ladder he found a Redeemed with no less than four crossbow bolts jutting from his shoulders, blood leaking from between clenched teeth as he attempted to haul himself up the first rung.

Vaelin hacked his hands off at the wrists and kicked him aside, scrambling up the ladder to the top to find the ground beyond the wall rendered into a scene of utter chaos.

Stahlhast and Redeemed battled alone or in small groups against soldiers from the Amber Regiments and a mingling of Sehtaku and Imperial troops. They stumbled over a carpet of bodies as they fought, many clearly nearing or even past the point of exhaustion. Some rolled over the corpses, clawing and gouging at one another. Beyond the chaotic melee he could see a more orderly contest had developed in the rough scrubland a hundred paces from the wall. A dense cohort of Stahlhast hurled themselves against the unyielding barrier of the Amber Regiments arranged in three ranks. Another contingent of the Imperial Host had formed up to the right to hold off a frenzied mass of Redeemed, Vaelin seeing the emperor's personal banner fluttering above their less orderly but still resolute ranks. The scene was different to the left of the Amber Regiments where Redeemed and Stahlhast streamed into open country, contested only by a few knots of conscripts, the black-song's warning note sounding loudest at the sight.

He paused to slice open the neck of a Stahlhast pounding a soldier's head against the wall before starting forward at a steady run. The song blared its bloodlust as he ran, keen to spur him into the midst of the nearest melee, but the warning note and the knowledge that something Dark lay ahead enabled him to resist it. He skirted thrashing combatants, leapt over warriors wrestling on the ground, killing any Redeemed who sought to impede his course.

The pitch of battle diminished as he crested a low rise, finding only a few knots of combatants in the plain beyond, but the black-song's recognition rose to its highest pitch yet when he focused on the cluster of tents a hundred yards away. This, he knew, was the site of Sherin's makeshift healing house, and the song left no doubt it was also where he would find the Darkblade's Gifted. A swirling dust storm covered the ground in front of the camp, but Vaelin made out dim figures amongst the maelstrom as he ran closer. His approach was interrupted by a body that came sailing out of the dust, meeting the hard ground with a crunch of breaking bones then rolling to a halt at his feet, a tangle of twisted limbs in a black robe. He had time to make out the face of Sister Lehun, staring up at him, wide-eyed and pale in death, before he leapt the body and hurtled into the whirlwind.

The gale-driven grit blinded him, birthing an instant of disorientation before he quelled it and gave himself over to the song's guidance. It led him on a wayward course, blaring loud to send him ducking a hefty chunk of indistinct debris that would surely have shattered his skull, screeching another warning that brought his sword up in time to stab through the chin of a stocky man who came lunging out of the haze, arms outstretched. Blinking away the needlelike scrape of the grit on his skin, Vaelin watched the man gurgle and twitch on the end of his sword, spitted from chin to nape. His eyes and face were that of the hopelessly insane, and Vaelin detected the echo of a prayer-chant to the Darkblade in the blood-laced words emerging from his mouth. Despite the imminence of his death he continued to reach out with both hands, trying to gain the slightest touch on Vaelin's skin. Although the exact nature of this madman's gift was unclear, Vaelin knew one touch from those hands meant death.

He twisted the blade, watching the final twitch of the Gifted's face before it slackened in death. Drawing the blade clear he let the song steer his steps, catching sight of a slender figure at the centre of this twisting fury. He charged towards it, the wind slackening as he slipped into the eye of the storm, finding himself confronted by a young woman of arresting beauty. She regarded him with a gaze just as insane and filled with love for the Darkblade as the man with the lethal touch, seemingly indifferent to the sword thrust the black-song guided towards the centre of her unarmoured chest. Just before the tip of the blade touched the thin cotton shirt she wore, her empty eyes blinked and Vaelin found himself lifted and cast away, swatted like a bothersome fly by the invisible hand of the woman's gales.

He landed hard, rolling across the earth until bringing himself to an untidy halt. The song swelled with vindictive anger as he forced himself upright, seeing the young woman through the gusting detritus, a slender shadow approaching with an unhurried stride. He crouched low, ready to launch himself at her, the song's rage allowing no caution now even though it seemed all such a course would achieve would be another swatting gale, probably with a few broken bones to go with it.

The woman's eyes appeared to shine as she came closer, her mad gaze entirely fixed on him with what he knew to be fierce recognition. The Darkblade had surely instilled his Gifted with a desire to kill the Thief of Names and now this one had a chance to honour her god. Her fixation was such that she failed to see the bulky shape to her rear and reacted far too late when something long and snakelike whipped out of the storm to wrap itself around her from ankle to neck. The whirlwinds faltered as the wooden coils tightened, Vaelin seeing the last, horrified rictus of her face before it seemed that every bone in her body snapped at once. She jerked, blood fountaining from her mouth before the coils slacked and retreated.

Vaelin saw Zhuan-Kai lean heavily on his staff as it resumed its normal shape. He tried and failed to remain upright, sinking to his knees with blood leaking from his nose and mouth. He met Vaelin's gaze, giving a hopeless shake of his head before sagging to the ground. Whatever had transpired on this field, it was clear the hulking monk had expended the last vestige of his blessing. Crouching, Vaelin pressed a hand to Zhuan-Kai's chest, sighing in relief at the swell of his chest and faint but present thrum of his heart.

Shredded grass and leaves fell like a green rain as the winds died, revealing a scene of carnage. The black-robed bodies of the Servants lay everywhere, surrounded by numerous slain Redeemed and Stahlhast. A strange, high-pitched laugh, only a note shy of a scream, drew Vaelin's eyes to the tents where he saw the abbot locked in combat with a tall, stick-thin man who bore no weapon. The abbot's sword was already bloody from tip to hilt, evidence of the many he had killed today, and he wielded it with peerless skill. The thin man, naked but for a few rags clinging to his skeletal frame, exhibited no caution at all as he advanced into the abbot's whirling steel, letting out another scream-like laugh as it tore at his flesh. Despite the blood flying from his wounds, the thin man advanced as if he were opposed by nothing more than a bothersome hail shower, forearm raised to ward off the worst blows before lunging forward. The abbot twisted aside, allowing the man's outstretched arms to slip by before whirling, reversing his sword as he did so, then stabbing it deep into his opponent's back. It should have killed him, but instead he laughed once more, Vaelin hearing the crack of dislocated bones as he turned his torso to an impossible angle, hand lashing out to clamp onto the blade of the abbot's sword. The abbot expended a precious, fatal second trying to tug the sword free, by which time the thin man's spine had twisted sufficiently for him to drive his free hand into the abbot's chest.

Vaelin saw it all as he charged towards them, too late to stop it. He saw the abbot look down at the hand that had punched through his rib cage. A resigned, bitter expression passed across the old man's face before defiance returned. He raised his face to the leering, giggling visage of his enemy and spat into it, lips moving in a final profane insult. The thin man dragged his hand free of the abbot's chest, blood jetting from the ripped vessels of the heart he held.

The skeletal monster spent a brief second regarding the organ in his grasp before tossing it away, turning in time to confront a second enemy. Chien ducked under a jab of the Gifted's arm, her staff-blade slashing across his belly before she rolled clear. Vaelin caught sight of the blood gushing from the thin man's gaping wound slow then cease, the half-emerged entrails retreating back into the body and the lips of the wound closing, sinew and skin knitting together. By the time Vaelin closed on him, the man's belly held no sign of a scar. He moved with a kind of insectile swiftness to avoid the slash Vaelin aimed at his neck, his shrill, delighted laugh sounding again before he replied with a kick, his leg emitting an obscene fleshy grind as it extended to twice its previous length. A last-second flare of warning from the black-song enabled Vaelin to dodge the kick, whirling as he did so to hack deep into the unnaturally elongated limb.

The thin man gibbered in either pain or delight as the blade bit home, then slashed at Vaelin's face with a whiplike arm before twisting away. The man's extended nails, now rendered into talons, nicked Vaelin's chin as he back-pedalled. Ducking under another lashing arm, he saw the thin man's leg wound mend itself just before Chien launched herself forward. She raised her staff-blade high in a two-handed grip, letting out a savage yell as she brought it down to cleave into the Gifted's shoulder. He howled and tittered in perverse triumph, Vaelin seeing the sundered flesh close around the blade, holding it tight as Chien tried to pull it free. The thin man's arm blurred, his taloned hand latching onto her forearm, claws digging deep as he gripped it with impossible strength. Vaelin saw the colour leech from her face as bones cracked and blood seeped forth in a torrent.

The black-song propelled him into a high, twisting leap, his sword sweeping up and down in a silver arc, severing the thin man's arm at the elbow. Chien collapsed, the clawed hand embedded in her flesh jerking spasmodically as it returned to its normal dimensions. Vaelin stooped to tug it free, casting the twitching thing away with a grimace of disgust. Turning to confront the thin man he found him regarding the stump of his arm with a puzzled frown, a crimson torrent pulsing from it until the flesh once again sealed the wound.

"So," Vaelin said, looking closely at the smooth stump. "You can heal it, but you can't grow it back."

The thin man let out a small, satisfied giggle, raising his brows at Vaelin with a smirk. It may have been the giggle or the smirk that did it, or perhaps both, but at that moment the black-song claimed him entirely. This time it wasn't like the Battle of the Dunes. Now there was no sense of being a spectator to his own actions. The world slipped into blackness, taking with it all sensation save a feeling of being adrift in a void. He experienced an absurd surge of gratitude at finding himself without a body. Here there was no pain, no rage, no all-encompassing desire to kill and hurt. Time became meaningless, his awareness reduced to just the very distant beat of his heart, which he lacked the inclination to measure. It may have pulsed a thousand times or twenty. It occurred to the very slight vestige of thought left to him that he may have died, that this was in fact death. True death, not the fickle vexations offered by the Beyond. If so, perhaps it was not to be feared. Perhaps it was to be welcomed . . .

"STOP!"

The world returned in a blinding, deafening rush, the pain and noise of it making him stagger. He felt a warm wetness on his face, finding his vision partially obscured by something red and viscous. A hand was clamped to his upraised wrist, holding firm against the downward stroke of his sword arm. Blinking the sticky, clinging matter from his eyes, he saw Sherin staring up at him, eyes wide but determined in a very pale face.

"That's enough," she told him in a coarse whisper, staring into his gaze and, apparently satisfied at finding comprehension there, releasing his wrist. She moved away quickly, and Vaelin watched her crouch by Chien's prostrate form. The outlaw woman was shivering, her skin bleached to an alabaster white and only a dull glimmer left in her eyes. Sherin looked briefly at the ruin of Chien's arm before gritting her teeth then clasping it with one hand whilst laying her other on the woman's forehead.

A rustling, scratching sound drew Vaelin's gaze away from the healing, and he found himself regarding the odd sight of a curiously pale spider tapping its legs against his boot. Its appearance was made doubly strange by the fact that it possessed five legs instead of eight, the tip of each featuring a fingernail. A surge of repugnance made him stamp his boot onto the thing, crushing it into the earth. But there were more. Small wriggling creatures of unfamiliar appearance littered the ground around him, some entirely red and glistening, others apparently fashioned from partially exposed and broken bone jutting from ripped flesh. Realisation dawned when he saw the head.

The thin man's eyes rolled up to regard him as he strode closer. Half his face had been hacked away and numerous sword strokes to the skull revealed the pink, pulsating matter within. Yet his lips, what remained of them, still managed to form a semblance of a taunting grin. It froze in place when Vaelin stabbed his sword through the exposed brain. As he did so the wriggling remnants of this creature ceased their obscene movements and lay still.

"Is any of that yours?"

Nortah stood a few paces off, bow in hand with an arrow resting on the stave that Vaelin knew had been pointed at him only seconds before. The poorly concealed fear on his brother's face, laced with a fair amount of horrified disgust, provided a paradoxical source of comfort. *At least he was willing to fulfil his promise.*

"Any of what?" he asked.

Nortah grimaced, gesturing to the gore that Vaelin saw covered him from foot to head. "I don't think so."

A low keening sound drew his gaze to the abbot's body where the surviving Servants had gathered. Vaelin felt a twinge of relief at seeing Cho-ka amongst the dozen-strong group, kneeling alongside Zhuan-Kai and Mi-Hahn. Zhuan-Kai wept openly, as did the others, whilst Mi-Hahn's face displayed only a faint sorrow as she reached out to close the abbot's eyes. *Time,* Vaelin thought, recalling his first meeting with the old man at the base of the temple, *is both precious and worthless. Eternal and fleeting. You may make of it what you will.*

Hearing fresh sounds of battle he looked to the east and saw mounted Sehtaku and a smaller number of Imperial cavalry charging full pelt through a rising pall of dust. "I think you've done your bit today, brother," Nortah said, stepping into his path as Vaelin started in the direction of the horsemen. "The tide's turned and the rest of the Darkblade's fleet is holding station a mile offshore. That lot are mopping up a few hundred Stahlhast who managed to grab a section of the wall."

Vaelin noted how he maintained a distance between them, just wide enough to raise and draw his bow before Vaelin could close it. "It's all right, brother," he said, sliding his sword into the sheath on his back. "I am . . . calmer." It was true; the black-song had subsided into a sibilant murmur, putting him in mind of a glutton's sighs after gorging on a copious feast. He watched Nortah relax, allowing his bow to fall to his side but leaving the arrow nocked. "The others?" Vaelin asked.

"Sehmon took a bad thump to the head but he'll live. Ellese is tending to him. Everyone else is fine; lost about half the *Stormhawk*'s crew and a few more of those pirates though." He winced as he surveyed the surrounding carnage with its many black-robed bodies. "Even so, we seem to have had an easy time of it, comparatively speaking. Looks like the emperor will need a few more Heavenly preachers to proclaim his divinity."

We needed them for more than preaching, Vaelin thought, grasping the heavy purse on his belt as his gaze settled once more on the cluster of surviving Servants. *Will this be enough?*

Nortah let out a weary sigh as a blast of inexpertly played pipes and bugles sounded from the direction of the wall. Through the fading smoke Vaelin could see the banner of the Monarch of the Benevolent Kingdom carried aloft by a group of well-attired pirates attempting, mostly without success, to march in step.

"Looks like there's a ceremony in the offing," Nortah observed, glancing back at Vaelin. "You might want to wash first."

◆ ◆ ◆

Tsai Lin spent over two hours secluded in his tent with Ell-Nestra, their discussion witnessed only by Zhuan-Kai and General Duhlan. Nuraka Shan was a keenly felt absence. The admiral's flagship had been lost to the inferno when the Darkblade sent his fireships against the Jade Fleet. Nuraka Shan's body, along with most of his crew, was yet to be found amongst the many washing up onshore. Luralyn's attempts to gain access to the emperor's tent had been met with a polite but firm refusal whilst Vaelin found he had acquired a new escort of Sehtaku from the Urikien Clan. They kept to a respectful distance but always maintained a circle around him. Heaven's Chosen, it seemed, was no longer as amenable to the advice of barbarians or foreigners but also was intent on keeping a close watch on those in his service.

Ell-Nestra emerged from the tent as the sky began to darken and the many columns of smoke from the funeral pyres rose to besmirch the reddened sky. He strode towards where Vaelin sat with Luralyn, Nortah and Alum. Ellese and Eresa had remained in the healing tents with Sehmon who, a tired and hollow-eyed Sherin assured them, would most likely lose his confused state of mind after a hefty dose of potent herbs and a night's sleep.

"My brother the emperor requests your presence," Ell-Nestra told Vaelin. "Just you and the good lady," he added when Nortah and Alum began to rise.

"His divine arse has risen too high for us now?" Nortah enquired, wisely switching to Realm Tongue although his caustic tone drew sharp glances from the nearby Sehtaku.

"I don't speak for my divine brother," Ell-Nestra said, evidently enjoying the moment. "But it behooves the wise king to keep his councils small."

"Eat," Vaelin said to the others, getting to his feet. "Rest while you can."

"Win a war for them and they can't wait to forget you," Nortah persisted, voice growing heated. "Always the way with kings."

"This war isn't yet won," Vaelin reminded him, starting towards the tent.

Emperor Tsai Lin, Heaven's Chosen and Divinely Blessed Monarch of the Jade Empire, appeared to have grown both considerably older and broader in Vaelin's absence. The sense of enhanced presence may have derived from the freshly stitched cut above his right eye, or the new armour he wore, a carefully arranged mix of plate and lacquered steel of both mainland and Sehtaku design. In any case, Vaelin knew the man he stood before was now truly a king in any way that mattered, with all the unstinting pragmatism and jealously guarded authority that entailed.

"You appear to have promised much in my name, Lord Vaelin," he observed in a tone that was mostly neutral save for a slightly curt edge.

"And delivered a great deal as a consequence," Luralyn said before Vaelin could answer. "You have a victory today, thanks in no small part to the alliance agreed by this man."

General Duhlan, standing to the emperor's right, stiffened in anger. "You appear to have forgotten the courtesies required of this court, woman. You will address Heaven's Chosen correctly."

"My people have rarely troubled themselves with courtesy," Luralyn returned. "Which perhaps explains why they found it so easy to conquer two-thirds of the Merchant Realms."

Her words provoked a poorly concealed laugh from the Monarch of the

Benevolent Kingdom, drawing a glower from the general, although any retort died on his lips when Tsai Lin raised a hand. "Rest assured, honoured lady," he informed Luralyn, "the service done by Lord Vaelin and yourself is appreciated. But today we won a respite, not a victory. Your brother lurks off our coast with much of his fleet and horde still intact. We, on the other hand, lost over half our strength holding this shore whilst, in your absence, the people of these islands have suffered greatly. You see, the Darkblade was not content to simply launch his invasion. For weeks the cursed Tuhla have been raiding at will throughout the Cantons. Villages and towns have been razed, men slaughtered, women and children taken away in chains. I have had to turn away subjects begging for protection, and punish those who spoke against me for it. All so I could keep this host in place on the promise that you, Lord Vaelin, would return with a stone that would end this war. And yet, instead of a stone, you present me with only a bag full of dust."

Vaelin felt a sudden weariness sweep through him then, something that went deeper than just the ache brought on by the day's exertions. *I am*, he decided as the black-song stirred from its slumber to voice a resentful growl, *very tired of kings.*

"You are right," he said, meeting Tsai Lin's gaze and striving to keep the rancour from his voice. "Victory yet eludes us and battle will resume shortly. The Darkblade knows where his sister stands and will come to claim her. I can feel his need for her. It quells all other impulses, even his hunger for conquest and his regard for her safety. Such unreason will work to our benefit."

"I see little evidence of unreason in the barbarian's dispositions," Ell-Nestra put in. "He's gathered his fleet into a great floating fortress, chained the ships together to fashion wooden walls. I don't relish hurling my lot against such a contrivance. Before we rounded the eastern shores of the Cantons I sent scout ships ahead to reconnoitre the sea to the north. They returned tonight with news of more ships sailing to join the Darkblade, ships flying the banners of the Transcendent Kingdom. All the Darkblade need do is sit in his man-made fortress and await reinforcements, unless you imagine his lack of reason will compel him to rash action."

Vaelin raised a questioning eyebrow at Luralyn, who responded with a guarded, sombre glance at the emperor. "In truth I don't know what he'll do," she said. "He may come for me before he's certain of victory or he may not. I do know that in all my years at his side, when it came to matters of war, I never saw him make a mistake."

"There you have it, my divine brother," Ell-Nestra said. "As I suggested earlier, our best course is to harry our enemy. The Transcendent Fleet is still two days away. We should use the time to send raiding parties against his fleet. The more soldiers we kill and ships we burn the better."

"And when the Transcendent Fleet arrives, my benevolent brother?" Tsai Lin enquired. Vaelin took some comfort from the hardness of the emperor's tone. *Failed to charm him, at least*, he thought, concluding that Tsai Lin's recognition of this newly raised king could in time prove to be little more than a temporary expedient.

"The Darkblade will have to break up his floating fortress to join with them, after having suffered our attentions in the meantime. There will be a period of chaos, and chaos in war always presents opportunity."

"Chaos is the heart of war," General Duhlan stated, his tone that of one quoting an old proverb. "However, I must advise you, Heaven's Chosen, that in such a battle it's always the side with the greater numbers that prevails."

"Numbers aren't everything," Ell-Nestra said. "Skill and courage matter just as much, and I'd match any one of my ships to three of theirs."

"That may be, but they have more than three to your one . . ."

As they continued to argue, Tsai Lin kept his gaze on Vaelin, brow furrowing in impatient expectation until he finally raised a hand. "Enough," he said, bringing their bickering to an abrupt end. "Lord Vaelin, at Keshin-Kho I heard my father once say of you, not without a certain grudging reluctance, that you were the kind of warrior I should fear more than any other. 'The strongest, the swiftest, the most courageous are all worthy of respect,' he said. 'But it's the opponent who knows the most tricks who's likely to kill you in the end.' Do you have a trick for me now?"

Vaelin nodded, hand moving to the purse once more. "I do. But I require certain things for it to work."

"And what might they be?"

"The *Stormhawk*, since she's the fastest ship in the fleet." He nodded to Zhuan-Kai, who had remained silent throughout, his heavy features still drawn in the kind of grief Vaelin knew could last a lifetime. The abbot may have been a hard man to like, and as far as he could tell, not mourned by the emperor he had worked so hard to raise, but the Servants had all loved him.

"I also require the Servants of the Temple," Vaelin added, "if they're willing, and all others within our ranks who possess a blessing of Heaven. And"—he held up the purse—"my bag full of dust."

CHAPTER THIRTY

S aikir appeared to view the prospect of battle as no more than a new game, fidgeting in excitement at Sherin's side, grinning and eyes alight with anticipation as he watched the sailors and soldiers ready the *Stormhawk* for sea. Uhlkar was a marked contrast to his adoptive brother. For the first time, Vaelin saw a glimmer of fear in his overlarge eyes, wide and bright in the pale head poking out from the thick layers of clothing Sherin had clad him in. Vaelin had expected more anger when he roused her from a brief slumber after a long day spent labouring in the healing tents. Instead, she listened in blank silence as he explained his intent before a dull sigh emerged from her lips.

"So," she said, "we are to become as he is, now? Children will fight our battles for us?"

"If there was another way . . ."

"What is it inside you?" she cut in, her gaze becoming more concerned and curious than angry. "What I saw yesterday . . ." She frowned, shaking her head. "I've seen you fight before, but that wasn't fighting. And it wasn't you."

"I told you, I took Ahm Lin's song . . ."

"Ahm Lin was never a monster." A flicker of regret passed across her brow as the sting of her words brought a wince to his face. "Do you think it will fade, just go away if you win this war?" she asked, tone softening a fraction. "Kill the Darkblade and the curse is lifted? Is that what you think?"

"I don't know. All I know is that he has to be stopped by any and all means, regardless of what it costs us. And I think you know that too."

She lowered her head, eyes closed and shoulders slumped under what he knew to be more guilt than she had felt before. "I'm going with them," she said. "And I'll hear no word to the contrary."

"You will be welcome," he said. "We'll need all our strength today."

The *Stormhawk* had to be towed out of the Jaigan-Shu harbour, three boats of sailors labouring against the changing currents to place her in the open sea. "Not much of a breeze today, my lord," Captain Ohtan said, eyeing the mostly cloudless sky as it lightened into the pale blue of morning. "It'll take us a good long while to get there," he added, nodding to the jagged silhouette below the horizon. The prospect of sailing alone towards the entire conjoined fleet of their enemy didn't appear to concern him as much as the lack of speed his ship would display in doing so.

"Stand ready, Captain," Vaelin told him. "The wind will arrive presently and we'll require our most able hand on the tiller."

Ohtan nodded and started towards the wheel, then paused. "Wasn't sure it was the right thing, y'know," he said, a tight, cautious smile bunching his beard. "Letting the Healing Grace put her hands on me. Seemed against nature, for I'd had all the days I was due. Thought it was past time for me to take m'self off and listen to the wife's nagging tongue for all eternity. Wasn't exactly true, y'see? What I said about wishing her dead. Might've said it, but I never felt it. When I got home to find her gone, I wept for a week." He looked down at his hands, smoothing the palms together, the fingers lacking the curled stiffness of age. "But I don't think she'd mind me sticking around a little longer, not when there's good work needs doing."

"No, Captain," Vaelin agreed. "I don't think she'd mind at all."

He moved to the bows where Sherin waited with Saikir, Uhlkar having reluctantly allowed himself to be placed in Luralyn's care. Vaelin lifted Saikir up onto the planking behind the bowsprit as the *Stormhawk*'s prow swung towards the clustered enemy fleet. "You know what's required of you?" Vaelin asked him.

"I know," he replied, his previous excitement now giving way to a modicum of trepidation. "*He's* there," Saikir said, pointing to the floating fortress. "I can feel him."

"So can I. Do this for us and you'll never feel his presence again."

"He was kind, when he found me." Saikir's features bunched as he sought to master unfamiliar emotions. "I didn't know why, because no one had been kind before. But it was a trick, a lie. He just wanted to use me for what I can do, like you."

"Except I haven't lied," Vaelin pointed out.

"No." Saikir looked at the sky then at the surrounding waters, still placid and barely troubled by the breeze. "But you aren't kind either." He turned to Sherin, the excitement slipping into a pale fearfulness until she moved to clasp his small hand.

"Don't worry," she told him, Vaelin seeing the guilt in her gaze as she forced an encouraging smile. "I'm here."

Saikir nodded, glancing at Vaelin. "How fast do you need to go?"

"As fast as you can make us."

The boy took a deep breath and turned his gaze to the *Stormhawk*'s listless sails, his smooth brow creasing in concentration. "Best tell everyone to hold on to something," he said.

The wind arrived without warning, a fulsome gust filling every sail in an instant. Water lapped over her bows as the *Stormhawk* lurched forward, rearing like a horse let loose from its tethers. The prow swung to port then back again in response to Ohtan's skilled hand. Waves rose around them as the wind whipped the sea, sending sheets of rain across the deck. Undaunted, the *Stormhawk* surged amidst the miniature squall as it conveyed them towards the Darkblade's fleet, the spiky silhouette looming closer with every passing second.

Through the rain, Vaelin could see the *Sea Empress* at the forefront of the assembled pirate ships and the surviving vessels of the Jade Fleet. They all sat low in the water, laden with the Amber Regiments, Sehtaku and most able contingents of the Imperial Host. Leaving the Emperor's Wall largely bereft of its most capable defenders was a gamble, but so was every other aspect of this plan. The fleet's sails were half-furled so that they inched rather than charged towards the enemy. If all went well, it wouldn't be wise for them to join the battle too quickly this morning.

The *Stormhawk*'s hull shuddered as she knifed through a tall wave, causing Vaelin to wonder if even so swift a vessel could take the strain of moving at such speed. However, she settled quickly, albeit with a few groaning timbers, and within the space of what couldn't have been more than a few minutes, the Darkblade's fleet lay less than a half mile distant. A glance at Saikir revealed a welling of blood on the tip of his nose that Vaelin knew would soon become a stream. He saw Sherin clasp the boy's hand tighter and felt the black-song sing its note of recognition as she allowed her gift to flow into Saikir, buttressing his strength. Sharing power between Gifted souls was something he had seen done only once years before and hadn't been sure how to impart the knowledge. Fortunately, it was a skill the Servants of the Temple had known for centuries and required only a short demonstration from Zhuan-Kai to master. The blood dripping from Saikir's nose was instantly whipped away by the wind, but Vaelin took satisfaction in seeing no more swell in its place.

Turning to the fast-approaching fleet, he saw it now lay only a few hundred paces off, close enough to see small figures clambering up ropes and troops assembling on the decks. A great many newly fashioned platforms were visible amongst the swaying forest of masts, each one holding at least a dozen archers. A scattering of small glowing specks lit the rigging as torches were touched to fire arrows. Within a few moments the air between the *Stormhawk* and the Darkblade's fleet would become a spectacle of flaming projectiles.

"It's time," Vaelin said, clasping Saikir's shoulder. The black-song flared as he did so, Vaelin feeling a faint draining sensation as a measure of his gift flowed into the boy to join with Sherin's. They both stiffened then, Sherin letting out a gasp whilst Saikir gave a pained sob. His eyes flashed at Vaelin in wounded rebuke, but finding only an implacable and unwavering purpose in the gaze that answered his, he gritted his teeth and shifted his attention to the sea beyond the prow.

Above him, Vaelin heard the snap of slackening rope and canvas as the wind propelling the *Stormhawk* abruptly died. Despite the sudden absence of wind she retained sufficient momentum to keep ploughing towards the floating fortress, although Ohtan was required to engage in some rapid spinning of the wheel when the water ahead roiled into a frothing, wind-lashed swell. Vaelin felt more of his strength seep into Saikir as he crafted the wave, drawing the water up into a slanted mountainous wall. Despite the power he borrowed from Sherin and Vaelin, fresh blood began to stream from Saikir's nose, his small form shuddering in their grasp so violently it seemed his bones would break. Seeing Sherin's stricken face, Vaelin reached out with his free hand to grasp her wrist, holding it in place before she could draw it free, keeping it there until Saikir let out a final, pain-filled shout and collapsed onto the deck.

The wave he had crafted sped away from them faster than any bird, an azure cliff of unstoppable fury, torrents of spume streaming from its crest and flanks. It exploded into white the moment it crashed into the outlying ships of the Darkblade's fleet. Even above the wave's roar Vaelin could hear the shattering of timbers and screaming of doomed souls. Debris churned amidst the fury as the wave swept on, the ships caught by its edges raised and flipped over, a dark cascade of Redeemed and Stahlhast cast loose from masts and decks. The ships at the outermost fringes of the floating fortress were spared the worst of the wave's strength, but many were dragged down by the chains tethering them to less-fortunate neighbours. Some disappeared beneath the surface with such swiftness Vaelin doubted any on board had time to leap clear.

The wave's ferocity only began to fade when it had neared the centre of the Darkblade's fleet, having torn a great rent through the mass of interlocked ships. They heaved as the wave ebbed, still possessing enough force to capsize a few, the chains once again spelling doom for many whilst crews worked feverishly to cast them off. By the time the last swell had risen and fallen, the Darkblade's floating fortress had been transformed into a disorderly crescent drifting in a sea littered with struggling Stahlhast and Redeemed, flailing hopelessly in the debris-strewn waters before their armour and weapons dragged them under.

"That was well done." Vaelin gave Saikir's shoulder a final squeeze, drawing a faint smile from his blood-smeared lips as he looked up from the cradle of Sherin's arms. Her eyes snared Vaelin as he started towards the mid-deck, full of accusation but also something worse: fear. She had seen the black-song's effect on him the day before, but now she had felt its touch. She knew what was in him, and it terrified her.

Vaelin tore his gaze away, severing her hold on him, knowing that to spare any time to face her judgement now would be a fatal indulgence. He strode to the mid-deck calling out to Captain Ohtan, "Maintain course! Take us straight towards the centre!"

The wind may have faded but the water drawn in the wake of the great wave ensured the *Stormhawk* made rapid forward progress, Vaelin making out the sight of a large warship at the centre of the shambolic crescent. The black-song's hungry growl left no doubt as to who waited aboard that ship. He could feel Kehlbrand's song now, lashing out across the water that separated them like the exploring tentacle of some nameless sea creature, searching with frantic need whilst also pulsing in rage. The note of respect Vaelin had heard after the drowning of Nuan-Khi was completely gone now, replaced by a seething, hate-filled wrath.

He went to where the dozen surviving Servants of the Temple were gathered around the mainmast. They were arranged with Zhuan-Kai and Mi-Hahn at their head. Eresa stood at Luralyn's side as always, both of them clasping Uhlkar's hands. Taking the purse from his belt and undoing the ties, Vaelin forced away a burgeoning well of doubt that this paltry gathering of Gifted souls would be enough. *It has to be*, he insisted, crouching to unfurl the purse on the deck, revealing the piled dust within. It stirred in the breeze, though not in a natural manner. Even though the wind was slight, it should still have whipped away a few grains from the pile. Instead they swirled at the air's touch, the grains sticking together as the pile rippled, creating the impression of a living thing.

It is a living thing, Vaelin knew, reaching out a hand, allowing it to hover an inch above the dust whilst he extended his other hand to Luralyn. She hesitated before taking it, her eyes flicking from him to the dust, then more reluctantly, to the fast-approaching line of ships beyond the prow. Her hand clasped his with hard, resolute strength, her other tightening on that of Uhlkar, who in turn gripped Eresa's hand more tightly. She reached out to entwine her fingers with Mi-Hahn's. The Servants of the Temple had already joined hands, creating a chain that ended with Zhuan-Kai. He seemed even more uncertain than Luralyn, fearful even. The abbot's death appeared to have left him bereft of more than just a lifelong friendship. What they were attempting had never been tried in all the many centuries of the temple's existence. This was the dawn of a new chapter in the history of his order, the start of a new journey, but without the old man's foulmouthed guidance, it appeared Zhuan-Kai was lost.

"The abbot always did what the temple expected of him," Vaelin said, staring hard at the monk across the circle of joined souls. "Now you are the abbot here, brother."

Zhuan-Kai's broad features betrayed a momentary shame before he moulded them into a purposeful mask and clasped hands with Mi-Hahn. With the chain complete, the river of strength began to flow, and Vaelin shuddered as it filled him, drowning out the black-song but also bringing with it a dangerously seductive perception of infinite potential. All the varied gifts of those he touched merging and blossoming within him birthed a near-irresistible impression of invulnerability. What need had he of this mere dust when power like this was within his grasp? With this he could crush the Darkblade like a bug, rend his army to shreds, stride across the sea to the Merchant Realms and take them, make himself a king above all other kings, no longer obliged to suffer their jealousies and petty games, be more than a king, be a . . .

". . . god!"

The word emerged from between his gritted teeth as a furious hiss, accompanied by a surge of self-disgust only partially mitigated by realisation. *This is what Kehlbrand felt when he touched the stone. All the Gifted souls the Stahlhast priests had fed to the tiger over so many years; a huge reservoir of power. That was the tiger's true gift. The delusion of godhood made real. But I have never wanted to be a god.*

He plunged his hand into the dust, letting the accumulated power flow through him. The world turned to darkness as his hand slipped into the grains, but it was a darkness filled with stars. They surrounded him, pulsing and flaring as a chorus of voices assailed him, a vast chorus of countless memories amongst which it was impossible to discern individual words. *So many,* he thought, wonder and regret rising in his breast. *So many voices, so many lives to cast into the wind . . .*

A familiar snarl banished his reluctance, the stars shifting and coalescing, first into swirling clusters then into one vast multicoloured spiral. *Not just lives,* he thought, recalling Keeper's words. *The gifts they carried in life, waiting in the stone to be awoken one last time. All will be dust in the end.* The spiral of stars glowed brighter in places and dimmed in others, forming into something he recognised, something that stared back at him, something that knew him. It snarled again, a deafening sound that banished the darkness and left him reeling on the deck.

He saw the others still gathered in a circle, now grown considerably wider, all eyes not on him but on the air above where the dust had lain. It was gone now, raised up into an amorphous, slowly revolving cloud. At first it drifted in an almost serene manner, sparkling as its grains caught the morning sun, but still somehow remained immune to the wind. Then it shifted, twisting and stretching, a deep growl emerging from its depths, a growl that grew, gaining volume until every soul on deck clamped their hands to their ears, whereupon it became a howl.

The sound of it was so all-encompassing Vaelin was rendered momentarily senseless, robbed of sight and hearing for the space of a heartbeat, and when they returned he found himself staring into a pair of yellow eyes. He had time to register the wolf's size, at least twice as large as he had ever seen it before, and real. This was not some ghostly apparition or mist-formed phantom. Its claws stabbed deep into the deck boards and its drool glistened as it fell from bared teeth. It was as real as anything else in the world.

The wolf raised its snout, nostrils flaring as it caught a scent, blinked once, then leapt over him, streaking towards the prow and disappearing from sight. Vaelin drew his sword and ran in pursuit, catching a glimpse of Sherin's face as she looked up from Saikir. He saw fear there, but also the strength that sustained her and the compassion that made her cleave to some vestige of regard for him, despite the monster inside him, a monster he was about to unleash. Then he leapt clear of the rail and her face was gone, replaced by a scene of utter chaos.

CHAPTER THIRTY-ONE

The *Stormhawk*'s keel had only just met the hull of a sinking freighter when Vaelin leapt over her bow, obliging him to scramble up a steeply slanted deck upon landing. He took a second to steady himself before sprinting forward as a cacophony of splintering timber and snapped rigging told of a falling mast. As it crashed into the deck behind he turned to see Nortah, Alum and Ellese leaping down from the *Stormhawk*'s starboard rails whilst the Servants of the Temple followed suit to port. He didn't wait for them, vaulting onto the next deck and running after the wolf, ignoring the shout Nortah cast after him.

As he ran he was assailed by the harsh grind of ships scraping together whilst tilted masts collided like the massed pikes of contesting armies. The chorus of screams from directly ahead cut through it all, being so numerous and so loud. As he pursued the wolf he bore witness to the carnage wrought by its passage across this shifting wooden field. Masts toppled like felled trees and sailors clung to the edges of shattered hulls whilst others stumbled about, eyes wide and screams issuing from their gaping mouths in an unending, ugly parody of song. Curiously, he saw no wounds on these screamers save those they inflicted on themselves. He ran past a woman clawing at her eyes then leapt onto a neighbouring deck to find himself confronted by the dead features of a Tuhla warrior, frozen in the act of screaming as he impaled his head on his own lance.

The screams and the tumult of destruction drew him on, leaping the dead and the debris, sidestepping the mad until, finally, he caught sight of the wolf. It moved like a blur across the deck of a long-hulled warship with many oars, transforming it into a shambles of shattered rigging, every oar rendered in turn into matchwood. The crew either fled over the side or tried vainly to fight, the jabbing spears and hacking sabres making no impression on the wolf's hide, and every soul that raised a hand to it was left maddened and screaming in its wake. The mere touch of the wolf, it appeared, was enough to rend all reason from minds in thrall to the Darkblade.

But not all were mad. Twice Vaelin was forced to halt his pursuit to cut down Redeemed intent on slaying the Thief of Names. The few archers that had managed to cling to the rigging also chased him with arrows, though the constantly shifting decks and the repeated flares of warning from the black-song enabled him to dodge every shaft. Up ahead he saw the wolf land upon the mid-deck of a tall warship, scattering wreckage and warriors like chaff. The force of the impact pushed the warship away from its closest neighbour, creating a gap between it and the deck where Vaelin stood.

He could only stand and watch the wolf leap clear of the warship, bounding on as it made for the large vessel at the centre of the disordered fleet. It was barely three hundred paces away, but Vaelin could see a great many Redeemed, Tuhla and Stahlhast surging towards it from either side. They scrambled from ship to ship with frenzied desperation, many falling into the sea or pushed aside by their comrades in their haste. A few dozen had already created a barrier between the fast-approaching wolf and the spot where the Darkblade surely waited, a barrier that grew thicker by the second.

The wolf charged into their midst, flinging many aside, sending others stumbling away in screeching madness. But still more poured in on the wolf's flanks, heedless of the danger as the wolf thrashed and tried to plough its way through the throng. Vaelin heard the Darkblade's song again, still riven with fear and frustration, but also a grim sense of triumph at having snared the tiger's enemy.

"Careful, brother!" Nortah dragged him aside as an arrow streaked down from the rigging of the warship opposite, missing Vaelin by the width of a finger. Ellese's bow immediately thrummed in response, and Vaelin saw a figure tumble through the matrix of ropes to plummet through a rent in the partially shattered deck below.

"We need to get across," he said, his own frustration mounting at the sight of the wolf being mobbed by ever more of the Darkblade's horde, so many that it was almost lost to view beneath the piling bodies.

The harsh grind and snap of twisting wood came from behind. Vaelin and Nortah quickly stepped aside as the mainmast of the freighter they stood on descended, swiftly but gently, to bridge the gap to the warship. It sprouted limbs as it settled onto the opposite deck, branches spreading and entwining themselves around the warship's masts and fittings, drawing it closer.

"Best hurry," Zhuan-Kai said, and Vaelin turned to see him palming the slick of blood from his nose and mouth. "He'll soon forget he's no longer a tree."

Vaelin paused before stepping onto the mast, taking the purse containing the gold nuggets from his belt and tossing it to Nortah. "Don't get greedy," he told him, starting across. "I'll want it back."

After he'd sprinted over the newly crafted bridge, the black-song rose with expectant ferocity, shouting with exultance as Vaelin hacked down three Redeemed who broke from the mob to bar his path. It wasn't as dominant now, filling him enough to guide his sword and warn of imminent danger, but still allowing full range of his senses. Parrying a lance thrust from a Tuhla, he heard a new note to the song when the Order blade sliced deep into his leg, a tone of mutual understanding. Today, it seemed, he and the song shared common purpose and it felt no need to seclude his mind from what it wrought.

He hurled himself into the mob, sword thrusting and hacking in a manner that matched swiftness with lethal accuracy as the song guided it unerringly to unarmoured or exposed flesh. He was aware of Ellese's arrows repeatedly flicking past to bury themselves in the throng, Nortah and Alum hacking away to his left. Off to the right, Zhuan-Kai's staff lashed out to snap necks and legs whilst the blades of Mi-Hahn, Cho-ka and the other Servants of the Temple rose and fell like a shimmering curtain to cut deep into the densely packed wall of bodies. Despite their efforts and the corpses and severed limbs piling up at their feet, he knew it wasn't enough. *Too many*, he thought stabbing his sword point through the eye of a gibbering Redeemed who lashed at him with clawed, skinless hands.

Above the frenzy of it all he could hear the Darkblade's song, its note of triumph keener now, shot through with the anticipation of looming victory.

Vaelin stepped back from the fray, letting his own song blossom, knowing Kehlbrand could hear the challenge in it. *Face me. We'll finish this. You and me.*

The Darkblade, however, replied with a taunting lilt to his song, rich in amusement. *Why bother? This will soon be over. But, Thief of Names, I do thank you for bringing me my sister.*

The black-song surged with a fresh crescendo of hate, a feral snarl rising on Vaelin's tongue as he prepared to throw himself back into the struggle, determined to carve a tunnel through the mass of flesh if he had to, then pausing as a curious hissing roar sounded from above.

The fireball arced down to explode in the centre of the mob, birthing an instant inferno and setting at least a score of Redeemed and Stahlhast alight. Another followed an instant later, bathing the rear of the mob in flame. Heat blasted Vaelin's face as yet more fireballs came streaking down, thick and oily smoke enveloping the scene.

"Back!" Nortah yelled, dragging him away as the barrage continued. Flaming figures ran through the smoke on all sides, some still possessing enough devotion to the Darkblade to continue fighting. "Oh, just die, you mad bastards!" Nortah grunted, ducking the axe swing of a large Stahlhast warrior, his armour and hair alight, then laying open his throat with a lateral slash of his sword.

Vaelin peered through the smoke, blinking against the acrid sting assaulting his eyes until he saw the signature bulk of the *Sea Empress* rising above the chaos of masts to the east. As he watched, the catapult on her fore-deck launched another fireball, the pirate ships on either side adding their own projectiles to the barrage. Dozens of blazing missiles arced high then plummeted down on the already burnt but still somehow resolute throng, birthing an explosion that sent Vaelin and Nortah sprawling.

When Vaelin rose, coughing, he saw Nortah and Ellese desperately try-ing to smother the flames covering Alum's back. Rushing to them, Vaelin added his hands to the effort, swatting the flames away and tearing off the sparse leather armour the Moreska preferred over steel. He jerked in their grasp, yelling through clenched teeth, smoke still rising from the raw, charred flesh extending from his upper back to the crown of his head.

An ear-straining growl and an accompanying shout from the black-song compelled Vaelin's gaze to the remnants of the mob, seeing a large shape emerge from the mound of burnt and twitching bodies. The wolf shook itself, casting corpses and debris from its fur like leaves. It started forward at a slow walk, hackles raised and head lowered. Standing directly in its path was a tall figure in black and silver armour with a large number of Stahlhast at his back. Beyond them Vaelin saw another figure tied to a wooden frame set alongside a black stone on a raised platform.

With a snarl the wolf launched itself forward, jaws snapping, only to rear back as the Darkblade slashed his sabre across its snout. The blade drew no blood, but Vaelin saw a deep rent appear in the wolf's fur-covered flesh. The wound leaked dust for a moment as the wolf retreated, shaking its head in confusion. When it crouched again, Vaelin could tell it had been diminished, the substance of it denuded, made less real somehow. The wolf bared its teeth and darted forward once more, its charge halted as Kehlbrand, moving with the speed and precision that only came from use of a song, hacked a portion of fur and flesh from its foreleg. More dust rose and slipped away on the wind, leaving the wolf again lessened in size, the extremities of its form becoming less defined. No other soul in this fleet could even scratch the wolf, but thanks to the song given to him by the tiger in the stone, the Darkblade could.

"Stay with him," Vaelin told Ellese and Nortah, rising from Alum's side. He scrambled over the smoking ridge of burning and squirming bodies, seeing the wolf rear back from another slash of Kehlbrand's sabre. Vaelin wasted no time in voicing a challenge, charging across the thirty paces that separated them with a wordless cry emerging from his throat as he allowed the black-song free rein. It was enough to get his enemy's attention.

Their blades met and rebounded with a loud clang, Vaelin pausing for a brief second to take satisfaction from the sight of Kehlbrand Reyerik's face. There were no sardonic grins or knowingly arched eyebrows now, no amusement glimmering in his eyes. Instead they glowed with hate, and the mottled flesh of his face quivered with the rage of a peerlessly arrogant soul finding itself thwarted.

"Hardly a godly aspect!" Vaelin grunted, bringing the sword up and down towards Kehlbrand's head. He wore no helm, and the prospect of seeing this false god's skull cleaved open brought an ecstatic trill from the black-song. Vaelin felt Kehlbrand's song shout a warning, and his sabre came up in a blur, driving the Order blade aside before he thrust at Vaelin's neck.

He twisted aside, whirling and crouching low to slash at Kehlbrand's legs, but once again his song enabled him to leap the blur of steel.

"YOU!" he shouted, the words emerging in a cloud of spittle as he gripped his sabre's hilt in two hands and hacked repeatedly at Vaelin's head. "ARE! NOT! SUPPOSED! TO! BE! HERE!"

Vaelin didn't retreat from the assault, instead dodging in a circle, allowing every stroke to miss him by mere inches. He could feel Kehlbrand's song becoming more discordant by the second, fed by its owner's rage, a rage he hoped would soon make him deaf to its meaning. He flicked a cut at Kehlbrand's outstretched arm, once again failing to connect but forcing him to abandon his attacks, voicing his anguish in a snarl as Vaelin heard his song descend into a confusion of rage.

Vaelin ducked low, feinting by allowing their blades to collide before drawing his down then up in a blurring slash at Kehlbrand's face. He managed to jerk his head back in time to avoid a killing blow, but not before the Order blade had scored a deep cut from jaw to brow, slicing through Kehlbrand's right eye in the process.

The black-song's shriek of exultant victory was so loud it threatened to rob Vaelin of his senses, even as it guided the sword towards the now-exposed neck of the Darkblade. He staggered clear of the thrust, spraying blood and gibbering incoherent rage, his sabre flailing about in a useless semblance of a parry. The black-song's shriek, however, abruptly shifted into a growl of warning before Vaelin could deliver another blow. He swayed back, the gleaming steel of a double-bladed axe slicing the air above his nose. The Stahlhast who wielded it continued to whirl, bringing the axe around again in an attempt to bury it in Vaelin's midriff. Something dark flickered at the edge of his vision accompanied by the now-familiar snap and grind of Zhuan-Kai's staff. One end had been moulded into something that resembled a huge, gnarled fist, which transformed the axe-wielder's skull into a compressed ruin despite the helm he wore.

As he fell, the other Stahlhast surged forward, some trying to place themselves between Vaelin and their god, others charging at the Thief of Names. Vaelin cut down two as they closed, each with a single song-guided stroke of his sword, the charge of their comrades coming to an abrupt halt as the Servants of the Temple rushed to meet them. He saw Cho-ka and Mi-Hahn fighting back-to-back, swords blurring like steel whips whilst Zhuan-Kai moved through the Stahlhast like a whirlwind, staff lashing like a cobra one second then hardening into a club to crush skulls and ribs the next.

Through the confusion, Vaelin caught sight of Kehlbrand being hauled to his feet by a Stahlhast before he struggled free of her grasp, cutting her down with frenzied strokes of his sabre. Vaelin started forward, driven by another joyous peel from the black-song, clearly delighted by the prospect of prolonging the Darkblade's end. He would hack each of his limbs off in turn, cut away the plates of his armour and torment his flesh with a thousand wounds. He would slice his guts open and laugh as this pitiful god wept at the spectacle of his own demise . . .

The song's joy ended as a large shadow passed overhead. The wolf still trailed dust as it leapt over the melee, reduced in size but retaining enough substance to scatter the few Stahlhast guarding the black stone when it landed in their midst. Vaelin watched it pause for a second to sniff the man tied to the wooden frame then lick his face with a quick dart of its tongue. With that it turned its full attention to the black stone, circling it, jaws quivering and teeth bared. It began to move faster, blurring as it gained speed, transforming into a silver-grey whirlwind that slowly began to constrict around the stone. The whirlwind's speed increased, tightening all the while until there came a final spasm of power birthing a thunderclap of displaced air that sent every soul within sight of it sprawling. Vaelin staggered but managed to remain upright, watching the now-glowing whirlwind as it seemed to merge with the black stone.

Vaelin had to shield his eyes from the brightness of the explosion, hearing the whistle of shards streaking through the air too fast to follow accompanied by the hard thwack of some striking armour and flesh. When he turned his gaze to the platform once more, no trace of the black stone remained. Instead, it was occupied only by the bound man and the prone form of a wolf, chest heaving in exhaustion.

Looking around, Vaelin saw most of the Stahlhast either lying slain or wounded, those still on their feet stumbling around in dazed confusion. Many wore the faces of those woken from a long, nightmarish slumber. Others appeared bereft to the point of madness, dropping their weapons to throw themselves from the warship's deck, a few sinking to their knees and weeping even as they drew daggers across their wrists or throats. One figure, however, knelt in a semblance of quiet contemplation, head lowered and appearing almost serene but for the blood streaming from the deep gash in his face.

The black-song thrummed with anticipation as Vaelin strode towards him, shoving aside the maddened or confused, none of whom were inclined to oppose him. *His fingers first*, the song cooed, sending waves of hunger through Vaelin's breast as he came to a halt before the man who had been a god only moments before. *One by one*, the song sang. *Then flay him, peel his skin away slowly, oh so slowly . . .*

The tumult of many raised voices and boots pounding on timber drew his gaze to the eastern arm of the sprawl of ships. A swarm of pirates was descending by rope from their taller vessels to join the several hundred others already rampaging across the mangled and overlapping decks of the Darkblade's vanquished fleet. Further north, Imperial ships were disgorging the Amber Regiments in a more orderly manner. Both forces advanced across the undulating wooden plain, sweeping away what little opposition they encountered from a few knots of Stahlhast or Tuhla, fighting, he assumed, out of desperation rather than fealty. The surviving Redeemed put up no resistance and milled about in shocked bewilderment, many stumbling into the sea or sinking to their knees to voice the abject madness of a bereft fanatic. The Darkblade's horde had lost its god.

Looking down at the kneeling form of Kehlbrand Reyerik, Vaelin felt no tune of recognition, no inkling that this was anything other than a man. No gifts. No blessings. No divinity. No song.

Quickly, the black-song's music urged as the Amber Regiments and the pirates swept ever closer. *Duhlan will claim him, or the emperor. He is ours.*

"You were right," Vaelin said, causing Kehlbrand to look up, sundered face and remaining eye displaying no emotion. "It was like fighting a child."

The black-song howled as he turned away, rising to a dangerous volume that caused him to stumble. Hearing a laugh he looked back, finding Kehlbrand regarding him with a sorrowful, almost regretful grin. "So," he said, the movement of his face causing a fresh cascade of blood to seep from his wound, "you think you saved them from me." His grin broadened, the sorrow in it giving way to a leering, depthless hate. "You're a fool, Thief of Names. I was saving them from y—"

Luralyn's dagger took him under the chin, the blow delivered with enough force to drive the blade up into his brain. Vaelin watched his eye roll back as she dragged the blade free, making sure to sever the larger veins in the process. She stood back as her brother's body slumped onto its side. Her face, besmirched by smoke and a spattering of blood, remained impassive, but Vaelin did see a small tear rise in her eye before she blinked it away.

"They will hate us for generations," she said, voice faint and hoarse. "The Stahlhast, for what he had us do. But at least it will be known that he fell to a Stahlhast blade in the end." Eresa came forward to take the dagger from her hand, and Luralyn pulled her into a tight embrace, her tears finally starting to flow.

Vaelin turned and picked his way through the still or writhing bodies to the platform, ascending the steps to regard the man bound to the frame. He knew this man's face, and his eyes, even though they belonged to two separate souls. The bound man offered Vaelin a grimace of greeting, features bleached and lips pale, the skin of his bare torso marked by many torments. "It seems," Obvar said, his voice little more than a whispering croak, "you get to kill me twice."

Glancing at the wolf lying close by, its form growing less substantial by the second, Vaelin recalled how it had paused to bless this man with its tongue, something, he knew, it had done before to a much more worthy soul. But who was he now to judge the worthiness of others?

"We are both children of the wolf," he said, drawing his dagger and severing the bonds around Obvar's wrists and shoulders. "And once was enough."

He left Obvar gasping on his hands and knees and went to the wolf, crouching to run a hand through its fur. It felt like gossamer, his mere touch birthing another tendril of dust to be scattered by the wind. It raised its head, regarding him with eyes that were no longer angry, the snarl vanished from its maw. Now all he felt from it was a great sense of age and weariness, plus a feeling of finality that brought a deep ache to his chest.

"Will I ever see you again?" he asked.

The wolf just blinked and lay back. There was a sound like a great many voices whispering at once, and the wolf slipped into a formless shadow that glittered as it twisted in the rising breeze to be borne away, subliming into a few dark wisps. As he rose to watch the last remnants vanish on the wind, his eye caught the familiar rectangle of a sail on the north-western horizon. It was soon joined by more, a wide procession that told of an entire fleet.

"Transcendent traitors," a gruff voice commented at his side. General Duhlan undid the clasp on his helm, removing it to reveal sweaty features. "Come to finish us off, I'd guess."

His armour bore the stains of recent battle, but from the determined, almost eager glint in his eye, Vaelin deduced he didn't feel he had had his fill for the day. Beyond him, Vaelin saw Tsai Lin standing in silent contemplation of the Darkblade's corpse as Sehtaku and soldiers of the Amber Regiments went about the grim business of methodically slaughtering the few surviving Stahlhast and Redeemed nearby.

"That isn't necessary," Vaelin told him, inclining his head to the killings. "Their god is gone, and I'd hazard many now have no notion of why they ever followed him."

"Gone or not, an accounting has to be made," Duhlan grunted. "Besides, can't leave them alive with another battle in the offing."

A small, sulky murmur from the black-song drew Vaelin's gaze to the eastern horizon where another procession of sails had appeared. At first he assumed it to be the rear guard of Ell-Nestra's fleet, or perhaps the slower Imperial ships, but then he noticed the size of the vessel in the lead, at least a match for the *Sea Empress* if not larger. It was too far off to make out the banner flying from her topmast, but he had no doubt it bore the sigil of the Greater Unified Realm.

"This war has just ended," he told Duhlan, meeting his gaze squarely to leave no doubt of his intent. "Now order an end to this slaughter or you will have another battle to fight, and it won't be with the Transcendent Fleet."

The general's face bunched in anger but a small twitch below his eye told of a harder realisation. Even a man whose pride matched his courage knew the certainty of death when he saw it. "It will be my honour," he said, "to suggest to the emperor that the first law of his reign should be the immediate exile of all foreigners, for they are clearly a pestilence upon our people."

He turned about and marched off, voice raised in command. "Sergeant, that's enough! Gather them up and take their weapons. And find some rope, a lot of it."

Vaelin went in search of Nortah and the others, finding them at the warship's bows clustered around Sherin as she ministered to Alum. He was mostly insensible thanks to the drugs she had made him drink, the burns on his back and head made glossy by the salve she applied.

"I would have healed him," she said, looking up at Vaelin with tired but guilty eyes. "But Saikir took so much . . ."

"I know," Vaelin said, peering at Alum's slack features. "Will he live?"

"With time and the right care. The scars, though." She gave a helpless shrug.

"Is it done, Uncle?" Ellese asked, nodding to the ships on the horizon. She held her bow ready even though her quiver was empty.

"It's done." Her eyes widened in surprise as he enfolded her in an embrace, pulling her close and trying to banish the catch in his voice that came from knowing he would probably never do so again. "We're going home, you see. Your mother's here."

PART IV

*If ever a man avows a desire for power, ask this of him,
"Have you friends?"*

If his answer is "No," then power is not for him.

If his answer is "Yes, I have many," then power is not for him.

*If his answer is "All the world is my friend, and I am a friend to
all the world," then power is for him, for he is both wise and a liar.*

—FROM "THE EMPEROR'S WISDOM—THE INSIGHTS OF TSAI LIN
THE GREAT, FIRST EMPEROR OF THE JADE EMPIRE"

Obvar's Account

All these years later I find there are few certainties left to me, a facility for end-less conjecture on doubtful remembrance being both the curse and the blessing of the old. But those certainties that linger are inarguable in their truth, the one that springs most readily to mind as I compose this account being that the man known to history as Tsai Lin the Great, First Jade Emperor and Exalted Chosen of Heaven, fully intended to kill me from the moment Al Sorna cut my bonds that day.

There are so many songs, odes and histories regarding the Battle of Tokira that adding yet another to these pages is surely a redundant exercise, even though I saw it all. I saw Kehlbrand finally succumb to madness when the wave sundered his fleet. I saw the destruction it wrought and the thousands it cast into the depths. I saw the Darkblade's duel with the man the Imperial scholars record only as "a certain foreign mercenary who did good service in the emperor's cause." And I saw the wolf.

Kehlbrand had been very keen to keep me alive to witness his final tri-umph, but, of course, that didn't mean I should be spared his judgement. Wak-ing to find myself somehow still drawing breath after killing our saddle brothers and suffering the attentions of the Redeemed had been a less-than-pleasant surprise. Kehlbrand, unfortunately, had found a Divinely Blooded healer amongst his vast collection of captives, a wizened, frail old wretch whose gift seemed at odds with the leering sadism I saw in his gaze. His power to heal, you see, was conjoined with the power to inflict pain. So, as he closed wounds, knitted bones back together and banished bruises both internal and external, he extracted a great deal of pain as his reward. It took days of this creature's attentions to return me to full health, all of it spent chained to a bed in Kehlbrand's tent palace where my screams echoed loud and long through vacant canvas halls. Fortuitously, whoever secured the chain had left it a few inches longer than it needed to be. Crushing the healer's twig-thin neck with it, after he had banished the last bruise from my skin, was all too brief an experience, but satisfying nonetheless.

Kehlbrand's rage at this murder was only marginally less than that provoked by my betrayal. I was beaten to senselessness and woke to discover I had been secured to a wooden frame at the side of his throne. He would sit receiving reports from servants and never once spare me a single glance throughout the many tortures inflicted upon my flesh. First there came men with whips, then men with very long needles skilled in finding nerves, then others with small flat irons they heated to a white glow before pressing to my skin. It would be a lie to record that I remained resolute in my defiance throughout this, for no man could. I screamed, I soiled myself in fear and agony and I begged whilst the man who I had once called brother refused to acknowledge my continued existence.

Yet, he still needed me. He was by then utterly friendless, shorn of family, shorn of every soul he had known as a child on the Steppe. Now all he had were those who worshipped or feared him, and most did both. He kept me with him, I believe, as a vestige of the true friendship he had lost, a reminder that the Darkblade had not always been a god. So, everywhere he travelled I went with him, carried upon my frame and kept alive through copious doses of foul-tasting medicines and the sustenance the guards forced down my throat. I was there to witness him draw ever more souls into the shadow of the Darkblade's love, swelling the ranks of the horde to its greatest number. I was there when the ambassador from the Transcendent Kingdom came to grovel out his master's acceptance of the terms Kehlbrand had dictated. And I was there the day his great fleet chained itself together to await the morning tide and renew its assault on the Free Cantons. This was to be the last day I ever heard his voice, for it was at the rise of dawn when he finally deigned to speak to me.

"It wasn't just the nun, was it, old friend?" he asked.

He stood atop the platform he had constructed on the deck of this warship, chosen by virtue of its size to carry the Darkblade on his voyage to victory. He stared out at the broad circle of tethered ships, flawless black and silver armour gleaming in the sun and long dark hair streaming from his face, still unscarred after all these years of war. The black stone sat to my right. It had become his habit to rarely place himself at a remove from this thing. It would be carted along during his increasingly brief forays into his wider realm, and he slept alongside it every night. Therefore, when it came time to set out upon this triumphant venture, it was inevitable that the stone would come too. I had been spared fresh torments for a few days so possessed more reason than was usual, enough to ponder whether I detested his presence more than my proximity to the black stone. It may have been a result of being placed in this body, some residual dread from my time beyond the wall of death, but being so close to the stone brought on a sense of fear and nausea sufficient to birth a tremble in my confined limbs.

"No need to shake so," Kehlbrand said, stooping to peer into my face. "It's merely a question, but I will have an answer. It wasn't just your unmanly attachment to that nun that made you betray me. Was it the man whose face you wear, I wonder? He's still in there somewhere, isn't he?"

I blinked swollen eyes and answered in a weary sigh, the ability to beg or plead having been driven from me weeks before. "Yes, part of him lingers, but that wasn't why. It wasn't Mai either, but she began it."

A frown of apparently genuine curiosity creased his brow. "How so?"

"Her eyes. At first there was just fear and distrust, as there should have been. But later, when she looked at me, in her eyes for once I was more than just your dog."

"Ah." His brows rose in understanding, a sad smile coming to his lips. "But what a fine dog you were, Obvar. The best of dogs, in fact. Until you chose to bite me. But don't worry." He turned about, eyes fixed on the land visible through the haze above the southern horizon. "I'll still have use for you, once you've been properly whipped. Luralyn will need a guard, a watcher. You'd like that, wouldn't you? I shall have to take your tongue, though. I don't think it would do for you two to converse."

A flurry of shouts from the warship's port side drew his gaze away. I craned my neck to make out the sight of a procession of ships dotting the sea beyond the gently swaying masts of the fleet. "So," Kehlbrand murmured, "the emperor decided not to wait. But, is he there, I wonder . . ."

He trailed off then, gaze abruptly shifting to the south, narrowing as he

searched the shoreline. My partially dimmed vision revealed nothing of interest until it alighted upon a lone ship, approaching so fast it appeared to leap
through the water.

"There," Kehlbrand breathed. "There he is, Obvar. I can't sense him but
who else could it be? But I can sense her. He brought Luralyn. A peace offering,
perhaps?" He gave a harsh, disdainful laugh, a laugh that choked to an abrupt
halt.

Imperial chroniclers have ascribed the wave that destroyed fully half the
Darkblade's ships to the Divine Hand of Heaven, reaching down in its boundless beneficence to gift victory to its chosen emperor. The truth is less widely
known, or believed, and needs little elaboration here. The events that followed
the wave's impact on the fleet remain a hazy mélange in my increasingly unre-
liable memory. There were screams, flames, battle and slaughter, I know that
much. But some things remain clear. Before he went to confront his end, Kehlbrand paused to share more words with me, and when he did, the face I looked
upon was that of a stranger.

The countenance of the man who had once been my friend and brother
had vanished long since, replaced by the malice and cruel humour of the
Darkblade. Now even that was gone. The man I beheld was as frightened and
despairing a soul as I ever saw. Also, I discerned from the unfocused gleam in
his eyes and the thin, whispering quaver that emerged from his lips, fully
insane. "He comes, old friend. I thought . . . I thought it was my mission to
make myself a god. But that was a lie . . . I see it now. I was created to stop him.
He is the true threat to this world . . ."

The rest of my memories of this event are a mangled collage of sensation
and images that may or may not be real. I recall the wolf, thinking at first that
it may have been some formless thing conjured by the Servants of the Temple.
But real it was, and I remember the touch of its tongue before the stone
exploded, a touch that seeped into me from skin to bone to whatever lies
beneath. Deep inside me the vestige of the man who had been Sho Tsai felt that
touch and, with gratitude, slipped forever into the void. I think I recall seeing
Kehlbrand die at his sister's hand, though she insists she stabbed him rather
than dousing him in oil and setting him alight. But, as I contended earlier, the
most real and true memory that survives is the intent upon the face of the
emperor when I looked up at him after Al Sorna cut my bonds.

I had never seen this youth before, except in the memories I shared with

Sho Tsai. Now those were vague, lingering like the faintest echoes. Even so, I knew instantly who he was. The eyes, the bearing, the set of his face. This was a king, an emperor, soon to be the only monarch left in the lands once known as the Merchant Realms. And he wanted very badly to kill me.

"You," he said, fingers flexing on the handle of his sword, "are not him."

"No . . . I am not," I agreed, the words emerging in a soft sigh as I sat back on my haunches. I met his gaze and didn't look away, deciding I had displayed enough cowardice recently. "He died," I added. "My condolences."

I saw the emperor war with himself then, the desire to expunge the abomination that my existence represented vying with an instinctive reluctance that came only from the fact that I wore the face of the father he had loved. In the end, he was spared the final decisive act, even though, now as then, I harbour no doubts that he would have performed it.

"Tsai Lin!"

The woman known as the Healing Grace strode towards us, the cheeks of her face hollow with near exhaustion, although this didn't cause her stride to falter nor diminish the tone with which she addressed the emperor. It was a scolding tone, the voice of a parent to a misbehaving child, which, to my great surprise, actually caused the emperor to retreat a step.

"This man is hurt and requires help," she snapped, crouching to help me up, assisted by a blond-haired foreigner who wore a markedly less compassionate expression. Nevertheless, he duly hooked my arm across his shoulders and dragged me away, hectored all the while by the Healing Grace.

"It appears . . ." I groaned to her, "I have more cuts for you to stitch."

The gaze she turned on me was wide with a desperate pitch of scrutiny, her eyes searching mine with an intense need I found painful to confront. What she searched for was gone.

"Mai . . ." I said, head lolling as a wave of utter weariness dragged me into a slumber from which I would be fortunate to wake. "I would . . . very much . . . like to see Mai . . ."

◆ ◆ ◆

I learned later there had been talk of punishment, or rather a correct and proper administration of the emperor's justice. I was, after all, none other than once-mighty Obvar, albeit confined within a stolen body. I had been at Kehlbrand's side throughout his initial conquests and done foul deeds in his name. In the guise of General Sho Tsai I had helped plan his conquest of two realms, resulting in great destruction and suffering. Upon being called to the emperor's presence, however, I was spared by personal appeals from the Healing Grace and one Mai Wehn, no longer a Servant of Heaven but still enjoying a great deal of respect from her former brethren, chief amongst them the new abbot of the Temple of Spears. Al Sorna also spoke for me, though from the chilled atmosphere in the emperor's chambers that day I find it doubtful his word held much sway.

"Your words are welcome as always, Lord Vaelin," Tsai Lin said, somewhat tonelessly as Al Sorna bowed. The emperor's gaze lingered only briefly on him before sliding to me. His expression was mostly blank but for a suppressed shudder that would probably never fade as long as he was obliged to look upon the face I wore.

"This one will be permitted to live," he said. "Where and in what manner will be decided later." He forced a smile and turned his attention to the woman at Al Sorna's side. She could easily have been mistaken for Stahlhast with the athleticism of her bearing and hair the colour of polished bronze, yet she spoke in a tongue only few present could understand. "For now, we must discuss these missives from your queen." Tsai Lin's hand played upon the letters on the tray at his side, elegantly inscribed in the script of the Merchant Realms. "Brought to us by her most excellent ambassador."

The bronze-haired woman listened to Al Sorna's translation before replying with a bow of her own. It was a stiff and awkward gesture, speaking of one with little liking for ceremony. Also, her rigid features told of a creditable suspicion of this place and everyone in it, not to say a deep desire to be elsewhere.

"However," Tsai Lin went on, slipping smoothly into the tongue of Al Sorna's barbarian homeland, "they appear to be addressed to a king who now lies dead amidst the ruins of his capital."

The bronze-haired woman betrayed only a slight surprise at hearing her own language before replying, "Word flies slowly across so broad an ocean, Highness. I assure you future correspondence from my queen will bear the correct forms of address."

"I have no doubt of it, honoured lady. I will personally compose a response that I hope you will convey to your queen with all despatch, there being many matters arising between us that require speedy resolution. Also, I have little doubt our foreign friends greatly desire to return home as soon as possible. Am I not correct, Lord Vaelin?"

"Quite correct, Highness," Al Sorna assured him with a bow. "Our queen's ships will depart, with your permission, on the morning tide."

I doubt anyone noticed my small sigh of amusement then, my distracting person having been consigned to the rear of the chamber. It did draw a questioning glance from Mai, however, who I placated with a vague shake of my head.

"Excellent!" Tsai Lin slapped the arms of his throne and got briskly to his feet. "As for tonight, you will be my most honoured guest. A feast the like of which, I am assured, has not been seen in the Free Cantons for generations has been prepared. Lady Reva of Cumbrael, I most humbly beg you take your place at my side."

◆ ◆ ◆

So I was allowed my life and to be permitted a scant few hours with Mai and the children, under the watchful eye of a substantial guard of Imperial soldiers, until Luralyn sought me out. The hour was late and she was accompanied by the Divinely Blooded former slave girl and a few monks and nuns from the Temple of Spears.

"We can't stay here," Luralyn told me in a brisk voice. I took note of the brief but wary glance she cast at the onlooking Imperial soldiers. "Nor can Mai and the children. Pack your things; the emperor has given us leave to depart. Best if we do so before less charitable souls persuade him otherwise."

We were escorted to the harbour of Jaigan-Shu where the surviving Stahlhast were arrayed along the wharf in chains. Counting them briefly, I found that there were barely enough to fill the war bands of two Skeld. "Most who lived through the battle were left mad," Luralyn explained, seeing the grimness of my expression. "Unable to even feed themselves. So it was with the Redeemed. The emperor granted them mercy."

"What will happen to them?" I asked, surveying the array of downcast faces, finding no more than a handful even vaguely familiar. Still, I did see some fortitude there, glowering defiance contesting with the shame of captivity. They were, at least, still Stahlhast in spirit.

"They belong to me," Luralyn said. "The emperor's reward for my service. We're going home, Obvar. All of us."

"Home? You mean the Steppe?"

"Yes." Her eyes narrowed as I let out a small laugh.

"I never told you, but Kehlbrand once had me touch the stone," I said, moving closer, voice lowered to a murmur. "It's how he was able to put me in this body. I can hear lies, Luralyn. And you just told a very big one."

She looked out at the ships in the harbour, the pirate vessels that had been paid handsomely to take us home, Imperial ships who refused to sully their decks with our presence, and the less familiar and much taller hulls of the foreign fleet that had arrived to scare away the Transcendent ships at the moment of the Darkblade's defeat. "Kehlbrand's great mistake was to forget that we are a people of the land," she said, "born to the Iron Steppe and bred to the saddle. We were never meant for war at sea. Taking and holding the northern provinces, however, was always well within our grasp."

I raised a curious eyebrow. "Taking and holding?"

"Although we won it at terrible cost, the fact remains that the Stahlhast now possess a huge swath of the north, from Keshin-Ghol to the eastern mountains and the coast. An empire of our own, an empire full of people who believe they were conquered by a god."

"And who better to rule them than the sister of a god?"

Her gaze grew sharp. "I never wanted to rule anything. All I ever wanted was to preserve our people and those I grew to call family, those we once enslaved. Now they are free and the Stahlhast no longer under the yoke of the priests or a false god. Together they could do great things, but only if they remain strong enough to stand against those who will surely come to regain what they lost. Tsai Lin will consolidate his power here then retake the Enlightened Kingdom. War with the Transcendent Kingdom will surely follow, and once triumphant, he will turn his gaze to the remnants of the Enlightened Realm and what lies beyond. The Kingdom of the North will need a general, Obvar. A general with the soul of a Stahlhast but the face those born to the borderlands will see as one of their own."

She looked at Mai and the children, Uhlkar and Saikir embracing the Healing Grace as she made her farewells. Saikir wept openly, clinging to the foreign woman's robe until Mai tugged him away. Uhlkar, as ever, was more reserved but did manage to conjure a smile as she knelt to pull him close. Nai Lian, the princess without a kingdom, stood off to the side, happily playing with her tiger-headed doll, although I did notice how she occasionally looked around with eyes that seemed much more knowing than a child's should be.

"And we'll need those with the Divine Blood," Luralyn added. "If we linger here much longer Tsai Lin's appreciation of their abilities may well overcome his compassionate impulses. And you know Mai will never leave them behind."

"I see you've acquired your brother's gift for manipulation," I observed, bringing a faint, shameful flush to her face before she straightened, fixing me with a commanding stare.

"Stay here and await an uncertain fate," she said. "Or come with me and build something worth preserving. The choice is yours."

"I think I preferred you when you were always on the verge of stabbing me," I muttered, moving past her to approach the ragged parade of chained captives. Spying one who had slumped to her haunches, staring miserably at the ground, I lunged forward, dragging her upright.

"Stand up!" I demanded, seeing her blink in surprise at the sound of her own language. "Are you Stahlhast or are you a dog?"

She blinked again before habitual aggression took hold. "I am no dog!" she spat, shaking herself loose. "Get your fucking hands off me!"

This brought an incensed growl from the other captives, chains jangling as they stirred, every face darkening as I stood back in satisfaction. Scanning each angry, unwashed visage, I knew that these had never succumbed to the Darkblade's love. Somehow, throughout it all, they had never fallen to the lure that snared so many of their kin, hence their lack of madness now the false god had fallen. Still, they had followed him, or rather followed their Skeld because they were Stahlhast who had been promised a march to the sea since birth.

"That's better," I said, jerking my head at the ships arrayed along the wharf. "See these? They're going to take us home, at least those of us willing to swear fealty to new Mestra Skeltir, the Queen of the Northlands. Any who don't will be left here to have their throats cut when these southland fuckers can be bothered to do so, and that's if they don't work you to death in their fields."

There was a fair amount of discussion, some of it violent, and a good deal of grumbling, but in time they all duly trooped onto the ships without exception. And that is where it began; the Great Northern Kingdom was born on a dock thousands of miles from its borders. All the greatness to come, all the wars we fought and cities we built started there with the sister of a slain god, a dead man in a stolen body and a few hundred chained captives clinging to the hope they might once again ride across the Steppe and regain a measure of renown. But that, honoured reader, is a story that sits outside the pages of this account, which has but one more tale to tell.

As I began to follow Luralyn up the gangway, I turned at the sound of a familiar voice. "Sho?"

The Healing Grace stood a few paces away, hands bunched at her sides and much the same desperation on her face as when she helped me away from the emperor's blade. Once, I knew, the sight of her face would have stirred a great many memories, and an ache to my shared heart that would be hard to bear. Even now, when those memories were just distant glimmers of a different life, it hurt to look upon her.

"I'm sorry," I said, shaking my head.

She came closer, eyes tracing over every scar, wrinkle and pore of my face. "Is there nothing . . . ?" she began, features tense with an implacable need to know, even though she surely dreaded the answer. "Is there no part of him left?"

I could have told her of the faint echoes that lingered, the depth of love Sho Tsai had felt for her loudest amongst them. But that would have been cruel, and I found I was beyond cruelty now. "There's nothing," I said. "He lingered for a time after I woke, but he's gone now."

She reached out to grasp my hand, pressing the palm to her face. The sigh that escaped her lips was as rich in sorrow as it was in need, and I felt a very faint whisper of familiar joy from deep within this body at the warmth of her flesh. She shuddered and closed her eyes, holding my hand in place for the space of just one more heartbeat before unclasping and turning away. She hugged herself tight, head sagging and slender shoulders jerking as she surrendered to her pain.

"I can't return him to you," I said, filled with a sudden urge to assuage her grief. Mercy is weakness, compassion is cowardice, I chided myself, but these were old lies now, the empty and best forgotten dogma of naive children. Whatever Kehlbrand had wrought upon us, at the very least he had ensured the Stahlhast were no longer children. "Too much was ripped away when I was forced into this shell. Were I to leave it, whatever remained would be . . ."

"I know." Her voice was harsh, thick with tears as it slipped into a whisper. "Just an echo of a man already dead."

"Yes, an echo, but one that sings loud enough for me to know that he would want you to return to your life, be a healer again, live in peace once more."

She raised her head, breathing deep and wiping her eyes before turning back to me. "I can never go home, not with the gift I carry. Besides"—her eyes roamed my stolen face once more, not searching now, just sad—"I don't think I could risk the chance that I might ever see you again."

She tore her gaze from mine and began to walk away, back straight and face set with purpose. "Wait," I said and she stopped, still keeping her eyes averted. "I also carry a gift," I told her. "Small and weak next to yours perhaps, but it has its uses."

Her face was guarded as she forced herself to look at me. "What gift?"

I began to smile but it froze on my lips. A smile from this face would cut her worse than a blade. "Lies," I said. "I can hear lies."

CHAPTER THIRTY-TWO

I didn't expect her to be completely safe when I sent her to you, but neither did I expect you to drag her halfway across the world to fight a
war."

He felt it would be wrong to think of Reva as having aged in the years
since he had last seen her, so vital and commanding had she become. The
many who gathered at the docks to watch her descend from the huge bulk of
the *King Malcius* could be forgiven for assuming her to be the fabled Fire
Queen of the Barbarous East herself. But, for all her vitality and the no-
longer-girlish shape of her face, Vaelin found the experience of conversing
with her differed little from much of their prior acquaintance.

"I didn't drag her anywhere," he said. "She came, very much under her
own agency and not without good reason. For all that she tries to hide it, she
has a good heart. You should be proud."

"I am, more than you could know. But I didn't just adopt a daughter, I
adopted an heir, one it appears I should consider myself extremely lucky to
find still drawing breath."

Reva turned to regard Ellese as she exchanged farewells with Mi-Hahn,
Sehmon standing at her side, head still bandaged and an apparently permanently bemused expression on his face. Sherin had advised that he was likely
to regain his full faculties in time, but would probably experience bouts of
confusion for the rest of his life.

"And what am I supposed to do with that one?" Reva enquired. "Since she refuses to be parted from him."

"A role in the Lady Governess's guard might be in order," Vaelin suggested. "He fights well."

"Boys." Reva shook her head with a sigh. "She collects them like pets. In time she'll need a husband. A Cumbraelin husband."

"Really? Like her mother?"

He saw an echo of her old self in the scowl she turned on him, although it softened soon enough. "The Blessed Lady is too holy to be sullied by matrimony, you know that."

"I do, it's in the Eleventh Book. Veliss is well?"

"Well enough, albeit considerably annoyed when I told her about this expedition. Less so when I said it was principally intended to return Ellese safely to our care. She loves her very much."

"So do I. I also know she wants no part of being your heir. In time, I'm afraid you'll have to find another."

Reva shot him a warning glare. "She knows her duty. As I hope you do, Lord Vaelin. Our queen summons you home."

"A summons I'll answer, once I've recovered my horse."

"Your horse." She raised a doubtful eyebrow. "I doubt she'll find that amusing when I try to explain your absence. When she returned from her Eastern Dominions to learn that the Tower Lord of the Northern Reaches had abandoned his post to sail off and embroil himself in someone else's war, it's said she actually raised her voice. Some members of the court are reported to have fainted."

"Master Erlin wasn't punished for bringing her unwelcome news, I trust?"

"No, but she did unnerve him somewhat. He was very frail last I saw, too infirm to face the journey back to the Reaches, in fact. She gave him a room in the palace and servants aplenty, although all he asked for was books, parchment and ink."

"I'll explain my own actions and stand ready to receive her judgement without argument."

"Once you find your horse."

"Quite."

The humour slipped from her face and she stepped closer, clasping his forearm. "I sailed a long way to fight a battle that had already been won. I did it on the queen's command, but I came for Ellese, and for you, for I feel we've been too long apart. Also, I know your sister will be anxious to see you home safe."

"I'll see her soon enough."

Her brow creased as the doubtful eyebrow became a frown, but she said no more. "Ellese!" she called out, turning and striding towards the gangway of the *King Malcius*. "Say what you have to say and get aboard or we'll lose the tide."

Ellese exchanged a final embrace with Mi-Hahn before rushing to Vaelin's side. "I wanted to sail with you on the *Stormhawk*," she said. "But Mother wouldn't hear of it." She cast a sulky grimace in Reva's wake. "I have a sense it'll be quite some time before she lets me stray beyond her sight again."

She looked down, eyes bunching against tears until he reached out to tease the mess of curls back from her forehead, saying, "I'm sure you'll find a way."

She pressed herself to him and hurried after Reva, taking hold of Sehmon's sleeve and tugging him along. He squinted at Vaelin as she led him away, his initial confusion giving way to recognition whereupon he waved, calling out, "Am I still pardoned, my lord?"

"In full, Master Vek!" Vaelin called back, returning the wave. "And know you'll always find welcome in the Reaches."

◆ ◆ ◆

Alum had to be carried aboard the *King Malcius* on a stretcher, lying facedown to spare his burns. His eyes were dulled by drugs as Vaelin crouched at his side, although they did betray a glint and a smile came to his lips. "Don't . . . feel bad . . . for me, my friend," he told Vaelin in a rumbling murmur.

"Your wounds . . ." Vaelin began only to fall silent at the Moreska's throaty chuckle.

"Another story," he said. "This one written on my skin . . . instead of the earth. Now . . . the Protectors will always find me . . ." His eyes closed and he slipped into sleep with a heavy sigh.

"Sherin offered to heal the scars, but he wouldn't let her," Nortah explained as two Realm Guard carried the stretcher up the gangway. "Something to do with clouding the Protectors' vision, apparently. She's already aboard," he added when Vaelin glanced around at the wharf. "A personal invitation from the queen to become Royal Physician is hard to refuse. And I doubt she feels welcome in the emperor's court these days. The ingratitude of kings is always a hard thing to see, brother."

"Kings are above gratitude," Vaelin said. "For them there is only loyalty, earned or bought. Tsai Lin learned his lessons well, and he has much to do." He nodded to the hulking ship. "You'd best get aboard. I'll see you in the Reaches once . . ."

"Don't speak another fucking word to me about your horse." Nortah met his gaze with moist and angry eyes until Vaelin looked away. "I would come with you . . ."

"You have a family waiting. In fact they've been waiting for a long time." He stepped forward and held his brother, his grip tight and fierce.

"What do I tell them?" Nortah asked in a hoarse whisper.

Vaelin released him and moved back, smiling in apology. "Tell Orven I'm sorry he'll have to sit on the Tower Lord's Chair a while longer, unless you'd like to relieve him of the burden."

Nortah shook his head. "I have a school to rebuild, amongst other things." He turned and started up the gangway then paused, taking a heavy purse from his belt. "Getting forgetful in your advanced age, brother," he said, tossing it to Vaelin.

"This feels a little light," he said, frowning as he hefted the bag, the gold nuggets clicking inside.

Nortah resumed his climb, Vaelin seeing the effort he made not to look back, his voice strained as he said, "You didn't think I'd do all this for no pay, did you?"

◆ ◆ ◆

Captain Ohtan guided the *Stormhawk* to a secluded bay ten miles to the north of Lishun-Shi, weighing anchor in the shallows where the ebbing tide allowed her to settle onto the shoreline. The night was clear and the moon bright, so there was no need for torches as sailors heaved a plank over the side to allow the Servants of the Temple to disembark, Zhuan-Kai and Mi-Hahn being the last to do so.

"It occurs to me," Vaelin said to the large monk, "that I never learned the abbot's name."

"None of us did," Zhuan-Kai replied. "He was there long before we fetched up at the gate. He was always just the abbot."

"Now the title is yours. Although he was a man with . . . admirable qualities, I hope you'll follow a less costly path."

"It wasn't his path; it was ordained by the temple. Now it ordains that we return." He hesitated, and Vaelin knew he was biting down on the words "without you." Zhuan-Kai smiled but it was a sad, vague semblance of his previous good humour. He had left the temple with close to five hundred brothers and sisters and would be returning with less than a dozen. However, Vaelin knew that in time the number would grow as the temple called others to climbs its tiers.

"You're not going back with them, are you?" Vaelin asked Mi-Hahn after Zhuan-Kai descended to the beach.

"Their temple is no longer mine to call home," she said. "It lies further north."

"Do you know how long you will stay there?"

"A day." She smiled, pausing to press a kiss to his cheek. "Then another, I imagine. Don't worry for me, brother. I have many pictures to paint." There was a pain in her eyes as she drew back, the same weight of guilt he had seen when they sailed north from the Opal Isles.

"It's my price to pay," he told her. "And I pay it willingly."

She nodded, forcing a smile as forlorn as her brother's. "I look forward to our next meeting. You know where to find me."

He watched her descend to join the others on the beach and tracked them as they crossed the sands to disappear into the tall grass beyond before glancing over his shoulder. "Are you here with a knife or a warning?"

Chien emerged from the shadows cast by the cargo on the foredeck, coming to his side with her staff in hand and a pack on her shoulder. "What makes you think," she said, "I am here to do anything but go in search of my sisters?"

"You seemed convinced of their demise not long ago."

"And I will be happy to find myself mistaken." She rested her staff against her shoulder, extending her arm, the sleeve drawing back to reveal the smooth, unmarked flesh. "A few marks, only visible in sunlight. And it's stronger than the other by a good deal."

"All the better to serve the emperor with. He was quick to recognise the need for a spymaster, and who better than you?"

Chien merely inclined her head before stepping onto the plank. "No knife. Just a warning."

"Don't come back?"

"Your presence . . . complicates things."

"It always does, wherever I go."

Chien's smile surprised him by being the only genuine one he had seen that night, even more so in its warmth. "I'd really hate to have to kill you one day," she said before leaping down from the plank. She moved across the beach in a rapid sprint, swallowed by the grass seconds later.

He watched the grass sway in the wind, allowing the black-song to rise as he searched. It had been truculent since the Darkblade's death, grudging in the guidance it chose to impart. *I denied it a death*, he concluded. *One it lusted for more than any other.* This then was the heart of the black-song, the truth that gave it substance. It fed on the deaths that he wrought, much as the tiger fed on the souls fed to it by the Stahlhast for so long. They succoured a monster, whilst he had birthed his own and would carry it throughout the years that remained to him, unless . . .

The song gave a small mutter as a section of grass swayed with greater energy, Vaelin peering closer then whirling around, hand reaching for his sword as an unexpected voice broke the silence.

"Did you really think you could fool me twice?"

Sherin stood by the mainmast, arms folded and head tilted at an inquisitive angle. He grimaced, shaking his head as the black-song failed to rise, as it had throughout the voyage from the Free Cantons even though she must have been secreted aboard somewhere.

"Nortah is generous with his gifts," she said, moving closer and holding up something small and shiny.

The purse was light, Vaelin recalled with a groan of realisation. "Captain Ohtan . . ." he began.

"Was kind enough to allow me to bunk in his cabin." She went to the rail, looking out at the shore. "People aren't always grateful when healed, but he's not a man to forget a debt." She turned to him with a raised eyebrow. "No horse, I see."

A snort and the scrape of displaced sand drew their eyes to the beach where Derka had emerged from the tall grass. He galloped towards the shore, tossing his head and voicing a loud, reproachful whinny.

"I didn't lie," Vaelin said. "Not about everything." He rested his hands on the rail, lowering his head. "Why didn't you go home?"

"What home? The Realm? I find I don't recall it with any great fondness."

"I have a very long journey ahead of me . . ."

"Good. I do like to travel. New places always bring something of interest."

"Sherin . . ."

"Or you could let me heal you. Banish that sickness inside you."

Looking up to regard her completely serious face, he shook his head. "Something comes back, remember? Besides, I suspect this may be beyond even your gift. This . . . sickness runs too deep, and it grows with every life I take, every cruelty I indulge. In time, I know it will make of me what Kehlbrand's song made of him and a new Darkblade will rise to plague the world."

She pursed her lips in brief consideration then reached into her sleeve to extract a vial. "A new recipe?" he asked as she handed it to him. "More potent, perhaps?"

"No, it's the same formula. The same as the one they gave you at the Temple of Spears, in fact. Just a mix of water and lavender oil, with a little minced cloves to put a sting on the tongue. It has no medicinal properties, Vaelin. It never controlled the song; you did."

He looked at the vial in his hand, watching the moonlight play on the viscous liquid inside. "The abbot," he said with a bitter laugh before allowing it to fall into the shadows below the hull. "It was never enough in any case. I should have known there was no quelling it."

"So you intend to run? Find some forgotten corner of the world to hide in? Waste all the remaining years of your life in seclusion?"

"There's no hiding from this. But there is a man, a man who has possessed the healing gift since birth, and his powers are . . . considerable. At the end of the Liberation War he set out to wander the earth, at my contrivance despite Lyrna's wishes, for she feared his power."

Derka came to a halt below, stamping an impatient hoof to the lapping water. "He seems a little excitable to spend much time in the hold," Sherin said. "But I have a concoction that'll calm him provided it's not too long a voyage."

"You don't understand," Vaelin told her. "I've tried to use the song to seek out this man, though it pains me. I've caught glimpses, and the sense of it leads me south but, in truth, I don't know where to find him. It could take a very long time, years perhaps."

Sherin raised her gaze from Derka, looking up at the stars. "Obvar told me something before he left," she said. "He told me Kehlbrand once made him touch the black stone and as a result he could hear lies. So, when you told the emperor you would shortly sail for home, he knew that to be a lie. But that wasn't the only lie he recalled. Sho Tsai's memories lived on in him, or a small vestige of them at least, and when he recalled those memories of me, he could hear my lies. Lies I told of the life I had lived before coming to the Far West, of the man I said I no longer cared for, hated in fact, for his betrayal. But I never hated you. Not for the briefest, most fleeting moment."

She lowered her gaze, Vaelin seeing her throat constrict before she asked, "Are you sure this man can cure you?"

"His name is Weaver, and if he can't, I doubt there is anyone in this world who can."

"Then," she said, moving back from the rail and meeting his gaze with a brisk smile, "we'd best get started."

Dramatis Personae

The Merchant Realms

Vaelin Al Sorna—Tower Lord of the Northern Reaches

Lord Nortah Al Sendahl—former Brother of the Sixth Order of the Faith; Sword of the Realm and hero of the Liberation War; renowned drunkard

Sherin Unsa—renowned healer known as "the Healing Grace"; former Sister of the Fifth Order of the Faith

Ellese Mustor—adopted daughter and heir to Lady Governess Reva Mustor of Cumbrael

Alum Vi Moreska—hunter for the Moreska Clan; friend to Vaelin

Sehmon Vek—former outlaw and indentured servant to Alum

Lian Sha—Merchant King of the Venerable Kingdom

Sho Tsai—captain in the Merchant King's Host; commander of the Red Scouts and former general of the Garrison of Keshin-Kho

Tsai Lin—apprentice officer in the Red Scouts; adopted son to Sho Tsai

Luralyn Reyerik—sister to the Darkblade, Kehlbrand Reyerik; Gifted seer of the Divine Blood

Eresa—former slave; Gifted and friend to Luralyn

Jihla—former slave; Gifted and friend to Luralyn

Chien—member of the Crimson Band Criminal Fraternity

Cho-ka—smuggler and member of the Green Viper outlaw band; former corporal in the Skulls Infantry Company

Johkin—smuggler and member of the Green Viper outlaw band; former soldier in the Skulls Infantry Company

Kiyen—smuggler and member of the Green Viper outlaw band; former soldier in the Skulls Infantry Company

Ohtan Lah—retired sea captain and cartographer

Nuraka Shan—governor of Huin-Shi, later admiral of the Imperial Fleet

Mah-Lol—Merchant King of the Enlightened Kingdom

Duhlan Sai—general in the Enlightened Host; Commander of the Amber Regiments

Urikien Sikaru—Sehtaku and later baron of the Urikien Clan of the Free Cantons

THE DARKBLADE'S HORDE

Kehlbrand Reyerik—Darkblade of the Unseen, Great Lord of the Hast and Leader of the Redeemed Host

Babukir Reyerik—younger brother to Kehlbrand and Luralyn

Obvar Nagerik—Stahlhast warrior of great renown; Kehlbrand's champion and saddle brother

Mai Wehn—formerly "Mother Wehn"; Servant to the High Temple of the Jade Princess; captured by the Stahlhast at Keshin-Kho

Saikir—member of the Darkblade's coterie of Gifted

Uhlkar—member of the Darkblade's coterie of Gifted

Nai Lian—captive; granddaughter to Lian Sha

THE TEMPLE OF SPEARS

The Abbot—Leader of the Temple

Zhuan-Kai—warrior and Brother of the Temple

Mi-Hahn—artist and Sister of the Temple

Dei-yun—blacksmith and Brother of the Temple

Lehun—cook and Sister of the Temple

Kish-an—healer and Brother of the Temple

OTHERS

Atheran Ell-Nestra—Pirate King of "The Benevolent Kingdom" of the northern Opal Islands; former Shield of the Meldenean Isles and hero of the Liberation War

Reva Mustor—Lady Governess of the Fief of Cumbrael; loyal vassal to Queen Lyrna Al Nieren of the Greater Unified Realm; adoptive mother to Ellese

Acknowledgments

For their efforts in helping me successfully bring Vaelin's latest adventure to a close, I would like to thank my US editor, Jessica Wade, and her tireless assistant, Miranda Hill, at Ace. Thanks also to my UK editor, James Long, at Orbit; my agent, Paul Lucas; and, as always, my proofreader Paul Field.